The Prince's attention was absolute and focused, ignoring all else except the warrior who challenged his authority. The intimidated mob gave way before his inexorable stride, as he walked boldly through them, fearless of any threat to his person. "Enigma Rise from out of Mist," Gralyre intoned resoundingly. Growling thunder replied from out of the sky, though there were no clouds above.

The Rebel stumbled backwards in time with Gralyre's advance, and the reverent crowd parted around both men.

"Spirit! Waken with a roar!" Lightening flashed, as Gralyre swung the great sword up before his eyes, in clear sight of the crowd. The dragon adorning the hilt seemed to come alive, its neck undulating along the glowing blade, its jaws gaping in a roar of defiance. "Dragon perched on vengeful fist!"

Lightning and thunder crashed overhead, shaking the roots of the mountain, and the crowd flinched with cries at the unprecedented din. The challenger tripped and fell to his back.

Gralyre brought the point of his five and a half foot weapon to a standstill less than a hair's breadth from the man's nose, where the sword remained extended without a quiver of effort. The Rebel froze, his fear panting from his lips.

Gralyre's voice quieted, as he finished reciting the famous stanzas of the prophecy. The silence of the street echoed the familiar words from the lips of all who watched.

"Fell Usurper rule no more!"

Other Books by L.G.A. McIntyre

Lies of Lesser Gods Series

The Exile

The Rebel

The Sorcerer

The Prince

The King – arriving in 2021

Children's Book

The Flying Giraffe

The Prince

Lies of Lesser Gods

Book Four

L.G.A. McIntyre

Per Ardua Productions Inc.

Vancouver, Canada

Published by Per Ardua Productions Inc.

www.perarduaproductions.ca

First time in print

Trade Paperback edition March 2020

ISBN: 978-0-9919120-6-3

eBook ISBN: 978-0-9919120-7-0

For Spencer

Writing Buddy

Distraction Specialist

I'll miss you.

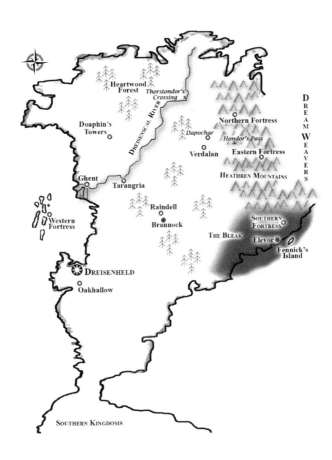

Prologue

The Bleak - Four days ago

Seen through the midnight occlusion of the drifting fogs of the Bleak, the lumenstone road ahead was clear to General Ryes' light-sensitive eyes, as he guided his men homeward to the Southern Fortress. The parallel, glowing rows of small stones that marked the edges of the path fluoresced in the weak light cast by the swinging lantern that hung suspended upon the rod over the head of his horse, growing brighter as he neared, and dimming to darkness after he had passed before flaring awake once more in the lantern light of the rider behind him. The faint dots to either side of the road seemed to hover in the shifting blackness, bounding the column of Rebels safely away from the dangers lurking within the dark mists. But how safe were they?

Not three days past, as reckoned by the resting circles on the lumenstone road, for there was no division of day from night in the Bleak, the Rebels had survived an enemy's ambush. Deathren by the thousands had swarmed them, controlled by one of Doaphin's Demon Lords. The Rebels would have perished had their mysterious travelling companion, Gralyre, not incinerated their foe within a cleansing storm of magical fire.

The Demon Lord's snare had been well baited, for somehow, after three hundred years, Doaphin's forces had finally discovered the secret to the Southern Rebels' ingenious navigation through the Bleak, and had removed the lumenstone road markers from the Crossroads of Banterlay.

When the small band of Rebels had encountered the gap in the bright, guiding stones, losing the road ahead, it had stranded them in place, frantically searching for vestiges of the trail in the disorienting murk, until the Demon Lord's trap had been sprung.

'Why now?' General Ryes lamented. *'After centuries, why have the roads been exposed now?'*

Lumenstones only glowed in the presence of light, and since Doaphin's demonic forces only had use for darkness, the secret pathways had never before been revealed. For three hundred years the Southern Rebels had remained hidden, even to the uncanny tracking powers of Doaphin's Stalkers, for the scents of human passage did not linger in this fusty climate.

The discovery of the Crossroads of Banterlay meant that the Southern Fortress was in grave danger, for the enemy needed only to follow the lumenstone-marked road back to the Rebel stronghold. This misfortune was a harbinger of their destruction.

Ryes took comfort in the fact that the Demon Lord had still been awaiting their arrival at the ambush, suggesting that the discovery of the Rebel roads may have been a more recent evil. There was a slim chance that his home still stood, and that his people yet lived. But for how long?

He had agonized over the delay but, as he had sworn to do, General Ryes had delivered the small band of condemned Northern Rebels to the beachhead across the inlet from Fennick's Island to begin their futile quest to recover the Dragon

Sword of Lyre. Despite the threat to his people, he had not strayed from his obligation to the rebellion.

Gralyre and his companions had always been destined for their fate, sentenced to death by Commander Boris all those months ago at the Northern Fortress, but they had been steadfast companions who had selflessly risked their lives for the good of all. Despite Ryes' suspicion that Gralyre was a collaborator, and his personal dislike of the man's arrogance, it had been no easy task to ride away, and leave the group to their doom. But having fulfilled his duty to the cause, General Ryes now had greater concerns. The path ahead lay clear, but it was not the one marked by the glowing, green motes of the road they now followed.

Ryes drew back on his reins, and brought his horse to a stamping, snorting halt. The beast sensed his unease, stepping and sidling, as it tried to continue onwards against the wishes of its rider.

"Da? Why have we halted?" Corr's face showed his concern, as he materialized from out of the mists and into the circle of light from Ryes' lantern. The horse Ryes straddled immediately calmed, nosing against Corr's animal for comfort.

"Is aught amiss? Is there something in the road?" Corr whispered, as he squinted into the gloom ahead. "Another trap?" All Southerners were cursed with overly pale flesh, the consequence of a lifetime spent in the darkness of the Bleak. Seen through the black haze, the weak glow from their combined lanterns lent Corr's chalky skin an oddly green tinge.

The rough hemp rope that connected Corr's horse to his father's had slackened to coil upon the ground. Behind, the safety line was taut, disappearing straight into the roiling black fogs, as though anchored to the mists instead of to the next horse in the line, and onwards in a chain spanning fifteen Southern warriors, the survivors of the nineteen strong who had entered the Bleak with the questers bound for Fennick's Island. The tether was necessary to ensure that no one fell behind or strayed away from the road into the dark mists.

The Southern warriors had noted that General Ryes and Lieutenant Corr had halted, and were doing their best to provide their leaders the privacy to speak. They rested their horses out of view, obscured by the Bleak.

The General took a moment to study his son, his Lieutenant. So alike were they in appearance that it often seemed as though he spoke through time to his younger self. They shared the same round face, the same receding blond hairline, weak chin and bulbous eyes, but most importantly they shared the same devotion to their people.

Ryes voiced his thoughts. "Three days back t' the Crossroads o' Banterlay. Five more t' our fortress from there, with the enemy sure t' be harrying us along our path, and perhaps four days or less until Catrian's storm smites us all!"

Corr worried his bottom lip with his teeth. "Even if we could reach it, and even if the fortress yet stands, there is no' enough time t' warn home o' the storm."

Masses of dark vapor drifted in nightmare shapes between the two men, unfurling menacing tendrils to brush against their flesh, suckling on the heat of their skin. A lifetime of conditioning kept Ryes and Corr from shrinking away from the clammy caresses.

"We must believe that they live, Corr," Ryes chided. "All is no' lost 'till we see it with our own eyes. But ye are correct. There is no' enough time if we ride the Crossroads, nor would we be likely t' reach home upon that path without Gralyre's sorcery t' protect us." He sighed gravely at the decision he must make. "'Tis only five days t' the fortress from here if we take the Rubicund Road."

Corr's eyes widened, and his throat bobbed, as he swallowed his unease. "The Rubicund Road? Through the dead mires at this time o' year?"

"We have those extra horses from Gralyre and his people. On the Rubicund Road we can make the fortress in three days if we do no' spare the animals. The Crossroads is compromised," Ryes championed his argument, "and o' a certainty we can expect an ambush along its length, but Doaphin's forces may no' yet have found the Rubicund. 'Tis our best chance t' reach our people in time t' warn them o' the storm. After that we must leave the Bleak forever! All o' us."

"Da!"

"'Tis time," the General decreed sternly, to convince himself, as much as his son, that his decision was purely altruistic on behalf of their people. "Our secret roads have been exposed! What safety we had is gone!"

He knew that his intent flew in the face of all Southern tenets. Their endurance of the Bleak was a dogma of defiance against the evils of Doaphin the Usurper.

Yet since his return, General Ryes had found sympathy for those of his people who had fled their homes for the outside world, and had been branded traitors for their crime of desertion. Upon every inhalation, he pictured the Bleak's foul, black miasma swirling within him, smothering all spark and spirit of life. The sensation was worse than it had ever been before because he had finally seen the sun with his own eyes, and breathed the crisp, clean breezes of the mountains to the north. No matter how deeply he inhaled now there seemed no air to sustain him, and he was often left gasping and breathless.

When he had been a young man, his father had warned him that, once seen, a yearning for the bright warmth of daylight could consume him. That was why Ryes had never before tested his mettle by leaving the Bleak for the outside world.

Having now spent most of the winter away from the shadowy mists, away from the stench of mold and rot, away from the choking reek of the smoking flesh of Deathren and Stalkers, and away from the clammy chill that iced through flesh to the very bones of a man, Ryes was unsure if he could ever be the leader that he had once been. How could he ask his people to live in the Bleak, when he was not sure that he could endure it any longer?

In his heart, Ryes could not believe that Catrian's oncoming storm would have any effect upon this ensorcelled land. The Bleak had been created to withstand winter squalls from the sea with nary a wisp of mist lost to the winds. Gralyre's desperate plan to rip back the curtain and expose Doaphin's creatures to the sun's cleansing rays, in order to clear Fennick's Island of Deathren and Stalkers, would fail.

Only a lifetime of darkness lay ahead if he stayed. At the thought, a claustrophobic suffocation came near to unmanning him, and Ryes shut his eyes briefly, the better to recall the pinks and reds of a golden orb rising from behind a blue mountain peak. The feeling of confinement retreated - for now.

During their journey north to attend Commander Boris' war summit, the colours and aromas of the world outside had overwhelmed him. Having previously known only the Bleak had made it impossible to withstand the sheer glory of a sunlit world that seemed to stretch forever: the arching blue expanse of the winter sky and the diamond sparkle of snowcapped mountains, the scents of drowsing forests upon an icy wind and the rustle of life within their branches, and the rush of wings as a flock of birds burst free from the earth and vanished into the sky! Though he had treasured every sensation, and had memorized every vista, Ryes had spent much of his time drinking deeply of the Northern Rebels' ale to dull the assault upon his senses.

"Ye heard Commander Boris at the war summit, Corr," Ryes reminded gravely, leaning forward in his determination to convince his son of his plan. "Doaphin's sword is falling. All humanity will die! I will gift our people a day in the bright sun afore that end!" The lantern light reflected twin fires of conviction in his eyes. "So we will leave, and march east through the mountains t' sanctuary in the realm o' the Dream Weavers, if they even exist. We will hold the passes open for fleeing Lowlanders for as long as we are able, just as we agreed t' do. And then we will finally be quit o' this desolate land, and its endless war!"

Corr's mouth tightened, but he gave his father a short nod of compliance.

Ryes smiled his approval, as he relaxed back in his saddle. "Good lad."

"We take the Rubicund Road," Corr called out to their waiting men.

"Aye Lieutenant," drifted back from the darkness, followed by echoed whispers of the order, as it was passed along the line of Southern Warriors.

"I will get the men turned back towards the ocean, Da." Once they reached the beach they would have to follow the shoreline east for at least a half-day in order to find the cairn that marked the trailhead of their new road.

"No," Ryes countered, "we will lose too much time backtracking. We will ride parallel t' the ocean from here until we cross the Rubicund's lumenstones."

"We canno' ride blindly through the Bleak!"

"Blind t' our eyes, but no' t' our ears. Ye can still hear it? The ocean?"

They held quietly for a moment while Corr cocked his head, his gaze losing focus, as he strained to listen. Faintly heard in the distance, the ebb and crash of waves whispered and sighed into his ears. "We should no' leave the road."

"We have already lost three days delivering Gralyre and his people up t' the madness o' Fennick's Island, and we would lose another day we canno' afford by returning t' the sea t' find the trailhead! We will listen for the tide, and keep it on our shoulder. It will guide us as well from here, as it would from there," General Ryes ruled. He wheeled his horse to the right, and urged it into an easy walk, boldly leaving behind the safety of the marked road before his son could convince him further that his decision was madness.

The throat of the Bleak promptly swallowed the General's horse and lantern, so that it seemed he rode through a roiling, misty cavern. Never before in his life had Ryes left the roads behind without a landmark to shepherd him, and surges of anxiety left his hands atremble upon his reins. Only the sounds from the distant tides would keep them from straying, a disaster from which they would never recover.

He glanced back, but his son's light had already vanished. Ryes had never felt so alone. Would Corr follow or insist upon keeping to the safety of the lumenstones?

Ryes was almost ready to turn back, and cede to his son's caution, when he felt small tugs upon the safety line as, one by one, his son and his other warriors fell in behind, committing their fates to his mad plan. He blew out a long sigh of relief, and traced the rush of its windy passage through the coiling whirls and eddies of the black mists. The General angled their travel slightly towards the distant rumble of the beaching waves to ensure that they did not stray too far inland to hear the guiding surge. Their course was set.

Though the threat of ambush would be lessened upon the new road, there were other perils to now consider. Alone in the darkness with his ill thoughts, the time elapsed slowly for Ryes, as his horse plodded carefully through the black mists.

The Rubicund Road was named for the blood-red clay of the dead fen it bisected for much of its length. The old-timers told tales of how the land had bled when Doaphin the Usurper had murdered the rightful King of Lyre three hundred years ago.

Whatever had birthed the Rubicund Fen, the crimson colour of its flesh made an attractive hearth. In the summer, the Southerners harvested its thick, red clay, shaping bricks and firing them in a hot furnace. These they then sealed with a spirit that was distilled from the thick growths of molds and mildews that claimed all surfaces in the Bleak. The red bricks became the only building material that could withstand the rot that would collapse a wooden structure within a fortnight. The clay was also used to fashion cookware, as iron rusted away if it was not kept well oiled.

As beneficial as the fen generally was, in the spring it became a danger to be avoided. The ground was prone to extreme flooding and shifting from the snowmelt runoff of the mountains to the north, making it impassable until the floodwater had ceased its rush towards the sea. Doaphin's creatures avoided the dead mire, lest entire units of Deathren be lost to the shifting ground, making it the Rebels' best chance at reaching home alive. Yet by that same danger, Ryes and his men might find themselves following the lumenstones into a muddy grave, or worse, the trail might be lost entirely, washed away by new-formed lakes or streams, stranding them in the darkness. Every summer teams of Rebels were sent to replenish lost stones, and to set a new road through the fen. Road building was not for men of feeble courage.

General Ryes was not much of a praying man, however he mumbled a quick petition to the Gods of Fortune that the Rubicund Road was still passable. Should the enemy have reached his fortress ahead of him, he might be arriving home only to the wraiths of his loved ones. Then what would it matter should he and his men die in their attempt to reach their people? The dangerous wetland was the only path left to them.

If he was steering his men true, Ryes judged that they would soon cross the twin bounding lines of the Rubicund Road but when the lumenstone markers failed to appear, Ryes grew afraid to blink lest it was at that moment that safety beckoned, and he missed it.

The General tilted to the side of his saddle, scanning the ground below for the lumenstones. His thundering heartbeat rushed blood through his ears, until he quaked with doubt that it was to this ebb and roar that he had been guiding his men eastward, instead of to the indistinct sigh of distant tides. Too much time had passed! Had he led his men astray? He had no choice but to continue onwards.

Finally, a dotted line of lights flared awake in the weak wash from his lantern, and the tightness relaxed from his shoulders. It was a road.

Ryes shared a concerned, tight smile with his son, as Corr and the rest of their men appeared one-by-one from out of the darkness. Though they were once more bound in safety by glowing lumenstones, it was possible that they had only traveled a wide arc back to where they had begun or stumbled upon an abandoned stretch of road laid down sometime in the last three centuries and then forgotten. There would be no telling if this was the Rubicund Road until they reached a landmark of either the fen or the Crossroads of Banterlay.

Trusting in the favour of the Gods, the General led his men inland. Urgency spurred every decision now, for they knew that time fought their steps. They pushed their horses into a rocking cantor, keeping their speed up for league after league, though it would not take much for a horse to pull up lame from a misstep in the darkness.

Their pace barely allowed the lumenstones the time to ignite, as they passed. They chanced straying into the treacherous mists, yet not a warrior complained. They all felt the same need to reach their families, and to discover the fates of their loved ones.

In the shifting blackness at the fringes of the circular glows of their lanterns, the ghostly trunks of rotting trees appeared and vanished in the midnight fog, as they rode through a long-dead forest. Their speed lent the woodland necropolis the illusion of movement, and the knowledge that another ambush could be awaiting them at any moment made the warriors constantly spooked by mirages of attacking phantasms. This road promised both safety and menace, yet they had no choice but to stay their course. Without the lumenstones to guide them they would never find their way home.

Whispers from out of the murk, echoes of the long dead, beseeched the warriors to abandon their lives and release their woes, while the claustrophobic mists pulled at their vision until they swore they could see the curling fingers of these same spirits dancing at the edges of their feeble tunnels of light, beckoning, always beckoning. It was the nature of the Bleak to confuse the senses. It robbed joy and destroyed hope, a rapacious vampire of all light within a soul.

Eventually, the lumenstones markers widened into a circle, denoting a safe place to rest. While half of the men spread tarps over the diseased sludge on the ground and flopped down to sleep away some of their exhaustion, the other half of the group guarded their repose against attack. It was to be only the briefest of stops, and it would not be until the next resting circle that the vigilant guards would have their opportunity for sleep, while the current dreamers watched over them in turn.

Their only light was the lantern that was always left burning to mark their exit path back to the road ahead. Without it to guide their direction when they set forth, they could unknowingly travel back the way they had come.

League after league passed in this fashion until, soon after their second brief rest stop, the ghostly trees vanished from around them, and they entered the Rubicund Fen. A small cheer erupted from the men at this confirmation that they had indeed been riding upon the correct road.

Their elation was fleeting, for as disconcerting as passing through the dead forest had been, at least it had provided a measure of bearing and progress through the Bleak. Without the trees parading past them, all sense of direction and movement vanished. There was no up, no down, no left or right and, despite the best efforts of their horses, they seemed only to be marching in place and never gaining a foot of ground.

The Southern Warriors paused to strap themselves to their saddles lest they succumb to the vertigo induced by the lack of a firm anchor for their sight. Isolated within the fogs, as each man was, should a warrior fall and be unable to call out, the entire column would pass him in the darkness, and never see that he lay in the road. They would not realize that a comrade was missing from his horse until the next resting circle.

Beneath the anemic wash of light from the bobbing lanterns suspended on the poles over their horses' heads, the wet ground was glossy and red as a battlefield, as though the recently slain lay just beyond view, pumping their lifeblood into the thirsty muck. Even the air now carried a tang reminiscent of blood, having adopted a harsh, rusty scent of corrosion, death and decay.

Their pace slowed to a laborious walk, as their horses did battle with the thick clay that followed each squelching step down with a sucking adhesion to prevent the next lift of a hoof. With every skirmish won, red filth spattered until the men and horses looked as though they had survived a murderous rampage.

The further they penetrated into the fen, the more gaps they encountered in the lumenstone markers. Stones were missing from one side of the road or the other, having sunk into the red clay or been washed away by muddy rivulets. The Rebels were able to determine the path forward until their worst fears were realized. The road vanished at the edge of a muddy lake.

They had no way of knowing how wide or deep the water was. Even if it could be forded, there was no guarantee that the trail took up again on the far side directly across from them. The markers might curve off in a new direction underwater or have been washed away completely. If that ensued, then they would have no choice but to backtrack to the ocean and, despite the danger of attack, find their original route home via the Crossroads of Banterlay.

While one man stayed ashore to anchor their safety lines and guard their horses, the others waded the icy water in divergent directions. Armed only with a coil of rope that they played out slowly behind them, they splashed through darkness, seeking a safe ford to the far side and, with luck, the continuance of the road ahead.

Further out, the water grew so deep that only those who could swim could continue onwards. The others waded ashore to report their failure.

After an hour with no safe crossing having been found, a new strategy was employed. They abandoned the road markers to follow the curve of the shore instead, picking their way carefully in the darkness using the watery landmark as their guide. It was a risky decision, but their only remaining hope of recovering the lumenstones. As they circumnavigated the lake, they discovered it to be at least five hundred feet in diameter, which explained the lack of a ford.

Their desperate gamble worked, and it was by the Gods' own sent fortune that allowed them to find the road again, intact, when they rounded the far side.

Obstacles were more numerous after that. They encountered patches of road that appeared sound until stepped upon, and then proved to be an illusion, an earthen slurry that retained just enough mass to keep the lumenstones suspended upon its crust while beneath it held the consistency of oatmeal.

Here they would dismount, and wade through the icy red muck, leading their animals while probing the ground in front of their feet with the rods from their lanterns to ensure that they did not step into a depth from which they would drown in the weight of the earth.

At the front of the column, Ryes had to be extra cautious to note the path ahead, for in the eddies of his horse's passage most of the lumenstones lost their tenuous grip upon the surface, and sank into the sludge, leaving the men in the line behind with no guide forward save for the pull of the safety line. The road was rolling up behind them, and there would be no easy way out of the fen should they be forced to turn back.

Fatigue took its toll on both the men and the horses. It was a long, grueling journey to reach the next resting circle.

It was bitter cold without the heat of a fire to warm them in their wet, muddy clothes but they could not chance the extra light in case the enemy was near. They huddled together to share heat, and only exhaustion allowed the fortunate half of the men, whose turn it was, to find sleep during their short break.

When they moved out again, their rate of travel was even slower and more arduous than the day before. The sound of flowing streams grew louder by the moment, and General Ryes recognized that they had been lucky to have made it this far into the fen, and they would be luckier still to exit before they were trapped by rising floodwaters.

The strenuous hours passed slowly, and though there was no day or night in the Bleak, Ryes had been born and bred in this darkness, and thus was able to judge time well enough. When the road lifted onto a small hillock, finally raising them above the sludge and onto solid ground, he sensed that another resting circle was nearing. His instincts proved sound when his lantern's light ignited a small ring of stones in the murk ahead, luring them to another cold, much needed rest.

This marked the end of the fourth leg of their journey home, and what Ryes estimated to be almost their third day of frantic travel since they had left the questers on the beachhead across from Fennick's Island. He had hoped to be home by now.

Ryes did not sleep at this stop, opting to join the men on guard duty so that one more of his warriors could rest. As he scanned the darkness for signs of attack, and listened to the soft snores of the exhausted men mingling with the low conversations of the other sentries, he fretted over their progress.

The time that he had hoped to gain with this new route was quickly slipping away. Indeed, the only boon was that they had seen no sign of the enemy's encroachment upon this road. The General's confidence that the Rubicund would ultimately prove safe from ambushes, if nothing else, was growing. Only the mad or the desperate would chance such a journey through the dead fen at this time of year, and Ryes grimly acknowledged which of those two criteria he met.

There would be one more resting circle before they cleared the fen, and then a half-day's journey to reach the fortress - if the exhausted animals could be coaxed to a canter.

Beset by urgency, it was not long before the General roused his men to ride. Their rest had been too short, but there was no help for it. They could not linger here when the floodwaters would soon wash away all chances of safe passage.

When they assembled to ride forth on their journey's next leg, General Ryes commanded that they should change the order of the line, so that it was the most exhausted men who were tucked protectively in the middle of the column between the warriors who had most recently rested.

It then fell to Corr, who had been one of the fortunate sleepers, to guide the column. Not heeding his own advice, Ryes positioned his horse directly behind his son's and, as they began their ride, felt the comforting tugs on the ropes that bespoke the other riders taking their places in line.

After a long time of staring into the hypnotically swirling, black mists, the General's head began to bob to his horse's gait. He would have whipped any man he caught napping, leaving them all vulnerable to attack, yet time and again he jerked alert when his chin met his chest. His secret crime was mortifying yet Ryes could not help it. He was utterly spent from the haste of their journey, and from giving up his last sleeping shift.

The rope between Ryes and Corr's horses gave a mighty jerk and a cry came from ahead. Had Ryes not been so tightly lashed to his saddle, he would have catapulted over his horse's ears when his animal balked.

His horse whickered in distress and set its hooves, pawing for purchase in the slick, red mud, as it was slowly drawn forward by a heavy weight upon the safety line.

Ryes blinked drunkenly, slow to clear the stupor of his exhaustion. He was uncertain of what he had heard for the mists were ever giving false whispers into a man's ear, and he had momentarily surrendered to a deep slumber. As seen by the weak glow of his light, the taut rope tied between his horse and his son's was hovering into the fog at a steep, downward angle. Ryes shook off his fatigue with the help of a zing of fear when he finally recognized that the danger was real.

"Corr has fallen! Tighten the line!" the General roared.

The warrior in the cue behind Ryes trotted out of the mists as fast as he was able, his speed hampered by his safety line pulling against the pace of the riders behind. By the time the Rebel drew even with Ryes' rearing, pawing horse a second man had ridden into the brighter circle of their combined light.

"Hurry!" Ryes urged.

The two Rebels flanked their General's horse, looping their tethers to his saddle to lend the power of their horses to the task. All three riders took up the strain, yet were still being dragged forward. Their horses were unable to find purchase, as their hooves churned and slid in the slippery, red clay.

"We need more draw!" Ryes shouted at the next warrior to appear. Ryes kicked his horse in the flanks, holding fast, as it jumped and pawed the earth, straining to haul the weight.

Alert now to the danger, the rest of the line of Rebels moved quickly to anchor themselves to each other's saddles, adding the strength of their animals to the cause, until they were finally able to halt their forward slide.

"Corr! Corr! Lad, are ye still there?" Ryes howled out into the blackness beyond their light.

"Pull! For pity's sake, pull me up!" Corr's terrified words were faint and eroded by the impediment of the shifting mists.

Ryes threw his reins to one of his men, pulled his dagger, and quickly severed the rope lashing his body to his saddle. As he slid off his horse, he jerked his lantern pole free of its special harness. When his boots hit the ground, he rushed forward with one hand upon the quivering safety line, and the other lifting his lantern high to light his way.

"Careful, General!" one of the warriors yelled, as he vanished into the swirling, black fog.

Almost to the moment, a yawning space opened at Ryes' feet.

He dropped his lantern pole, as he began to pitch forward. Grasping at the low rope with both hands, he fought his own momentum to keep from tumbling off a cliff.

Momentarily suspended out over the edge of a chasm, Ryes watched his falling light, and a shout of denial burst from his lips when Corr was revealed in passing as it fell. Ryes threw himself backwards before he followed his lantern unto his own death.

"Bring me another light! Hurry! But be wary o' a cliff!" he cried back at his men, as he rolled to his belly in the thick muck, and wormed his way back to the precipice by feel alone.

A warrior ran from the murk with two lanterns swinging on their poles, one cupped beneath each armpit. Warned of the danger ahead by the greater illumination, he fell to his knees, and crawled the final few feet to his General. He stabbed the butts of the poles deeply into the red clay, so that the lights were suspended out over the rim of the cliff to reveal the extent of the peril to their eyes.

Corr had been taken by a large sinkhole. His horse had broken its neck in the fall, and hung limp as a bird, dangling upon the safety line far below the cliff edge. Corr clung to its bridle, his legs kicking in space. "Da! Da! Pull me up!" he screamed when the weak light appeared overhead. His face glowed blurrily, worm-white in the light, as he stared up towards safety.

"Hold fast, Corr! Do no' let go!" Ryes glanced over his shoulder, back into the swirling fog where he knew that his men were straining to hold the dead weight of the horse from falling.

They could not cut it away without losing his son. "Bring me a rope!" he roared.

"We have ye, Corr, we have ye, son," Ryes chanted the reassurance until a nudge came upon his shoulder, and he accepted a long coil of rough hemp rope from the newcomer.

Standing together with his two warriors, bracing to take up the strain of Corr's weight, Ryes lowered the rescue line to his son. He watched tensely, shouting encouragement, as Corr tangled his hand around the rope, and released his grip upon the bridle of his dead horse.

Like a released pendulum, Corr's momentum swung him into the weeping wall of the sinkhole, and a large slab of ruddy earth broke away at his rough impact. Corr yelled, as he was pummeled in a muddy landslide. Somehow, he maintained his grip upon the line.

Overhead, the rescuers were now standing upon a bit of undercut earth, their own danger great, as the fought to save the General's son.

"Quickly! Pull him up!" Ryes urged. With three men on the line, they easily hauled Corr up and out of the sinkhole.

Ryes knelt and grabbed his son in a hug, helping him clear the lip of the pit and, as his men continued to pull, was dragged unceremoniously along with Corr through the red mud towards the safety of firmer ground. Behind them all, the last bit of earth at the rim of the hole crumbled into the depths, taking one of the suspended lights with it.

"Cut the line!" Ryes ordered, to relieve the strain upon the steeds holding the dead weight of the hanging animal suspended in the sinkhole.

One of the warriors pulled his dagger, and sawed through the rope holding the unfortunate beast, allowing it to fall back into the abyss. They did not hear it strike the bottom.

Ryes spied his second man edging towards the lip of the hole to reclaim the remaining lantern. "Leave it, Sarten!" Even as he cautioned his man back, the sinkhole shifted again, consuming another foot of earth from the edges.

The warrior, Sarten, stumbled back towards firmer ground, as the last pole slumped, setting the lantern to swinging wildly before it cartwheeled away into oblivion, and plunged them all into darkness again. "We have lost the light!" Sarten called back to where the rest of their party waited.

Cocooned in the sinister mists, Ryes held his son tightly while awaiting the slowing of his thundering heartbeat. Against his chest, Corr's body shivered and heaved with heavy gasps. In the darkness, with no eyes upon him, the young warrior could be weak in his father's arms, a boy soaking in comfort after the terror of the last few moments.

Ryes pounded his son's back in rough solace, producing wet, squelching sounds from the coating of thick, red clay. "Rest a moment Corr. Rest here," he whispered. "I thought I lost ye, boy!"

A bobbing light grew brighter from out of the mists. "Do ye have him? Is the Lieutenant safe?" The Southern Rebel asked, as he slid through the red muck towards the men.

"Yah, we have him!" grinned Sarten, his teeth flashing white in the filth that spattered his face.

"Thank the Gods!"

Following the man with the light, the other Southern Warriors gathered, expressing relief over the favorable outcome.

The General had still not released his son.

"I am alright, Da. Let go. I can stand." With the light upon them once more, Corr seemed embarrassed to show such vulnerability in front of their warriors.

Father and son arose from the muck looking like ancient spirits of death, caked as they were from head to toe in the blood-red clay of the mire. Despite Corr's avowal, Ryes kept his hand firmly gripped around his son's upper arm. The instinctual fear of a parent made it impossible to release his boy just yet, lest his safety was a trick, and the ground devoured him once more.

When Corr began scraping layers of mud off of his face, and flicking the handfuls to the ground, Ryes finally allowed his men to edge him away. The Southern warriors gathered around their Lieutenant, and pounded his back with rough affection, trading insults and laughter in the time honoured bonding of men who have faced and conquered death.

While they were occupied, the General assessed the magnitude of the challenge that they now faced. Aided by the radiance of their accumulated lantern light, the lumenstone road clearly vanished over the lip of the cliff, yet the greater intensity of light was unequal to the task of spanning the sinkhole to spy its far side, nor to show the depths of the abyss below. The cliff's edge vanished beyond their pooled light, to the left and right, showing the dimensions of the chasm to be vast.

The General saw two choices before him.

He could send a man to walk each direction, and then lead the group to whomever found the road first. Though it could cut their search time by half, it would mean sacrificing a warrior to abandonment, and possible death within the Bleak.

Alternatively, he could trust to luck, pick a direction, and send only one man. If the Gods were kind, the scout would find the continuance of the lumenstone markers on the first try, and no one would be left behind.

Perhaps one of the other Generals of the Resistance would have made the pragmatic decision to lose a man to gain time but Ryes was not of their ilk. The Southerners were a small group, an extended family as much as a fighting force. There was only one decision that Ryes could stomach. He justified that their numbers were too few to be short a warrior should they need to fight their way through to the fortress at the end.

While he debated, more earth sloughed into the sinkhole. If it were to be done it must be done quickly for, minute-by-minute, the sinkhole was taking more of their hope away from them. Ryes bade a man to step forward, choosing one of the warriors who had aided in his son's rescue.

"Go left, Sarten. Keep well clear o' the edges in case it caves further, and work your way around t' the far side. If… *when*… ye find the road again, blow your horn, and we will follow your lumenstone trail t' come t' ye."

As a signal, the horn would be safe. The thick mists of the Bleak scattered sound. Though Sarten's blast might tell the enemy that the Rebels were in the area, a fact that they likely already knew, Doaphin's forces would be unequal to the task of tracking the signal back to its source.

Sarten's red hair and pale blue eyes glowed eerily in the lamplight, as he nodded his compliance to his General's orders. It was no easy thing to leave the group and set out alone without a safety line. If aught happened to the sparse trail of lumenstones that he would drop every few feet as he walked, he would be lost, wandering until the oil in his lanterns failed, and then groping blindly through darkness until hunger, exhaustion or a misstep took his life.

From their stores of supplies, the General passed Sarten a large pack of lumenstones, and an extra lantern. The other warriors slapped his back, and wished Sarten luck, as he clipped his two lanterns to his belt, one alight, and the other in reserve should the first fail.

"See ye soon, lads," Sarten grinned with bravado, his teeth flashing white through his wiry, red beard. He shouldered his pack of stones, and stepped boldly into the Bleak.

After he was gone, they doused all but one lamp to conserve fuel, as their stores were running dangerously low. The sinkhole had claimed four lanterns, and Sarten, seeking the new route, had taken away two more.

Knowing that the scout would be gone for a while, the men

took the opportunity to rest and eat. Periodically, the sinkhole would shift and widen, a hungry monster feeding an insatiable appetite. They were safe for now, having made their camp far back from its crumbling edges.

Too much time passed without the beckoning sound of a horn. Both shifts of men slept, and the warriors began to despair that Sarten was lost. They looked to Ryes to make the difficult decision to abandon their wait for the sounds of running water grew ever louder, and the edge of the pit drew ever nearer.

"Da?" Corr prompted at last.

Ryes stared grimly after the direction that Sarten had taken. He could not afford to send a man to look for him. His moon-shaped face fell from the sorrow of another good man lost. Save that it had provided his men the time to recuperate some strength, he might as well have searched both bearings at once. "We seek in the other direction," he announced finally.

"Here!" a Southern Warrior named Andel volunteered immediately. He collected sacks of lumenstones and an extra lantern from their depleted stores. After saying his farewells, he stared into the roiling mists for a long moment before striding away from his comrades.

The men grew solemn, as they watched Andel's bobbing light vanish into the misty Bleak. The lone lumenstone that he had dropped to mark his path dimmed to darkness, a frail breadcrumb guarding against their oblivion.

"Andel will find the road, Da. The Gods would no' have allowed us t' make it this far without getting us the rest o' the way home."

Ryes shook his head, and his reply was enameled with the vivid colours of cynicism and grief over the loss of Sarten. "Would they no'?"

Their wait began anew.

The subdued Southerners sat in darkness and listened to the sounds of streaming floodwaters grow to a roar. Each, in their own way, reconciled themselves for what was to come. If they were cut off from their path forward, then they would have to turn back, and hope that there was still enough of the Rubicund Road remaining to follow out of the fen. If the road had been obliterated, then their deaths were a certainty. Worst of all, they would have to abandon the Southern Fortress to its fate, condemning all whom they held dear.

"General! A light!" pointed a warrior. "'Tis Sarten! He is alive!" His excited announcement was almost eclipsed by the now thunderous sounds of cascading water.

Sarten staggered into their rough camp, exhausted from the nerve it had taken to walk through the darkness alone for so long. He threw himself to the ground when he reached the safety of the group, and the Bleak's mist billowed away from his body, sending echoes of his movements rippling outward. By the weak light of his lantern, Sarten's pale blue gaze passed with deep thankfulness over the faces of his comrades, as he accepted a cup of ale from Corr.

"Sarten, what did ye find? What happened, man?" Ryes demanded. "Ye were gone for so long that we feared the worst!"

"There is no way around the sinkhole, General." Sarten paused to take a deep draught from his cup. "No' in that direction, at any rate. 'Tis massive! I skirted the edges o' the pit, like ye said, until I came t' a river flowing into it. I followed the banks for a while, but it had no end, so I waded in, 't cross it. It did no' seem so deep, so I kept going, but it soon turned t' a lake o' mud, and I feared I would drown."

His clothing was still saturated, his red hair pasted tightly to his scalp. He began to shiver violently, as his body cooled from his long ordeal. Noting this, one of the men draped a woolen blanket over Sarten's shoulders.

Despite the white mold that ate at the fibers of the weave, Sarten sighed deeply, and curled into the musty warmth while he continued his tale. "The current took me and I lost my light. I was tumbling and fighting t' keep my head up. I do no' know how long it was afore I found solid ground again, and pulled myself out o' the water." Sarten's shivers grew with his remembrance of terror. "It took a while t' relight my spare lantern because everything was wet. By then, I was far off the trail o' lumenstones that I had dropped, and I did no' know which direction it lay, so I guessed, based against the current o' the river, and trusted t' the Gods. They finally led me t' cross my trail." He hung his head in defeat. "I am sorry it took me so long t' return. I am sorry I failed ye all."

"Ye were fortunate, Sarten. Truly, the Gods were watching o'er ye," Ryes advised the exhausted man kindly. "The river could have carried ye into the pit." His words were interrupted by the distant blare of a horn.

"Was that...?" Corr held a hand up for silence from the men, as the faint blare sounded again.

"Andel! He has found the road!" General Ryes crowed, and bent down to clasp Sarten's shoulder. "Can ye ride, man?"

Sarten's guilt ebbed, as he was relieved of the responsibility for their survival. "Aye! Anything t' escape this cursed place!"

The Rebels mounted quickly, and followed the sparse trail of green, glowing stones that Andel had dropped.

They were awed by the massive size of the rift in the landscape. More a canyon than a hole, they could hear rivers of water thundering down into it. It was staggeringly good fortune that Andel had recaptured the road back to the Southern Fortress.

When they finally caught up with the scout, Andel was sitting on a rock and grinning in welcome. Glowing at the edges of his light lay the parallel rows of stones that marked the reappearance of the road. Better yet, they could clearly see the ancient, rotting trunks of a dead forest.

"We did it, lads! We made it out o' the fen!" Andel pumped his fist in victory.

"'Tis less than a day t' reach home from here!" Corr announced, and the men rejoiced that the dangerous Rubicund Road lay behind them. Encrusted in the filth of the clay, as they all were, and grinning hugely in their relief, the red earth now felt less like the bloody wounds of a battle lost, and more like the war paint of victorious conquerors.

However, the delay to rediscover the road had cost them, and the men now held meager hope that they would arrive in time to alert their kin to the oncoming dangers. But that slight chance was enough to hasten their pace. Now, as they neared the end of their long journey, that slim hope remained the only coin in their exhausted purse.

Corr, who was boldly riding point again, was the first to see the carpet of glowing stones that lay in the road ahead, spread thickly as a welcoming beacon to all returning travelers. The Southern Rebels mined lumenstones from a pit to the east of the Southern Fortress. Sacks of the smaller stones were given to travelling warriors to ease their passage through the darkness of the Bleak while the larger blocks were kept for the building of avenues and streets. For a society birthed in darkness, it was light that they revered most.

Different hues of lumenstones bloomed in Corr's lantern light, revealing a gem-like mosaic depicting the Gods of Fortune. Curse, Fate, Blessing and Hope threw their dice carved of the bones of man, using the stars as their wagers. "We have made it, lads! We are home!" Beyond the sigil, the road became a wide, glowing river of large square lumenstone pavers. From here to the gates their passage would be afloat upon radiant light.

The fortress was now only a league away, and the customary hushed conversations were abandoned, as the Southern Warriors, who had been away from home for most of the winter, began to swap jovial banter about the people they had missed most, and what they would do first upon their arrival.

Abandoning their customary single file line, they clustered

upon the widened road, pushing their exhausted steeds into a rocking canter, as they raced each other to the fortress gates. The horses caught the spirit of the men, tossing their manes and prancing their hooves in celebration of the greater illumination.

A few minutes later General Ryes held up a clenched fist, and reined his horse in. The conversations faltered, as fear found fertile soil in which to root once more. Muffled by the thick fogs, they could hear echoing concussions.

Corr's eyes crinkled with equal parts terror and sorrow. "'Tis an attack! We are too late!"

General Ryes grimaced. "Curse the luck! Dismount. We lead the horses from here. Arm yourselves, keep quiet, and be prepared for an attack! This close t' the fortress the enemy may have posted sentries upon the road!"

soca

The Southern Warriors lost all anticipation for their homecoming; the lumenstone pavers no longer celebrated their return. Doaphin's war was upon them.

All lanterns were snuffed save for the General's. Holding his sword in one hand, and his horse's reins in the other, Ryes led his line of warriors towards the sound of battle.

His men crept forward in blindness, lightly touching their saddles for guidance. In their free hands they gripped short swords in order to defend themselves from ambushes. Bows and quivers, gifted to them by the Northern Rebels, were slung over shoulders.

Soon, the acrid smoke emitted by the burning flesh of amassed Deathren stung their noses, and set their eyes to watering. Despite being shielded from sunlight by the billowing black clouds of the Bleak, the creatures still smoldered during daylight hours. The odour of rotting, smoking corpses thickened the air until the men were forced to breathe through their mouths to keep from choking. There had to be thousands attacking their home for the reek to be so strong!

Explosions from a Demon Lord's magical barrage upon their fortress made them flinch with dread. The din masked the slight sounds made by their horses' hooves striking the lumenstone pavers, though it mattered little, for the arrogant enemy had not bothered to post sentries.

A flickering burn pushed back the thick mists ahead, and General Ryes dowsed his lantern, for they no longer needed its guidance. The smoke from fires now overlaid the sinister odours of Deathren. The Rebels abandoned their horses upon the road, and slunk forward to peer out at the battle from the thinned fringes of the nebulous wall of black fog, where they were still shielded from the eyes of the enemy.

Leaves of fragile ash drifted down from the sky, and wisped oily smudges upon their faces and clothes, unheeded in their dismay. Ruddy light shimmered against their pallid skin, bloodying faces misshapen by grief, as they stood in mute witness to the end of their world. Ahead, the traitorous lumenstone road was an excited jubilee set aglow by the lights from the fires, as it travelled in a rainbow arc of mosaic designs down into a small valley, and betrayed their gates to the army that besieged them.

The distilled spirits that they painted onto the red bricks from which they constructed their homes slowed the growth of decay, but the substance also invited flames to burn at a heat that could melt stone. And burn it now did. Brick buildings shattered, and spread further destruction after each salvo of sorcery from the Demon Lord.

The intensity of the heat blasted back the Bleak, lifting the thick smog to a higher ceiling, and pushing it away to the sides. The flickering reds, yellows and oranges of the fires illuminated the roiling black clouds of ash and mists, so that to their eyes it seemed that Doaphin's army had built an impenetrable barrier of flame around their stronghold. Their fortress was a flashing ruby wrapped inside a fiendish box.

Despite the bloodshed, Corr was stirred by his first sprawling view of his fortress, never before seen in its entirety from afar. There were the familiar streets and crossroads, homes and halls. Now nothing but fuel for the flames. His heart broke to know that he would never walk there again. He had not known that his home was so beautiful.

Tall, thick walls of red brick yet stood in proud protection encircling the burning fortress. Armed warriors yet hurled debris, spears and arrows down at an unstoppable enemy that clambered over each other, like angry insects from a kicked nest, in frantic bids to reach them.

The Deathren shrieked eerily of their insatiable hunger, as they crashed in endless waves against the fortress defenses. Only beheading, sunlight or flame could stop the reanimated Demon Riders. The Southerners owned no such weapon to defeat such an army, and so could only keep knocking the creatures down from their walls. Unable to die, though riddled with arrows and spears, the Deathren attacks were unrelenting. Corr was overcome by the brave yet futile defiance of his people, and his vision blurred with tears for the approaching, inevitable end.

The small group of Southern Rebels watched helplessly, as their defenses failed. A collective moan of despair burst free from the throats of all, as they watched the masses of howling Deathren swarm through the shattered gates. Screams followed, floating to their ears from over the distance: women, men, and children. They were all being slaughtered and fed upon. There could be no retreat or escape, for to flee into the Bleak without the benefit of the marked roads was as much a death sentence as staying to face Doaphin's army.

One warrior openly wept into his hands, no longer able to withstand the horror. "Gods! They are dead!" His wife and child had been awaiting his return.

"General, we are too late! We canno' help them! We have t' save ourselves!" urged another.

General Ryes glared at his warriors, quelling their lamenting. "Those are our families! Our friends! We will no' abandon them, whatever the cost the Gods demand!" He turned back to the destruction, blinking heavily to hold back his tears. He flinched when another concussion thundered, and another plume of fire geysered up from within their ruined walls.

"Warriors o' the South!" Ryes' voice cracked, and he cleared his throat to bark more strongly, "Ready your bows! If we canno' save them, then pray the Gods grant us the luck t' avenge them!"

The men nocked arrows, standing at the ready within the threshold of the mists, lest the enemy sense their presence. More than one arrow clacked against the yew of a bow from the tremors in their hands.

"Aim for the Demon Lord. He is controlling the Deathren. See there! On that rise!"

In the distance, the Demon Lord paid scant mind to the fact that his forces had breeched the gates. Magical fire continued to wreath his hands, and he attacked with joyful abandon, flinging balls of fire up to the sky to rain down upon the fortress, massacring Rebels and Deathren alike with the same disregard.

"With him gone, the Deathren will be as like t' turn on the 'Riders and Stalkers, as t' kill our own. Some o' our people might escape in the chaos!"

"Aye, General!" the men answered as one, and their aims shifted towards their target with military precision.

"I make it… ninety yards," Corr announced hoarsely, as he stared down the shaft of his arrow at his target. It would take a miracle sent from the Gods to make that mark. Southern Warriors never practiced for distance shooting. There was no need of such marksmanship in the Bleak, where visibility was the distance between a horse's ears and its tail. That they were even carrying weapons capable of such a feat was due to having travelled in the bright world outside, where game could be hunted from afar. Corr raised his aim, trying to judge the trajectory his arrow would need to reach his target.

Ryes turned for a last look at Corr, a pause on the cusp of battle. For a moment, the gazes of father and son spoke the volumes of love and respect that there was no time left to utter. Now was their only chance to strike, while the Demon Lord was distracted. If he was not killed outright, Ryes and his small band of Southern Rebels would be crushed by the Demon Lord's retaliation within the next few moments.

"Fire!" Ryes bellowed.

Their bows sounded deep thrums, and the sixteen arrows flew away to be lost to the ruddy darkness; sixteen chances to avenge their loved ones.

They waited out the heartbeats it took for their flight of arrows to reach their target, praying throughout to the Gods of Fortune for a boon, for the luck it would take to save them all. They did not bother to run. There was nowhere that they could retreat to fast enough that the Demon Lord's magic could not reach them.

A gusty breeze swirled the mist, momentarily occluding their target. The stirring was their only warning before a blast of wind plucked up people and horses, tossing them aloft upon the currents. The army before their gates vanished into the maelstrom of Catrian's storm.

Flailing through the air, Corr snagged the branches of a dead tree. It uprooted, and both he and the rotted trunk went tumbling. The vicious currents reversed to slam him into the ground, and the wind's invisible hand dragged him along the slick, moldy earth to smash against an outcropping of large stones.

Corr scrabbled for purchase against the slime that coated the rocks, and jammed his fingers into narrow cracks lest he be sucked upwards again. He hugged a boulder with all of his might, arms and legs clenched tightly, yet could barely withstand the gale force of the tempest that tugged and spun around him.

Debris whipped against his body, a lashing of pain that demanded a choice between anchoring himself or shielding his flesh from harm. It took every fiber of muscle to fight the onslaught in order to wedge his body deeper into the protection of a crevice.

The storm had a voice, a scream of wind that was louder than anything Corr had ever heard. It spoke of destruction and hate, grief and retribution. Having so recently felt those very things, Corr readily recognized the wailing for what it was. It was the sound that his soul had made when he had watched the gates of his fortress fall.

The Bleak was streaming away. The heavy curtain of mist was drawing back to reveal the brightness of daylight. Caught up within the circling funnels of the storm, Deathren and Stalkers flamed to dust in sparkling bursts, as rays of sunlight found them.

Corr flinched when a body smacked down against the stones

beside him. In the growing light, the Demon Lord's crushed and bloodied face grimaced up at him. Corr bellowed in alarm, his cry lost to the roar of winds, before the maelstrom sent the body cartwheeling back up into the sky. Three Rebel arrows had pierced the evil sorcerer's chest, and it gave Corr a burst of righteous pride that it had been his men, and not the happenstance of Catrian's storm, that had ended their enemy.

The tempest passed over them quickly, drawing up the Bleak as it went. It hastened out to sea, towards Fennick's Island in aid of Gralyre's bid for the Dragon Sword of Lyre.

Corr's ears rang from the sudden hush in the wake of the screaming wind. His breath rasped harshly, as he waited out the moments to ensure that it had truly ended. After a time, he struggled to dislodge himself from amongst the rocks. Pain shot up his leg from a deep sprain to his ankle, and he collapsed back onto one of the stones that had shielded him.

The Bleak had vanished. Sunshine blasted, bright and hot, into the blight left behind by centuries of darkness. Corr blinked heavily from the pain of daylight suddenly searing into his sensitive night vision. Yet the tears that seeped from his eyes were wrought from much more than this, for of his fortress nothing remained save a field of smoldering wreckage that was scattered as far as he could see. Brick walls had not been strong enough to withstand the cyclonic force of Catrian's storm.

From the small rise upon which he sat, Corr had an unimpeded view to the far western horizon, where the path of the storm's eye had actually scoured the land down to the bedrock, creating a wide, open road flowing north to south. As he gaped at the destruction, he lamented that so much devastation could be wrought by a storm that had dealt them only a glancing blow.

Bit by bit, battered Southerners stirred from their hiding places. They were the lucky ones, like Corr, who had found a way to anchor themselves against the pull of the winds.

Except for a select group of warriors who had held the privilege of seeking supplies in the lowlands, few of the inhabitants of the Southern Fortress had ever felt the heat of sunlight, or experienced the open expanse of a world without the claustrophobic mists of the Bleak wrapping them tightly in its diseased embrace. It had been thought a kindness to deny them the sun, for one could not crave what one had never known.

The sudden shattering of the mask to reveal the true face of the world sent many of the survivors into an hysterical panic or a religious ecstasy, for fear that the bright light heralded their deaths. Others seemed too dazed to respond to the sudden glory of the world, and picked aimlessly through the burned rubble, or sat as Corr did, in abject shock.

As Corr watched, a Demon Rider crawled out from under a collapsed outer wall, where it had sheltered from the winds. The survivors immediately pelted their enemy with loose bricks. The 'Rider tried to shield itself, but soon succumbed to the stoning. A warrior stepped out of the small crowd, and lopped its head with his sword, preventing its rebirth as a Deathren at the setting of the sun.

"Lieutenant Corr, sir?"

Corr blinked upwards at a man's dark silhouette against the bright, blue bowl of the sky. It was Sarten, one of the small band of warriors that he had travelled with.

"Thank the Gods ye survived, sir!"

Corr had not heard him approach, and wondered how long he had been gaping at the devastation, mindless of all else. "Have ye found others? My father?"

The Southern Rebel shook his head in the negative. Various hues of red coated his face, creating a startling contrast to the Southern whiteness of his light-deprived skin. Blood washed his left cheek from a gash near his eye, and dried crimson mud, the filth accumulated through days of hard travel through the Rubicund Fen, encrusted his auburn hair. "No one. I…" Sarten's shoulders heaved. "Do ye think the Bleak is gone forever?" His face was filled with dread at the abatement of the darkness, even as he lifted it towards the benediction of the sun's warmth.

"We can only hope, Sarten. 'Twas magic what made it, and magic what destroyed it." Corr extended a hand. "Help me up. We need t' gather our people." Together, the men hobbled down the short hill into the thick of the devastation.

It took time for Corr to calm the survivors. There was much work to be done which was a blessing, for it distracted them from their sorrows and terror. Though all Deathren and Stalkers had been destroyed by the overwhelming appearance of sunlight, any dead Demon Riders not carried off by the winds of the storm would need beheading to prevent Deathren attacks upon the survivors after nightfall. Any surviving enemy also needed to be found, and put to the sword.

Search parties were formed to seek survivors within the collapsed rubble that was all that remained of their homes. Few of their own were unearthed, and only one other 'Rider was found alive and swiftly dealt with.

It was fortunate that few Demon Riders had been present at the battle. By this time of year, most of the 'Riders stationed in the Bleak would have been ferried over to Fennick's Island to await their opportunity to seek the Dragon Sword of Lyre during the Spring Solstice.

Catrian's storm had been deathly efficient in its purpose. Of the Southerners who had survived the fires and the Deathren attacks, more had been killed by the winds and taken into the sky to never be seen again. Though they searched until sunset, and found many bodies, Corr knew in his heart that his father was one of those who would be lost forever.

Bodies of friends and family were carted into the heart of their destroyed fortress, and placed in a mound. From there, they would await the turning of the world, while marking the passing of the People of the South.

As they all gathered in sorrow for their fallen, Corr performed a quick head count, and found their dearth of numbers heartbreaking. Far too many had travelled to the side of the Gods. Less than a fifth of the five thousand residents of the Southern Fortress remained.

Their population had never been large, for the Southern

Rebels were sickly from lifetimes spent in darkness. Few babies were born to them, for children bespoke a hope in the future, and theirs was a dark world that none would wish upon an infant. It had been a point of pride that they had remained in the Bleak to do their duty for the rebellion, though it meant disease and poverty to rival that of the meanest lowland village. Most had not minded the promise of an early death, and many had hastened to meet it - anything to escape the Bleak. Corr's own mother had taken this path to the Gods when he was but a child.

Still, there had been beauty in their world. Oil lamps had ever burned along the avenues of their fortress to fuel the intricate patterns of luminous mosaics carpeting the streets that they trod upon. Gone now. Never to be seen again.

Their red hearths had ever glowed with the welcoming heat of peat fires to drive back the insidious damp. Music, deep and dark as their world, had comforted them of an evening, played quietly on lutes within closed halls to ensure that the sound would not carry to the ears of their enemies.

All but the memory of their homes had vanished into the whirlwinds, evaporated along with the fogs of the Bleak, as though they had never been aught but imaginary abodes of mist and shadow.

Corr was too numb to grieve. He had to maintain a strong face for the sake of his remaining people.

That night the survivors slept where they fell, while the few remaining warriors, Corr and Sarten among them, stood guard against any Deathren attacks. It was possible that some dead

Demon Riders would have been missed during the searches, hidden in the rubble, but the night was blessedly quiet save for occasional moans of pain and quiet sobs. Cascades of stars watched over them from the skies above, the first to be seen in this land for three hundred years.

The following morning, the bedraggled survivors of the Southern Fortress scavenged what they could from the rubble in preparation for their departure.

Doaphin's forces in the south may have been decimated, but Corr could not rely upon this for long. Soon enough Doaphin's battalions would return, and the remnants of the Southern Rebels had to be far and away by then. They could not afford a fight, not with so few warriors, and with wounded, children and the aged to protect. All they could do was run, as fast and as far as their injuries would allow.

Corr sent a rider ahead on their one surviving horse, charging the courier to reach the Rebel rendezvous north of Verdalan. Commander Boris had to be informed of the death of Corr's father, General Ryes, and that the south could no longer be relied upon to fulfill their part of the rebellion's battle strategy.

Commander Boris was depending upon General Ryes to open and hold the eastern passes in the southern Heathren Mountains into the realm of the Dream Weavers, so that Lowlander refugees had a path of retreat ahead of Doaphin's oncoming genocidal war. But not enough Southerners remained to perform this vital task. What few warriors Corr had were needed to guard his fleeing people against attacks. They were now the refugees in need of succor.

Corr walked amongst the remnants of his people, doing his best to bolster them for the long journey ahead. They were looking to him to know what to do, and he had no plan beyond marching back north towards the other Rebel strongholds. Despite his father's comments to him on the road, Corr would not gamble upon the existence of the legendary Dream Weavers, using the safety of his remaining people as the wager. North had to be their direction. He could only hope that the extra mouths would be welcomed within either Commander Boris or General Kierdenan's forces.

The Southerners travelled not as a strong army in proud ordered formations, but as a straggling, shambling mob of defeated refugees. They used the new road left to them by the storm, a straight, wide path that the wind had scoured into the earth, to guide them north towards the promise of sanctuary.

The saturated ground, overshadowed by the heavy fogs of the Bleak for three centuries, was drying quickly in the cleansing heat of direct sunlight, emitting a stench of long dead things. The white mold that coated all surfaces was dehydrating into mummified paper, and blowing away in the gentle puffs of swirling breezes.

As the first day progressed, and the strong sunlight continued to bake the earth into a cracked desert devoid of life, dust from shuffling steps arose to hang in the air, surrounding their slow progress with a further choking misery.

In front of Corr, an older woman stumbled to her knees,

dropping the basket that she had held balanced against a hip, and strewing her few pitiful possesions. Corr paused to help her, while others continued to shuffle past, too dazed by their own woes to notice the misfortunes of another.

"The Gods bless ye, General. We are all sorry for the loss o' your Da!" Her face was flaming red from the burn of the sun, a match to Corr's own, though he had gained some pigment during the journey north to the war summit to help him withstand it.

He grimaced at the title she gave him, the promotion. He was a fraud. His father had been General, not he. Corr shifted her attention back to her own woes. "How are ye getting on? Do ye need a turn on the wagons?"

Culled from the wreckage of their fortress before they had abandoned it, a few iron carts used in the mining of lumenstone ore were being pulled along by the stronger survivors to allow the lame and injured to rest from time to time amidst the piled baggage and belongings. Other carts carried what little food had been scavenged.

"Gods bless ye, General," she repeated, and gave him a familiar pat on the cheek. "I do no' need it yet."

Corr, after helping her to stand, continued to limp forward. The ache in his calves and feet told the tale of this difficult trek. His sprained ankle was a stab of pain with each step, and the deep bruises sustained from the impacts of wind-driven debris ached with each movement.

He did not seek to ride upon a cart, and instead welcomed the agony, as an outlet for the grief that he could not yet release.

CHAPTER ONE

Above the Heathren Mountains - Now

In mere hours, the magic-borne sphere shuttled the champions of Fennick's Island north over the same distance that had required a journey of months on horseback. Seen through the transparent surface of the orb that suspended them aloft, the rushing ground far below was only a quick plummet away. The wind was a constant thrum, as though they were caught within a broken minstrel's harp that had but one note to play.

The small group's acute terror of Gralyre's strange magic lessened into weary acceptance, as the evening elapsed towards midnight, for such intense emotion could not be sustained. Exhausted from their ordeal on Fennick's Island and this strange flight through the sky, and with no food to eat, they rested where they could find space, trying their best to avoid bumping the legs of the unmoving animals.

Though the horses were held immobile, their eyes rolled fearfully at the people amongst them, beseeching an end to their imprisonment. Even Little Wolf appeared to be only a stuffed and mounted trophy, taken by a huntsman eager to impress his neighbours with his prowess in taking a black wolf.

The hum of the wind altered pitch, as the orb slowed, and their flight drew to an end. A new fear swept the small group then, for Gralyre was steering them into an army that was amassed in the valley below the ruined walls of the Rebel's Northern Fortress.

Rewn stood next to Gralyre, unable to awaken his friend from the spell of the Dragon Sword, though he shook his shoulders and shouted for him to return. Stymied, Rewn confronted the others. His brown eyes were rimmed red within his exhausted, white face, as he pleaded with them to keep their faith in Gralyre. "'Tis a mistake! Gralyre would no' deliver us t' our enemies!" His voice echoed strangely in the spherical space of the invisible orb. Like all of them, he was ragged and filthy, and his brown hair was blackened by sweat and dirt to a colour deeper than its original hue.

Jord's ever present daggers flashed in the moonlight, as he pointed one at the nearing campfires. "Then what do ye call that?" The evidence was clear to them all. He tossed back his overlong, ragged brown hair, briefly revealing the sneer of betrayal beneath his large nose before he turned away. He tottered between the oddly still horses towards the other side of the sphere to collect his pack. The concave curve of the invisible floor, and the speedy passage of the land far below, made walking a dizzying experience.

Rewn's face clouded with doubt. The constant drone of the wind continued to change pitch and volume, as the orb decelerated and descended. His stomach rolled into his throat, as they dropped towards the ground. The bright dots of campfires drew nearer and clearer. Battle would soon be upon them.

"Gralyre, can ye hear me? Ye must waken!" Rewn roared while shaking Gralyre's arm again.

Like the animals, Gralyre stood as a statue, and his body scarcely shifted with the violence of Rewn's jostling. His hands melded to the glowing Dragon Sword of Lyre that he held aloft before his torso. His rapturous face ran with rivulets of sweat, as if he were experiencing great pain and pleasure in the same moment. His blue-black eyes had rolled back in his head, leaving the whites exposed, eerie and foreign, yet his balance had never faltered as the hours had elapsed.

"Leave him! He canno' hear ye, Rewn! Ready your weapons!" Dotch ordered the group at large. Older in years and experience than the others, he assumed command. "Do no' lag nor await each other! Scatter t' divide their attention, and do what ye can t' fight free!" He tested the smoothness of his sword's release from its sheath by plunging the hilt a couple of times. Satisfied, he slung his pack over a shoulder. "We will meet up at the south gate o' the fortress. If I do no' make it…"

"Do no' worry Dotch. Whatever comes, whoever survives, we will find and protect your family," Aneida vowed, for she was now alone in the world save for her friends within this sphere, and they were made all the more precious to her for it. Only hours earlier, she had watched her sister, Mayvin, die in an avalanche of stone. Aneida's cheeks were still streaked with the dirty paths of shed tears.

Dotch shoved an urgent hand through his short, salt-and-pepper hair, sending the short strands into further disarray. "Ella is smart. She survived the attacks. I know she did." If faith could make it so, his wife and sons would be found safe. He tried to swallow past the constriction in his chest that had manifested in the moments after they had flown over the ruined fortress walls.

"What o' Trifyn?" Saliana's grey eyes grew round with dread. "He canno' run!" Her fine, white-blond hair was caught up in a rough braid, similar to the plait in Aneida's red tresses, and it swung forward, as she placed her palm over Trifyn's brow. As she evaluated his fever, she was careful to avoid the deep, crusted gash in the bowman's cheek, sustained from the lash of a rope during Catrian's storm.

One of the missing sleeves from Saliana's grey frock was bound over the dire wound on Trifyn's thigh. His blood had seeped through the makeshift bandage since she had affixed it in place, and had oozed down off his upper leg to drip against the transparent surface of the orb. The pool of red lent shape and form to the invisible.

Though Saliana quivered from the hours of strain spent ignoring that she had nothing beneath her body save for a long drop to a certain death, she bore little resemblance to the meek young woman who had begun this journey.

"I will no' leave him," Saliana whispered, as though not yet believing that she was going to sacrifice herself so. One of her hands drifted to the hilt of the blade that was shoved through the belt at her waist. The sword gifted to her by Mayvin before she had died.

Aneida bent to shake the bowman's shoulder, and Trifyn

mumbled, a moan of pain, but otherwise he did not stir. He had fallen into a stupor not long after their magical flight from the south had begun. He seemed even younger now, his blond hair pasted thickly to his scalp from the sweat of his fever. His hand clenched around the polished yew of his bow that lay at his side, his fingers scrabbling occasionally, as though he drew it in his dreams. Blood and dirt soiled his broken nails, bespeaking the fight for survival on Fennick's Island that had brought him to this state.

Aneida straightened, and her finger played over the long, thin scar that spanned her neck from ear to ear. The other missing sleeve from Saliana's torn dress was bound around a wound on Aneida's upper arm. Her chin jerked once in a nod of acceptance, as she came to her decision, "I will stay with him. Ye go. Ye run."

"No!"

"Do as I say!" Aneida flicked her thick, red braid over her shoulder, and braced her feet aggressively.

"No! I am the healer. He is my responsibility. Ye go! Ye are the better fighter. Ye have a chance t' make it! Take it!"

"I know I am the better fighter, that is why ye are going and I am staying!"

"Ready yourselves!" Dotch roared, interrupting their budding argument over who would be the martyr. Treetops and moon-dappled rivers spun past before they dropped in a last stomach-churning arc. They halted with a lurch that toppled all save Gralyre and the animals to their knees.

"Gralyre!" Rewn yelled in a last attempt to awaken his friend.

The sphere rent with a thunderous clap.

They fell the final foot into the woodland clearing, writhing with pain, as the pressure in their ears equalized to their new altitude. Released from the magic that had bound them still all night, the horses bucked and neighed, running dangerously amuck through the tents and campfires of the army that they had landed amidst.

Little Wolf howled and snapped, as he fled into the moonlit forest at a ground-scratching run, putting as much distance as possible between himself, and the fearful journey that Gralyre had taken them all on.

The ragged party lay in the loamy dirt, drawing upon the air with harsh gasps. Despite their intentions, there was no fight left within them. The pain in their ears, and the sudden stillness after the rushing movement, assailed their senses with waves of vertigo. They listed helplessly, as unknown soldiers ran past seeking to corral the horses ere they could do damage.

Dozens of rows of cone-shaped tents surrounded them, evenly spaced amongst the trees. Most were blooming with the light of lanterns, as the occupants awakened after the group's loud arrival.

"Ah, Gods," Rewn moaned, as he spat at the dirt. His back arched, and he began to heave in great rasping spasms. He glanced up to meet Gralyre's concerned gaze, but it was too soon to move, and he was caught by another retch.

Now released from the sword's will, Gralyre's expression

was without guile. Whatever was to come, Rewn was certain that he had meant no harm - just as with the destruction of Fennick's Island, and the resulting tidal wave that had almost claimed their lives shortly after they had recovered the Dragon Sword of Lyre.

Rewn's gaze shifted to the sword that lay in the dirt at Gralyre's side. The Maolar silver of the magical blade was dulled and metallic now, glowing with nothing more than reflected moonlight. It was an unfathomable tragedy that they had survived all of their epic trials, only at the finish to deliver the powerful weapon unto Doaphin.

Rewn shivered and heaved dryly, drawn back to his misery. The yawning motions of his mouth and throat had the unexpected benefit of popping his ears to relieve the pressure and pain.

Saliana began to sob, rocking against her drawn up legs with her face buried in her hands so that she would not see the end when it came. Would the Demon Riders take her for the Tithe or just kill her? What would become of Trifyn'?

By her side, the bowman lay still and silent. Saliana was thankful that he would be unaware of his death when it came. How could Gralyre have betrayed them so?

To Saliana's left, Jord was suffering from a similar malaise as Rewn. He coughed and groaned, his hands digging deeply into the dirt in an effort to anchor to stillness and hold back his heaves. He was aided in this by the fact that they had eaten nothing for days.

Between dry retches, Jord tried to study the gathering of strange warriors, but the flickering torchlight of the woodland clearing kept lurching and spinning. They were not 'Riders, and no attack had come as yet, but he would be more confident in defending himself if he could stop the world from pitching.

The strange warriors were tall men of dark hair and tawny skin. Most sported quivers on their backs, and knocked bows at the ready. They stood guard in a loose semi-circle, and remained vigilant though the small group was obviously no threat to them.

Aneida's grief-filled roar made Jord's head lurch in drunken alarm to find her. He was in time to watch her stagger away from Dotch, careening from tree to tree to keep from falling. Her sword dragged loosely behind her, as she vanished into the bushes. Her repetitious bellows bespoke pain and madness, and echoed throughout the forest as she fled. The strange warriors made no move to stop her. Why were they not attacking?

Dotch watched after Aneida with great concern, all the while hugging a thin sapling in order to stay on his feet. His sword had never made it out of its scabbard. "Sorry, sorry," he kept repeating, though the reason for his regret was not readily apparent to Jord.

After a short wait, an older man pushed through the encircling warriors. He paused to scan the scene while wiping a hand through his neatly trimmed, white beard to shake out the crumbs from the mouthful of food he was just swallowing. Against the thick whiteness of his hair, his eyes were a startling blue in his healthily tanned face, as he evaluated the ragged group laid low before him.

Unbent, though approaching his later years, he was as tall as the men around him. Clad in a loose linen tunic and brown trousers, topped by a simple leather jerkin, nothing about him was indicative of status, yet the deference shown to him by his men betrayed him as their leader. They parted to make way, as he strode forward with the confidence of his station. His tall, gnarled staff tapped softly to the rhythm of his easy steps. His comfortable old boots made little sound upon the soft needles of the forest floor when he halted in front of Gralyre.

Gralyre dragged himself upright, wavering though he used the massive Dragon Sword of Lyre as a crutch. Manfully, he stood straight, in order to meet the older man's assessing gaze. His black hair and his beard dripped with sweat from the exertion of his magic over the past hours.

"Welcome to the army of the Dream Weavers, my lord Prince."

Rewn's eyes clashed with Jord's. "Did he just…?"

"Prince?" Jord wheezed, finishing Rewn's sentence. "'Tis no' possible! Dream Weavers?"

Gralyre's midnight-blue eyes rolled white, as he toppled backwards into the dirt. His great strength, at last, was spent.

"Hmph," the older man grumbled before he turned his attention to the rest of the weary arrivals, and expanded upon his greeting. "You are *all* welcomed to the army of the Dream Weavers. Tents and beds have been prepared. You are expected."

With a soft creaking, the men holding knocked arrows relaxed their bowstrings. A babble of conversation began, as most of them dispersed back to beds or to the duties interrupted by the startling arrival of Gralyre's party.

Dotch was still having trouble catching up. He was shivering from the cooler temperature of the mountain glade. "Dream Weavers?" he mumbled, as he released his tree. He staggered a step before the ground seemed to sway out from under his boot, and he fell to his knees with a jarring impact.

One of the tall warriors leaned forward with a friendly grin, and helped him to stand. "Dream Weavers?" Dotch repeated, the shock of it overwhelming all logic. Not only were they safe but they were also among powerful allies of song and legend.

The warrior nodded.

"What...?" Dotch stuttered. "Jord," he hissed to the side, "did he call Gralyre *'Prince'*?"

Jord nodded mutely, still regarding the company suspiciously. He slowly pushed himself up to rest his rump upon his heels.

Dotch turned back to the warrior who had helped him to stand. "I canno' stay here!"

The warrior backed away, holding out his hands and shrugging to indicate that he did not understand.

Dotch turned frantically towards the man who had welcomed them. "Sir, please! My wife and family! They were in the fortress! I have t' get t' them. Please," Dotch begged, "a horse!"

The leader regarded him with compassion. "You must rest

first. Return to the fortress in the morning light."

Dotch's jaw jutted stubbornly. "No. I must go now! I must get t' them!"

"Rest. What was to be has already happened. If they live, yet will they live in the morn. If they have perished, a delay of hours will not change their fate. You must eat and rest, to gain strength to face what comes in the morn."

Dotch shook his head in frenzied denial. "No! My sons… my wife...!"

"*Bou-te-deva*!" The elder ordered softly in the Dream Weaver tongue, and the warrior who had so recently helped Dotch up, now gave him a little nudge to the centre of his chest.

Too weak to overcome the sudden challenge to his balance, Dotch's arms momentarily windmilled before he crashed onto his back.

Jord snarled at the unprovoked attack, and dove forward to hover protectively above Dotch's heaving chest. Knives flickered into his fists, and he waved them erratically, blinking heavily to try to focus his vision. "I will kill the next man t' touch him!"

The leader's mouth tightened. "You are in no danger from us, but have no strength remaining," he chided reasonably. "Abide with us this evening, restore your strength, and we will aid you in your search in the morning."

Dotch passed a hand over his eyes, voicing a guttural growl of frustration.

Jord leaned closer to whisper, "We will steal a couple o'

horses, and…"

"No. He is right, Jord. I am no good t' Ella until I have rested." The Dream Weaver had made his point.

They were interrupted anew by a female screech of joy. "Rewn!" Dara, Rewn's younger sister, flew across the clearing towards them.

Rewn opened his arms in time to catch her, as she barrelled into him, sprawling him backwards into the dirt.

"Gods! Ye are safe! Thank-ye! Thank-ye!" Dara was hugging and kissing him, and weak as he was, all Rewn could do was chuckle and hug her back.

His hand fisted into her brown tresses as, overcome by a reunion that he had never imagined would come again on this side of life, he found himself sobbing quietly against his sister's shoulder.

The Dream Weaver leader beckoned one of his men forward from out of the loitering onlookers. The newcomer wore the long leather smock of a healer, and toted a leather satchel over one shoulder that he rooted through, as he neared. He was a man of middle years with a pleasant face cast in lines that exposed an amicable nature. He was as dark of hair as the other Dream Weavers, and as deeply tanned and fit with health.

The leader held out his hand to accept a small, wooden vial from the healer, before kneeling next to Gralyre's prone form. He unstoppered the small flask, and pressed the lip of it under Gralyre's nose.

Gralyre moaned and sputtered, as the acrid fumes within the

vial drew him awake.

The leader turned slightly to address the healer in the language of the Dream Weavers, motioning him towards the unconscious Trifyn.

Saliana shied away from the approach of the stranger, watching suspiciously, as he lifted the bandage on Trifyn's leg to peer at his wound. After evaluating the nature of the injury, the healer charged a couple of waiting warriors to gently lift the unconscious Trifyn from where he lay in the dirt.

Saliana lost her timidness in a rush of protective ire, and rose to stagger after the Dream Weavers. "Where are ye taking him?" she demanded fiercely. "Dotch! Jord! Help me! Where are they taking Trifyn?"

"Ahhhhrg!" Jord yelled aggressively, and lashed out at a Dream Weaver who had bent down to help him to stand, forcing the warrior to leap back from his flashing blades. "Do no' touch me! Dotch! They are taking Trifyn!" Jord crawled roughly towards Saliana, scrabbling across the forest floor in an effort to catch the men bearing the bowman away.

Dotch lunged, and caught Jord's ankle, halting the knifeman's forward progress. "We are safe, Jord," he announced sternly. "Saliana," he looked towards the distraught woman, "ye are both safe." He cupped one of Jord's hands where it was fisted around a dagger. "Put those away now, lad. Ye are amongst friends."

Jord stilled with indecision, his dark brows wrinkling above his prominent nose, as his innate suspiciousness warred against

Dotch's reason. "Ye are certain?" The people that Jord trusted numbered fewer than he could count on one hand, but after all that they had been through, Dotch was prominent among them.

"Aye."

"How do ye know?" Saliana challenged, still fretting and frightened, as she watched Trifyn being toted away to a place unknown.

"Rewn's sister seems fine. And Gralyre trusts them. He has left with the leader."

Saliana glanced around wildly, just in time to see Gralyre disappear into a far tent.

The Dream Weaver healer turned to face them then. His brown eyes were kind, and he folded his hands benignly at the waist of his long leather apron. "Be at ease." His voice held a strange, yet pleasant accent, more pronounced than that of the leader. "All is well, I assure you. Your friend is injured and in need of care. My name is Ninrhar and I am a healer."

"I am Dotch, this is Jord," Dotch volunteered, indicating his travelling companions as he named them, "and Saliana is our healer." Jord's knives vanished, and Dotch, taking that for a sign of capitulation, hauled Jord up.

Dotch slung an arm around Jord's back to steady them both. Though Jord stiffened at the touch, he seemed to accept that he needed the temporary support.

"You must all be hungry." Ninrhar motioned to the Dream Weaver warrior who Jord had so recently threatened.

From a careful distance, the warrior mimed eating, and

motioned them to follow after.

"Food," Dotch and Jord breathed reverently. Their last meal had been taken on the beach before escaping the tidal wave from the sinking island - one seventh of a ration of salted meat that Rewn had saved to share with the group.

"It is safe," Ninrhar urged. "A meal has been prepared for your arrival."

"Rewn, are ye coming?" Dotch called out.

"In a while." Rewn mumbled against Dara's shoulder. Still overwhelmed by his good fortune, he was not yet ready to release his sister.

Though not wholly at ease, Dotch and Jord went willingly enough after that. Had the Dream Weavers meant them harm there would have been no need for such pretences.

Only concerned with Trifyn's wellbeing, Saliana ignored the invitation for food. "Can ye help him?" she tested the Dream Weaver.

"You have been tending to him? You are a healer?" Ninrhar asked Saliana in lieu of reply.

Guilt shamed Saliana to be labelled so, for really she was only an apprentice, and had deserted the Rebel fortress well before she had learned much at all. "I was training t' be one," she demurred.

The Dream Weaver smiled. "Then you must come with me, for there is much for you to learn."

Saliana returned his smile hesitantly. "Really? Ye would teach me?"

Ninrhar shrugged. "Knowledge to a learner is as water in the desert if one is thirsty." He nodded, as though the oblique statement explained all, and encircled Saliana's waist with a strong grip to support her, as they followed after the men who were even now stepping through the flap of a nearby tent with Trifyn's body suspended between them.

Saliana glanced back once more before passing through the flap into the healer's tent, to see that only Rewn remained where they had been dropped by Gralyre's magical orb. He was well occupied embracing Dara. Everyone was safe, for now.

She was suddenly overcome by the knowledge that they had survived their quest for the Dragon Sword. New tears began to slip down her cheeks. She had spent months preparing to die, only now to realize that the Gods had gifted her, gifted all of them, with more life.

All save for Mayvin. Now that the danger had passed, she had time to remember her friend and to grieve. Poor Aneida. What was she to do without her sister?

The healer's conical tent was ten feet across, and bright with light from the lanterns set around the perimeter of the circular space. There was no furniture on the earthen floor, only a pallet of heaped furs that had been placed in front of a small brazier for warmth and comfort. Leaving Saliana to grasp the centre post for balance, the Dream Weaver healer directed his men to place Trifyn gently upon the waiting bed. Saliana sniffed, and brushed her hand across her face to staunch her lingering teardrops.

One of the warriors dropped a bucket of water, and a leather satchel next to the bed before collecting his companion and leaving. Saliana shrank away from the men's path, as they brushed past her on their way out of the tent.

Ninrhar motioned Saliana to join him, as he knelt by Trifyn's side, and gently unwrapped the bandage from around his wounded leg. "From an arrow?"

"Aye"

"'Tis a fine bandaging," he complimented.

Saliana blushed, as she sat at his side. "Thank-ye. I did no' have much time."

Ninrhar smiled, as he noted her missing sleeves. "Ah," he nodded. "You made due with what you had, and you kept him safe and alive. This is no small feat on a battlefield."

Saliana dipped her head, as embarrassed pleasure washed over her. She was unused to praise.

After thoroughly scrubbing his hands with a bar of lye soap, and rinsing them in the bucket of water, Ninrhar reached within his satchel for a crisp, clean linen that he folded and placed beneath Trifyn's injured leg. "Tell me of the first step in treating wounds?" He asked conversationally, as he worked.

Saliana bit her lip. "Stop the bleeding?"

Ninrhar eyed her sharply. "Are you sure?"

Saliana drew a breath for courage. "Aye. Stop the bleeding."

Ninrhar's eyes crinkled, as he smiled approvingly. "There. Now you are sure. How do we stop the bleeding?"

"With a hot brand."

Ninrhar's brows rose in amazement. "Is that what is still done in these lands?"

Saliana nodded. It was what she had been taught during her aborted apprenticeship. She had witnessed the practice while at the fortress, and had used the same technique upon wounds great and small, as they had travelled south to Fennick's Island.

Ninrhar leaned closer to examine Trifyn's wound. "Yet, you did not burn him."

"There was no time. We were fighting the 'Riders, and then Gralyre used magic t' whisk us off the island, and then the island sank with a huge wave, and we were fleeing inland from it…"

Ninrhar waited patiently, as her tale gushed forth in a spew of disjointed events. Saliana noted his expression, and her nervous chatter ground to a halt.

Ninrhar placed his hand gently over hers. "Be at ease. Burning a wound is not a sound treatment, for it will nearly always cause a later infection. It is of benefit only if the blood is spurting, and you have no way to apply a tourniquet. Better than searing flesh, binding a wound tightly closed with a clean cloth is usually enough to eventually stop the flow of blood. You would not have helped Trifyn had you burned him, but only made his injury worse. Lean in and smell it."

Saliana bent and immediately detected the scent of corrupted flesh. She gasped, for into her mind's eye, it was now Mayvin who was lying before her with her shoulder split and broken, slowly dying from the poison of her wound, while nothing Saliana could do could save her. She blinked quickly, and the mental image dissolved into the teary sheen of her grief. Even if

Mayvin had not sacrificed herself to save them, she would not have survived her mortal injury.

"Be not afraid." Ninrhar patted her hand kindly. "I will cleanse the wound now."

The healer's palms hovered above the gash in Trifyn's thigh, and he slowly played them back and forth, yet never touched the injury directly. Yellow pus began to flow out of the tear in Trifyn's flesh, oozing thickly from the wound, and sliding off the smooth muscles of his leg to soak into the clean linen placed beneath. The smell of rotting flesh thickened the air.

Saliana's hands rose to cover her mouth. "Ye are a Sorcerer!" she squeaked.

Ninrhar did not reply, his attention focussed solely upon his task. Slow minutes passed, and the pus gave way to watery, bloody discharge. When finally only thick, normal blood seeped from the wound, Ninrhar withdrew his hands.

Saliana gulped, as she eyed the jagged puncture in Trifyn's thigh. "Could ye no' have healed it all the way?"

Ninrhar smiled, and used a clean cloth to blot at the beads of sweat that had collected upon his upper lip from his efforts. "I encouraged Trifyn's Godsmagic to repair his direst injuries. The poisons in his blood will be left to his body to heal, so that it might grow stronger from the fight."

"Fighting makes us stronger?" Saliana frowned in confusion.

"Of course. Think of your own trials. You survived, and now are stronger than you would ever have been without them." As Ninrhar spoke, he lathered a cloth in the bucket of water, and began to cleanse away the filth and bloody discharge from in and around Trifyn's wound.

"Also," Ninrhar continued to lecture, "it has been found that without the fear of pain breeding caution in battle, over time a warrior healed of all suffering gains an inflated sense of invulnerability. They take senseless chances, and die all the sooner for it."

Ninrhar rinsed the cloth, generously lathered it once more, and tackled the dirt upon Trifyn's face. He gently washed the crusted gash on Trifyn's cheek in order to examine the depth of the wound. The skin knitted shut beneath his hands, as he worked. A few more passes with the soapy cloth removed the last of the scab, leaving a narrow pink scar in its place that faded rapidly from sight.

A crushing sense of inadequacy sagged Saliana's shoulders. "Ninrhar, I can ne'er do what ye have done," she admitted quietly. "I have no magic."

Ninrhar laughed, his head thrown back in amusement. "Young miss, there are few who can." He rinsed the cloth again, leaving swirls of red in the sudsy water. "I will teach you of the true magic of healing, with techniques and ointments and potions. All I have done can be accomplished through these. It is just that we will be marching to war soon, and this young man must be made hale by then."

Determination etched Saliana's features. "Teach me all!" her words were uncharacteristically fierce. Never again would she lose a friend through her lack of knowledge.

Ninrhar reached into his bag, and drew forth a shimmering Maolar needle attached to a fine line of silken thread. "Then I will begin with teaching you of the importance of cleanliness, and then show you how to darn flesh to aid the knitting of deeper wounds."

෪ଓ

Dara could not stop hugging Rewn. She smoothed his lank brown hair back from his face, and rocked him in her arms, as tears of happiness fell freely. Laughter bubbled up, for she had never thought to see her brother again. Against all odds, he had returned victorious from Fennick's Island.

Granted, Rewn was a wreck. His already lean frame was now gaunt, and his pleasant face showed a hardness that had never lived there before. He shivered violently in the wake of the fearful journey, but Dara did not care. He was alive, and he was home. "Oh, I am glad t' see ye!"

Her smile lit up his world, and Rewn was sore glad to see it. It had been a long time since he had last seen her happy. Not since the attacks she had suffered at the hands of the three Rebel Stewards had she looked thus.

Leaving Raindell ahead of her family, Dara had been sent to the safety of the Northern Rebels to escape Doaphin's Tithe. Upon arriving at the fortress, instead of finding sanctuary, as a Lowlander, she had found prejudice and abuse. Without her family, she had been vulnerable to attack, and the three Rebel

Stewards had forced her to trade her body for food and shelter.

When he had finally arrived at the fortress, and discovered what had befallen her, Rewn had enlisted Gralyre's aid to ensure that her abusers had paid for their crimes. Dara had been long recovering from the horrors of her ordeal. Rewn would always carry the guilt that he had not been there to protect her.

Rewn smoothed back her long, brown hair, and gave her a noisy buss on her cheek. "Dara! I am glad t' be seen!" He returned her grin with a shaky one of his own. "Help me up."

Dara slung his arm over her shoulder, and hauled him upright. He had lost more weight than she had thought. Never before would she have been able to lift his larger frame so easily.

Rewn groaned like an old man, as he arose. "Where is Dajin? And what are ye doing here instead o' at the fortress? Though I thank the Gods 'tis so, and ye are safe!"

Dara huffed out a breath to blow an errant strand of brown hair away from her cheek, as she walked him through the encamped army. "Dajin is this way. Ye will want t' see him first, and then I will take ye t' get some dinner. Did ye no' know that I am a heroine?" she continued casually, and her smile was mischievous, as she watched him closely from out of the corner of her eye.

Rewn glanced down at his little sister with a teasing smile of his own, pulling her close for a squeeze. "Really? And what have ye been after doing while I have been off battling Demon Lords, Stalkers and Deathren, and winning a fabled sword from a nefarious labyrinth? Oh, and returning t' tell the tale o' it?"

"Well, Dajin and I have only rescued the Sorceress Catrian from assassins and traitors, and certain death from Stalkers. Two o' the beasts attacked us in the woods after we fled the battle up at the fortress. Dajin was swatted unconscious by one, so I killed it with my puny dagger t' save him, but the second Stalker escaped me." She heaved a mock sigh, as though disappointed.

Rewn stumbled them to a halt, as he dug in his heals. "What? Ye did what...? Ah, ye are teasing me."

Dara shook her head. Her mouth smiled still, but her eyes were serious.

"Well. Well now."

Dara burst into tears, and Rewn hauled her into a protective hug against his chest. His exhausted brain was still trying to assimilate her words. "Did ye say ye killed a *Stalker* with naught but a *dagger*?"

A laugh burbled through her weeping, and she leaned back in his embrace. She wiped away the wetness on her cheeks with the back of her hand. "I got it in the eye, just as it was charging us. O' course, the Dream Weavers had already filled its hide with arrows."

"Do not believe her modesty. The beast was not mortally wounded. She delivered the blow that felled it."

"Jacon!" Dara blushed and dipped her head, scrubbing at the last of her tears, as she disentangled herself from Rewn's hug. Together, they reeled unsteadily to meet the Dream Weaver warrior who had come upon them so quietly.

Rewn felt a brother's protectiveness surge to the fore at the man's possessive gaze upon his sister. Keeping a proprietary arm around Dara's shoulders, he unconsciously rose to his full height, though still an inch short of the man standing before him.

"Hello, *belitar*. This is your brother returned?" Jacon reached out a hand with easy camaraderie, and Rewn automatically clasped it. "'Tis good to meet you, Rewn. I am Jacon, son of Gedrhar who greeted your arrival. You will want to see your brother, Dajin. He is recuperating from his injuries born of the Stalker's attack. Dara will show you. We will talk soon, you and I." Jacon gave Rewn's hand a meaningful squeeze before he released it, and turned away.

Rewn's, "Nice t' meet ye," stumbled forth a bit late, but Jacon heard it, for he turned back and smiled before his eyes shifted warmly to Dara.

Dara blushed again, though she held his gaze.

"I will see you tomorrow, *belitar*? At breakfast?"

"I wish t' be with my brother, Jacon," she blurted harshly. She frowned, knowing that her response was out of proportion with the lack of threat. Why could she not act normal? "Perhaps after, though?" she equivocated, taking pains to sound more herself, though her chest tightened for agreeing to see him at all.

"Perhaps we will walk together?" Jacon suggested, and his smile broadened before he continued on his way.

"Anything else ye want t' tell me, little sister?" Rewn probed meaningfully.

"No! Nothing!" Dara's blushes increased, and there was no horse in the land strong enough to drag the truth from her lips.

She was broken inside. *'Belitar. It means beautiful.'* What made this lovely endearment so fearful a thing?

"Dajin is this way," Dara sidetracked Rewn, as she made for the tent where their brother had been housed after being healed of his injuries. "There will be room for ye t' rest in here as well," she chattered, as she pushed into the tent.

They caught Dajin standing shirtless next to a lantern, twisted at the waist to examine the colourful and painful bruises that marked the spot where the Dream Weaver healer had mended his broken ribs earlier that day.

"Demon take ye, Dara! Can ye no' announce yourself?" Dajin snarled, barely glancing at her, as he bent painfully, and reclaimed his shirt. He did a double take, as his mind registered the man that his sister was supporting. His threadbare shirt slithered from nerveless fingers.

He had seen that Rewn and the others had returned; the concussion of magic announcing their appearance had echoed loudly throughout the vale. But Dajin had thought it of no consequence, opting to stay inside his tent instead of running forth to greet Rewn, as Dara had done. Yet, having his brother standing before him, returned from the dead, broke through his indifference with a rush of feeling akin to a flood shattering a dam.

"Rewn." Dajin mouthed. His siblings swam in and out of focus from the tears of emotion that caught at him unawares. "Rewn!"

"Hello, little brother," Rewn grinned. He released Dara, and tottered to Dajin, pulling his stunned brother into an embrace.

For a long moment Dajin returned the hug, overcome that Rewn had survived.

"We made it, Dajin. And we got the sword!" Rewn's voice was rough with emotional pride, as he thumped Dajin's back with a closed fist. He felt renewed at being near to his family once more. It was a gift that he had not expected to ever come again. His gratitude for this extra time with his loved ones was immense. "And ye would no' believe it, but Gralyre is the Lost Prince!"

"Gralyre is the Lost Prince?" Dara chortled. "I knew it! I just knew it was him!"

At Rewn's heartfelt words, Dajin's thoughts clotted with envy, strangling his joy at his brother's unexpected survival.

Always, Rewn had to flaunt his valour! Rewn had travelled into certain death and returned! Rewn had quested for the Dragon Sword of Lyre! Rewn's name was now tied to a legend, to the tale of the Lost Prince himself!

'Where is my glory?' Stolen by Dara, his own twin! She had robbed him of his due when she had killed a Stalker with naught but a dagger, and left Dajin nothing to show for it but ridicule and broken ribs!

Dajin pushed roughly out of Rewn's arms, making his weakened brother stagger back a step. "The two o' ye conspire t' ensure that I have nothing!" His face, so alike to Rewn's, twisted into malcontent lines.

Rewn's smile faltered. "Dajin?" His brown eyes searched his

brother's seeking answers for the absurd accusation, and physical rejection.

Dara sighed heavily. "Dajin, do no'!" She had already been privy to Dajin's caustic rants, and easily recognized the signs of his oncoming blast.

"The pair o' ye make me sick! My family," he sneered. "Ye," Dajin motioned to Rewn, "with your important friends who take ye on important quests! And ye," Dajin motioned to Dara, "who seek t' overshadow my deeds! The two o' ye do nothing but take from me, until I have nothing!" he roared. "Get out! Leave me be!" Dajin rushed forward, and pushed Dara.

Taken by surprise, Dara lost her balance, and fell to her side, but as Dajin turned to do the same to Rewn, he was met with a fist. Dajin's chin snapped upwards, and he fell to the thick furs carpeting the floor of the tent.

Rewn could neither believe his eyes nor his ears. His hands still clenched, he scowled at Dajin who lay before him nursing a bloodied lip. His brother's face was contorted from the pain in his jostled ribs, but he made no sound, as he glared back.

Rewn shook his head, dumbfounded. How had a joyous reunion suddenly turned into a bloody battle? Dajin had long been angered at the world, but when had those resentments spilled over to include his family? Rewn relaxed his fists, and held out a hand to help Dara to stand.

Dajin's harsh pants filled the space between the siblings, as he recovered from Rewn's blow, and the stabbing pain in his ribs. "Thank-ye for making my point for me," he sneered finally, wiping at the blood that dripped from his lip onto his bare chest. "Now get out. And take that traitorous whore with ye."

Dara gasped, her eyes misting from remembered humiliation. Given what had happened to her, it was the worst insult that Dajin could have used.

Rewn started towards Dajin again, as rage overcame his exhaustion. Brother or no, nobody spoke of Dara in such a fashion!

Dara's clutching hands on Rewn's arm held him back. "Leave it, Rewn! Let it go." But her voice was full of hurt from Dajin's vile insult, provoking the exact opposite reaction in her protective sibling.

Rewn reclaimed a measure of physical control but he would not allow Dara to lead him from the tent just yet. "Dajin! What is rotting in your maggoty brain? Ye hit your sister? Ye accuse us o' harming ye?"

Dajin's sneer twisted into petulant defiance. "Ye think I do no' know what is going on? But I do! Oh, I do! Ye both think ye are better than me! Ye think me a coward! 'Tis obvious that I will ne'er be anyone, and I will ne'er have anything with the two o' ye around. Ye will both make sure o' it! Why did ye have t' return, Rewn? Why did ye no' just die? I wish ye were dead! I wish ye were both dead!"

Rewn's face greyed, and he stumbled back, as from a blow.

Dara was horrified, as she quickly got an arm around Rewn's back to support him. "Rewn, he does no' mean it." She turned to her twin and hissed, "Dajin, take it back!"

Knowing he had gone too far, Dajin's gaze fell, yet his mouth set mulishly against any apology.

"He meant it." Rewn glared down at Dajin, willing his little brother to look at him, to face him, to ask forgiveness. The silence stretched between the siblings, and Dajin's words hung with a life of their own, twisted creatures set to breed dark offspring.

Dara could bear the tension no more. "Come, Rewn. I will billet ye. Come on," she drew her stunned brother from the tent. "Let us find ye something t' eat."

Dajin stayed on his back, waiting until they had left before he stood. The taste of blood filled his mouth, and he spat defiantly, his spittle chasing the direction of their retreat.

෨෬

"Ye did no' come back t' the tents, so I brought ye a plate."

Aneida glared at Jord, a wounded animal huddled in the darkness of the forest. Her face was ravaged with her grief over the death of her sister. In the play of the moonlight that filtered down through the forest canopy, Jord could see that her cheeks were wet with tears, glistening tracks of silver against her skin.

Aneida was the one who laughed at death during the height of a battle. She was the one who attacked, not the one who retreated. To see such an expression of misery upon the brash woman's face was disturbing. Jord shifted his weight from one foot to the other, uncertain of how to proceed, as he studied her bent shoulders.

Ignoring her unspoken wish to be alone, he set his jaw, and strode forward to sit a foot away from her upon the trunk of the blown over sapling that she had claimed. It bounced lightly from his weight, as he slapped the tin plate of food into the space between them. "Here it is anyway. Ye should eat."

"Go away."

"No."

Aneida turned on him, her teeth bared, "I said go!"

"I said no," Jord growled back.

"What do ye want from me?" Aneida cuffed the plate so that it flew into the bushes with a sharp clang, abruptly ending the argument.

Jord just stared at her without responding. He did not offer condolences, empty words of pity that they were. He sat as still as the darkness. For once, even his knives were not at play through his deft fingers.

The mere fact that Jord's entire focus was upon her made Aneida's shoulders heave, before her torso buckled from her pain. "She is gone, Jord! Mayvin is gone! What am I t' do? She was all I had!"

"Ye are no' alone. Ye have us. And now that Gralyre has the Dragon Sword…"

"That thrice damned sword! 'Tis treacherous! We should ne'er have quested for it! Mayvin would still be alive!"

"Ye left afore ye heard," he persisted in the face of her rant.

Aneida sniffed loudly, and rubbed a filthy sleeve across her eyes. "Heard what?"

"That Gralyre is *him*, the Lost Prince. And it is a Dream Weaver army out there. Some would say that the prophecy has been fulfilled."

Aneida sneered. "Is that supposed t' give me hope in a pretty future? Ye do no' believe in that demon dung any more than I."

She pounded her chest, punching herself repeatedly, as though the physical pain could help the emotional one. "Mayvin is dead! She pulled a mountain down upon an army o' evil! She died! This is all there is, and all there ever will be. Doaphin's war will consume us all, no matter that the Lost Prince has reclaimed his sword. And I! Do no'! Care! Not anymore! Let him come! Let us be done with it at last!"

The silence between them stretched. Clouds found the moon, and buried it in darkness. The night settled about them, as they drifted in memories of the quest for the powerful sword that had come at such a steep price.

When Jord tried to reach Aneida again, his voice had adopted a pensive cadence, monotone from the horrors he recounted. "I failed, back on the island, did ye know? I failed the very first trial, and the veil was pulled back, and Doaphin's madness was revealed t' me. Ye were no' inside the Labyrinth. Ye did no' see the horror o' it; the bones o' millions o' his own, those that he had sacrificed for three hundred years, stretching t' all horizons, piled so deep that the ground could no' be seen, and the bones shattered underfoot as ye walked. I was alone there, amongst the dead for hours, until Rewn and then Dotch failed their trials and joined me.

"We were doomed t' die in that accursed place at sunset, just lay down and turn t' brittle bone like the millions who had come afore us. But then Gralyre reclaimed the Dragon Sword, and he found us, and he saved us all."

Aneida's harsh, irritated sigh sought to interrupt him, but Jord ignored it. "From out o' the millions o' dead on Fennick's Island, the Gods chose *us* t' survive. I have been asking myself why."

"I am in no mood for riddles."

Jord's dark eyes glittered from the shadows that hid his face. "I do no' know what horrors lie in your past. I see the scar across your neck, and I know 'twas a knife that made that mark. And Mayvin, with her voice stolen from her." Jord brushed against her hand then drew back, what in another man would have been an embrace. "Mayhap one day ye will tell me o' it." He shrugged. "I care no'. 'Tis your secret. But ye survived. That is what is important. I recognized it in ye from the first moment we met. Evil marks a soul forever, and gives ye a kind o' fearlessness, because if ye survived the worst then ye can survive all else."

"Ye are talking shite!" Aneida snarled.

Jord's jaw flexed, as he fought to hang onto his temper, pursuing his point. "'Twas no' in vain that we suffered and lived through Fennick's Island. 'Twas the Gods, do ye see? Forging us into their weapons, by setting us trials that should have broken us. Out o' millions, we are the ones who survived."

"Are ye saying that the Gods discarded Mayvin because she was a broken weapon? No' deemed worthy t' save?" Aneida screeched. She launched off from the deadfall, slamming Jord from his seat. They tussled in the underbrush, as her fists hammered blindly at his face.

Finally, Jord was able to capture her hands in his. He rolled then, pinning her to the ground, and giving her a little shake, rattling the bushes around them. "I was no' finished!" he yelled in her face.

"Get off o' me! Leave me be!" She roared and bucked.

"I am saying that Mayvin *was* good enough. That she was forged by the Gods for *just that moment*, t' save us all so that we could continue! We are the ones who survive! And we survive only because o' Mayvin."

Aneida coughed out a gasp of grief. "We survive," she echoed numbly.

Jord's chest heaved from the exertion of pinning her long enough to make her listen. "Aye," he puffed.

Aneida's fists relaxed, as the fight suddenly ebbed from her body. She seemed to shrink beneath him. "I do no' want t' be the one who survives. No' again. No' without her."

Jord released her, and sat up. "Ye must."

"T' what end, Jord? What do the bloody Gods want from us?"

At last he looked away from her, staring out into the darkness. "I am no' a hero. The others can fight their wars o' magic and power, and Gralyre can feast upon his demon-humping sword, for all I care. But ye and I? We are going t' kill Doaphin. For all he has taken from us. That is why the Gods have spared us."

Aneida drew a shaky breath. "Aye. I can live for that," she whispered before her grief overcame her, and she curled into a ball of pain.

Jord stayed at her side, as she sobbed herself to sleep. He remained to watch over her for the remainder of the night.

☘☙

Sethreat waits patiently in the shadowy darkness. He spies on the Dream Weaver army from a small, bushy knoll beyond their sentry lines. The flickering fires of the enemy are an insult to the darkness. Would that they were smothered for all time! Humans exist for but one purpose, and Sethreat's hunger for the taste of their flesh is extreme. But the Master has other plans for Sethreat this night.

The winter has waned, and the snows have mostly vanished from the high woodland valley, but the night chill still harkens back to the cold season. Sethreat is made sluggish by the icy air, and by injuries too new to have healed. It licks fitfully at a seeping wound caused by a Maolar weapon, and grumbles softly at the aches of other injuries, those delivered by the Master's punishing hand this very night. Sethreat's execution was stayed at the last possible moment by the thunderous arrival of the travellers from Fennick's Island.

The Master still has use of It. Use is life. It lives to obey the Master's will. The Master grants life, and the Hunt continues.

The Man is within easy reach now. Sethreat needs only to reach out and claim him, and return him to Dreisenheld. Upon success, the Master will be pleased, and the reward shall be great! Perhaps even a youngling to despoil!

Thoughts of the dark pleasures to be found in the bowels of Dreisenheld, where the cold of winter, and the burn of sunlight never reach, set the spines on Sethreat's back aquiver with longing. And so It passes the time, as the Dream Weaver army settles slowly back into slumber, quieting from the stir caused by the late night arrivals from the south. Clouds hide the face of the full moon, smothering the forest in cloying darkness. As the night advances, so too, finally, does Sethreat.

Sethreat's preternatural senses pierce the darkness with sharp clarity, and It slips with confidence between the alert warriors of the Dream Weaver sentry lines. The Humans never hear a sound from Its clawed feet. Despite Its injuries, Sethreat owes an unnatural allegiance to stealth.

Though they never realize how closely death passes, one Human shivers, and peers deeper into nearby shadows. Some prey can sense the evil that brushes past them in the night.

On any other foray, Sethreat would glut upon murder. But not this night. This prey has teeth that can bite back, Maolar weapons that can pierce Stalker hides and bring death. Only the Man matters. Once he is returned to the Master, Humans will be of no further use, and there will be slaughter enough to sate all.

Clear of the watchful sentries, Sethreat snuffles deeply of the clear night air, sifting through the collective odour of amassed humans for the one It seeks.

It has found Him at last! Entwined with Sethreat's remembrance of the Man's scent is the magical flavour of the ailing Sorceress from the fortress. There is power emanating from a second Sorcerer, a male, the one that the Master spoke of. And the sword. A locus of power! It forms a mental image of prey huddled together, fearing Its deathly arrival. Has the Master arranged it thus?

'Hail the Master! Praise the Master!'

This night, Sethreat will destroy all of the Mater's enemies! It will glut upon the sick Sorceress and the Rebel Sorcerer to speed Its healing! It will take the Sword and the Man captive! The Master will honour It above all others! Sethreat will live in exalted servitude at the Master's feet forever!

Oh, to loose a howl of triumph to waken all the vermin! To watch them spill from their tents with fear laden screams! To rampage and slaughter at will!

The Dream Weaver's Maolar weapons caution Its desires. *'No! Cannot roar! Cannot mindlessly break bone and rend flesh!'* Only the Sorcerers will feel the crush of Its teeth this night. Only they will feel Its ebony claws ripping them apart!

It strains to resist the snores, sighs and odours that permeate the air. It creeps towards Its prizes. It slinks quietly from shadow to shadow. Only the prey matters. Only the Man. Only the Sorcerers. Restraint is Its pathway to eternal glory.

Sethreat arrives outside a tent, a clone to all others save for the delectable triumph that waits within! To tease Its hunger with anticipation, Its forked tongue patters the air; the prongs at the tip soak up the flavours of what is to come. A tang of suffering trembles upon the currents - the Sorceress; a familiar perfume from the battle at the fortress.

'Still ill. Still defenceless. Once before, she didst escape but now she hast come back. The Master hast willed it so. Hail the dark Master!'

It is an oddity that only one other Human resides within the tent. Is it the Man or the Sorcerer?

'Both! The Rebel Sorcerer is the Man!'

The armoured ridges on Sethreat's back flair with Its surprised excitement. Its body arches back, Its throat elongates, and Its lower jaw dislocates in visceral desire to feast. Thick ropes of saliva drip onto Its powerful torso. Jaws snap and double rows of razor teeth gnash with Its instinctual response to carnality.

'The Master wilt eat of the Man's power, and the Man wilt lament that he hast ever sought a path of defiance!' Urine streams, hot and thick, splashing quietly to the forest floor to mark the kill.

Savouring the anticipation, Sethreat slowly extends a long, sharp talon to slice through the canvas fabric of the tent, all that separates It from Its triumphant victory. It croons softly, keening and quivering with excitement.

Green sparks hiss and snap, and the tip of Its nail shears off.

The snippet hits the ground, smoking along the smooth surface of the cut.

Sethreat rears back, rumbling softly, as It raises Its truncated talon before Its reptilian eyes. It is nothing. The claw will regrow. Not so, had it been the entire hand.

It picks up a fallen stick, and tosses it lightly at the tent. The small branch strikes the canvas, unharmed, and skids softly down the fabric to the ground. Sethreat collects the severed tip of Its talon, and tosses it in a like manner. It flares brightly and vanishes before reaching the side of the tent.

This snare is made for It alone, lethal to Stalkers, and harmless to all others. Had Sethreat not stopped to savour Its kill, this trap would have taken more than Its talon. *'What trickery is this?'* It senses nothing of this magic.

Ambushing Sorcerers while they slumber is not the same as engaging in battle with an unknown sorcery when injured from the Master's beating. It must retreat, though the rising frustration of being denied the end of the hunt is overwhelming. The night is wasted! Instead of glory, Sethreat courts the Master's rage and retribution with Its failure.

Yet, a secret has been discovered. The Prince and the Rebel Sorcerer are one! Knowledge to bargain away to the Master for more days? Surely, the Master will forgive every failure this eve. Usefulness is life. It lives to serve.

❧

It was nearing dawn when Little Wolf passed like an unseen shadow through the Dream Weaver army to return to Gralyre's side, after fleeing from the magic that had transported them all out of the path of the tidal wave. His panic had subsided, and he had found a rabbit to sup upon.

He followed the trail of something foul, fresh with the taint of the beast that had left it, tracking it to the tent where Gralyre lay sleeping.

Little Wolf chuffed softly, as a shape shifted within darker shadows. But it was not the evil one, only an older man who was crouched over something on the ground.

His scent was calm, unafraid, and carried an undertone of lightning after a storm that Little Wolf had come to associate with beings who wielded magic. Gralyre sometimes smelled of this.

Little Wolf started when the stranger spoke. *'My name is Gedrhar. Come here, Wolf. Tell me what you make of this?'*

Little Wolf's head dipped in confusion. Few spoke to him as Gralyre did, or knew that he could understand. He approached cautiously, but the reek of urine on the ground was a clear contrast with the clean odour of the man crouched beside it. There was nothing to fear here.

Little Wolf concentrated to share his thoughts, as he would if he were speaking to Gralyre. *'A hunter of the night stood here. It sought to claim the tent.'* He lifted his leg, and covered the scent with his own mark, reasserting his territory.

"'Tis as I feared, wild one." Gedrhar stood, dusting his hands, as Little Wolf bypassed him to paw at the dim green shimmer of magic that overlay the outside of the tent.

'This smells of you.'

"That is because I placed it there." Gedrhar considered the wolfdog closer. "Odd that you can see it. That should not be. You are no longer what you were. You have become more than a mere beast. But you know that."

Little Wolf met the Dream Weaver's stare directly, not responding.

Gedrhar smiled and nodded. "Keep your secrets then. I bid you good ev'en, Wolf." He reached over to pluck the green shield, drawing it towards him as though it were a bit of cloth. It turned into a vapour that flowed back into his hand, and sank into the skin of his palm. "No need for this now. You will guard him till morn."

Little Wolf watched Gedrhar walk away, before he nosed aside the flap of the tent, and slipped within with a quiet rustle. He padded softly through the thick furs that carpeted the floor, and stopped short at the glint of discarded metal.

He lowered his snout so that he could snuffle at the Dragon Sword, and a low rumble of disquiet escaped him at the ozone of magic that infected the air around it. To his senses it seemed almost a heat wave of power surrounded the blade. It smelled bad, and not bad. Both. Neither. It was not to be trusted.

The ruby eyes of the dragon adorning the sword's hilt were aglow, painting red tips into Little Wolf's thick, black fur. The wolfdog took several cautious steps back, and edged sideways, placing his body protectively between Gralyre and the weapon.

He stared at it for a time, but the sword seemed to remain inert. Little Wolf finally circled three times, and lay facing Gralyre, ignoring the sword so that he could evaluate another turn of events.

Covered in lush furs, Gralyre slept on the low pallet with Catrian held protectively within the circle of his arms.

His master had taken a mate. Little Wolf approved.

CHAPTER TWO

Within the Wizard Stone

The large, ruby pommel stone of the Dragon Sword of Lyre glows red, and the soul of an ancient sorcerer looks out from his Wizard Stone, upon a world unseen for three hundred years.

The thralls scream and lament, as usual, trying to escape their compacts, but they are easily mastered and muzzled. Their company is tiresome. Countering their petty insurgencies has been his only distraction for an age.

His awareness returns to the scene outside his stone. Piles of deep, soft furs of bears and lynx separate him from the sleepers, beings of immense power. The red glimmer from the ruby burnish the two with a soft flush of colour. The woman, the man, entwined they make a handsome pair, and a union of the two would yield powerful issue. A contingency for the future, perhaps?

He has tasted vicariously of the life to come through Gralyre's use of the sword's magic, and is eager for more after his long fast. So much time has been lost! Always, Gralyre has been troublesome to control, yet the connection has finally been forged, and every hour sees the conduit grow stronger. Every use of the sword's power binds the Prince more tightly to his fate.

It takes little effort to traverse the conduit, and slide smoothly into Gralyre's memories of the past. To gain victory, the Prince's will must be softened. He must be made to remember… and to forget.

ഇരു

Gralyre's Past

…The wind blows cold and hard, shaking and bending the forest with its rush and roar, a phantom team towing an autumnal chariot, while summer's bright beauty flees before its inexorable charge. The scudding clouds hide all light save that of the many campfires that dot the valley amongst the genuflecting trees.

My army is oddly still and silent. There is neither song nor laughter echoing in the night. But then word has just reached us, brought with the arrival of the Court Sorcerer, Fennick, that Dreisenheld has fallen, and my father is dead.

I lean morosely against the poles supporting the canopy at the entrance of my pavilion, and watch the night, not grieving, yet disquieted by my own dispassion. I raise the tankard of dramhale to my lips, and take a bracing swig of the burning liquor. 'Tis not a pleasant taste, both sweet and bitter against my tongue, yet it suits my mood and need this night. I drain my cup, and hold it out to my page, who is quick to refill it. The fumes of alcohol momentarily compete with the fresh gusts.

I have ordered a tot for all, and I imagine quiet cups raised in respect. How many eyes turn towards the largest pavilion, at the centre of their camp, where their Prince has become their King?

The wind roars and rails through the forest. No quiet whispers and sighing in the boughs for this, the eve of the falling of a kingdom.

A lantern approaches, the light bouncing and rocking, telling of a warrior moving at speed.

Something has happened.

Gods, could there have not been but one night without an attack? This of all nights?

The monsters strike from darkness. His army has been forced to cede their daylight to necessary sleep, becoming as nocturnal as the evil they fight, that they will be alert during the darking.

The warrior skids to a halt, and drops into a bow, panting mightily from his haste.

"Speak."

"My Prince... My King... Majesty... My sincere grief for you upon the death of your father. Long Live the King!"

"Thank-you, soldier, but you have not run here to tell me this. Stand and share your news."

"Our lines have been breached by one of Doaphin's creatures, one of the big, scaled ones. It has asked for parlay, and bears a truce flag."

"Where is it now?"

"Ten men armed with Maolar tipped spears guard it."

Vigilant warriors watch the perimeter of my army. The picket lines run three deep, and I am confident that the creature will be held. I had not known that Doaphin's creatures could speak. I am curious to discover what it wants.

"Bring it to me. And post more men. It could be a diversion. A raid could be imminent."

The warrior bows, "Yes majesty," turns, and runs.

For a moment, I watch the warrior's light bobbing and weaving towards the edge of my army's encampment, before I push back through the curtains into my pavilion.

I barely notice the lavish fixtures and comforts that befit my station, nor my page who has quietly entered in my wake. Thickly piled silk rugs cover both floor and walls, blocking all but the heaviest pushes of the persistent wind. The large room is divided by a black damask curtain, left ajar from the passage of servants at work. Beyond the curtain, my bed awaits, already turned back for the coming of daybreak when I will retire. The gold embossed rods from the warming pans peek out from under the fine linens and coverings of black sables. The gilding on the handles is a stark contrast to the dark bedding.

I catch my reflection in an ornately carved mirror hanging above a polished cabinet containing my royal raiment. Within the silvered surface is a man clad in black from head to boot, a tall man of commanding presence and solemn bearing. I am already clad in mourning for the grief I have yet to feel.

Using the reflection, I spy upon the table in the corner where Fennick, newly arrived from Dreisenheld, and still wearing the stains of travel, sups heartily on roasted meat and wine. He has aged poorly since last I saw him. His hair has whitened, and his tall, thin frame is made even more cadaverous by the sagging dissipation on his face.

"You should not allow it entry. 'Tis likely an assassin."

"Then I will kill it, afore it kills me." I am unsurprised that my brief words with the soldier outside have been overheard. I ignore the Sorcerer's counsel for another deep draught of dramhale. The liquor's burn seems the only warmth within me this night.

Wrought iron sconces, affixed to posts at all four corners of the tent, illuminate the jewels adorning my tankard, as I drop into a large oak chair that is piled deep with red cushions. The Dragon Sword hangs in its sheath over the back of my throne, a blatant proclamation of my birthright and power. My page takes up position at my left elbow. I wait.

Under its heavy guard, and the inviolable rules of parlay, the beast is brought safely to stand before His Majesty.

I pass the jeweled tankard to my page, as my men escort Doaphin's messenger to a halt in front of me. My army has been battling these reptilian killers for over a year now, and my men are all well versed in how dangerous it is. The Maolar spears that pen the beast never waver in their diligence.

The creature bows, as best it can while avoiding the sharp metal tips. "This one's name is Sethreat, my King."

My new title, growled from the throat of this creature, is repulsive to me. "I do not call myself King. Not until Doaphin lies shattered upon the bloody rocks of Dreisenheld will I call myself by that title."

Sethreat laughs, hissing slyly. "Then 'tis well that I bring thee terms of surrender... Prince." Its tone is an insult.

My men begin a stuttering cheer of excitement, but I chop my hand through the air, and they falter to silence. There is more to this play of words. "Speak your terms!"

"My Master cares naught for the fate of thy men. If thou comest with me now, thy men shalt live. 'Tis thee who must bend a knee."

The warriors guarding the creature lose their brief dream of peace in a wave of protective ire for me. They shove closer with their spears. Maolar lance tips prick the creature's flesh, raising little hisses of smoke with every contact.

"Parlay!" It roars, as its flesh blisters from the touch of the magical metal of the Dream Weavers.

The creature's pain brings a small pleasure to the dismal night, yet the rules of engagement are clear, and parlay protects the messenger. I relax my men with a slight nod, and they withdraw their weapons by an inch, so that they no longer touch Sethreat's scaly flesh, yet still hover at the ready, a ring of lethal Maolar to keep it in check.

"What possible reason could you give to compel me to an act of such lunacy?"

"My Master will spare thy beloved." Though no smile can live on that reptilian snout, Sethreat's tone is slick with enjoyment, as it watches the impact of its words strike with the precision of poisoned darts.

Rage suffuses me at the insult, and despite the fact that

Sethreat speaks under the protection of parlay my hand travels over my throne to touch the hilt of the Dragon Sword. Perhaps it is the drink, yet I cannot stand a moment more of the beast's enjoyment at my expense!

Without removing my gaze from the nightmare that has invaded my world, I draw my massive blade, a menacing rasp, as I stand slowly from my throne. My movements are deliberate and overtly threatening. "Your words reek of corruption. She died at the King's bedside when Dreisenheld fell."

Grating chuckles grind from the creature's throat, despite the implicit promise of my bared blade. "According to whom?"

"Fennick!" *My head snaps towards the corner of the room, where Lord Fennick, the kingdom's court sorcerer, the man who has brought me news of my father's death, sits quietly sipping wine and watching the unusual summit play out.* "You told me she was dead! You saw her fall!"

Fennick sighs heavily. "The beast lies, my Prince, as it must." *His tone is bored and unconcerned.* "'Tis its nature to deceive. Princess Genevieve is no more. This I promise you."

Sethreat unslings the pouch it carries upon its shoulder. "Proof for thee, Prince." *It tosses it towards my feet.* "Thy lady yet lives."

The sword is light in my hand, as I skewer the bag ere it can touch the floor. With a quick flick of my wrist, the sac splits, spilling golden tresses out onto the rich carpeting. Light from the flickering sconces plays through the loose, blonde curls, as they drift to a rest, fluttering in the fitful currents of the night wind that have managed to infiltrate the tent.

I consider the curling locks, matching colour and length to my memories of my lady. "'Tis no proof. You could have easily shorn her after her death."

"Look thee closer."

What devilry does the creature seek? I use the point of the Dragon Sword to sift through the masses of hair, until I spy the folded parchment.

At a gesture, my young page darts forward to retrieve the message, and delivers it into my waiting hand. The note is wrapped with a golden chain bearing a sparkling teardrop sapphire that I had gifted to Genevieve as a betrothal promise.

I lean my sword back against my throne, and flip the note open, quickly scanning the contents. The drink churns in my guts as I read, for a bright smear of red stains the page, a delicate fingerprint from the Princess.

My Beloved;

Alas! I was sore afraid to end my own life ere the keep fell, and now they have taken me. They have told me of my fate and I cannot bear it! Doaphin has surrendered to madness! Forsake me not! Leave me not to suffer! Please, in the name of our love, do whatever is asked of you!

I know you will come for me, my love. I know you will rescue me. I await you.

Your Princess, Genevieve

I recognize the ornate, curling script from other notes she has sent to me. The dramatic professions of love, and the self-serving tone are purely Genevieve's own. "You are wrong Fennick. She survived the fall of Dreisenheld. By her own hand 'tis so."

Fennick shrugs, an odd reaction. "On his death bed, the King bade me to abandon him, that I could bring you our news, my Prince. You know this. What happened after is conjecture. The lady refused to leave with me. What more could I have done?"

"Enough!" *Would the dolt reveal all in the presence of an enemy spy?* "This is not a conversation for the ears of many."

My attention returns to Sethreat. "What assurances does Doaphin make that the Princess shall be released if I comply?"

"NO!" *Fennick finally takes notice enough to abandon his board and stand, toppling his chair in his urgency.* "Do not be a fool! You cannot bring the sword to…"

I silence the Sorcerer with an imperious glare. "I am not my father, wizard. If I wish your counsel I will ask for it." *Power. It is mine now, not Fennick's. It is a heady realization, and I am not sure what I will do with it yet…*

෫ඏ

Within the Wizard Stone

The ruby on the Dragon Sword glows brighter, as the ancient sorcerer exerts a subtle burst of power. It would not do for the boy to remember it all.

Asleep on the pallet, Gralyre tosses his head with a soft moan, as his memory shifts and reshapes.

"On his death bed, the King bade me to abandon him, my Prince. The lady refused to leave with me. What more could I have done?"

"You did enough!" Gralyre inclines his head regally. "We will speak of this later."

Gralyre's attention returns to Sethreat. "What promises does Doaphin give that the Princess shall be released should I comply?"

"My Prince, no!" Fennick careens his chair over when he stands. "The danger is too great!"

Gralyre looks to the Sorcerer. "Fear naught, my old friend. I know you seek only to protect me, but you must follow my lead in this…"

The Sorcerer's soul withdraws from Gralyre's dreams, returning to his Wizard Stone. He cautions himself against altering too much too quickly. He must be patient.

The thralls rail and curse at him. They are working together now to use the magical umbilical cord that he has established to Gralyre's Godsmagic to escape their imprisonment within the Wizard Stone. They seek to usurp his claim upon the new vessel.

'You are my slaves! My food!' he reminds them. He shreds their minds, and scatters them to the far corners of his cold realm. Their brief revolt is quelled, and they will be a long time

coalescing their souls back into viable beings. Fennick enjoys the quiet while he can.

The glowing ruby adorning the sword dims to normalcy, reverting the weapon to a benign though powerful presence lying amid the furs on the floor.

Gralyre must never sense his tampering until it is too late, and his transference is complete.

🙰� இ

Gralyre's Past

...Sethreat bares its teeth. "My Master promises that if thou dost not comply, thy lady will suffer all manor of atrocities for thy defiance. My Master shalt entomb her alive and aware, a butterfly in amber for all eternity. She wilt witness all depravities yet ne'er shut her eyes against it. The eons shalt pass, and she will descend into madness. Only thy surrender wilt release her."

My sword leaps back to my hand, and the tip comes to rest against the creature's neck. The lights from the sconces sparkle along the Maolar blade, collecting in the ruby eyes of the dragon so that they seem to glow with a malevolent sentience. My men shift to the side, opening a channel in the ring of Maolar that I may reach my enemy.

Sethreat stiffens, lifting its chin up and away from the lazy curls of smoke drawn from its skin by contact with the razor-

edged Maolar of my sword. "Parlay," it still has the gall to claim.

"A counter offer for you to take to your Master!" I am so maddened that I can barely relax my clenched teeth enough to utter my threats. "Doaphin's days wane. When he is dead I will rescue Princess Genevieve, if she yet lives, but I will not sell the lives of my people for her. I do not accept his terms."

Sethreat gnashes its double rows of serrated teeth, creating a horrifying snapping and grinding sound. "No! Thou must cede! Thy Master commands it!"

"Doaphin is not my master!" I roar, and slash a strip down the beast's cheek for its insolence, coming dangerously close to violating the sanctity of parlay by injuring the messenger. The tip of my Maolar blade hisses and spits from the taint of the creature's black blood now adorning it.

Sethreat claps a powerful, clawed hand against its wound to snuff the burst of flame left in the sword's wake. "Thou canst! I am inviolate under the flag of truce!" Smoke curls from around its long talons.

I sense that the beast is finally afraid. Its failure terrifies it more than my sword does. I will use both weapons against it!

I slice the other side of Sethreat's reptilian face, raising more flame and smoke, and drawing yet more black blood. "Show Doaphin your wounds, and tell him that I am coming. And that he should be afraid. This is my reply."

I am through with this mawkish play! I turn my back insultingly, and throw the order to my men over my shoulder.

"Take it to the edge of camp and release it. If you see it again, kill it on sight." I turn, sink into my throne, and rest my bared blade across my thighs. "This parlay is over!" The Stalker's black blood soiling the tip of my weapon ignites in a burst of flame, punctuating my edict. In moments, the blade has cleansed itself of the creature's contamination.

Sethreat lunges to attack but halts prudently at the prick of ten Maolar tipped lances, a cage through which it cannot reach me.

As my men prod the creature to move away, I lean forward and mockingly drag a finger down each cheek, mimicking the wounds I have dealt the Stalker. "One day, I will see you again, beast…"

₧₧

Gralyre's dream thrust him from deep sleep to confront full wakefulness. He sat up with his heart pounding a rough tattoo from the memory. He had a name. He had a past with no dark wall sealing it away. He was finally whole. With the speed at which everything had happened, there had been no time to reconcile it until now.

Gralyre dropped his face into his hands, and scrubbed at his beard. Would that he could reach within, and tear his past away once more!

Disturbed from where she slumbered at his side, Catrian mumbled, "What is it?"

Sunrise glowed against the smooth, oiled canvas of the cone shaped tent, bringing soft light to the darkness within. Outside the sounds of men awakening to morning routines were beginning to echo softly in the forest clearing, as the Dream Weaver army stirred.

Gralyre gazed down at Catrian in concern. The soft glow of light from the sunrise brought radiance back to her skin, an illusion of health, yet could do nothing to disguise the weight she had lost. She was so frail. Her cheekbones were sharp blades above sunken cheeks, and her eyes were recessed deeply from starvation and fever. Catrian's appearance was a stark reminder of how nearly he had come to losing her forever.

"'Tis alright. Just one of my dreams." It had been so vivid, this memory from his past, and it had left behind a sinister foreshadowing. "Sleep." He reclined, and drew Catrian back into his arms, pressing a soft kiss to her cheek.

Gralyre turned his head, and met Little Wolf's steady gaze. The wolfdog had been waiting patiently for him to awaken, and his tail thumped happily into the muffling furs, as his presence was acknowledged.

Sleep no more. The world is new and green. Stones and death are banished. Home awaits!

Gralyre's worries eased, and he smiled fondly at the bit of wolfish poetry. To Little Wolf it seemed a miracle that the Bleak and Fennick's Island had been supplanted with lush, green forests, literally overnight. They had indeed returned home.

'Go, Little Wolf. Run in the forest. I will meet with you later.'

'Your mate will join us?'

Gralyre's heart thumped for what he knew was to come, and he armoured his intensions away from the dread of it. *'No. She is still too weak.'*

Little Wolf clambered to his feet, and after giving the Dragon Sword in its bed of furs a wide clearance, danced lightly out into the dawn. His tail was held high and happy, and waved in great circles.

Gralyre lay still for a long while, a stolen indulgence. He savoured Catrian's warmth as she slept, cherishing their closeness, and watching her face by the light that grew steadily brighter with the advance of the sunrise. Her scent surrounded him, the unique blend of heather and wilderness, magic and woman. He leaned nearer to her golden brown hair, and breathed deeply, steeping his memory with her essence so that he would never forget.

Catrian smiled softly, and her hand slid into his loosened shirt to rest above his heart. Her fingers curled possessively into the black hairs of his chest. He had never disrobed from his long journey. Nor bathed. She wrinkled her nose for a moment before deciding that she did not care.

"You must sleep some more," he bade softly, as the heart resting beneath her hand shattered. The longer she slept, the longer he could stave off the inevitable. His eyes burned, as he stared into the bleakness of his future. He had thought that the answer to all of his problems lay in the reclamation of his memory. Instead it had bred a whole new host of evils.

"How can I sleep a moment longer? I ne'er dreamed it possible that ye would survive to return, nor dared hope that we would be as we were last night." She whispered earnestly, and nestled closer. "If I am wrong, and this is a dream, do no' waken me."

Gralyre gave her a gentle squeeze, careful of her frailty. "'Tis no dream. I am here." He too luxuriated in memories of their tryst within her Wizard Stone, where their souls had merged as one in absolute perfection. Last night, he had dared to dream of forever, despite the looming war against Doaphin's oppression.

After a moment's consideration, Catrian pushed herself shakily up on an elbow to look down at him from above. Her brow knit with confusion above her hazel eyes, her gaze clear of fever though she was obviously still weakened from her long illness. "Gralyre, how are ye here?"

He caught her eye, and deliberately turned his head, drawing her gaze towards the glint of metal in the soft furs across the tent, where he had tossed the Dragon Sword the night before after replenishing her Godsmagic and saving her life.

Five and a half feet of glittering Maolar lay in isolated splendour upon its bed of furs. The wings of the dragon were furled open to form the guard. The tail of the dragon wrapped the hilt as an ornate grip, holding the cabochon-cut ruby pommel stone safely within its coils. The dragon's neck snaked down the massive blade for six inches. Its mouth was open in a roar, displaying sharp little teeth. The glitter of red rubies in its eyes matched the massive jewel of the pommel stone.

The Dragon Sword's draw was suddenly more persistent than ever, an addictive need that briefly supplanted Gralyre's longing for the woman in his arms. *'What am I thinking? Anyone could have stolen within the tent, and taken it while I slept!'* He was shocked by his internal struggle to remain passive beneath Catrian's slight weight, instead of shoving her away so as to arise, and go to the blade.

Catrian gasped, "Is that...? Gods! Gralyre! The Dragon Sword?"

Gralyre blinked, and looked away from the sword, reclaiming his discipline, and suppressing his craving for the powerful talisman. He was thankful that Catrian was too weak to sense the conflict within him. Chuckling awkwardly, he smoothed an errant golden-brown tress from the side of her face, and tucked it behind her ear. Instinctively, he knew that he must distract her keen mind from noticing his growing obsession. "'Twas how I reached you in your Wizard Stone. Without it, you would have been lost to me. I would have been lost."

At his fervent declaration, Catrian's smile of excitement faded. Fascinated by his sincerity, she forgot to ask how he had discovered Fennick's word of power, the word which forced the Wizard Stone to obey his will, the word that would protect him from possession by the ancient soul within the stone.

Instead, she searched his midnight-blue eyes, compelled to the truth in response to his confession. "Only ye could have reached me. I did no' want t' return t' a world without ye in it. I thought ye were dead."

Gralyre lifted his shoulders off the furs, and captured her lips in a long, soft kiss. His need for the sword was supplanted by a more pleasurable desire.

Catrian drew away before he did, propping her chin on her hands atop his strong chest, as he relaxed back against the bedding. The rise and fall of his breath was a powerful tide that rocked her gently, as her gaze roved over his face, and then around and over the strange surroundings, the foreign, cone-shaped tent, and the furs. "Gralyre, this is no' my home. Where are we?"

"We sleep amongst a host of Dream Weavers."

Catrian frowned. "Ye jest!" she dismissed.

Gralyre smoothed the wrinkle from her brow with the light touch of his finger, drawing it down her straight nose, and resting it against her full lips to still her questions. "Dream Weavers," he confirmed, relishing the warmth and silken quality of her skin.

Catrian's gaze lost focus, as she tuned her magical senses to the activity around them. She grew excited, and broke into a wide grin. "Dream Weavers!" she crowed, and rolled onto her back, laughing.

Gralyre rolled with her, drawn to her joy, his own lips twitching into a smile, though his words were worried. "You should not use your magic until you are fully recovered."

Catrian rubbed her hands up over his shoulders. His lean muscles were easily felt under the tattered shirt he wore. He had lost weight during the quest for the Dragon Sword. "Do no' fret!

I am better and better by the moment. I never dared hope that allies would appear now, when we need them the most! Gralyre, how long was I ill? What has happened? Tell me all!"

Gralyre's expression became haunted, and his tone bleak. "You have been ill since the storm you created to save us on the island. 'Tis a day past the Spring Solstice, I think."

Catrian grimaced. "So long… Gods know Boris will have something t' say about this," she carped on a sigh. "We must be travelling towards the gathering o' the Generals then? When did we find the Dream Weavers? Or did they find us?"

Gralyre shook his head. "I do not know. I had more important things on my mind last night when I arrived. Like saving your life." He pinned her head between his large, warrior hands, and leaned down to rest his brow against hers. "Catrian, you used all of your Godsmagic. You almost died. I almost could not reach you!" His tone was fierce, as his whisper soft words brushed against her lips. "Never do that again! Not for me."

Her face glowed, as she looked up at him, so close to each other that they shared the same breath. "Do ye no' know that I would sacrifice all for ye?" Her voice was just as soft as his had been, as she ran her fingers into his thick, black hair to cup and knead the back of his head.

Gralyre's eyes drifted closed from the pleasurable sensation of her fingers gently massaging his scalp. He nestled his lips to hers in the softest of kisses, schooling himself to gentleness. His body urged him to pursue much more, though his mind recognized her fragility beneath him.

'Tell her,' his conscience demanded, sapping his ardor.

He levered away, rolling to sit up with his back turned. Gralyre could not look at Catrian, and find the courage for what he must do.

"There is…" he drew a deep breath, and glared upwards through the open peak of the tent at a blue sky. "I must tell you…" He could not find the words.

As the pause lengthened, she prompted him to continue. "Gralyre?"

"My memory has returned," he blurted, coming at it obliquely.

"I remember. Ye told me last night, in my Wizard Stone." She grinned cheekily. "We were a little distracted, and did no' finish our conversation." Catrian sat up, and circled his torso with her arms, squeezing him tightly. "Gralyre! I am so happy for ye!" She kissed his neck below his ear, smiling possessively, as he shivered in reaction to the sensation. "Who are ye? Where did ye come from? Tell me all! Is Gralyre your real name?"

As she spoke, Gralyre gently disengaged her embrace, and surged out of the bed, pacing a few steps away. He would never do what he must with her touch upon him.

He kept his back turned, as he bent and reclaimed the sword that he had flung aside the night before. He froze in place as it whispered to him of the pleasure of unleashing its might against the world.

"What is wrong?" Catrian asked, as a strained silence fell between them. She reached out with her consciousness, questing gently for entry into his thoughts, but his mind was sealed tightly against hers.

At the caress of her mind's touch, Gralyre was suddenly furious at her unwelcomed, attempted intrusion. He turned on her, holding the sword angled threateningly. "After all this time you still do not trust me?" he accused fiercely.

Catrian reared back in shock at his sudden, and inexplicable rage. "Do no' talk t' me o' trust," she reproached. "No' now. No' after all we have been through and all that we mean t' each other."

Her expression penetrated his ire, shaming him. Uncertain what to do with the blade, Gralyre shoved it through his belt loop, though the point of the long length dragged upon the furs. As his hand released the hilt, his anger drained, leaving him as confused by his outburst as she was.

Catrian sat amongst the bedding, tense with concern. "Please Gralyre! Let there be no secrets between us!" Fear made Catrian's throat tighten. "Is it bad? Were ye… are ye… aligned with Doaphin?"

"Gods no! 'Tis not that!"

"Then what? Gralyre? Tell me! Let me in. Let me see."

Gralyre sighed harshly, and rubbed his face. Why was he railing against her request? Only the night before their souls had twined in a harmony of which there was no denying. He had nothing to hide from her… except for the truth that he was avoiding like a coward.

Gralyre turned to Catrian then, standing tall, and braced for her pain. He dropped his impenetrable shields, and at last she was able to see the truth for herself.

"I am the Lost Prince."

Catrian's jaw sagged slightly, and she slowly drew herself up onto her knees. "Impossible," she murmured, though she could see the truth of his pronouncement within his thoughts.

"In the Labyrinth, when I reclaimed my sword its power shattered the wall within my mind that was keeping my past from me. I am Prince Gralyre, heir to the throne of Lyre. There is no doubt."

Catrian shook her head slowly, unsure of the changes in the world while she had been ill, but he spoke truthfully. His memories were there, free at last. "'Tis impossible!" she repeated, even in the face of uncontroversial proof. "But somehow, with all else that has happened...?" As she withdrew from his mind, words failed her, and she gestured to the tent of the Dream Weavers, and at the sword hanging at Gralyre's side.

"Gods!" she breathed, as she absorbed the full import of what he had shown her. "The prophecy has come to pass! You have returned!" Catrian gave a choked, little laugh but her wonder faded, as the near brush with disaster derailed her thoughts. "Gralyre, Boris sent ye t' your death! We could have lost ye! Lost all!"

"Shh. We have the sword. That is what matters. All is well," Gralyre soothed.

It was then that Catrian noted his stern features that were so at odds with his gentle words. "What is wrong? This is a great thing, Gralyre, why are ye no' happier?"

"I have remembered that which I wish I could forget," he began haltingly. He watched her face closely, as she sagged back against the bedding. Her eyes narrowed, and her breath visibly hitched.

"Princess Genevieve," Catrian whispered intuitively. Of course she knew of the Princess. Everyone knew of the legend. It spoke of the great love that the Lost Prince had held for the beautiful woman.

"Genevieve," Gralyre acknowledged. Gods! He would rather face a legion of Stalkers than cause Catrian this pain!

Catrian began to shiver, as she realized that she was about to lose him forever. Gralyre was saying goodbye! She panted shallowly to keep the acute agony inside, and stared down unseeingly at her fingers that were clasping and unclasping in her lap. With a concentrated effort, she stilled the telling movement.

His heart shattered upon seeing her obvious pain. "Catrian, I cannot abandon Genevieve in Dreisenheld, trapped by Doaphin's magic," he explained, as gently as he was able. "I am honour bound to rescue her, and once she is rescued, I am honour bound to marry her. I was never free to be with you!"

"Honour bound t' save her? Aye. That I can understand," Catrian tried to agree reasonably. Her blood roared through her ears, and her shivers intensified. "But it has been hundreds o' years! Surely your promise t' wed her has passed?" her voice cracked on the last. Her ears rang with shock. Her illness was quickly sapping strength from her quivering flesh. Gralyre was right; she should not have used her magic so soon.

"No, not hundreds of years! 'Tis been only months for me, though who knows how long for her? Doaphin promised that she would be aware of all. Gods! Please understand." Could she not see that hurting her like this was tearing him apart?

Pride bolstered Catrian from a place deep within, and she found a burst of strength in her hurt. "Understand what? Ye have made this decision ne'er once asking what I want!" She drew a breath of restraint. Her voice quieted to an urgent plea, as she came as near to begging as she ever had in this life. "Gralyre, please! We go t' war. We have so little time! Let us be together until what end comes!"

"I cannot!" he bellowed in response to his overwhelming desire to relent, and to be with her as she offered. "I am the Prince! I was never free to love you!" His hand slashed violently to punctuate his words. "I was never free to make you my own! I cannot, I will not, allow you to be seen as less to me than you are!"

Pure rage spewed volcanically through Catrian's veins, supplanting her need to continue to beg him to change his mind. The son-of-a-whore had pledged his love to her! Genevieve be damned! Catrian had seen inside Gralyre's heart, and knew of the depth of his feelings for her. If he thought for one instant that he was going to get away with ruining both of their lives.... Her control evaporated, as her emotions overtook her. "Get out!" Catrian snarled.

He stood there, staring at her in helpless confusion with his handsome face, and duplicitous heart, and her fury crackled into pure magical force, filling her hands. "Get out!" she roared again like a lioness.

Lightning flashed from Catrian's fingers, and Gralyre dove for the opening of the tent, propelled by the din of an exploding fireball. Where he had been standing, a blackened crater now smoked and sputtered. The burning furs raised a terrible stench that filled the space with acrid smoke. The clouds churned through the open flap in Gralyre's wake, and up through the smoke hole at the tent's peak.

"I hope I singed your arse!" Catrian shouted crudely after him then flopped back onto her pillow. She gasped heavily, as what strength she had mustered suddenly drained her limbs so completely that she could barely twitch.

The lingering stench of singed hair and shattered dreams taunted her weakness.

CHAPTER THREE

Gralyre glared back at the tent.

'I am the Prince! How dare she! She could have killed me!'
Though in hindsight he suspected that was not quite true; she
had given him fair warning, and her aim had been slightly off.

The sound of hearty laughter interrupted his dark confusion,
and Gralyre pivoted to see Rewn doubled over, with his hand
weakly patting at the shoulder of a grinning Dream Weaver. His
face lively with mirth, Rewn pointed wordlessly at the curl of
smoke escaping through the top of Catrian's tent.

Gralyre's face heated with embarrassment. The entire army
must have heard the detonation of Catrian's magic!

"Gralyre," Rewn chortled, as he wound down, "…the look on
your face!"

Gralyre's mouth tightened at the ribbing. He stood taller, as
regal outrage pulsed to life. "You *dare* to mock your Prince!" He
rested his hand menacingly upon the hilt of his sword.

Rewn's eyes widened at the aggressive gesture, and his face
drained of all amusement. "What?" His consternation was well
seasoned with tension, as he straightened. "No. Gralyre, er, I
mean… Prince Gralyre…" He glanced away.

Rewn's change of demeanour penetrated Gralyre's
indignation with a spear of contrition, and his hand slid limply
away from the Dragon Sword. A lifetime of royal entitlement

warred with the abiding affection that he bore this man. Reason returned, and Gralyre shook his head to relieve a sudden spike of pain in his temples.

'What am I doing? Rewn is no enemy!' It was the second time that morning he had been unusually wroth with those he loved.

The Dream Weaver warrior filled the awkward silence that remained. "Prince Gralyre. Highness, we had no time yestereve to introduce ourselves." He bowed. "My name is Jacon, son of Gedrhar." He straightened and nodded towards the thin trail of smoke lofting from the tent. "Your lady would appear to be recovered from her ordeal." His expression was perfectly bland.

Gralyre nodded curtly in response. His Lady. He could never claim her as such. His mood soured further.

Jacon supplied an old Dream Weaver proverb. "It is a wise man who knows when to flee the anger of a woman." He bowed again.

Rewn aped Jacon with a self-conscious bow of his own. "Your Highness, I am sorry that I offended ye."

'A Prince is never wrong; a Prince never apologizes! To do so is to question the very Gods who have anointed his soul's destiny!' It was a tenet instilled into him since birth.

Even so, shame flooded Gralyre's conscience with a surge strong enough to bathe his face red with his disgrace. Rewn was a true friend, seeking his company without avarice or guile. Gralyre could not recollect having shared such a bond with another. He had always been isolated by his station.

Gralyre shook his head regretfully, and stepped forward to grasp Rewn's shoulder, lifting him from his bow. "No." Gralyre fought every ingrained royal disposition to voice his apology. "'Tis I who am sorry. You need never…" Ruing his overreaction, he glanced away, gritting his teeth until muscles jumped in his jaw. "Never," he repeated with a little shake of Rewn's shoulder, unable to find the words.

Rewn grasped Gralyre's hand tightly where it rested on his shoulder. Their gazes met for a long moment with the friendship of men closer than brothers, men who had saved each other's lives, laughed together, and had survived together. "Come, Prince Gralyre," Rewn smiled hesitantly, "we were just about t' find breakfast."

Having had no victuals for days, Gralyre's hunger clawed urgently at the suggestion, and the beckoning aroma of food wafting on the breeze set his stomach to baying loudly in agreement. "Thank-you," he said, for more than the invitation, for the gift of a true friend who would forgive him all.

As they walked across the encampment, Gralyre looked out over the familiar vista of encircling mountains that protected the hidden valley of the Rebel's Northern Fortress. Why were they still here? The Rebels had not yet mobilized for war. He would demand an accounting from Commander Boris before the day was out!

Dream Weaver warriors went about their morning duties: feeding horses, sharpening pikes, fletching arrows, and practising their martial arts. Their numbers had to be at least five thousand strong. As Gralyre passed them, they halted their chores to stand and bow in deference.

This was familiar pageantry. Gralyre nodded his head regally to each of them in turn, unaware that Rewn was gaping at the spectacle.

The soft cadence of the Dream Weaver language washed around Gralyre, and he realized that he understood most of what was being said. He remembered a time from long ago, of his mother speaking to him in the tongue of her people.

His nursery had been a bright room with polished parquet floors, and blue enamelled walls. Murals of fanciful creatures had been painted into window alcoves. The vistas beyond the precious panes of glass had been of the blue ocean, and he had thrilled to the sight of ships with billowing sails anchoring in Dreisenheld's harbour.

He and his mother had often sat in a deep window seat, propped by soft goose-down cushions bound in blue silk. Her arms had held him warm and secure while the soft murmur of her voice, in the language of her youth, told him of heroes from long ago ages and far away lands.

The recollection was comforting.

Another hunger pang drew Gralyre back to his present. They approached the Dream Weaver kitchens, the cookfires that fed the army. Unlike in the west, where every warrior spent precious time cooking for themselves, the Dream Weaver army's meals were prepared and served centrally by a small company of cooks. This efficiency freed warriors to attend to martial tasks.

Jacon lead them over to one of the cookfires, and nodded slightly to the men who already breakfasted there.

Gralyre made the traditional greeting and introduction in the language of the Dream Weaver people, as his mother had taught him. "I am Prince Gralyre of Lyre. My sword is sheathed; my hands are open in friendship. This is my companion, Rewn Wilson."

The warriors stood and bowed, making their own introductions after their custom. "We welcome our friends to our table. I am Arock D'Maru and this is my brother Shefon. These are our cousins, Warfon and Padfor. We offer our meal and friendship."

"Eat heartily, my friends," Jacon bade. "I have matters to attend, and will take my leave."

Gralyre hardly noted Jacon's departure, as his attention was fully captured by a cook approaching their fire. He eagerly accepted one of the plates the man carried, which was mounded with scrambled eggs and salted pork. His first heaping bite was shovelled into his mouth ere he had seated himself fully upon a convenient stump by the warmth of the fire. A moan of pure pleasure rumbled out of his chest at his first taste of food in days.

Rewn seconded the sound, as he chewed and swallowed. "Here, try this." He passed a toasted heel of bread slathered with butter into Gralyre's eager hands.

It was warm and crunchy, soft and rich, and Gralyre had never tasted anything so good! He made an effort to slow his chewing, lest the food rebound from his shrunken stomach.

As they ate, soft murmurs drifted around them from conversations at other fires. Gralyre indulged in memories triggered by a scent, or a noise. His past was his once more, waiting to be rediscovered, no longer hidden away. What had been sundered was now made whole.

The Dream Weavers finished their breakfast, and left Rewn and Gralyre alone at the fire. Without the sound of their conversation to fill the air, Gralyre finally noted the silence that spanned him and Rewn. Though Rewn had accepted his apology, something heavy now lay between them.

"Are you recovered from our journey from the island?" Gralyre asked clumsily around a mouthful of food, taking refuge in trivialities. He had been so preoccupied with saving Catrian the night before that he had not stopped to see to the welfare of his companions. "I know that you were all troubled by its speed," he downplayed politely, for he knew that the journey had terrified them. Added to his reaction to Rewn's jest this morning, and it was little wonder that their easy friendship was suddenly strained. "But how convenient to travel that far of a distance in mere moments."

Rewn's fork suspended, halting halfway to his mouth. "Gralyre, um, Prince Gralyre," he corrected, "we were aloft for most o' the night."

Gralyre frowned in confusion. "No… it was surely only a few minutes, at most."

Rewn's loaded fork returned to his plate, untasted. "What do ye recall o' it?"

"A kaleidoscope of movement, colours and speed. I heard the group screaming, frightened. All I could do was hang onto the sword until its spell was done."

Rewn stirred the eggs on his tin plate aimlessly, as though having suddenly lost his appetite. "Ye gathered us up into an invisible sphere o' air, with nothing beneath but the open sky. The horses and Little Wolf could no' move. Ye stood like marble, holding the sword for the entire journey. Ye ne'er shifted, no matter how we called out or shook ye. This went on for hours. Ye truly remember none o' this?"

"No. Nothing." Gralyre was horrified, yet had no reason to doubt Rewn's account. How had his perceptions of the event become so skewed? A deep unease swirled within Gralyre at how thoroughly the sword had subverted his senses. The magic had taken him completely.

"We are fine," Rewn blurted to distract Gralyre from his obvious distress. "It was a shock, but all things considered, ye are right, 'twas better than travelling months by horseback, or drowning in a flood!" Rewn tried on a grin.

It was a poor effort. Peering closer, Gralyre could see that his friend's face was etched with sadness. There was more here than what he was revealing. "Rewn, what else has happened?"

The sound of their names being called delayed Gralyre from pursuing the matter further.

They arose to greet Dotch, as he jogged to meet them, but Gralyre and Rewn's smiles of welcome faded when they noted

Dotch's distress.

"I am returning t' the fortress," Dotch announced urgently, as he neared, "I have t' find my wife and family. I must know that they survived the battle!"

"A battle?" Gralyre snapped with concern.

"Aye, the fortress has been destroyed," Rewn supplied.

Consumed as he had been by the intense magic, Gralyre had not noted the destruction of the fortress, as they had passed over it the previous night. This was the first he had heard of an attack. "Was it Doaphin?"

Memories assailed Gralyre then, of a slight man, with sly, sharp features, and thinning blond hair. It was disconcerting to discover that in his past he had met and spoken amicably to the creature responsible for all the ills that plagued his realm.

Doaphin had arrived from the Southern Kingdoms, as part of Princess Genevieve's retinue. Had Gralyre known then what would come to pass less than a year later, he would have slaughtered the Usurper at first sight, and his father's treaties be damned!

Rewn quickly summed up what he had learned. "Sorry Gralyre, Prince Gralyre," he corrected himself once more, "I thought that ye had been informed. 'Twas no' Doaphin, but that rutting bastard, Kierdenan! He attacked the fortress two nights past, on the eve o' the solstice. Bloody damned traitor! What evil could drive a man t' betray his allies?"

Gralyre scowled. "I do not know, but he will answer for it." Gralyre gripped Dotch's arm firmly. "We will help you find your family, Dotch. This need not be done by you alone."

"Come, Dotch," Rewn added, and tossed his half-finished plate to the top of the stump he had so recently occupied. "We will borrow some mounts."

Dotch closed his eyes, lifting his face skyward, as he tried to control his dread. "Thank-ye! Thank-ye both!"

"Give me a moment to make arrangements for Lady Catrian's care. I will meet with you both at the paddock," Gralyre promised.

Rewn bowed, and Dotch watched him with confusion before the light of understanding suffused his face, and he performed his own awkward genuflection. "Sorry. I forgot ye are... who ye are. What do we call ye now?"

Gralyre froze, as ingrained protocols warred with his close relationships with these men. He had been a Prince born to rule but he was now a creature far removed from royalty. An exile? A rebel? A sorcerer? A prince? Who was he? Who was he to become? Somehow, he had to discover a way to merge this messy chimera into one being.

"Call me Gralyre," he decided carefully, "as you would of old." He waved his hand to give them their permission to depart, an imperial gesture as natural to him as breathing, and never noted that he did so.

Gralyre went in search of Gedrhar, and found the elder kneeling in the dirt, mumbling to himself, and using a stick to draw on a patch of dusty ground.

Gedrhar glanced up from his intricate dust drawings. "How is

Lady Catrian?" he asked, speaking in the tongue of the Dream Weavers.

Gralyre replied in kind. "She is better, but should rest. Will you send food to her? I must go to the Rebel fortress to find Commander Boris and General Matik." While he spoke he examined the swirls in the dirt, but could make no sense of the symbols that Gedrhar had etched.

The old man nodded while sitting back on his haunches and picking up a tankard of water from which he drank heartily.

Gralyre turned to leave, but paused as something occurred to him. "By the way, how did your army enter the vale past the Rebel outposts?"

Gedrhar regarded Gralyre for a moment before answering. "I have been searching the Heathrens for you and the Rebellion since the onset of winter. I had a general location of this fortress, based upon my sense of Lady Catrian's use of magic, but when she fell ill, her magic ceased, and I could no longer find her.

"Then, about a sennight ago, my scouts chanced upon the signs of an army advancing in this direction, so we followed after it. When we arrived at the pass to the south, we discovered all within had been slaughtered."

"Demons take Kierdenan!" Gralyre interjected.

"The sentries had not long been dead. We stopped to amass the slain, and to build a cairn before marching onwards across the valley."

"Thank-you for seeing to our fallen," Gralyre inclined his head sadly.

"The battle at the fortress had commenced before we arrived. Not knowing whose side we should support, we chose to stay hidden and neutral until such knowledge became clear."

"And has it?" Gralyre asked, seeking words of assurance and commitment.

"Of course. You are my kin, and the rightful King of Lyre. The Dream Weavers stand ready."

Gralyre angled his head. "My thanks, Gedrhar."

As Gralyre turned to go, Gedrhar's words followed after. "Be on your guard at the fortress, for there are mutinous words hidden within the storm. The Dreamers speak of it."

Gralyre nodded to humour the elder, and strode away. Weaving between the trees and tents, he headed for the makeshift corral where Rewn and Dotch awaited him. "*Mutinous words hidden within the storm?* What does that mean?" he muttered in disgust over the cryptic omen. Ever were Sorcerers tricksters with their words and actions, and not to be trusted!

Gralyre's pace stuttered, as he realized that he was now a member of the Sorcerer ranks. As was Catrian. Where had he arrived at his foul opinion of magic? It was not just Doaphin, but something else…

"Gralyre!" Rewn hailed, interrupting Gralyre's musings, and the stray notion slipped his grasp, a slippery eel seeking deeper waters in which to hide.

Rewn had a sack slung over one shoulder. "Food," he replied to Gralyre's raised brow.

"Better ready another mount!" Jord called out, as he arrived.

"Ye did no' think that ye could leave without me, did ye?" He clapped Dotch on the shoulder. "With more eyes, we will find your family all the faster."

"Thank-ye, lad." Dotch's voice was strained with worry. His disarrayed salt-and-pepper hair bore witness to the number of times he had pushed his hands through it, seeking calm. He passed a set of reins to Rewn, and grabbed the leads of two other horses, guiding them out of the paddock.

"I saw that brother o' yours, Rewn," Jord mentioned amicably, as he saddled his horse. "He looked like he had been chewed up and spit out."

"He was attacked by a Stalker," Rewn grunted, not elaborating. Despite his exhaustion, Dajin's viperous words of the night before had made sleep impossible. He did not want to talk about his brother. He needed time to adjust to the bitter man who had supplanted the boy he had known.

"Dajin is injured? How badly was he hurt?" Gralyre asked with concern.

"He is fine." Rewn hung his food sack from his saddle horn, and heaved himself atop his horse. As exhausted as he still was, he had to grip hard with his thighs to keep from sliding off the far side.

Intent upon sharing the remarkable events, Jord did not note Rewn's unspoken cue to let the matter rest. "'Twas Gods' own luck that he lived! Stalkers were drawn t' the fighting up at the fortress. They were killing everyone!" Focused on fastening a stubborn buckle, Jord also missed seeing Dotch's face tighten with alarm.

"Rewn's brother and sister saved the Sorceress from Kierdenan's warriors, and then carried her off into the forest. A couple o' the Stalkers followed after them." Jord stiffly boosted himself up onto his steed, and groaned mightily, as a joint popped. "I heard your sister killed one with a dagger," the knifeman whistled low in appreciation. "Right through its eye!"

"Aye," Rewn agreed, a genuine smile finally lightening his face. "That she did. She protected both Dajin and Catrian."

"Then I owe her everything." Gralyre was never so thankful that this remarkable family had taken him in, and given him warmth and friendship when he had no memory of who he was, and had nothing with which to repay them. Their selflessness towards a stranger in this time of want and war was truly extraordinary.

As Gralyre straddled his horse, thoughts of family made him long for the soft bed he had left that morning, and the beautiful woman within it whom he would never be with again. He sighed heavily, and glanced up to see the three men smirking at him. They had caught him with his heart in his eyes, as he had unconsciously stared towards the tent that he had shared with Catrian.

"What?" Gralyre snarled disparagingly.

"I heard that the Lady Catrian is recovering," Dotch mentioned casually, his woes ebbing slightly in the face of Gralyre's good fortune. He tossed a hidden wink at Jord.

"I heard the same thing," Jord mused. "We did no' see ye last night for dinner, Gralyre," he trailed off suggestively, a teasing smirk flashing beneath his impressive nose.

Royal ire tried to assert itself, but Gralyre was so gladdened that his friends were treating him as old that despite himself he felt the pull of a grin.

"I am sure that was the Sorceress' tent that we saw ye leave this morn," Dotch deadpanned innocently, looking to Rewn for confirmation.

"Big smile on his face," Rewn embellished, holding his hands wide apart to show the size. "Big!"

Jord snorted. "Could no' have been so big," he leered the double entendre, "she tried t' kill him."

Dotch stroked his chin. "Is that where that crack o' thunder came from?"

Gralyre's eyebrow shot up, his face daring them to utter another word. "Remind me to beat you all senseless later," he warned drolly. He kicked his horse in the ribs, and rode haughtily to the forefront.

Rewn doubled with laughter, and Jord guffawed loudly, as they followed.

Gralyre's proud exit was ruined when Saliana stepped into his path, forcing him to rein in sharply or run her down.

"Where are ye all going?" she demanded.

Briefly, Gralyre informed her of the plans for the day.

"Let me gather some medicines. The survivors will have need o' a healer." Saliana wheeled to run to the tent she had shared with Dara and Rewn, but skidded to a halt to turn back and glare at them all. "Do no' leave without me!" she ordered, her finger wagging.

The men sat their horses, chaffing at the delay, and Gralyre suddenly saw an opportunity to get some of his own back. "Saliana has certainly changed since we rescued her from Raindell, Rewn," he mused, as he watched her trim back and swishing grey skirts disappear into her tent. He made sure that he could watch his friend from the corner of his eye. "She seems very interested in keeping you in sight."

"Me? No," Rewn denied. "She just likes t' be underfoot."

Dotch took up Gralyre's cue, for he had no loyalty when there was an opportunity to rile the younger men. "I would be careful, were I ye, Rewn. That girl is hunting. A woman who has set her heart on ye is more persistent than a Stalker, and harder t' shake than Deathren!" he teased. "'Tis how my wife caught me."

Mild panic vised onto Rewn's innards. Saliana was as a sister to him! Certainly he had never thought about her much at all, and if at all, only in passing.

Jord fought it for a moment before surrendering to laughter at Rewn's disgruntled expression.

For a moment Rewn forgot about his troubles with Dajin, to wonder what the men were seeing that he did not. His jaw snapped shut on his retort, as Saliana emerged from the tent. He watched her like a caged bird would a stalking cat, as she hurried to the corral, and retrieved a horse. A cold shiver rattled his backbone, as she turned to glance back at him with a smile.

But she was not looking his way at all. The Dream Weaver

Healer, Ninrhar, had intercepted her, handing her a heavy pack, and giving her a fatherly pat on the shoulder before seeing her mounted.

Gralyre decided to change the subject to relieve Rewn's dark frown. "What has become of Trifyn and Aneida?" he asked after the rest of his companions.

"Well," Dotch leaned forward to pat his horse's neck, "The Dream Weaver warriors took one look at Aneida, and started t' follow her like sniffing tom cats. The leader, Gedrhar, explained t' me that the Dream Weaver men place women warriors at about the level o' goddesses."

"They best watch themselves or she will snap off the parts most dear t' them!" Jord grinned, and his knives came out to spin lazily through his fingertips.

"And what of Trifyn?" Gralyre asked. "How is his leg?"

Saliana heard his question just as her horse came abreast of theirs. "He is resting now, but his wound went bad afore Ninrhar ministered t' it. Even with healer's magic, he could no' remove all o' the corruption. Trifyn has got the blood fever now, and 'tis up t' his own strength t' heal or no'."

A deep rage boiled over in Gralyre, as another memory from his past sifted to the surface. "Damn them, the evil, worm eating beasts!" he snarled. "They rub their own filth upon their weapons so that even a cut can kill!"

Into the silence that followed his outburst, Saliana blurted, "Ye are the Lost Prince? Truly?"

Gralyre inclined his head in a regal nod. "I am."

Saliana licked her lips nervously. "Oh! All right. 'Tis a fine thing then." Her horse stomped impatiently, and she squeaked, teetering unsteadily while clutching at her heavy pack to keep it from tumbling to the ground.

Rewn sighed in exasperation, and pulled the healer's bag from her arms. "Here. Give it t' me. I will carry it for ye." He strung it to the opposite side of his saddle from the bag of food he already carried.

Gralyre, Jord and Dotch exchanged wicked grins, as Saliana smiled warmly in response to Rewn's gallantry.

"Are we going or no'?" Rewn demanded huffily.

CHAPTER FOUR

Dreisenheld

Boom... boom... boom... boom... boom...

The Master's will drives the thunderous impacts of a million boots. Demon Rider foot soldiers, twenty-five abreast in ordered lines that stretch to the horizon in a thick, red swath, lock step to the beat of deep drums. Each soldier holds a pike, so that it seems a forest of leafless trees are on the move.

Boom... boom... boom... boom... boom...

The Master's red banner snaps smartly throughout the throng, held aloft by standard bearers. The bright sunlight pierces the clouds of dust kicked up by the army to illuminate the golden crown that is suspended between the venomous fangs of entwined black serpents.

Boom... boom... boom... boom... boom...

Riding the perimeter of the host to either side, the cavalry spans fifteen abreast, tens of thousands of horses restlessly pawing at the marching pace. The armoured steeds with their metal clad riders flash brilliantly in the sunlight, a stark contrast to the red uniforms of the foot soldiers.

Boom... boom... boom... boom... boom...

From where Doaphin oversees the deployment, from horseback atop a rise overlooking the Dreisenheld River valley, the marching army bears a startling resemblance to an enormous silver vein pumping poisonous blood. The *boom... boom... boom...* of the drums is the measured pulse of the Master's black heart.

The earth shudders from the rhythmic progress of the soulless millipede. The vibrations travel up through the hill upon which Doaphin watches, and small stones rattle together, the pebbles singing a lament of the oncoming ruination of mankind.

The billowing dust allows Doaphin to track the army's progress across the leagues by following the snaking brown clouds towards the eastern horizon.

The Stalkers and Deathren will not march until sunset, and their numbers are equal to what lies spread before Doaphin in the valley below. The Master's army has been departing since midnight, and still the vast numbers have yet to ebb.

Boom... boom... boom... boom... boom...

Overkill. Unwieldy. He is tasked with swatting a gnat with a mountain. But the Master's will is to be obeyed. Without question.

Twenty Demon Lords flank Doaphin, each of the corrupt sorcerers to command a different battalion of the Master's army. He ignores them all. As Supreme Commander, they are there to do his bidding, and will await his pleasure.

The sun rises higher into the sky, and the day grows warmer, but Doaphin still sits his horse, counting the lines, as each begins its march. He refuses to doff his heavy helmet with its ridiculous crest of red-dyed feathers to the demands of the heat. His endurance is not for the creatures surrounding him, the Demon Lords in their court raiment, unprepared and unclad for war, who snidely whisper amongst each other about his ridiculous stance. It is for the one who watches from Dreisenheld Castle. The one who sends him to his doom.

Boom... boom... boom... boom... boom...

'Demons take Fennick and his curse!' Doaphin lifts his gloved hand, rubbing it to relieve the ache in the withered flesh. It is a stark reminder of his past defeat. His thoughts grow oily with uncertainty, as he considers the threat tendered by Fennick's prophecy. *'What a strange thing it is to feel vulnerable in the face of such power.'* Already, Gralyre has recovered the sword. How long will it be before the *'Dragon perched on Vengeful Fist'* comes for him?

Gralyre and the sword must not return to Dreisenheld and the Master. He missed his chance to stop the Prince from claiming Fennick's Wizard Stone. He will not fail again.

Boom... boom... boom... boom... boom...

Doaphin watches and waits, until the day wanes. The rearguard and wagon trains are only now leaving the marshalling grounds from the plains overlooked by the capital city. Their departure is hampered by the churned ground left in the wake of the hundreds of thousands who have marched before them.

Lastly come the drovers, and their herds of cattle, goats and horses set to feed the hungry mouths of the juggernaut. The food will nourish the army for less than a fortnight, and then their sustenance will be derived from, and of, the people that they are set to slaughter.

It is finally time for Doaphin to depart. He can delay no longer.

Doaphin wheels his horse for one last look at the city, which is commanded on a rise by the royal castle of Dreisenheld. The red rays of the setting sun and the heat that has claimed the day both work to magnify the air, drawing the spires of the citadel closer so that he can clearly see the lone figure standing atop the castle battlements, dominating all.

The vast army marching to war is as nothing when compared to the might of the Master. Doaphin's mouth tightens with resolve. If the spirit is made corporeal, and the Master gains the power to leave Dreisenheld, the world will drown in blood and death forever. Gralyre cannot be taken alive. He and the sword must both be destroyed.

"Find your battalions." Doaphin does not turn away to ensure that his order to the Demon Lords is heeded. Instead, he listens to the pound of retreating hoof beats with his gaze steady upon the small figure in the distance. Alone now atop the hill, Doaphin salutes the Master, and awaits an acknowledgement.

When it comes, the powerful blow knocks him from his saddle to the ground. The ridiculous helmet flies from his head with the impact, and cartwheels down the hillside. The red-feathered crest is ripped and soiled by the time it strikes the rocks at the bottom.

His horse screams with pain, and explodes in a pink mist of flesh and bone. For a moment Doaphin fears that the Master has sensed his treasonous thoughts.

Mocking laughter erupts from the air, followed by a dire warning. *'Do not fail us.'*

Doaphin cowers in the spring grasses amongst the guts and bones and carnage, as all that remains of his steed rains down upon him. "My life is yours, my Master. Mankind shall die, and I will return with Gralyre and the sword. I swear it!"

Only when the cold chill of the Master's presence fades does Doaphin dare to rise from his abasement.

Bloodied and shaken, he uses his magic to call another horse from out of the drovers' herds. When it arrives, he transfers his previous mount's gore-soaked saddle to the new steed, though the horse protests and sidesteps the stink of death.

Doaphin rides to war with as much dignity as has been left to him, abandoning the ornate helmet with its tattered red feathers to the lengthening shadows beneath the hill.

෫෬

Verdalan

The spring day was sunny and warm with a blue sky, as crystalline as water, arching high overhead. The privation of winter was only a memory, and summer was as yet only a sultry tease of the relenting of want and hardship. It was a day to be breathed in with gratitude for yet another year's victory over the long, dark cold.

But that lovely sun was a thoughtless token from Gods who had not turned their attentions to the lives of men for far too long. They had missed the signs that their greatest creation was losing its fight to exist. So while that bright glory bequeathed its warmth and promise of life, it left not the smallest shadow for mankind to hide within, when murderous gluttony erupted in the streets of Verdalan.

"Kill the Humans! Kill them all!" The exhortation from the throat of one Demon Rider became the rallying roar of the many. In reply, the shrieks of the dying spurred humanity into a frenzied flight to escape the killing grounds, but the city gates had been sealed upon the Master's edict. There was no resistance to the slaughter. It had long been outlawed for mankind to carry swords. No human would be spared. Verdalan was to be cleansed.

The city streets bled. Scarlet rivulets flowed into the channels between cobblestones before streaming away into cracks and drains, those safe havens where victims had been unable to conceal themselves from the annihilation. The blood rippled in the sunlight as it coursed, juddering with a beating pulse from the impacts of darting feet.

A Demon Rider wrenched its sword from the chest of a gasping man, and paused to savour its kill while pandemonium swirled around them both, slayer and prey. Their stillness was a reef of calm eternity within a turbulent ocean of violent moments, until the man shattered the lull by dropping a small bundle of rags from his slackening arms, and collapsing into the street.

The man had risked all to retrieve these humble things from his hovel, only to have his desperate flight ended with his meager treasures scattered beneath stampeding boots.

His fallen body dammed the rivulets of blood in the street so that they began to pool around him: his blood, his neighbours' blood. The red womb of humanity cradled his passing.

Released from its fascination, the Demon Rider leapt forward to slay a shrieking woman who was scrabbling in the filth at the curb to squeeze herself into an open sewer grate to escape the massacre. Leaving her body poised on the cusp of safety, the Demon Rider then darted after yet another fleeing victim, reveling in its rampage, rejoicing in what it had been bred to be.

Yet, pockets of safety were to be found for those who knew where to look. Beneath Verdalan's ramshackle buildings, beneath even its sewers, where a fortunate few had found temporary refuge from the slaughter in the streets above, lay an elder realm of which only a select number were aware. The bones of an ancient city lay buried beneath the streets of the current one, its presence long forgotten from age and cataclysm.

Impassible ruins and collapsed passages defined most of the vestiges of this lost civilization save for a lone architectural wonder - a vast, ancient cistern. The decaying beauty of this bygone era put to shame the horrors and ugliness assailing the world above.

The manmade, underground lake gently lapped against stone pillars of carved magnificence where torches in iron sconces burned brightly to reveal crisscrossing pathways of jewel-coloured mosaic steppingstones that spanned the water for hundreds of yards. These paths led towards small chambers, dry sanctuaries within the cistern, whose purpose and use were lost to antiquity. Light and shadow mirrored in the waters, as above so below, with only a thin, rippling seam to anchor illusion to reality.

The cistern's ceilings vaulted high, vanishing within the domain of darkness that held the subterranean realm in crumbling repose. Now and then, tiles rained down, and shattered the reflections, sending echoes roaring throughout the standing pillars, as a warning that one day even their mighty strength would fail. Time would tolerate no challengers.

One of the mysterious cistern chambers bloomed brilliantly, shining a beacon of light across the stilling black waves of the watery expanse. The tall silhouette of a lean man appeared at the entrance, as all grew quiet again except for the relentless drip of water, and the murmur of men's voices speaking of rebellion and war.

"Are ye satisfied, Laurazon? I told ye, 'twas just a bit o' roof falling. 'Twill happen a dozen more times afore ye depart."

General Laurazon's keen blue gaze continued to scan the torch-lighted darkness for hints of movement within the dancing shadows. "Ye will forgive me, Baldric, if I am no' as confident o' our safety as ye, given what is occurring above."

Laurazon found it curious that even in the stillness of this subterranean haven, a breeze could still thread its way into these dark ruins to keep the torches flickering. If a breeze could do so, why then could not the evil that reigned over them also find its way into General Baldric's hidden lair?

"My men are shepherding as many t' safety into the sewers as they can. The 'Riders might find their way beneath the streets, but they will no' find us." General Baldric's deep voice carried the certainty of his fanaticism.

Laurazon propped a lean hip against the chalky stones at the doorway of the ancient chamber, and crossed his arms to wait out the seconds. His tall, slender frame camouflaged a coiled strength that could explode into movement at any given moment. Beneath his dark hair, his watchful gaze scanned patiently for movement within the cistern. His caution was rooted in reason, not the illusion of belief.

The sound of dripping water spurred his imagination. For a moment the General envisaged it to be the blood of the innocents dying in the streets above, somehow seeping through the deep darkness, just as the breezes had, to befoul the pristine waters of the cistern with clouds of red. It was not an unlikely notion. Sensing no further movement in the darkness, General Laurazon finally turned back towards the light.

His gaze flicked over the teeth that embedded every surface of the chamber. He had heard the rumours, but until now had thought them exaggerations. Molars, bicuspids, and incisors embedded every surface of the room. They gleamed from the walls and ceiling, from the long table and eight throne-sized chairs set around the board, and even from the floor on which they trod. The teeth were meticulously worked into patterns, swirls and whirls that created a dizzying vista. The accumulation had to account for thousands of Demon Riders. It was a disturbing outward symptom of General Baldric's inner madness.

The only relief for the eye was a brass ewer filled with water, and a motley collection of goblets that shone golden at the centre of the tabletop. It was a startling burst of colour in the otherwise glowing, ivory room.

Though Laurazon's face did not reveal his thoughts, it was perhaps the fact that his regard lingered for a heartbeat longer than was needed upon the macabre sight that prompted General Baldric to comment.

"My furnishings are no' t' your liking, General Laurazon?"

Laurazon shrugged with disinterest, an elegant shifting, as he glided towards his seat at the table. There was no benefit to giving the man his true opinion. One could not win an argument with an obsessed lunatic. "I was only marveling at your commitment. It must have taken years t' gather so many," Laurazon commented politicly.

Baldric brushed a large hand down the length of his black, silky moustache, from lip to chest, combing through the thin strands to remove any snarls before giving the ends a haughty flick. "It did no' take so long as ye would think!" His swarthy face, animated with enthusiasm. "This chamber is but one o' many I have decorated with the teeth o' our enemy!"

General Laurazon's second in command, Lieutenant Pedric,

filled a cup with water from the copper ewer, and set the goblet on the toothsome tabletop in front of Laurazon as he resumed his seat. Pedric's face was perfectly bland, as he inquired in a quiet murmur, "All clear?"

Pedric was deceptively pleasant of face and manner, behind which he masked a pragmatic killer. Of average looks, height and coloring of brown hair and brown eyes, there seemed nothing remarkable about the Lieutenant, an illusion that had felled many an adversary. A better man in the fight there was none. Laurazon trusted him implicitly.

"Aye, Pedric, for now. But we should no' tempt the Gods by lingering longer than we must," Laurazon commented, before asking of their host, "When will it be safe for us t' depart?"

The rest of Laurazon's company, twenty warriors in all, had been taken elsewhere along with General Baldric's entourage, presumably to eat and sleep to recover from their long journey out of the mountains after attending Commander Boris' war summit. They had entered the city that morning, only to find themselves trapped, as Doaphin's purge began.

Baldric quaffed deeply of the water from his goblet, and waved towards the man at his shoulder. "Come nightfall, Iptus will guide ye and your men out o' these tunnels." Without looking, he held up his cup to be refilled.

Lieutenant Iptus, holding a second brass ewer ready, stepped up to General Baldric's elbow, and poured. Baldric's second was a twitchy man of slight stature whose duties seemed more suited to that of a valet than a Lieutenant of the rebellion's spy network. His eyes were ever moving, and his body was ever shifting, as though his mind was telling his feet to go and stop in the same moment. Laurazon often wondered how much of Lieutenant Iptus' nervous strain was caused by the madman he served.

Encouraged that the water was untainted by Baldric's drinking of it, Laurazon finally lifted his cup, and took an exploratory sip. He had little trust in his unpredictable host, despite their common allegiance to the rebellion. Baldric had insisted that these waters held restorative powers. Laurazon was skeptical of the claim, but had to admit that the cool wetness was welcome at the end of their difficult trek.

"Leave this night?" Pedric jumped into the conversation, "Is that wise? Stalkers and Deathren will be deployed t' track any humans who try t' escape. How will we get beyond the walls?"

Baldric's face hardened with hatred, and his hand fisted around his goblet. "Doaphin's creatures will be glutting themselves upon the flesh o' the city with their gazes turned inwards at their debauchery. My tunnels are safe. 'Tis a route oft used. They will no' notice ye. We have horses waiting beyond the walls t' bear ye and your men home. I have a hall in need o' enameling, and revenge t' take!" His eyes ignited with the flames of a zealot.

Laurazon lowered his goblet carefully, back to the toothy tabletop, and brushed his stained sleeve across his mouth to blot the moisture left in his beard by the water. "Ye are no' leaving the city with us? Who will see t' Verdalan's survivors?"

"Ye deal with them. Ye lead them t' safety."

Laurazon suppressed all signs of anger behind a bored façade. Losing some of his men to this task would leave the rest of them vulnerable, as they travelled northwest across the country to home. "Am I mistaken in my remembrance that 'twas ye who Commander Boris charged with relaying refugees t' the mountains?"

At his side, he could feel echoing waves of aggression emanating from Pedric who, taking his cue from Laurazon, also presented an outward calm and unthreatening manner.

"Would ye have me leave an entire city o' the enemy at our backs?" Baldric demanded.

"If they ne'er know we are here," Laurazon started to argue prudence.

"Exactly!" Baldric smiled. "They will no' be expecting an attack!"

Demons take Baldric! This was not the time to tip their hand! This was a fight to save living humans, not useless real estate. They had neither the numbers nor the time to take back the city! If Verdalan was lost, then let it be lost! Such self-indulgence on the cusp of war was folly! If the Spymaster were to be captured here in Verdalan, the entire Rebel strategy would be betrayed. But then conceit seemed the cornerstone of Baldric's nature.

Despite their weeks of hard travel, General Baldric appeared as clean and fresh as when they had left the safe haven of Commander Boris' fortress, while Laurazon and Pedric had allowed the road to hold sway in the name of speed; their clothes were stained from the hard trek, their chins were bearded, and their hair tangled.

Of a morning, Baldric would refuse to budge until Iptus had painstakingly shaved his chin around his impressive moustache, and braided the straight black strands at his temples to keep his long hair in order.

Every regrettable delay now played out its consequences in the streets above. How many could they have saved if they had only arrived a day or two earlier?

"Sir," Iptus interjected nervously. "We can spare five men t' take the survivors t' the Heathrens."

Baldric considered for a moment, before grunting and waving his hand in consent.

"Haloo-o-o-o!" echoed from across the cistern's cavernous space, and the Generals and their Lieutenants leapt forward to crowd the doorway to the chamber. Swords were drawn in readiness.

"General, should I douse the light?" Pedric asked.

"Too late," Laurazon replied to his man's question. In the far distance, a torch bobbed upon the mosaic steppingstones of the pathway to their bright chamber.

"No need. 'Tis my men," General Baldric announced with certainty, and sheathed his blade. "'Riders would no' use a torch t' see in the dark, nor announce themselves."

Baldric's words were proved true when two bloodied warriors, with their arms supporting each other's staggering weights, resolved upon the mosaic pathway. "General!" the one holding the torch hailed when they saw the men awaiting their arrival, "General Baldric!"

The other warrior clasped his free hand against a wound in his gut. He stumbled over the remaining distance to the cistern chamber, and only the strength of his companion held him upright and upon the pathway.

Baldric blocked their entrance into the dry room. "Who are ye? Tell me your names."

"This is Kevoy, I am Avan," the torchbearer replied. "We were stationed within the hidden wall passages at the 'Rider barracks when it began. Please, let us pass! Kevoy is hurt. He must rest."

"No' yet! Where is it? Where is my tribute? Give it t' me!"

The gravely injured Kevoy swayed, barely conscious now, only held erect by Avan's support.

Standing at Baldric's back, Pedric's hand toyed with the dagger at his waist. On his face, the congenial mask had slipped to reveal the predator beneath, a look that Laurazon knew well. Pedric's had reached his final endurance for the Spymaster's capriciousness. It was well that they were parting company with Baldric this nightfall.

For a moment, Laurazon considered the benefits of gutting the Spymaster. It would eliminate the obvious danger that the lunatic posed with his quest for personal glory. On the other hand, the spy network that Baldric commanded was integral to the rebellion's war strategy. Throwing it into disarray would cause more harm than good. Laurazon gave his lieutenant a slight shake of his head, and Pedric's hand slid reluctantly from the hilt of his weapon; his face became bland and unremarkable once more.

Needing an empty hand with which to work, Avan doused his unneeded torch into the water off the landing to the chamber, raising a spit of steam as it sank from sight. He reached within his companion's shirt for a small leather pouch, joining it with one of his own.

"Here, General. Your tribute." Avan's face was without expression, though there was tightness about his mouth that spoke of hatred. He shifted the weight of Kevoy's arm over his shoulder so that he could toss both sacs to Baldric. Kevoy cried out at the rough jostle this made.

Baldric caught and weighed each with a small shake, producing the sound of pebbles rubbing together. It took no guesswork to divine the contents of those purses. "Ah...Well done men." His flat black eyes adopted a faraway gleam, and he stepped backwards into the chamber, finally clearing the doorway for his wounded to reach sanctuary.

With the aid of Laurazon, Pedric and Iptus, the injured spies limped to the table, where they collapsed in exhaustion. Blood marred the pristine white surfaces in their wake.

Baldric frowned, and motioned to Iptus, who drew a rag from his vest, and set obsessively to scrubbing and sopping up the trail of red from the doorway.

"We had t' fight our way through the streets t' reach the passages t' below!" Avan announced, his body aquiver from unspent adrenalin. "Everyone is dead. Women! Children! The 'Riders are sparing no one! So many bodies. So many," he shuddered. He reached for the brass ewer, and sloshed a healthy serving of water into a tankard, holding it to his injured companion's lips with trembling hands. "They ne'er had a chance. They had no warning, no weapons. They could no' defend themselves!" Tears rolled unchecked down his cheeks, his grief seeping out without him seeming to realize it.

"There is more," Kevoy gasped out after he had taken a pull of water. He pushed the tankard away, wincing deeply, as he clutched at his side where blood seeped between his fingers from a mortal wound in his guts. "I heard the orders myself, when they arrived from Dreisenheld. Doaphin has commanded the garrisons t' empty. Any towns, villages, or holds in their paths are t' be razed."

"Where? Which ones first?" Baldric demanded.

The spy's face crumpled in horror. "All o' 'em! All at once! What is happening here is taking place all across Lyre!" His words ended in a racking cough that erupted mists of bloodied phlegm that spattered the gleaming ivory surfaces around him. His eyes rolled back and he slumped.

"Kevoy! Kevoy!" Avan shook his friend's shoulder, but one look at the spy's face revealed that he had passed beyond the cares of this world.

"Damn the Gods on their thrones! What is happening, General?" Avan demanded. "Doaphin orders one human t' be left alive at each massacre with a message, '*The Lost Prince*

pretender must bring the sword t' Dreisenheld or all will die'.
What madness is this?"

General Laurazon met Pedric's surprise with his own. They leaned their heads closer, as Laurazon murmured, "How does Doaphin know? We have told no one yet."

"General Chartrin?" Pedric suggested just as softly. "Travelling the rivers, he must be half-way t' the coast by now."

In answer to Avan's question, General Baldric announced, "The Lost Prince has returned, and may even now have the Dragon Sword in hand. Doaphin's reign will soon be over."

It was the beautiful lie that Commander Boris had ordered the Generals to spread. It sounded ludicrous to Laurazon's ears, especially as Baldric uttered it without any conviction, yet Avan sat straighter, and a sliver of hope seemed to ease his grief.

"Gods! Truly? He has returned? He seeks the sword?"

Laurazon's clever mind turned the incongruity from side to side, considering all angles. If the lie had not yet been told, then how had Doaphin known to warn the 'Riders to seek a pretender? Against all odds, had Commander Boris' mysterious warrior actually won the Dragon Sword from Fennick's Island? Or was there a spy in their midst, leaking information to the enemy?

"Look at what has become o' my table!" Baldric sneered at the fine red droplets left behind by Kevoy's death rattle.

ເ໑ຕ

Deep in the Lowlands

General Chartrin stood in the prow of his longboat, keeping watch on the patterns of flowing water, as his men rowed tirelessly to increase their speed down the broad river. The planks of the decking pushed up against the soles of his feet, rising and falling with the surging currents.

Gods! How he had missed the water!

Chartrin gloried in the rush of wind through his hair, from the vessel's sustained speed that was over twice that of a horse at a gallop. The river was a tireless runner that required no rest or sustenance, unlike the steeds that had borne them less than eight leagues a day during their descent out of the mountains after the war summit at the Northern Fortress.

When Chartrin glanced back down the length of the longboat, sunlight winked from the jewels in his ears, and in the lengths of thick gold chains around his neck. The flashes from the gaudy trophies of war were matched within his wind-tossed, golden hair.

Forty feet away, in the aft of the longboat, Lieutenant Jon manned the rudder, steering by the hand signals that Chartrin made, warnings to avoid water hazards such as deadfalls, sandbars, rocks and whirling eddies. Where General Chartrin seemed made of sunlight riding on cresting waves, Lieutenant Jon was like a quiet pool at midnight. His black hair was clubbed back from a narrow, austere face that was intent with concentration. He met Chartrin's reckless grin with a somber nod of his head, what in another man would be a whoop of joy.

Spaced evenly between Chartrin and Jon, ten benches spanned the hull of the longboat, seating their twenty men who plied the oars. Many had shed their shirts in the warmth of the day and, with both callused palms pressed firmly to the shanks of their oars, they pushed and pulled in a tireless, sweeping rhythm. The oar ports were padded with rags to muffle the sounds of the men's rowing, so that only a quiet splash, quickly lost within the natural rush of the water, betrayed their passage, as they sculled down the broad river through the lowland forest. The men did not speak. Silence was their ally, as they slipped unseen through enemy territory.

Rowing inland against the currents in the fall had been a slow and arduous process, especially as they had been carrying the weight of cargo and horses. They had left their longboat safely beached and hidden for the winter in the thick forest at the edge of a mountain lake where, according to the ancient chart by which the General had steered, the waterways ahead would have grown too steep and rough to be of further use.

From there, they had continued on foot into the mountains towards the Northern Fortress, trailing the pack horses that had carried a tribute of supplies and valuables for Commander Boris; the plunder from raids upon Doaphin's ships.

Their return journey, descending from out of the Heathren Mountains, had taken the back-half of winter. Fortunately, they had arrived to find open water on their lake, and were able to launch their longboat immediately.

General Chartrin had opted to loose their horses into the forest to fend for themselves. Without the weight of plunder and animals, the longboat now held a draw of no more than the depth of a man's chest, giving them access to the shallowest of waterways. The cargo hold up the centre of the boat was hatched over, and empty of all but food and bedding, and the square sail and rigging that they would raise when they finally reached the open sea. Until then, the thick mast at mid-ship remained bare.

With the additional rush of the spring melt swelling the rivers and lakes, they travelled over twenty leagues per day save for when they were obliged to take the weight of the boat onto their shoulders to carry it overland to the next body of water in the chain that would eventually take them home to the sea.

Speed was their highest priority, as they hastened to warn as many settlements as possible of the oncoming genocide, and to spread Commander Boris' lie that the Lost Prince had returned to fulfill Fennick's prophecy.

Some Lowlanders heeded them and chose to flee. Often, they aided the cause by sending runners to warn neighbouring villages, before they packed up and started their journey east towards the Heathren Mountains, and their eventual sanctuary in the legendary realm of the Dream Weavers.

And some did not.

Chartrin and his men had been driven from more than one waterfront village by Lowlanders too terrified by their blind obedience to Doaphin's dogma to trust the Rebels' claims.

Chartrin's Rebels had no time to linger, and convince them

otherwise. The Lowlanders would be delivered of the consequences of their own actions. They had the knowledge that they needed to save themselves, should they so choose. Chartrin's conscience was clear.

As General Chartrin travelled beyond the continental midpoint, he would begin directing evacuees northwest towards the coastal fishing town of Ghent, where his ships would be waiting to ferry them to safety onto the islands of the Western Fortress, an archipelago lying in the seas beyond Dreisenheld.

The further the Western Rebels distanced themselves from the Heathren Mountains, the more obvious spring's flirtation with summer became. The forest glowed, reborn after the long winter. The green raiment danced upon woodland fingers to the music of the light breezes, flashing like emeralds in the intermittent sunbeams. The forest canted over the waterway in a greedy search for more light, creating a green tunnel of life through which the sparkling river flowed.

One could almost forget that this land was afflicted by the demon blights of oppression and death until periodically, along the banks of the river, they passed the ruins of townships and villages. 'Twas a common enough sight in the Lowlands.

Doaphin's Tithe, that perversion that demanded the lives of fertile women every thirteen years, had seen to it that few children were born to mankind, and Lowland villages had been abandoned, as populations had depleted. The few townships that had resisted the heinous tithe were marked for their honourable defiance with burned and shattered buildings. In the end it was a futile posturing, for with either condition, revolt or submission, the results were exact. Mankind drifted near the shores of extinction in the land of Lyre.

Brought from his musings by the faint scent of wood smoke upon the breeze, Chartrin made a sharp gesture towards the right bank of the river. He felt the instant response of the longboat, as Jon obeyed the silent command, and shifted the rudder. The General held up a closed fist, and his men lifted their oars, allowing the longboat's momentum, and the currents to carry them to an exposed sandbar at the river's edge.

Chartrin's boots hit the shallows at the very moment that the hull beached on the gravel embankment. His men followed closely, vaulting lithely over the gunwales. With the ease of long practice, they hefted the longboat to their shoulders, and carried it inland, into a copse of bushes where it would remain hidden.

Chartrin withdrew an old roll of velum from inside his loose shirt, pulling it open to study the ancient chart that was inked upon its surface. Lieutenant Jon drew closer to his shoulder, that he might also view the map.

Though the chart Chartrin steered by was from the days of the Lost Prince, it was still unerringly accurate. It was disturbing to see how populous these lands had once been. The ancient map now bore multitudes of little blots of red ink to mark the towns that were no more. They easily outnumbered the tiny black crosses indicating those that still survived.

"I make our position t' be near Frenton, " Jon advised quietly, leaning past Chartrin's shoulder to trace their route upon the line representing the river they were currently travelling. "'Tis the only village nearby."

Chartrin nodded. "Aye, but we have no' made that distance yet. No' t' be near enough t' smell their hearth fires." Chartrin re-rolled the chart carefully, his face grave with thought.

Jon stepped back. "We could take a chance, and continue downriver t' the village."

"No. The smoke could be from a patrol, and if the 'Riders see us pass by, they might follow us back t' the village. It would go badly for the Lowlanders."

"The smoke could be from the far side o' the river."

"Unlikely. The village is on this bank. 'Tis more likely that a patrol would be riding on this side."

"If we canno' pass them…" Jon trailed suggestively.

"Then we have t' kill 'em!" Chartrin concurred with a flash of teeth. "Ye two," he singled out a couple of his men, "stand guard. The rest o' ye follow me. We need t' discover who is tending the fires."

Keeping to the cover of trees, they tracked the source of the wood smoke downriver. The odour grew steadily stronger until they could see smoke drifting between the trunks of the forest giants. The blue haze filtered the sunlight, revealing pillars of light that seemed solid enough to support the weight of the sky.

Voices echoed ahead, and Chartrin, walking in front, was first to spy a flash of red through the trees, a stark contrast to the greens and browns of the underbrush. Chartrin motioned to his men to take cover. He had been correct, but took no joy in it. A patrol of at least sixty Demon Riders, in their crimson uniforms, was taking its ease around a campfire in a clearing on the banks of the river.

Slowly, in order to minimize noise, Chartrin drew his curved cutlass from the scabbard at his waist. His warriors aped his gesture. He felt them there at his back, a ferocity of purpose, each of them eager to spill the blood of their enemy. The 'Riders might outnumber his eighteen men three-to-one, but the element of surprise was on their side, and his men were eager for a fight.

Raising his hand, Chartrin held his men for a moment, savouring the tension of their eagerness echoing his own. With a gesture, they were loosed. They sprang from cover with howling battle cries.

It was a short and bloody fight, a butchering, more than a battle. The 'Riders had been unprepared to meet the armed Rebels.

In the aftermath, Chartrin wiped his bloodied sword across the back of a felled 'Rider, and ordered, "Check the bodies and the saddlebags o' the horses. Take anything o' use."

Lieutenant Jon approached a small cast iron stewpot that was burping over the fire. "What are ye eating for breakfast?" he asked, as he bent and lifted the lid. He grabbed a stick, and gave the grey, watery broth a stir. Severed fingers of varying sizes swirled around in the resultant currents.

"Mercy from the Gods!" Jon snarled, as he reared back. He gave the vessel a kick with his boot, and steam hissed off the hot coals, as the liquid spilled into the flames of the campfire, dousing it.

"*Help. Help us. Save us.*" The voice was urgent, though weak as a whisper.

"Jon!" Chartrin motioned his man to investigate.

The Lieutenant, with four warriors at his back, leapt lightly over a fallen tree to discover three men trussed upon the ground. Their hands and feet had been severed.

Jon beckoned to Chartrin. "General! One yet lives." He whipped his belt from around his waist, and tightened the band around one of the injured man's seeping wrists, while another Rebel did the same for the other arm. "Get his ankles!" Jon ordered more tourniquets.

With one look, Chartrin could see that there was little point. The ground was thick with clotted blood. Bloated flies rose in clouds of joyous abandon at the bounty that they had found.

The Lowlander lay still as death, his strength depleted by his call for help. Beneath the grime of extreme poverty, his flesh was grey. His eyes and cheeks were sunken from starvation, and his clothing was ragged and bloodied.

"Who are ye? Where are ye from?" Chartrin asked loudly, though he had already guessed the village of Frenton.

Through lips that were tinged blue with his approaching death, the wounded man whispered, "They killed everyone. In every house. I do no' understand. We obeyed. We did no' defy Doaphin. No reason. Everyone... dead."

The man panted for a moment. His quivering, emaciated arm, ending in its bleeding stump with a belt tight around it, lifted to the side, and thumped down upon the chest of one of the dead men laid out beside him upon the bloody earth. "My boy, my boy... the Prince is going t' save us," he sighed before his shuddering breaths stilled.

Chartrin shrugged away the fevered raving, as he straightened from where he had crouched to hear the dying man's final words. He met Jon's sorrowful gaze, and a bone deep weariness settled deep into his soul at the loss of yet more human life.

He turned away, and his gaze landed upon the dead 'Riders. "Finish them!" Chartrin snarled at his men, and watched with deep satisfaction, as the creatures were removed of their heads, preventing their Deathren rebirth when the sun left the sky.

Jon unfastened the tourniquets from the dead man, returning the belts to the warriors who had donated them. "What shall we do with them?" he indicated the bodies of the three humans.

Chartrin shook his head. "We have no time t' send them off proper. Leave them. Let the forest cleanse them."

One of the Rebels suddenly pounced onto a small bush. There was a startled yelp, and a short tussle, and he pulled out a raggedly dressed boy of about ten years, who had clean tracks upon a filthy face, telling of the heavy fall of tears. "General! We have a stray!"

Chartrin motioned, and his man brought the struggling youngster to stand before him. "What is your name, boy?" he demanded, not unkindly.

"Nyal." The boy looked up into Chartrin's face with deep dread. "Are ye going t' kill me?"

Chartrin sighed deeply, and placed heavy hands upon the boy's thin shoulders. "No."

"Did ye kill my Da?" The child looked beyond Chartrin at the dead bodies, and his chin began to quiver.

"No, we killed the 'Riders. Your Da died o' his wounds," Chartrin guessed rightly that one of the wounded at the campfire had been his sire. He moved his body to block the mutilated dead men from Nyal's view.

The boy nodded, his chin dipping low and staying there, as he stared at the ground in shame. "I am glad ye killed the 'Riders. I could no' figure out how I was going t' do it by myself."

Chartrin squeezed the boy's narrow shoulders. "Good lad. Ye are a good lad." He cleared his throat. "What can ye tell me about what happened in Frenton?"

Nyal's face went blank with the trauma of remembrance. "The 'Rider Captain stood in the square, and he made us gather, and then he told us that we was all going t' die because o' the man pretending to be the Lost Prince. He pulled me aside, and said that I alone would live, and he made me learn it, the message, t' tell everyone I should meet."

Chartrin's eyes narrowed, and his hands flexed upon the boy's shoulders. "What was the message?"

"*The Lost Prince pretender must bring the sword t' Dreisenheld or all will die.* Then they… they… killed…"

Chartrin released Nyal and straightened, uncomfortable with the boy's grief. He needed no more information. "Feed him," he motioned to one of his men, who handed the boy a ration of salted venison.

With a quick dart of his hand, Nyal snatched the offering, and bolted back into the trees.

"General?" the Rebel warrior asked if he should go after the boy.

Chartrin waved his hand dismissively. "Leave him." The fleeing child had relieved him of the obligation to care for him. "Boy!" he yelled loudly. "Go east. Make for the Heathren Mountains and the Rebels. They will help ye!"

He motioned to Jon to join him, and together they stepped away from their men for a quick discussion.

Jon's somber face grew even more so. "General, I thought the man was ranting in his death, but the boy has confirmed his words. The lie could no' have reached here ahead o' us. The enemy can no' know that we sent an imposter for the sword. What is happening?"

Chartrin played with a ruby bauble that hung from one of the many thick, gold chains around his neck. "Boris has a spy in his camp," he decided.

Jon stiffened, offended to his very core. "Who? Only the Generals and their Lieutenants were at the Commander's table. Only they knew o' the lie that we agreed upon. Perhaps a servant?"

Chartrin shook his head. "Catrian ensured our privacy. Only we who were there know the truth o' it."

"General, that Gralyre fellow was a suspected spy."

"General Ryes was keeping him in check for the duration o'

the journey south. Gralyre would no' have had an opportunity t' betray us."

"He was a Sorcerer," Jon argued.

"And is surely dead by now. I fear we must look elsewhere."

"Or…"

"Speak your mind, Jon."

"Solstice has come and passed. Do ye think that Gralyre lived? I mean… 'Tis no' possible, but…" he stuttered.

"Ye think he has claimed the Dragon Sword?" Overtaken by surprise, Chartrin laughed heartily, and clapped Jon on the back. "Is he the Lost Prince as well? I have ne'er known ye t' be sentimental!"

Jon nodded somberly. "As soon as I said it aloud, I could hear the foolishness o' it. So there is a traitor. Who?"

General Chartrin shook his head. "Who can say? All I know is 'tis no' thee or me." He thumped Jon on the chest. "Come. We need t' get back on the water."

Their hike back upriver to their longboat went faster, as they were able to abandon caution for speed. With the patrol gone, there was nothing more to fear.

When they arrived at the longboat, the two men who had been left on guard held a familiar, small figure struggling between them. Nyal stilled as they approached, and glared defiantly up at Chartrin through the rat's nest of his filthy, brown hair.

"We caught him trying t' stow away," one of the Rebel guards announced, giving the boy a shake that made him stumble to keep his balance.

Nyal licked his lips. "Ye are slow!" he announced boldly.

Chartrin snorted. "Why are ye here, boy? Our business is done."

"Ye must take me with ye," he announced. "Ye robbed me o' the 'Riders, and my vengeance! Ye owe me!" he finished cockily.

"I owe ye dead 'Riders?" Chartrin threw back his head and laughed, and his men laughed with him.

It would seem that the Gods wanted this one protected. "Hop aboard, bilge-rat."

CHAPTER FIVE

The Rebel Northern Fortress

Rugged mountains encircled the vast, heavily forested valley, a natural barrier of protection for the Rebels' Northern Fortress. Doaphin's Demon Rider troops remained a constant threat but cold-blooded creatures, such as Stalkers or Deathren, could not easily survive the snow and ice of the high passes, and so they seldom ventured into the mountains to trouble the Rebels. They preferred to keep to the warmer climes of the lowlands.

The cold that protected the people of the Northern Fortress from their enemies was also their greatest weakness, for though there was plenty of game to be hunted, the elevation was too high to grow crops. In order to survive the brutal winters the fortress was reliant upon scavenging grains and edibles in the lowlands during the summer. Even so, many of their people still died of starvation before winter's end.

At the north end of the hidden valley a tall, craggy peak scraped clouds from the blue sky, and wrapped them around its shoulders like a nebulous cloak. The Northern Fortress rested high up the mountain upon an enormous plateau jutting from the steep slope above the treeline. At the mountain summit, neatly stacked tree trunks awaited a flame, a signal to the other Rebel troops in the area should there be need. The north side of the fortification nestled into the chest of the mountain cliffs while the tall, wooden palisade walls protected all other approaches, and commanded clear views of the entire valley. From three gates set in the walls, switchback roads snaked down the skirt of the mountain into the treeline, before winding through the forested valley towards the outer defences, a day's ride away to the east, west and south.

The Rebel outer defences each housed a garrison of fifty warriors to guard the only three passes through the encircling mountains to the outside world. Should an enemy attempt to infiltrate the valley, the sentries would use bits of mirror to flash a warning back to the fortress.

The switchback roads up the mountainside also served a protective purpose. With no straight path to follow, aggressors would be without cover as they climbed towards the fortress, prey to archers upon the walls, and forced to contend with massive boulders that the Rebels had amassed near each gate that, with little effort, could be rolled downslope to crush enemies.

All of this foresight and preparation had come to naught. The fortifications designed to repel Doaphin's hordes had never been used. General Kierdenan's warriors had taken the fortress under the treacherous ruse of kinship.

The Dream Weaver army had camped in the wooded valley less than a league to the west of the Rebel fortress so, although they had gotten a late start to their day, Gralyre, Dotch, Rewn, Saliana and Jord made good time through the sun-dappled forest towards the switchback road leading up to the east gate. They spoke little, each consumed by their own cares, leaving the sounds of the awakening forest to fill the silence between them.

The birds warbled from within the bushes, enjoying the anonymity provided by the budded leaves to pitch woo to their mates. The air was steeped in the sweet perfume of the trees, as sap thawed and flowed. Underlying it all was the gentle hum of newly birthed insects, a droning hymnal of praise lifting towards the sun that had only just cleared the tall peaks of the encircling mountain range to kiss the valley below in warmth. In the darker shadows, stubborn drifts of snow and ice still cowered, fearing to melt away, as they one day must.

Through gaps in the treetops, the companions began to glimpse the devastation that they would find when they reached the fortress. Now and then, when the breeze eddied in just the right direction, the sweet forest aromas were tainted by the sinister scents of war. Whiffs of acrid smoke from the fires still burning in the fortress were well seasoned with the rot of death. 'Twas a reek that the group knew well after their brief stay upon Fennick's Island, where millions had died in service to Doaphin's obsession with the Dragon Sword of Lyre.

Little Wolf loped from the underbrush to join them, having tracked their progress from the Dream Weaver encampment. His tongue lolled from the exertion of his run, and feathers and twigs matted his thick, black fur. The sudden appearance of the large predator made the horses snort and sidle before Gralyre calmed them.

Little Wolf shared the thrill of his morning hunt, using the wolfish poetry to which he was prone, a mixture of words and images that somehow conveyed his exhilaration. *Running circles in slippery dew. The hare escapes. A pheasant flies into my teeth!*

'Next time we hunt together,' Gralyre promised him.

There were powerful, destructive forces now at his command, but Gralyre's favourite talent would always be his ability to commune with animals. There was something grounding about the uncomplicated joy of Little Wolf's lupine thoughts that placed the cares of this world into a manageable perspective. Little Wolf remained unaffected by Gralyre's royal elevation, and so Gralyre could simply be himself, without fault or consequence.

The wolfdog still had vivid, fearful recollections of the magical journey from Fennick's Island, but Little Wolf lived so completely in the present that already those memories were fading.

Mid-morn was upon them before they finished their climb up the switchback road to reach the fortress, where the totality of the destruction became clear.

The massive gates through the palisade wall hung askew, their hinges strained past the point of carrying the weight of the large timber doors. Gralyre and his companions passed through the wall unchallenged, and paused on the far side, as they were overcome by what had befallen their home.

The eastern gatehouse was shattered and burned, as though it had been struck by a giant's fiery hammer. The inside of the wall was blackened, and much of the walk encircling the top of the palisade had been consumed. Wreckage of tents and carts was strewn everywhere, and the companions had to pick their path with care to make their way deeper into the ruination.

Tendrils of smoke curled lazily from embers that still glowed red-hot from the infernos that had ravaged the fortress in the wake of the battle. The light breeze drove clouds of ash and smoke into whirls and twists, the agitated ghosts of the desolate slain.

The silence was shattering, bereft of the songs of spring from the forest below. Gone was the familiar background hubbub of the large thriving community of eight thousand people.

There were a few survivors about, poking and digging through rubble. Their clothing was blackened with soot, and their faces dirty and streaked with blood and tears. They eyed the small band of armed riders with the defeated acceptance of yet another invading force to be endured, and did not seek to hail them as they passed.

"Would that I had killed Kierdenan when I had the chance!" Gralyre snarled.

Kierdenan had attempted to stop the quest for the sword by assailing Gralyre's small group with accidents, an attempted poisoning, and finally an ill planned ambush that had been meant to claim Gralyre's life. It had been General Ryes of the South who had pardoned Kierdenan's sedition, saving his neck from Gralyre's avenging sword. Behold what General Ryes' lenience had brokered.

"I am sure your family came through, Dotch," Rewn comforted. His voice was overloud in the hushed stillness. He shook his head, unknowingly contradicting his reassurance, as he tried to reconcile what he saw before him with the memory of the large, organized fortress that they had left behind only a few short months ago. Entire neighbourhoods, where once avenues of tents had been pitched with military precision, were now blackened wastelands of charred posts, the scorched fingers of hidden hands begging for mercy from the Gods.

"I hope ye are right, lad," Dotch rasped, as his horse sidestepped a bloated body with an arrow lodged in its chest. Dotch turned his head away in sorrow, breathing through his mouth to avoid the stench of the warrior's death. "Kierdenan deserves t' die for this! I will hunt the demon-humping bastard down myself!"

"And we will help ye!" Jord vowed. His knives snapped into his hands and vanished, again and again, the speed and aggression of the distracted movement speaking of his agitation.

"'Tis best if we divide, and search separately," Gralyre directed, his face tight with compassion for Dotch. "We can cover more territory." After seeing the aftermath of the battle, he held little hope that his friend would find his family alive.

"I am going t' the centre square," Saliana announced. Although the past few months had seen her confidence grow, she still failed to meet their eyes when she spoke, a habit learned over a lifetime. She received her medicines back from Rewn.

"Let any injured ye pass know that I am there, and can help them," she instructed.

"Take the food." Rewn leaned over, and transferred his sack to hang off her saddle. "We will see ye later tonight. Be careful."

Saliana nodded, and steered her horse towards the middle of the fortress.

Rewn's troubled gaze followed after her. "Will she be safe?"

"The people need her help, Rewn," Gralyre reassured, watching Saliana's horse wend its way through the smouldering debris. "I am sure she will be made welcome."

Dotch claimed the East Sector for his search. "We lived near here. I will check our tent first." His panic seemed to vibrate the air around him, having grown apace from his first view of the destruction.

"I will stay with ye Dotch. Ye should no' be alone if ye find they are…." When Dotch's expression turned bleak, Jord made a vague gesture with his hand, and his gaze dropped.

"I will take West Sector," Rewn volunteered.

Gralyre nodded. "That leaves the south for me. That suits, for I left some items behind that I would reclaim. We will meet back with Saliana tonight at the centre square. Dotch, we will send word to you if we discover anything afore then." His concerned midnight-blue gaze met Dotch's. "If we do not find them before it grows too dark, we will begin anew tomorrow, in North Sector."

Excepting the most dire of circumstances, it was unlikely that Dotch's wife would have sought that direction in which to flee the fighting. North Sector abutted the mountainside where there was no exit from the Fortress. "The Gods favour your search, Dotch."

₧₧

Saliana arrived at the centre square of the fortress to find that a makeshift infirmary had already been attempted. A chorus of pain and suffering shattered the desolate silence that held court in the rest of the fortress. Throughout the large open space of the square, disorganized rows of injured lay upon ash-dusted ground. Few of the patients had received treatment of even the meanest bandage. Infected wounds, left to fester in the warm sunlight, intensified the stench of rot.

Saliana scanned the area to see if there was someone in charge to whom she could speak. The wooden buildings bounding the square, that had once housed stores of weapons and food, were now blackened, smouldering shells. Near the remains of one such structure, she spotted an octet of begrimed and bloodied women sitting around a small, smoking campfire.

They ignored the screams and cries for help from the afflicted. It was obvious to Saliana that, having assembled some of the wounded, they now had no strength remaining to give further aid. Indeed, the women looked as though they needed succour themselves. Their faces were blank with shock and loss in the wretched aftermath of Kierdenan's treacherous attack.

Pity twisted within Saliana's heart. They had more need of

her, and the Dream Weaver medicines that she carried, than she had thought possible. She clicked to her horse to move it forward, and steered carefully down the narrow aisle between the crooked rows of the injured towards the women and their campfire.

Finding a cleared space near to the small group, Saliana slid from her horse, and reached up to her saddle to unhook the sack of food, and her medicine bag.

A large woman had noted her arrival. She leapt up from the campfire, and barrelled forward while shouting, "Who are ye, then? Who! Who are ye?" She halted mere inches from Saliana with her chest ballooned in aggression.

Saliana averted her gaze. "I am Saliana Greythorn, lately o' this fortress." Her voice emerged a nervous quiver, as she shied from the confrontation. "I am here t' help ye. I have food and medicines." Saliana tried to step around her, but the larger woman shoved rudely back into her path.

"I do no' care! Ye are no' welcome here!" She flicked a backhanded slap at Saliana's soot-free, grey skirts. "'Tis plain t' see that ye have no' been here with us. Ye have been hiding in the woods with *her*, with the *witch*!" She grasped Saliana's collar, and shook her roughly. "Catrian summoned Stalkers and Deathren and Demon Lords t' attack us!" her voice rose shrilly.

"She never!" Saliana protested.

But the woman ignored all in pursuit of blame for her pain and suffering. "Is that why ye are here? Have ye come t' finish what she started? Are ye here t' try t' kill us?"

Saliana struggled free of the larger woman's hold, but by then the damage had been done. The overwrought accusations drew the other women to their feet. Showing solidarity with their own, they moved to flank Saliana in a rough circle, spitting insults and abuse, venting their woes upon the stranger in their midst.

"Lowland whore!"

"Demon lover!"

Saliana's heart pumped wildly, as the group pressed closer, blocking her avenues of escape.

Someone yanked the reins of Saliana's horse from her grasp, dragging it away, but she did not turn to see what had become of her steed, knowing to keep her attention on the immediate threat posed by the larger woman.

Shoved from behind, Saliana stumbled forward, only to be thrust back again. The conditioning of her upbringing came back to haunt her, and she could feel herself curling inward for protection, passively awaiting the violence to run its course.

But Saliana was no longer the fearful, abused girl she had been all those months ago in Raindell when her father had sold her for a copper to the Lord Collaborator at the Mid-Winter's Moon Festival. Since then she had faced a platoon of Demon Riders, fighting shoulder to shoulder with the Lost Prince! She had fought Deathren and Demon Lords. She had ridden to, and returned from, Fennick's Island!

Saliana threw down her medicine bag next to the sack of food, and her voice rose over the squawks of the women. "I am Saliana Greythorn, healer t' the Lost Prince!" she announced grandly, though her heart flitted about like a caged butterfly at her loose use of the truth. "He has returned, and he has brought the magic Dragon Sword o' Lyre with him from Fennick's Island."

The group, having momentarily quieted to listen to her words, jeered and shouted louder at her ridiculous assertions.

Saliana had to yell loudly now for her words to be heard. "Listen! He learned o' your hardship when he arrived last ev'en, and ordered me t' help as I could," she freely embellished. "Even now, he rides through the fortress seeking survivors!"

"What offal!"

"Ye are cracked!"

Saliana could not really fault them. She had just announced that a fable had stepped out of myth and legend. No wonder they were now looking at her as though she had lost her mind.

"If the Lost Prince returned, *ye* certainly would no' ride with him!" the larger woman contested snidely. She circled Saliana with a prideful strut. Her friends shouted approval, tightening the circle about the combatants, glad for the entertainment to distract them from their ills. "He would no' have such a puny, worthless lass!"

Angry faces crowded Saliana's line of sight every which way she turned. The ring of hollering people reminded her of a cockfight she had witnessed as a child, and how the men had yelled to incite the birds to greater violence. Her opponent was taller, heavier and stronger. Her braying performance to the approval of her friends was the only reason she had not yet sprung an attack.

Aneida and Mayvin's tutelage on dealing with animals arose in Saliana's thoughts. '*Strike first, strike hard, and make sure they canno' rise.*'

Rage and fear tunnelled Saliana's vision. Her fist lashed out, clouting the larger woman in the nose, and knocking her flat afore she could utter another disparaging word.

The encircling women stuttered to an uncertain silence, as their champion was unexpectedly felled.

Riding high on the crest of her ire, Saliana hauled her opponent up by her greasy, soot-matted hair, eliciting a screech in protest. The woman reached up to claw at Saliana's tight grip.

"I am the personal healer t' Prince Gralyre!" Saliana shouted into her face. "I have come t' lend myself t' the sick and hurt o' this fortress, and ye greet me with this?" she demanded, anger flashing from her grey eyes like lighting in a storm cloud. She no longer resembled the meek victim she had first appeared.

Saliana flung the woman away, her long journey having given her muscle beyond the ordinary. Carefully, she wiped her hand clean along her grey skirt.

The felled woman shrunk back into the arms of three others who had been her companions at the fire, mewling quietly, as she wiped at her bloodied nose. Like all bullies, once defeated she revealed a craven nature. They murmured and soothed her, as best they could.

A strong, deeply masculine voice suddenly cracked like a whip over the heads of the small group. "Have you a problem,

Mistress Greythorn?"

By Gralyre's side, Little Wolf moved two heavy steps forward. The wolfdog's black-furred shoulders stood almost to the belly of Gralyre's horse, and he appeared even larger, as his hackles bristled. His nasty growl echoed Gralyre's tone in no uncertain terms.

Gralyre, having arrived in the middle of the fortress, as he travelled towards South Sector, had watched as Saliana had neatly dealt with her challenger. Yes, he mused, she had certainly changed from the scared girl they had rescued from Raindell.

Saliana scanned the group at large with a hard glare. "No, my lord Prince. We were only discussing our recent journey from Fennick's Island." The unmistakable glint of the naked Dragon Sword that swung from a loop on Gralyre's belt, lent credibility to her claim.

The corners of Gralyre's eyes crinkled, though his face was sober, as he nodded his head regally towards her from the back of his horse. "Carry on then," he commanded, before addressing the small group of women.

"Saliana Greythorn is my personal healer. She has generously agreed to help you in your time of need. I will hear of it if she is ill treated!" His imperial glare seared away the last of the crowd's backbone.

Little Wolf snapped a vicious bark in concurrence, showing the ivory length of his teeth. The women shrank away, unwilling to be in the path of the beast should it be loosed.

"Thank-ye, Prince Gralyre." Saliana curtsied. The women witnessed her action, and began to awkwardly ape her.

Satisfied that the situation was now in hand, Gralyre nodded once more to Saliana before riding onwards.

Little Wolf trotted forward to nose against Saliana and accept a scratch of his ears before hastening after Gralyre.

The women gaped at the affection the vicious beast showed Saliana. A babble of wonderment replaced the screaming of moments before.

"The prophecy! Oh, Gods! That I should live t' see this day!"

"It was him! The Lost Prince has returned!"

"'Tis no' possible!"

"But he has the sword! He has come t' save us!"

"He looked at me! Did ye see?"

The veneration even spilled over to include Saliana.

"Sorry, Lady..."

"My humble apologies, Lady." One woman even tried on a bow for Saliana as though she were royalty too.

Saliana's jaw sagged, and a hot blush washed her cheeks before she gathered her wits. She retrieved her medicine bag and the sack of food. "Now," she declared firmly, as she strode forward, and the women fell back respectfully, "where can I help?"

She left her sack of food by the cookfire, and a couple of the women ushered her towards the first row of patients.

Saliana was horrified by the conditions. The injured lacked even the rudest of comforts. They lay upon the cold, hard earth, coated in the filth of ash and gore from the battle. In this row alone, at least two of the wounded had quietly died, and been left to rot by the sides of those who were soon to follow should nothing be done. She could see that burns were the most common, but so were bloody gashes from the battle with the invading Eastern Rebels.

The worst were the children, crying for a lost parent, or more alarmingly, quiet and staring with shock from their terrible injuries. Saliana dismayed at the numbers she faced. She had only ever treated one person at a time, and simple hurts at that. She was overwhelmed by the scope of these injuries.

Where was she to begin? After her boasts, the women were now looking to her to lead, and after only one night observing Ninrhar, she saw her previous knowledge as a healer for all its primitiveness.

Though the Dream Weavers could use magic to cure, Ninrhar had informed her that it was generally a gift reserved for dire injuries beyond the scope of mundane healing arts to aid. For all else, they used cleanliness: boiled water, boiled linens, and strong spirits to cut infection. They used needles and thread to rebind wounds, and herbs and potions far in advance to anything that the Rebels owned, to improve the body's spirits, and to fight corruption in the blood.

Now she understood why Ninrhar had passed her this medicine bag today. He must truly be a sorcerer to have known how deprived the conditions would be in the wake of the battle!

Ninrhar had emphasized cleanliness above all else the night

before, as together they had tended Trifyn's infected leg. So she would begin by cleaning every wound, and every patient! If nothing else, it would make their suffering more bearable, and perhaps slow the infections until Ninrhar arrived.

"Ye men there!" she called out to a few loiterers who wandered among the wounded. "Find tarps! I want a roof over all of the wounded within the hour!"

"Right away, miss!" They set off in search of any canvas that may have survived the flames.

"We can help. What do ye want o' us?" Asked another man, indicating back over his shoulder at a score of warriors who had gathered near the women's small campfire, as the rumour of food had quickly spread.

Saliana's patients were lying in piles of black ash upon the hard earth. "Cots, blankets, linens, clothes, and food. Find it all and bring it," she listed.

"I do no' know that we can, miss."

"Why is that?"

"Kierdenan's Rebels have taken West Sector, and they have seized all that we have left for their own use. We will be hard pressed t' find bedding, let alone food."

"Do what ye can," Saliana advised on a sigh. "There are plenty o' upturned wagons and carts. Perhaps something can be fashioned from them?"

"Right ye are, miss." He motioned his group to his side, and they left to scavenge what they could.

Water was at least something that was in good supply. The

small stream that bisected the fortress had thawed, releasing the burbling waters that flowed past the laundry works. Saliana appropriated the large iron kettles that had survived the flames that had gutted the laundry, and all of the strong lye soap that could be found in the rubble.

As supplies trickled in, and more people gathered, Saliana employed many of the idle folk to scrub and boil linens that were then strung on lines in the late-morning sun and wind to dry. Others were tasked to bathe the injured of as much filth as possible using boiled water, soap and clean rags.

Little enough food had been found to supplement what Rewn had thrown in his sack, but Saliana bade others to set up cook fires to feed the people who had begun to gather. What they had, they would mete out to as many as they could. Saliana had faith that Gralyre would find a way to feed everyone when he returned in the evening.

Saliana assigned the most able bodied among them to comb the fortress for more wounded. Yet another team was tasked with carrying the dead outside the walls. Later, a funeral pyre would be created to light the lost back to the Gods.

In the midst of the bustle, it was Saliana who unbound filthy, putrid bandages, and cleansed wounds as best she could. After discovering fine Maolar needles and thread in her borrowed medicine bag, she tried her hand at stitching the worst of the gashes closed, as per Ninrhar's instructions of the night before. After the first stomach-turning attempt, she started to become quite proficient, telling herself it was not unlike darning a tear in cloth.

The burns were the worst of it. There was no flesh remaining to sew over these wounds. She could do little besides douse the patients with the strong Dream Weaver teas, made from herbs that she recognized, to induce sleep so that their pain would be lessened, as she cleansed their injuries of filth.

There were ointments in the medicine bag that she did not know, and that she dared not use. Instead, she covered charred flesh lightly with fresh-cleaned linens to repel the flies that circled in clouds over the wounds, first dampening the cloths before applying them so that they would not adhere onto the seeping burns. The cool, wet cloths also seemed to soothe her patients' pain to a small degree.

Oddly, the wounds infested with the larvae of the flies showed the least amounts of corruption. She wondered at this, and determined to query the Dream Weaver healer when next she had opportunity, even as she engaged in the stomach turning task of painstakingly plucking maggots from the wounded arm of a warrior.

"Thank the Gods for your kindness, miss," the man croaked, as she treated him.

Saliana felt like a fraud, as he watched her in awe. She was only doing what little she had been shown in the Dream Weaver camp, or what common sense now seemed to dictate. What she had gleaned was as nothing when compared to the vast stores of the Dream Weavers' lore, but because of her boasts of being healer to the Lost Prince, all that she did and said was being treated as pearls.

Gralyre sought familiar landmarks, as he searched through the South Sector. His purpose was twofold. Foremost, of course, was to find Dotch's family, but he was also seeking the tent that he had shared with the Wilsons, in order to reclaim the belongings that he had left behind before he had been sentenced to die on Fennick's Island.

Where once had stood a thriving neighbourhood there was now only a desolate, burned wasteland, making it difficult to accurately judge where their tent had been pitched. Gralyre relied heavily upon Little Wolf's senses to guide him, as they criss-crossed South Sector's razed neighbourhood.

With every survivor that he encountered, he asked after Dotch's family, to naught but negative answers, shrugs and sympathy. There seemed little hope, and Gralyre's heart grew heavy with sorrow for his friend. He prayed to the Gods that one of the others were having greater fortune in their search.

Many of the tents in the fortress had been dismantled in preparation for the march to war, before Kierdenan's traitorous attack had disrupted the Northern Rebels' departure. The remaining homes were to have housed the women and children in safety behind the stout walls of the fortress while the men were away fighting. That would no longer be possible.

The oiled canvas pavilions had gleefully accepted the

invitation to burn, flames leaping from one to the next in an unstoppable conflagration. Left behind were deep piles of grey ash, and the twisted, blackened bodies of those who had sought refuge from the battle. So many of the remains were small, child sized, and a deep anger fermented within Gralyre at the injury done to the Northern Rebels by General Kierdenan's betrayal.

Eventually, Little Wolf flagged a wooden stump that had sat before their cookfire. Remarkably, it had remained untouched by flames.

Gralyre dismounted to examine it closer, and enjoyed a moment of triumph when he found a familiar divot in the bark of the wood. It was the puncture mark made from a crossbow bolt, a missed attempt at murder.

At the height of winter, when food had grown scarce, thieves had attacked in the night, intending for Little Wolf to be their next meal. Gralyre and Rewn had fought them off, but in the heat of the skirmish, Gralyre had defied Catrian's edict and used magic to defend their lives. He had endured her punishment for the transgression in the form of a sound whipping.

As Little Wolf sniffed around the perimeter, and began to renew old scent marks to reclaim his past territories, Gralyre assessed the remains of their tent. A blackened centre post, four charred corner posts, and some iron stakes were all that remained to mark the area where their home had stood. The large, wooden bins, where once food, weapons and bedding had been stored, had been reduced to bits of charcoal within a mound of ash. A lazy tendril of smoke still curled from a surviving ember.

All that Gralyre owned in the world, those items that had been on his person when he had awakened with no memories in a lowland forest almost a year ago, had been buried for safekeeping beneath these bins. He had not trusted that Dajin would respect and keep his property safe. Gralyre could only imagine the vainglorious havoc that the younger Wilson brother could have wrought had he gained possession of the royal seal of the House of Lyre.

Gralyre grasped a bit of melted metal that may have once been the lid to their kettle, and set to digging into the gravelly earth where he judged the storage bins to have once stood. The rocks still retained warmth from the inferno that had consumed the tent. If the heat had been too intense, even as deeply as he had buried his sheath and chain mail, there would be little for him to recover but twisted slag.

His makeshift shovel scraped against oilskin, and he pushed away the loosened scree to unearth the first bulky bundle. Gralyre was encouraged, for the package did not appear to have been scorched by the heat of the fires above it. To be certain he tore through the wrapping until his hands were filled with the rich gleam of his Maolar chain mail.

It was as pristine as the day it had been gifted to him by the Dream Weavers, a royal offering crafted by his mother's people. As Gralyre stroked his hand over the smooth metal loops, he vividly recalled the day it had arrived, and the hope that the accompanying cartloads of weaponry, and promises of aid had given him.

Maolar was the only metal that could slay Doaphin's beasts, and the Dream Weavers had sent all that the King's forces had required. But by the time the King had relented, and asked his allies for aid, it had been far too late. The King had denied the danger for too long, and provided their enemy with the time needed to entrench deeply into their kingdom.

Gralyre sighed heavily, as he draped the gleaming armour over the stump. A ray of sunlight found the chain mail, flashing against the intricate loops of metal so that it appeared crusted in gems.

In hindsight, perhaps he should have taken the chain mail and his other belongings with him to Fennick's Island, but Gralyre had elected to leave the relics of his past behind in relative safety. His reasoning had been simple, and poignantly human.

He had not wanted to pass unremembered from this world.

Should he have died in his attempt to reclaim the Dragon Sword, there would have been nothing left behind to mark his passing; no headstone, or tomb, nor even a carved wooden icon to show that he had ever existed.

So he had awaited a moment when he had been alone in the tent, and he had buried his belongings deeply under the storage bins. He had imagined that perhaps, in the far future, someone might unearth these relics, and marvel at the mystery of them. Perhaps they would even think of the Lost Prince, or of a man named Gralyre, and wonder if it had been he who had left them. It had been a small solace, as he had bravely faced his execution.

But a God's Jape had been played upon those who had sought his death, for now the Dragon Sword had been reclaimed, and the looming wall overshadowing his past had toppled to reveal the truth. He was the Lost Prince. There was a reckoning coming, and he had need of his belongings in the battles ahead.

If he remembered correctly, he had buried his sheath just to the right of the chain mail. Gralyre widened his hole, and unearthed the second, longer roll of oilskin. This bundle was not as intact as the first. The wrapping was charred in several places.

After unrolling the packet, he examined the scabbard's four feet of black, tooled leather for damage. The sheath was attached to a thick baldric that was designed to support the weight of the Dragon Sword against his back. He discovered only a bit of scorching on one side of the tough leather, which would not effect its use.

Tucked into the oilskin package beside the scabbard and baldric was his wide, black leather belt that concealed his purse. Some of the coins within had welded together, the gold more apt to soften in heat, but he counted himself blessed when that was the extent of the damages.

Within the purse, he sought the scrap of cloth depicting his family's coat of arms. When he had awakened in the forest, alone, terrified and covered in gore, his first thought was that he was a deserter from a battlefield. He had picked this crest off the chest of his vest, and tucked it into the secret purse for safekeeping. With new perspective, Gralyre re-examined his crest, and was reminded to check upon his other precious relics.

He slipped his fingers into the secret pocket worked into the tooled design on the black leather scabbard, and drew forth his ring, and the last letter he had received from his father, the King.

Gralyre swivelled the plum-sized sapphire on the ring of state, revealing the seal of his kingdom, the seal of his ancestors, etched into the embossed white gold, a match to the crest he held in his other hand. He rasped his thumbnail over the dragon defiant, roaring a challenge with the crown in one talon, and a sword in the other. How confused he had been a year ago, to find the crest cut from his leather vest echoed within this kingly jewel. What had made no sense then, was now exceptionally clear. This letter and this ring were his only proofs of birthright, the last fragile tethers to his claim upon his vanquished throne. He supposed they were fitting remnants of a lost prince.

Gralyre pushed his left index finger through the loop of the ring, and held out his hand, considering the large blue gem that now adorned it, the royal seal of Lyre, his now, along with the crown.

How many times as a boy had he stood in his father's library, staring at this blue jewel glinting in the firelight on the King's left hand, as judgement was pronounced upon him for some minor infraction?

...Pain from a lash. Count of four. Count of five. The dark, the rats. Cold, so cold...

At Gralyre's hip, the ruby adorning the massive sword briefly glowed red. A quiet hum filled Gralyre's ears, dampening the dark memory to a blurred, indistinct thing that he could not quite bring to mind.

His gaze lit upon his extended hand, and he grew confused as to why he had raised it so. Time seemed to have taken a leap forward. What had he been thinking about? He must still be exhausted from the trials of the Labyrinth.

Something about the ring was disquieting so he jerked it from his finger, and pushed it, along with the letter and scrap of cloth back into the hidden pocket on his scabbard.

He was not yet King, not until Doaphin was dead, and his lands cleansed of the evil that roamed it freely. Only then would the ring return to its rightful place on his hand.

No longer having a reason to hide, Gralyre boldly wrapped his wide leather belt around his lean hips. Determination defined every line of his strong face, as he donned his Maolar chain mail, girding himself for the battles ahead. With the ease of familiarity, he sunk the four-foot blade of the Dragon Sword into its scabbard. He slung the baldric over his head, and settled it from left shoulder to right hip, shrugging the familiar weight of the sword into position against the centre of his back.

The massive sword was five and a half feet from its tip, which brushed Gralyre lightly against the back of his calf, to the ruby cabochon pommel stone of the dragon-adorned, two-handed grip that rose tall behind his head. Made of shimmering Maolar, the Dragon Sword of Lyre weighed less than five pounds, perfectly balanced for attack or defence.

For the first time in almost a year, since Gralyre had awakened in that far, lowland forest, everything he owned was returned to its rightful place. His path ahead was clear. He had his realm to reclaim, and his revenge to take.

ഌരു

Heaped debris blocked Rewn's forward progress from the main thoroughfare into West Sector. His first thought was that it was just the same wreckage that he had been picking his way around since leaving the others, yet beyond the barricade he could clearly see that the fires had not reached very far into this neighbourhood.

His exhausted thoughts were just catching up to the fact that the barricade had been piled purposefully, when a man arose from behind a tipped cart with his crossbow aimed, and his finger upon the release. "Stand there!"

"What is this?" Rewn asked wearily, as he leaned forward, and rested his elbows over the pommel of his saddle. He had been through too much in past weeks to work up the energy to feel more than exasperation. "Why have ye blocked the road?"

"Everything beyond this point belongs t' Commander Vetroy and the Eastern Rebels!"

Rewn's brows rose. "*Commander* Vetroy? The last I saw o' him he was just Kierdenan's second, a lieutenant. How is it he is now the Rebel Commander? Where is Boris?"

"Boris is dead!"

Rewn straightened at the unfortunate news. "And General Matik?" he asked carefully.

"They are both dead."

These were dire tidings indeed. After what they had put Gralyre through, Rewn held no grief for either the Commander or General Matik, but he had respected them. Without them the resistance would have devolved further into banditry than it already had. Already, the Rebels were as close to a plague upon the lowlands as Doaphin's forces were. What would become of the rebellion without them?

"I still fail t' see how Vetroy replaced Commander Boris. What o' General Kierdenan?"

"Kierdenan was killed by the Stalker that the Sorceress called t' her aid when the General and his men fought outside her tent. That makes Vetroy the highest ranking officer alive in the fortress. That makes him Commander o'er all the Rebels."

Rewn lips hinted at a small smile, for hope yet prevailed. "No' anymore."

Movement caught at the corner of Rewn's eye, and as he turned he realized that the warrior in front had been holding his attention to give his partner the time to flank him. He was too late to duck the butt of a spear that exploded pain in his face, and quieted his thoughts to darkness. He never felt the ground catch him, as he sagged out of his saddle.

ഐൽ

Jord's knives came out of hiding to flicker through his fingers, around and around, juggled negligently, as he was accustomed to doing when he was troubled. "'Tis for the good, Dotch. If they are no' here, then they escaped the fighting and fires. That man we met said he saw women and children flee out East Gate during the battle. We did no' pass anyone on the way in, but we were no' looking either. They are likely hiding in the thickets."

The remnants of Dotch's tent had held no dead. His family had not taken refuge there. Neither mentioned their encounters with the blackened bodies lying within the ashen remains of other dwellings who, so badly had they been burned, would never be given names.

Until all avenues of search were exhausted, Dotch refused to consider that his family was part of the nightmare that they had ridden through. His mouth thinned glumly, and he nodded tightly. "As ye say, lad, let it be so!"

They mounted up from their brief stop, and soon passed back through the East gate, gladly leaving the desolation behind.

Though the roadbed was comprised of rocks and loosened soil, their own tracks from earlier could be seen to overlay faint, older imprints that were still present, even after the days had passed. Jord leaned out from his saddle to peer closer at the ground. "There are lots o' tracks. Small and large footprints both."

Dotch made his own evaluation. "They would no' have gone far. No' with little ones in tow."

They kicked their horses into a trot, following the steep switchback road down the mountainside, and into the treeline. There were clear signs of a trail, now that they were searching for it, that they followed into the forest; broken foliage and overturned stones that told the story of fleeing people. Soon after they entered the shadows under the trees, they heard hushed voices, and happened upon the rude camp of the ragged survivors.

When the two warriors rode into the small clearing, some of the refugees scattered into the trees, intent only upon self-preservation. They did not linger to see if the men meant them harm.

About thirty women and children remained, huddled together in trembling terror, too exhausted or injured to flee.

"Is Ella among them, Dotch?"

"I do no' know!" Dotch swung down off his horse, his gaze scanning frantically over the sooty faces of the people who faced him. "Ella! Is there one among ye named Ella? Demin? Kentle?"

Jord dismounted, and caught the trailing reins of Dotch's horse before it could wander. "We mean ye no harm," he called out to the trees. "Ye are safe. Come on back!"

After a long pause, small clusters of women and children began to materialize from out of the bushes.

"Who are ye? Is it safe t' return t' the fortress?"

"Is anyone still alive?" Another woman asked.

A little girl tugged at Jord's sleeve. "Do ye have food?"

His face blank of emotion, Jord gave her the bit of ration that he had saved from his breakfast afore he had set out that morning. He was no stranger to starvation, and had spent more days than he could count with hunger gnawing at him when he was this little one's age. As an adult, he was seldom without a scrap of food secreted on his person.

She stuffed a bite of bread into her mouth, and ran to keep the rest of what he had given her out of the hands of some larger boys who gave chase.

Dotch's gaze settled upon a petite woman who had emerged from the trees with two young boys clinging to her ragged and singed skirts. Her dark brown hair was matted with twigs and all matter of filth. His breath suspended in joyful recognition.

She stood still, save for great shudders that wracked her slight frame. Tears cut paths down her soot-smeared face.

"Ella!"

His voice calling her name seemed to bring her back to life. "Dotch!" She cried out, and ran towards him. "Ye are alive!"

Dotch threw himself forward, and grabbed her into his arms. "Ella!" He held her head pressed tight to his heart, while her feet dangled in the space as he rocked her. "Thank the Gods! Thank the Gods!"

"Da! Da!" The boys careened after their mother.

Thirteen-year-old Kentle was faster, five years older than his younger brother, and quickly outpaced Demin to reach his father first.

Dotch caught and lifted one boy in each strong arm, pressing them up under his chin. His eyes met Ella's and he smiled.

"I did what ye said. I kept them safe!"

"Well done, lovey. Well done!" His lips captured hers in a long kiss.

Jord's gaze met that of a woman who had tears streaming down her face from witnessing the happy reunion. He realized that he was grinning like a fool, and quickly quieted his expression to something more manly and stoic.

ဆာထ

The conditions for the wounded had improved dramatically. The scavenging parties were returning, and tarps were now being erected over the sick. The worst of the injured now also lay on boards instead of the cold earth. Most had been bathed, and campfires had been lit at regular intervals to provide additional warmth.

It was later in the afternoon, and Saliana was gently feeding tea to a burn victim, trying to ease the poor woman into slumber. Her patient had only a few clear patches of skin remaining, and in places her flesh had burned deep enough to char bone. It was amazing that she yet lived. There was little that Saliana could do beyond gifting her sleep to escape her agony.

The woman's one good hand arose to grasp Saliana's arm, spilling the tea that would ease her pain.

Saliana tsked under her breath. "Marta, please take this, and refill it for me?" She asked one of her assistants, as she passed the tankard she had been using.

"Right away, miss." Marta dashed to where the potent tea was steeping in a porcelain crock, set upon a stone near to a fire to remain warm.

"Uhhhh!" the woman moaned through the melted, raw skin of her mouth.

Saliana gently squeezed the hand that clawed and clutched at her arm, almost the only flesh remaining intact on the woman's body. "Shh. Soon ye will sleep, and this pain will fade."

"Uhhh, uhhhh, uhhhh!"

Saliana saw that the ruined mouth was trying to form words. "Shh. Do no' try t' speak. Let the tea do its work."

But the woman was insistent, staring feverishly into Saliana's eyes. And suddenly, with a gasp of horror, Saliana recognized her patient. "Oh Gods!"

It was Mistress Patiana the Healer, whom Saliana had apprenticed with afore she had chased after Rewn on the epic journey to Fennick's Island.

"Mistress Patiana!" Saliana's tears started, the first she had shed this day, releasing a bottleneck of grief at her inability to help the woman who had gifted her life with a purpose. "I am sorry. I am so sorry that I canno' do more for ye!"

Mistress Patiana convulsed, her back arching, as she let out a pain filled screech that silenced all in the vicinity. She fell back upon her bedding, and breath stirred no more.

Marta returned with the filled tankard, and awkwardly placed her hand on Saliana's heaving shoulders. "I am sorry, miss. Ye knew her?"

Saliana nodded, unable to prevent her shuddering gasps, as an awful truth exploded in her mind. Mistress Patiana had been too injured to survive, and Saliana had known it. She had wasted valuable time easing Patiana's suffering, as with other dying people before her, when she should have been helping those who might actually have a chance to live. On the far side of the equation, there had been those who, though in pain, were not in any immediate danger and could have awaited treatment.

A maternal ruthlessness arose in Saliana, as she gently placed Mistress Patiana's uninjured hand back to rest upon her burned chest. Many would die today, who might have had a chance at life, if only she had reached them in time. To save as many as possible she was going to have to make hard choices. Hence, she would have to decide who was to be abandoned as a lost cause, who was to be treated, and who was to await her attentions though they suffer. The numbers were simply too great for Saliana to do anything less.

After drawing a long, shuddering breath, she regained control. Marta's comforting touch fell away, as Saliana sprang to her feet, and dashed the last of her tears away.

"There are so many more that we need t' help. Mistress Patiana would no' wish me t' waste time with useless weeping. Please have the men carry her t' the pyre. There will be grief enough for all when we say farewell t' our fallen."

Saliana smoothed the fabric of her grey skirt with a violent snap of her hand, and moved on to the next patient in a seemingly endless parade of gore and death.

CHAPTER SIX

The Dream Weaver Army

The gaping, jagged wound of grief within Aneida was awaiting her, a precipice inviting her to fall.

'Mayvin is dead. How am I to bear it?'

She stared fixedly into the cookfire's dancing flames, and pushed the food that she had been given around and around upon her tin plate. It had been days since she had last eaten, but the scent was nauseating. How could she eat, when her sister lay buried beneath a mountain of stone? Even the island was gone, claimed by the ocean, as though it had never been. As though Mayvin had never been.

Aneida coughed, choking upon her grief, thunder before an onslaught, but the storm was not quite ready to break. She set the food aside.

Two Dream Weaver warriors came to the fire and sat, staring at her with smiles, and speaking softly to her in their own tongue.

She could not understand their words, but their body language was clear enough. She needed only to reach out to them to receive all of the comfort that she could desire. But as with the food, the thought left her sickened. How could she continue life without Mayvin at her side? It seemed such a betrayal to feel cold, or hunger, or lust, or anything of pleasure or need when Mayvin would never feel such as this ever again. She was dead, and Aneida wanted nothing more than to join her.

Aneida thought of her sister's hand language, the code they had developed after Mayvin's voice had been stolen. Who would share secrets with her now? To whom would Aneida confide?

Mayvin, I miss you! Aneida signed, though the Dream Weaver warriors had no understanding of the complex gestures.

Madness!

Without further response to their overtures, Aneida stood up from the fire, and wandered away. For as long as she could remember, it had been Mayvin and her against the world. Together they had survived the horrific night when the Tithe had come for them. They had survived their losses and their injuries, and then the journey into the mountains in search of the Rebels.

Jord had been right. Aneida and Mayvin had been survivors. But this was different. Now Mayvin had fallen on Fennick's Island. Lost. Forevermore. The strength required to survive again, without Mayvin at her side, was more than Aneida wanted to muster.

Aneida realized that she had ceased walking, and had been staring blindly into a thicket, when she was pulled back from her dark thoughts by the commotion of the Dream Weaver army breaking camp around her. She watched as the last of the tents were knocked down and stowed. The activity must have been ongoing for hours, and she had not noticed until now.

Gralyre, and the others had left without her that morning,

bound for the fortress, and she had little doubt that this would be the Dream Weavers' ultimate destination as well.

Aneida caught sight of three men lifting an unconscious Trifyn into the cramped bed of a small, one-horse cart. It had been well padded with thick furs to cushion the bowman from further harm while they relocated. He had yet to awaken, and the men were very gentle, as they laid him upon the furs.

Arms crossed, Rewn's brother waited impatiently off to the side for the men to finish settling Trifyn. "Are ye going t' stand there, or help me up?" Aneida heard Dajin carp loudly. He reached out a hand for a boost into the sick-cart. Perhaps the foreigners simply did not understand him, but to a man they turned away, leaving Dajin to clamber into the bed on his own.

As Aneida approached the cart, and witnessed Dajin's ease of movement, she judged him hale enough to ride a horse, and wondered why he had chosen not to.

"Aneida," he called out as she neared, "we are moving up t' the fortress, though I do no' see the point o' it!" Dajin winced, and clamped an arm to his side where his once broken ribs had been healed to little more than bruises. He faded into the furs beside Trifyn, as though unable to endure further pain.

His actions seemed overly dramatic to Aneida, and she made no sound of sympathy. She had none to spare. Mayvin had taken a blade to her shoulder that had split it to the bone, and she had never complained, not once, though riding had to have nigh destroyed her.

"Bloody bastards did no' heal my ribs properly. They still

hurt!" Dajin groused. After a pregnant pause failed to give birth to a compassionate reaction, he continued, "'Twas a Stalker that did it. Two o' them, actually," he boasted. "No' many can claim t' have survived the attack o' two Stalkers!" His face fell when she still did not respond favorably.

Aneida had never been one to offer sops to a man's ego, and her grief made her even less inclined to do so. She would have left Dajin to his swagger, yet instinct made her loath to leave Trifyn alone with Rewn's narcissistic brother.

"I will drive," she announced, and motioned to the wagoner to pass the tethers. With a nod, he dropped the reins, and hopped down from the cart, leaving her the driver's bench.

Catrian approached the back of the cart on the arm of a Dream Weaver, her steps hesitant and feeble. Aneida rolled her eyes, as Dajin sat straighter, and assumed a manly pose. Now she understood why Rewn's brother had not chosen horseback.

The warrior helping Catrian up into the wagon bed motioned at Dajin to move aside to give her room to recline next to Trifyn. The cramped space held room aplenty for both Catrian and Trifyn to lie comfortably upon the cushioning furs, but Dajin's presence made the fit too tight, and he was forced to retreat to the driver's bench next to Aneida.

"Thank-ye," Catrian gasped out on a sigh of exhaustion, as she collapsed beside Trifyn. The short walk from her tent to the cart had finished her, and she welcomed the opportunity to recline again.

"You are welcome, Lady Catrian." The warrior saluted

smartly before he was off to find his place in the ranks, as the Dream Weaver muster continued.

Catrian's eyes were fluttering closed when Dajin spoke loudly to rouse her.

"Ye look better than ye did when I rescued ye from the fortress." His smile was overly wide, as he mined her for the ore of appreciation.

"Thank-ye for rescuing me, Master Wilson," the Sorceress said politely.

Petulance curdled Dajin's face when further lauding was not forthcoming. He turned away, arms crossed mulishly, and talked no more.

Five thousand strong, the army rode out, with packhorses strung behind them carrying their tents and supplies. The padded wagon bed that was to save Catrian and Trifyn from jostling was only moderately successful. The route through the trees to reach one of the switchback roads up the mountainside was difficult terrain for the small cart to pass over. Ten men walked with the cart, five to a side, using brute force and pry bars to lift it up over rocks when the wooden wheels became jammed in crevices, and the horse could not pull it free. Theirs was the only wagon, an impractical conveyance in the mountains without a road. Aneida was left wondering where the Dream Weavers had found it.

The rough journey eventually awoke Trifyn, when at a particularly hard jostle, he cried out in agony, grasping at the bandage that encircled his thigh.

Catrian propped herself upright, and drew Trifyn's head into her lap so that she could soothe him. Having succumbed to a bout of weakness before they had begun the journey, she had now reclaimed a short burst of strength, but the day had already taught her that her frailty would return quickly. Gralyre may have replenished her Godsmagic, but her body had lain still as death for many days, and it would be many more before she regained her strength of old. The use of her power that morning had left her insensate for hours.

"It hurts!" Trifyn moaned, his head thrashing. Beads of sweat had gathered upon his forehead.

"We are all hurt," Dajin sniped without pity, angered at the care that Catrian was showing a man who was nothing to her, who had not even saved her life. During another rough jostle, Dajin slouched back with a dramatic moan, a wasted effort, as Catrian did not even glance up from comforting Trifyn.

"Ye will have t' do better than that," Aneida whispered to Dajin with a shadow of her trademark, wicked grin.

"Shut up," Dajin snarled back as quietly, blushing red.

Catrian brushed Trifyn's blond hair from his eyes, and rested her hand against his fevered brow. "Shh, hush now. All is well."

Trifyn relaxed under the pleasurable coolness of her gentle caress. His glassy blue gaze roved Catrian's face, seeking reassurance. "My leg?" he whispered.

"Still there."

"I am so tired. Am I dying?"

"No," she reassured softly. "Ye just have a bit o' fever. Ye will be back on your feet in no time." But he did not look well. Bright splotches of red glowed in both cheeks though the rest of his face was grey and pasty. A sparse, blond beard had overtaken his chin, reminding Catrian of just how young the warrior was. He swallowed with difficulty, and began to cough, so she reached for a skin of water that the Dream Weavers had tucked in beside them.

As she tipped a thin trickle of liquid between Trifyn's chapped, trembling lips, Catrian sought for a rope of hope for him to clasp to keep from falling into death's comforting embrace. Having so recently been faced with a similar choice, she knew how important it was.

"Ye are a hero, Trifyn, did ye know that? Ye no' only retrieved the Dragon Sword, ye brought the Lost Prince back t' the world. Ye have saved us all!"

"The Lost Prince? Who…? 'Tis Gralyre," Trifyn guessed with a weak grin, though his pain seeped through each quivering syllable he spoke. "I knew it was him! I knew it all along." His words bore the naiveté that had been his before the quest for the sword had burned most of his youth away.

The cart rocked, and Trifyn gritted his teeth against his agony. His frame trembled with long, racking shivers. Prudently, Catrian set the water aside lest he choke upon the trickles she was giving him.

Catrian bent closer to his head where it rested in her lap, her words softer, and for his ears alone. "Prince Gralyre needs ye, Trifyn. He needs ye by his side t' kill Doaphin. So ye have no choice but t' heal. I will no' lose him, and so I will no' lose ye."

Understanding softened the lines of suffering from Trifyn's features. "Ye love him."

Catrian nodded. "Aye." She glanced away from his innocent blue gaze, assailed by memories of her fight with Gralyre that morning.

"Then I will recover, and keep him safe for ye, Lady," he vowed softly, his words trailing away, as he fell unconscious once more.

Her own strength now spent, Catrian removed his head from her lap back to the soft furs, and sagged down beside him. She pillowed her cheek against her forearms, as she regarded the felled bowman. "I will hold ye t' your promise," she warned softly.

ഇൽ

Dotch and Jord led the women and children that they had discovered in the forest back into the relative safety of the ruined walls of the fortress.

In vivid contrast to his dread of that morning, Dotch was now utterly content. His wife, Ella, shared his saddle. She was a warm weight against his back, as she hugged him close. Dotch's two sons rode with Jord.

Saliana ran forth to meet them when she spotted their horses entering the square from out of the wreckage of the eastern thoroughfare. From her labours of the day, her dress was spattered with blood, and her fine, blond hair wisped free from its braid. Her hands covered her smile of excitement, and forgetting herself in the moment she squealed and bounced, "Dotch! Ye found them!"

Dotch waved at her, as he halted his horse. He offered Della his hand to help her to slide from the back of the saddle before joining her on the ground. His arm remained wrapped around his wife's waist, as he walked towards Saliana.

Jord dismounted, and reached up to catch the boys, as they leapt down at him. His head craned around before he looked back at Saliana. "Where are the others?"

Saliana could not stop grinning. "Ye are the first t' return." She gave Ella's hand a friendly little squeeze. "I bet ye are famished."

"We all are. There was no time t' gather food afore we fled, so the boys and I have no' eaten for days."

"And rightly so!" Dotch growled, as he gave Della a little squeeze of affection. "We saw the ends o' those who thought t' delay for belongings."

Saliana's smile faded, for she had been treating many such injuries all afternoon. "We have no' much, but we can fill your stomachs for tonight." She clapped her hands for the attention of her aides, and the men watched in quiet amazement, as she sent people scurrying to fetch food and water for their supper.

"This canno' be our little, Saliana!" Dotch joked to Jord with a nudge of his shoulder.

Saliana heard his rib, and grew flustered by the sudden

attention. "I will have beds readied for ye." She fled from the men out of habit, seeking to fade into the background, but a woman grabbed her arm as she passed, not allowing her the escape that she sought.

"Which one is he? Which one is the Prince?" the woman asked in a loud whisper.

"Neither o' them. He is no' here yet," Saliana told her briskly, but she brightened anew, as she saw the familiar figure riding into the square from out of the southern avenue, with the big, black wolf at his side. "No, wait. Here he comes."

Gralyre's shoulders seemed even broader with the adornment of the enormous blade slung across his back. Having donned his Maolar chain mail, and properly sheathed the Dragon Sword, he appeared every inch the warrior prince of legend.

"He was a huntsman for South Sector!" the woman exclaimed in recognition. "He is the one that everyone said was a lowland spy," she grouched, disgruntled at the thought that they had all been duped.

"He was in disguise," Saliana explained with an airy wave. Where was Rewn? The hour was growing late, and a hint of unease feathered her thoughts.

"Food for ye, Lady."

Distracted from her concern, Saliana swung around to find that a young man stood close, holding a bowl of gruel and a chunk of bread for her dinner.

Saliana had already seen the quality of food to be had, and knew that this ration was the best of the fare. Tired as she was from fighting with the spectre of death all that long afternoon, she smiled warmly in thanks. No one had ever waited upon her.

The young man smiled back.

As he left, Saliana was charmed to realize that no man had ever looked at her with admiration either. The sensation was heady. There were other men in the world besides Rewn Wilson! Mayhap it was time she took a look around.

ଧେ୦ଔ

When next Catrian awoke, the sun was spending its last rays in sparkling, pink prisms upon the glaciers of the jagged mountain peaks above them, spreading bright halos against the rouged clouds of the aged day. The front of the Dream Weaver column had reached the switchback road leading up to the fortress, and the wagon now glided smoothly over the well-packed trail.

Catrian shouldered the blame for the fall of her fortress, as the cart rose higher up the mountainside with each curve of the road. She could have stopped this battle ere it had begun; if only she had not been so consumed with fear for Gralyre's life that she had spent her Godsmagic to the point of death!

Soon, she could clearly see the smashed gatehouse and the scorched, askew gates that should have been sealed against the approaching Dream Weaver army. Catrian breathed shallowly through her mouth to avoid the intensifying odours of death and smoke. Her anxiety and guilt grew apace with their approach to the fortress, and she braced for the worst.

Jacon dropped back to ride beside the cart, as they neared the broken gates. "Lady Catrian," he called out, "would you prefer that we remain outside the walls? We can make camp on the field outside your western gate?"

Mutely, Catrian shook her head. No.

Jacon, his face expressionless, spurred his horse forward to address Aneida. "Be on your guard," he advised before cantering ahead of the cart to lead the column of Dream Weaver warriors into the fortress.

Aneida snapped the reins to encourage the horse and cart through the open gates in turn.

"Ah, Gods!" Catrian cried out when she bore witness to the destruction that had befallen her home and her people. It was far worse than her imaginings.

Aneida heard Catrian's cry, and glanced back over her shoulder to warn, "'Tis worse ahead."

For once, Dajin was sober and silent, as he absorbed the chaos and death surrounding them.

"Be brave, Lady Catrian," Gedrhar advised kindly from where he rode beside the cart.

Catrian set her jaw, and steadied her sorrow, keeping her gaze fixed upon the devastation. She owed her people not to flinch from their pain. That it had come from betrayal at the hands of the Eastern Rebels, their allies, was a sour medicine to swallow. She had known of Kierdenan's ambitions, but the man had managed to mask the extent of his cravings for power.

If only she had scanned deeper into Kierdenan's soul when last they had met at Boris' war council! If only she had not been distracted with anger by the obscene thoughts that the Eastern General had assailed her mind with! In hindsight, she recognized that he had done it on purpose to divert her attention.

Her guilt was a poisonous snake uncoiling and rattling within her chest, striking fangs into her heart, over and over, with each regret, and with each body that they passed.

ഞ്ഞ

Intense pain hammered at Rewn's temple. It throbbed in time to his heartbeat, and reached fingers down his neck, and into his shoulders, digging deeply with icy claws. His thoughts were jumbled and confused, making it difficult to make sense of how he had come to be injured.

The familiar musty odour of old canvas teased at his nostrils and that, combined with the dimness beyond his eyelids, told him that he was within a tent.

But they had lost all of their supplies on Fennick's Island, and he had not eaten since…

…This morning… This morning I ate at a cookfire, wonderful food… Dream Weavers… Gralyre is the Lost Prince!

The flash of clear memories helped him to focus upon the here and now: the devastated fortress, the search for Dotch's family, and the barrier to East Sector. It had been no tap that had put him out. He supposed he was lucky that they had not stove his head in.

Rewn heard a hollow rattle followed by the sound of dice hitting a hard surface. He had been listening to it for some time, though it had made no sense to his scrambled thoughts.

"Dogs and horses. Ye owe me twelve now. Ye have no luck today, Oren."

"It will turn." The dice slid back into the leather cup, and the rattling began anew. "What do ye say, Hermot?"

"God's Eyes."

"Ye sure? 'Tis a fool's bet."

"Just throw the bones. We will see who is the fool."

Rewn tried to raise his hands to rub his aching temple, but as he shifted, he realized that he was bound tightly to a chair, and his wrists were tied behind his back. His hands were tingling with pins and needles, slowly losing feeling, as they were starved of circulation. He flexed to test the bindings, and stabs of pain lanced up into his skull, wringing a soft moan from his throat.

Rewn peeled his eyes open, but when the injury to his head made his sight dance a jig, he quickly clenched them shut to control the wave of nausea that afflicted him. He tried again when his queasiness had abated. As his vision settled and adjusted to the dimness, his gaze found two men sitting at a table in the far corner of the tent throwing dice.

His moan of pain had been noted, and had prompted one of the men to abandon the game. The Eastern Rebel walked to the entrance, and pulled back the loose tent flap. The burst of brighter light made Rewn wince.

"Tell the Commander that he is awake," the Eastern Rebel told an unseen presence.

There was a short delay, before the flap rustled open once more. Wisely, Rewn closed his eyes against the glare this time, awaiting the dimness to return against his eyelids before discovering who had entered.

"Vetroy," he growled his recognition through his gritted teeth. Gods! How he wished for his sword, and the freedom to swing it!

Vetroy was kitted in chain, the armour hanging low enough to cover his upper thighs. From his belt, a longsword dangled on one hip, and a dagger on the other. He eyed Rewn slyly through the long, blond hair that hung low across his cold, blue eyes.

"By the Gods," Vetroy mocked, as he pulled off his leather gauntlets, and slapped them against a palm. "Do ye know who this is, Oren?"

Undeterred by his man's shrug of disinterest, Vetroy continued. "This Lowlander filth is Rewn Wilson, him that was supposed t' be dead on Fennick's Island. So why is he no'?"

"Do ye want me t' ask him for ye, Commander?"

At Vetroy's nod, Oren took a quick stride forward that ended in a clout against Rewn's ear. "Why are ye no' dead?" he shouted.

Rewn's chair rocked from the blow, and his stomach roiled at the intensifying pain. He gasped and reeled, unable to think, as blackness dotted his vision. He felt as though he were sliding into a dark pit. Through a high-pitched drone in his ears, Rewn heard Vetroy caution, "Gently, Oren. If he dies we do no' gain answers."

Vetroy pulled up a vacant chair, and set it opposite to Rewn's, waiting patiently while Rewn righted himself.

The other sentry, Hermot, sat alone at the table in the corner, throwing his dice with an air of boredom, as he awaited Oren's return to their game. He swept the bones together, shook the cup, and threw them, over and over. The clacking sound was a surreal backdrop to Rewn's interrogation.

"I warned ye no' t' cross me, Rewn Wilson!" Vetroy snarled, as Rewn's focus returned. "Ye and your Lowland spy friend, Gralyre, murdered my men on the road, and left them to be fed upon by wild beasts! Ye humiliated my General! I told ye that there would be a reckoning!"

"Your men ambushed us. They meant t' kill us!"

Vetroy easily sidestepped the shaky provenance of his allegations. "Ye will answer for your crimes. But first, I want t' know how ye came t' be here, when we left ye on the way t' your death on Fennick's Island? Even if a dirty, Lowlander weakling like yourself could have survived the Bleak and the island both, ye would no' have been there and back in such a short time. Which means ye took the coward's road. Ye pissed your britches and ran. I suppose it would no' have been so hard t' elude General Ryes, and his pasty Southern Rebels. Did ye kill them too?"

A slow rage seared Rewn's pain to insignificance. "I am no' a coward, Vetroy! And neither are the men and women whom I travelled with t' Fennick's Island. We have been through such danger and hardship, as would kill a lesser man such as yourself! 'Twould seem t' me that cowardice is attacking your own when they think ye an ally! Just as you tried t' murder us on the road south! And just as ye attacked this fortress!"

Oren's face tightened, and red seeped up to his hairline. Even if Vetroy did not care, his men were obviously shamed by their part in the attack upon their allies.

Vetroy chose to answer Rewn's accusations by lashing out with his heavy gauntlets. Pain snapped into Rewn's cheek from the whip of the leather gloves.

"As I said, ye would no' have been t' the island and back in the time since we left ye. Have ye no defense, coward?"

Rewn grimaced, trying not to swallow the blood that filled his mouth from a new cut inside his cheek. He turned to the side and spat. "'Tis a magic sword, Vetroy," he reminded snidely. "How do ye think we returned so quickly? It brought us home in a single night."

"Impossible. Ye think me a fool? Where is it then?" Vetroy sought to shatter Rewn's alibi. "Where is the fabled Dragon Sword?"

"With the Prince, o' course." Rewn laughed harshly. "He is *lost* no more."

Vetroy laughed with him, though there was no amusement in the sound. He glanced up at Oren with a shrug. "He is mad!"

Rewn's laughter stilled to bared teeth, for he felt every bit as insane as Vetroy named him. "Even now, the Prince rides through the fortress with an army o' Dream Weavers at his back, witnessing what your foul betrayal has wrought! Ye will have much t' answer for."

"Then I will kill him, the same as I did Boris. The old man's meal was done, but he was too greedy t' step away from the table. 'Tis a time for a new Commander."

"And ye think it should be ye?"

"Aye, I am the Commander now!"

Rewn recognized the defensiveness in Vetroy's posturing that belayed the surety of his words. Even if the Lost Prince had not returned, still the other Generals of the Resistance would have some contention with Vetroy's coup.

"Prince Gralyre will dispute your claim. Were I ye, I would start running. If ye are very lucky, he will be too occupied with killing Doaphin t' chase after ye." Rewn smiled coldly, his teeth awash in blood from the cut inside his mouth. "For a time."

Vetroy's teeth flashed in response, gleaming whitely in the dimness of the tent. "Tell me ye are no' trying t' pass that ragged swordsman ye travelled south with as the Lost Prince returned? The Lowlander spy?"

Rewn shrugged. "I will no' convince ye o' anything. He will do that on his own. Ye will soon see for yourself."

Vetroy stood and drew his dagger. "I have had enough o' your lies. 'Tis a coward's death for ye, Rewn Wilson, if for no other reason than t' avenge the good Rebels ye murdered on the road. Hold him!"

Oren took up position behind Rewn's chair, and clamped a strong forearm across his brow.

Rewn tried to flinch away, to dodge, as Vetroy's dagger neared his vulnerable neck, but Oren's strength easily held his head still, and the chair's bindings took care of the rest of his body's resistance.

Vetroy placed the tip of his blade at the hollow of Rewn's throat, and began to push forward - very slowly. There was no mercy in the artic depths of Vetroy's eyes. This execution was going to play out for as long as he could make it last.

The pressure of the dagger's point was hard and choking, and growing more so with each miniscule increment of the slow thrust. The pop of Rewn's skin as it split was a small relief that bloomed into more pain than he could have thought possible. It was torture in the greatest sense. This was to be no quick beheading. Vetroy wanted to feed upon Rewn's terror. He intended to sup upon each morsel of agony.

Hermot's dice had ceased to clack against the tabletop, and a thoughtful expression had overtaken his air of disinterest. "Commander, is this the same Gralyre what defeated the field at Boris' tournament?"

The pressure on Rewn's throat eased minutely, as Vetroy, distracted by Hermot's question, relented slightly. "What o' it?"

Rewn gagged and tried to struggle, but Oren stilled his head with a flex of his forearm. His contortions seemed only to sink the dagger's tip further into his throat.

Hermot scratched at his brain cap. "I have ne'er seen a

swordsman as good. I know he is no' the Lost Prince, but he is dangerous, and this man is his friend. He could do a lot o' damage afore he was put down. Ye may need the prisoner alive for bartering, t' make Gralyre give up the Dragon Sword."

Vetroy considered for a moment. "Ye make a valid point, Hermot." The dagger's pressure vanished from Rewn's throat.

Oren's forearm released his forehead, and Rewn wheezed and coughed, as he was free to move his head once more. The flow of the blood from the deep gash in his neck gushed thickly to dampen his shirtfront. The dagger had done its damage. His wind whistled from his neck, as much as from his mouth. It was a mortal wound. His death, it would seem, had only been delayed.

Vetroy glared down at Rewn. "The gods grant ye luck today, Lowlander. Ye will no' die yet. No' until ye have played goat for us." Maximizing the insult, he wiped his dagger upon Rewn's sleeve, leaving a thick smear of blood, before sheathing his blade with a rasping click.

Rewn grimaced, as he choked on his blood and gasped for air. Vetroy deserved every ill that was about to befall him!

At that moment, a young Rebel burst through the tent flap. "Lieutenant!"

"How many times do I have t' tell ye? Call me Commander."

The Eastern Rebel frowned, thrown for a moment, before affecting a sloppy salute. "Commander!"

"Report!"

"A large host has entered through East Gate."

"Demon Riders?"

"No sir, they are human."

"Where in all the hells did they come from?" Vetroy pivoted to address Oren. "Rouse our warriors! We have a fortress t' defend."

"Commander?" the young Rebel tried to reclaim his leader's attention.

"And Oren, bring the Lowlander coward with us."

"Yes, sir." Oren saluted smartly, and motioned to Hermot to help him drag Rewn up out of his chair.

"Lieutenant Vetroy? I mean Commander? Commander Vetroy, sir, there is more," the Eastern Rebel continued to badger.

"What!" Vetroy snapped with a beleaguered air. "What is it?"

"She is with them, sir. The Sorceress. She has come back!"

Vetroy's eyes glowed with satisfaction. "She should have kept running! If she has returned, then all is no' yet lost."

಑಑಑

"Kentle, Demin?"

"Ye Da?" They answered Dotch in unison.

Dotch chuckled at them. He would never grow tired of being back with his family. "I want ye t' meet someone."

He led his boys over to where Gralyre was preparing a feedbag to place over his horse's nose.

"Dotch!" Gralyre hailed, as they approached. "These are your sons? Ye found everyone safe?" He quickly finished buckling the horse's feedbag in place, before stepping forward to meet them.

"Aye!" Dotch puffed proudly.

They clasped arms, and Gralyre grinned, his dark cares abating for the moment. "By the Gods, this is happy news!"

"Your Highness, I would like ye t' meet some very important men. This is Kentle," Dotch squeezed the shoulder of his eldest, "and this is Demin."

Both boys bore a strong resemblance to their father, with matching squared chins and high cheekbones.

Demin's little neck craned back so that he could look up, and up, to meet Gralyre's eyes.

"Lads, I want ye t' meet..." Dotch's polite introduction was rudely interrupted by his youngest.

"Ye are the Lost Prince!" Demin announced with certainty. "My Da went with ye t' fetch your sword!" He well remembered the day when his father had left for Fennick's Island. The grief of watching him ride away would stay with him for all of his years. At the time, Dotch had told him that he quested for the Dragon Sword with the Lost Prince, and had pointed out Gralyre. It had never occurred to Demin that his Da would have lied to spare his son's sorrow.

Gralyre crouched so that he was more at level with the two boys. "If it were not for your father's bravery, I would not be standing here. He saved my life, many, many times."

Kentle and Demin's faces shone with pride, and they stared

up at their father with brown eyes made round by awe.

"Is that your wolf?" Demin asked, pointing, as Little Wolf came to Gralyre's heel and sat.

Little Wolf's ears were tilted up, tall and friendly, as he regarded Dotch's pups with a quizzical intensity.

"This is Little Wolf," Gralyre said.

His head tilted to the side, as Gralyre spoke his name, and his tail swept the ground in a gentle rhythm.

"Hello, Little Wolf!" Demin patted the wolfdog on the side of his snout, fearlessly, a feat that most grown men would never attempt.

Little Wolf slurped his face with his long tongue, leaving a wet slurry behind that a giggling Demin had to wipe away using his sleeve.

Finally finding his voice through his awe, Kentle asked shyly, "Is that the Dragon Sword?" and pointed at the hilt that arose above Gralyre's shoulders.

At Gralyre's solemn nod, he asked, "Can I hold it?"

Dotch stiffened for he recalled Gralyre's possessiveness of the blade on the beachhead beyond Fennick's Island. "Ah, boys, I do no' think…"

But Gralyre surprised him by standing and shrugging off the baldric. In a practiced move, he freed the sword from the black scabbard in a rasping song of destruction. The blade was still ringing, as he tossed the leather aside, and touched the tip to the earth, silencing it. The towering, shimmering weapon dwarfed the two boys.

With his mouth tilted mischievously, Gralyre released his hold, and the Dragon Sword began to topple towards Kentle.

With a little cry of excitement, the boy leaped forward and caught the hilt, stopping the blade's fall. He gaped, as the weight came to a rest against his shoulder. Kentle chortled gleefully, and Gralyre shared a grin with Dotch.

Demin reached out with far more caution than he had displayed with Little Wolf, and petted the head of the dragon on the hilt that rested upon his brother's shoulder. He snatched his hand back, as though the figure would snap at his little fingers.

The boys shared an excited giggle, and Demin did a little jig of pure happiness, the coltish innocence of a rambunctious child.

"Alright boys, give the Prince his sword back," Dotch advised, "I see his dinner coming."

Gralyre reclaimed the Dragon Sword, sheathed it, and snugged it back into place at his back.

"Thank Prince Gralyre, and go find your mum."

The two boys beamed and thanked Gralyre, before bolting like runaway horses back to their mother with the tale to tell.

As Dotch turned away to follow his sons, Gralyre called out, "I meant every word I said."

Dotch blushed, and ran a finger around his collar. "We are well even then, for I would no' be here with my family, had ye no' rescued us from that bone yard on the island." He hesitated before leaving to add, "My boys have been through a terrible time. Thank-ye for letting them touch the Dragon Sword. I know what it means t' ye."

Gralyre grimaced at the remembrance of his poor behaviour back on the beach. "The magic in the blade is very powerful… and I…"

But Dotch was backing away, placing distance between them. "No need t' explain," he bowed awkwardly, "er, your Highness - Gralyre" he corrected uncomfortably. "I will leave ye t' your dinner."

Gralyre's hands fisted, as he watched Dotch return to his family. There was no denying that a barrier of station and power now stood between him and his companions, but worse, he was not certain that he should seek to breach it.

As the Prince of Lyre, he was accustomed to deference, the *your Highness* this, and the bowing that. Gralyre had only to think back to this morning, and his unreasonable anger at Rewn's teasing to prove this. In the past, he had expected the proper, respectful address, and had been outraged when he had not received it. But the lost warrior he had been for a year was deeply ashamed of his unwarranted responses. Had he been himself, he would have laughed with Rewn, and responded with a quip of his own.

'Had I been myself,' Gralyre mused.

Who was that? The Prince, the Warrior, or the Sorcerer? Would he return to his familiar customs of old, or keep faith with who he had been gifted to become when he had lost his memories?

"Food for ye, your Majesty," a young Rebel announced, as he arrived at Gralyre's side.

Gralyre scowled at the irony of the moment that so perfectly echoed his thoughts. "Majesty is reserved for the King. I am a Prince. The proper address is Highness." Of course they did not know of regal protocols. These people had not had a king in three hundred years.

The Rebel thought himself Gralyre's target of displeasure for his unknowing insult, and babbled nervously, "There is no' much food t' be had, Highness." He tore a hunk of bread off a loaf that he carried under his arm, and passed it over with a wooden bowl of thin stew. "Most o' it was packed away and sent ahead o' our march t' war."

Little Wolf reset his paws to face the food, and licked his chops noisily. His black nose quivered to the scents upon the air.

"And what were those left behind to have survived upon?"

"Mostly destroyed in the fighting and fires. What was left o' that has been taken by Kierdenan's men."

"The Eastern Rebels are still in the fortress?" Gralyre condemned. "Where are Boris and Matik? Why have they not ousted them?" He would have their heads for dereliction when next they met!

"I am sorry, Prince Gralyre, I thought that ye would have been told. They are both dead. They were ambushed on the walls." The young warrior's shoulders slumped. "We were betrayed by our own. 'Twas traitors that opened the gates t' let the Eastern Rebels in t' kill us."

Gralyre regretted his shortness. "I did not know that they had died. Thank-you for telling me." His duality of disposition would quickly become a hindrance if he were to constantly have to atone for his royal overreactions. "I vow that I will set it right."

The young Rebel's face shone with faith. "I know that ye will, Prince Gralyre."

Gralyre was distracted from the conversation when a flash of Catrian's anguish bled through. She had entered the fortress, and borne witness to the devastation.

His heart twisted with sympathy for her pain. Despite their fight that morning, their magical interlude the previous night had left them irrevocably linked.

Returning his attention to the young warrior, Gralyre advised, "Be not concerned with food. The Dream Weavers are arriving now, and they have supplies aplenty to share with us."

The Rebel's eyes adopted a dazed glaze. "Dream Weavers!" he echoed softly. Like every person alive, he had been weaned upon the fabled tale of the Lost Prince, and of his allies in the fight against evil, the Dream Weavers. Had someone told him yesterday that such as this was like to happen, he would have scoffed and named them mad. Now, for the first time in his life, hope began to paint a vivid colour on the horizon of his drab future. Though he did not immediately recognize the sensation for what it was, he found himself hoarding that bright spot like a miser with a shining jewel.

The Rebel bolted to spread the word about the Dream Weavers' arrival.

As Gralyre watched him go, a weary protectiveness arose for

the young man, and for everyone else in his realm, for these, the remnants of his people. Doaphin had to be defeated, but it was a sickening tragedy that young men such as this one would lead the charges in the battles ahead, and would likely never live to see the changes that they wrought in the world.

Pain shot through Gralyre's temple, a flash of vision of Catrian being pelted with filth from the street. His hand loosened in response, sending his bowl of gruel tumbling to the ground.

Her voice echoed into his thoughts. *'Why are ye doing this?'*

"Gralyre, what is it?" Dotch called out, as Gralyre yanked the feedbag from over his horse's nose, spilling the remains of oats onto the soot-encrusted earth in his haste.

"The Dream Weavers have entered the fortress. Catrian is under attack!"

Dotch leapt up. "Jord!" he shouted to the knifeman. But Jord was already reaching for his tethered horse, while shoving a last bite of bread into his mouth.

Gralyre vaulted to his steed's back, galloping out of the square without benefit of a saddle or rein.

Little Wolf followed, stretching out into a long stride to keep pace with Gralyre's horse.

"Be careful," Ella admonished, and gave Dotch a quick buss on his lips before he too swung up onto his horse, meeting Jord, as they raced after their Prince.

ℰℛ

The Dream Weavers created a stir, as they paraded six abreast through the ruined east gate, five thousand strong, with a pack train of supplies winding down the switchback road into the tree line below. Their progress was slowed by the necessity of clearing rubble from their path, as they moved forward into the Northern Fortress. Refugees gathered to watch, as word spread of the foreign army's arrival.

Catrian called forward, "Aneida, we must find Commander Boris and General Matik. I must know o' our losses, and what we must…"

"Witch!"

Catrian swiveled in surprise at the loud insult, and was in time to receive a clump of offal in the centre of her chest. She watched uncomprehendingly, as the wet muck slid off her breasts, leaving a dark stain upon her homespun shirt. Thus distracted, she never noted the oncoming rock that struck her between her shoulder blades. She cried out at the painful impact, twisting around to see who had thrown the stone, slow to realize that she was under attack.

"Get down!" Aneida cautioned Catrian, as she hauled the horse to a halt. Objects flew threw the air, clattering down upon the sick cart. "Take these!" she tossed the reins into Dajin's surprised hands. Aneida drew her sword and stood, crouched in readiness to dive into the fight.

Dajin dropped the reins, and quietly slid off the wagoner's seat, flattening his chest to the floorboards to reduce the size of the target he made. Above him, Aneida bellowed, "The next bloody coward t' throw a stone at the Sorceress gets a sword through their guts!" The cracks and thumps of flung stones answered her challenge.

Word spread quickly that Catrian had reentered the fortress, and it drew combatants at a run from all corners with weapons drawn to repel her magical menace.

"Come and reap your rewards, ye cowards!" Aneida goaded the mob, ducking and bobbing to avoid being struck.

The Dream Weavers still entering through the gates halted the rear of their column to protect the men and supplies that were still upon the switchback road.

"*Gra-ee-ai partoo ey,* Catrian!" Jacon ordered, and the entire front column of Dream Weavers swarmed their horses to encircle the sick cart protectively. With bows drawn, and arrows ready to fly, they pressed their mounts outwards, forcing the crowds back. They were unwilling to engage in battle if they did not have to. They had come to offer aid, not slaughter allies.

Cries of outrage from the gathering survivors peppered the air with the promise of violence, but in the face of the mounted army, and with no clear leaders rallying them, their attacks momentarily stalled.

Catrian met the maddened gaze of an older woman, who screamed so violently that spittle sprayed from her lips. "Murderess! Murderess!"

"I have done nothing!" Catrian cried out in shocked confusion. Her protest was lost to the howls of the mob. In the urgency of the dangerous moment, Catrian forgot the lesson of only that morning, that she had not the strength of old, and instinctively erected her magical blue shield to surround the wagon and protect against further projectiles. A foul mass struck her magical barrier and slid away, leaving a black smear against the blue, crackling surface. Were she hale, her shield would have been strong enough to incinerate anything that touched it, even unto melting arrow points that hit its surface.

Her potency was draining rapidly, and her magic began to flicker and fail. There was a battle brewing, and Catrian despaired, for the last thing she wanted was to bring more hardship to her people. She gasped for breath, and her heart raced, as her Godsmagic ebbed. Blackness ate at the edges of her vision. If she spent any more power she would return to the state from which Gralyre had rescued her the night before.

"Sorceress," Gedrhar yelled to be heard, from his place at the side of the sick cart, "you are not yet recovered, and dare not use your Godsmagic. Release your power. Trust us to protect you."

Catrian gritted her teeth at her uselessness, but did as he asked. As she released her hold on her magic, she was overcome by such weakness that she collapsed into the furs beside the still comatose Trifyn. Panting from effort, and struggling to remain conscious, Catrian grasped the side board of the cart bed, and weakly drew herself up to peer over the edge.

From there, she watched Gralyre race from out of a side street, his horse frothing from the speed that he had demanded of it. Dotch and Jord rode in hard at his back, and Little Wolf claimed the rear.

Gralyre's furious gaze met Catrian's, as she lay in the wagon, breathless from her exertions. He clearly sensed her dismay at the accusations that were being flung at her, along with aught else that the mob could lay hands upon.

Already there were hundreds of angry people gathered and armed for battle, with more pouring into the wreckage-choked lane by the moment. When sufficient numbers had amassed, a riot would be inevitable.

Gralyre assessed the situation with a sweeping glance. The forefront of the Dream Weaver column was safeguarded at the sides by heaps of rubble, and at the rear by the singed palisade wall and the gate where the bulk of their army had not yet entered the fortress. The majority of their Rebel opposition had gathered to block their path forward.

Gralyre vectored his horse between the pressing mob and the clustered Dream Weavers. He indicated the sick cart with a slash of his hand, to send Dotch and Jord to aid Aneida in protecting Catrian and Trifyn, leaving him to concentrate on quelling the mob.

Gralyre's horse reared, as he drew it to a halt. Showing impressive horsemanship, he tightened the grip of his thighs to maintain his seat without the benefit of a saddle. He shrugged from his baldric, and flung the scabbard away from the Dragon Sword with a flick of his wrist, as the beast danced and pawed at the air. The front lines of the angry mob of Rebels were forced back to avoid its flailing hooves.

Rising to an imposing height above the heads of the people

who sought to bring harm to his Sorceress, Gralyre raised the Dragon Sword aloft. His rearing horse let loose a long, challenging whinny, while in Gralyre's hand the sword ignited with a fiery brilliance that cast new shadows, apart from the setting sun. Shattering prisms of reflected light sparked from his glittering Maolar armour, surrounding his body in a nimbus of godly light, so that he was difficult to look upon.

From where he crouched near Gralyre's pawing horse, Little Wolf loosed a primal howl that lent a wild danger to the moment. As the wolfdog's voice rose above all others, every Rebel ranged against them fell silent in primitive dread.

Gralyre let the tension build, imprinting his heroic image upon the crowd's imagination, before commanding his horse to drop to four hooves. Augmented with a bit of magic, his voice thundered over the people, uncontested. "I am the Lost Prince Gralyre, returned!" he declared theatrically. "By the Dragon Sword of Lyre, I proclaim the innocence of your Sorceress! Catrian Kinsel is, and ever has been, your greatest ally in your fight against Doaphin."

There was no mistaking the famed Dragon Sword of Lyre, that fabled weapon that they had been told of all their lives. The mob's aggression buckled under the weight of their recognition and awe. Hushed whispers of confusion supplanted the shouts of rage from moments before. Wonder began to glow in some of the faces assembled before Gralyre, as the miracle of hope took root in their hearts. However, for most of the mob, the pragmatism of survival still needed more proof than one man's word. Gralyre was claiming the impossible, even if he wielded the magical blade of the Lost Prince.

A lone Rebel showed the bravery to step to the forefront of the throng, and to shake his sword threateningly at the man claiming to be the Lost Prince. "Ye are wrong!" Compared to Gralyre's amplified, resonant tones, his voice was reedy and small. "'Twas Catrian who summoned the Stalkers! 'Twas what we all heard t' be true. She is evil!" Angry shouts of agreement came from his supporters within the crowd.

Catrian's shoulders sagged at this betrayal. Magic was always viewed with suspicion, and she had always known that she walked in borrowed shoes that would remain hers only so long as she remained of use to the resistance. Boris, her own flesh, had told her as much. Still, it was a bitter schooling in the fickle trust of her people. After all that she had sacrificed, it had taken little more than a rumor for them to turn upon her.

"Heard from whom?" Gralyre sneered regally in response to the Rebel's assertion. "From the same betrayers who opened your gates to your enemies? Or from the Eastern Rebels who attacked without cause, and still occupy your homes?" Gralyre's voice softened dangerously, "Ask who would benefit from besmirching the Lady Catrian's honour?" He scanned the crowd, not yet satisfied with the number of shamed gazes that darted and dropped away from his imperious glare. "'Twas not she who summoned Stalkers and Deathren into this fortress. My people, you have been eating from a dish of lies!"

The defiant Rebel selected another lance from the arsenal of his argument. "Says ye! We have only your word that ye are the... Lost... Prince!" His words trailed nervously, as Gralyre abruptly dismounted, and stalked towards him.

The Prince's attention was absolute and focused, ignoring all else except the warrior who challenged his authority. The intimidated mob gave way before his inexorable stride, as he walked boldly through them, fearless of any threat to his person. "Enigma Rise from out of Mist," Gralyre intoned resoundingly. Growling thunder replied from out of the sky, though there were no clouds above.

The Rebel stumbled backwards in time with Gralyre's advance, and the reverent crowd parted around both men.

"Spirit! Waken with a roar!" Lightening flashed, as Gralyre swung the great sword up before his eyes, in clear sight of the people. The dragon adorning the hilt seemed to come alive, its neck undulating along the glowing blade, its jaws gaping in a roar of defiance. "Dragon perched on vengeful fist!"

Thunder crashed overhead, shaking the roots of the mountain, and the crowd flinched with cries at the unprecedented din. The challenger tripped and fell to his back.

Gralyre brought the point of his five and a half foot weapon to a standstill less than a hair's breadth from the man's nose. There the sword remained, extended without a quiver of effort. The Rebel froze. The fear panting harshly from his lips sounded loudly into the quiet, expectant hush of the crowd.

Gralyre's voice quieted, as he finished reciting the famous stanzas of the prophecy. The silence of the street echoed the familiar words from the lips of all who watched. "Fell Usurper – Rule. No. More."

Gralyre hefted the blade and, with all the power of his massive shoulders, drove the point into the ground between the Rebel's outstretched legs. A concussion detonated outwards, knocking all before him to the ground, yet not affecting the amassed Dream Weaver army at his back. Broken carts, ash and debris flew outward from the force, like the ripples in a pond after a stone has pierced its surface.

"Gralyre, no!" Catrian whispered, shocked to her core, and anxious for the lives of her people. Even though they had attacked her, they did not deserve death! They had only acted from ignorance and fear!

Gralyre folded his hands atop the hilt of the impaled blade, and stared dispassionately at the screaming, terrified people who were now groveling for his mercy. Ash and dust slowly settled over them all like a thick blanket.

Gralyre's voice easily arose above the din, his volume augmented by the magics at his command. "Harken to me, my people! Listen! Listen! Heed my words! Now!" he thundered.

The people went mute, frozen in huddled terror from the wrath of the Lost Prince.

"My name is Prince Gralyre of Lyre, son of Bylyre, son of Raylyre, son of Chrylyre, unbroken sons of the kingship of Lyre for seventeen generations! I swear by my sword that I will fight for you until my last drawn breath, and unto the death of the usurper, Doaphin!"

"Spare me, my Prince," the chastised Rebel cried out from where he cowered on the ground at Gralyre's feet. His hands covered his head fearfully. "Mercy! I did no' believe 'twas ye!"

"Will you fight by my side?" Gralyre demanded of him.

"Aye!" the Rebel vowed fervently. "Aye, I will! I will!"

"Then all is forgiven! Rise and join me - Warrior of Lyre!"

With great hesitation, the man cringed as he stood, as though to be upright would be to give terrible offence.

"Do you vow to help me cleanse our lands of evil?"

"Aye!" This time the man's voice was strong and sure, as he gave his oath of fealty to his Prince. Tears rolled down his cheeks, as he became overwhelmed by the truth of the legendary warrior standing before him.

Gralyre's midnight-blue gaze rose to pass over the awed gathering, an imperious challenge, and more voices joined that of the warrior standing before him.

"Aye!"

"My sword is yours, my Prince!"

"I will, my Prince! I will fight!"

"Then rise up and join with me, Warriors of Lyre!" Gralyre invited, and throughout the throng, in twos and threes, Rebels stood, and shouted their vows of allegiance.

"Will you help me drive my Dragon Sword into the heart of our enemy?" Gralyre roared.

"Aye!" even more screamed and stood. Weapons were reclaimed to shake at the sky, at each other, and at the Prince.

"Then arise! Arise and stand with me, Warriors of Lyre!

Death to Doaphin!" Gralyre bellowed at them, and jerked the Dragon Sword from the earth to stab at the sky.

All present roared their fealty, as the last of the people surged to their feet to meet their Prince's boldness with their own. "Death to Doaphin!" They screamed in agreement, and stabbed their own weapons skyward in mimicry of their Prince.

"Death to Doaphin!" Gralyre shouted again, and lighting descended from the clear sky to detonate along his weapon with a thunderous roar, throwing harsh blue light throughout the throng. Gralyre pointed the Dragon Sword at the newly minted Warriors of Lyre, and sparks of fire danced along the tips of all of the weapons held aloft. "Death to Doaphin!"

As the magic of the Dragon Sword sanctified their blades, the people were overcome with fervor, a howling cacophony of defiance against the evil that threatened all mankind. Fear was a thing unknown, for their Lost Prince was with them.

Catrian felt eyes upon her and glanced up to meet Gedrhar's gaze. She knew that her face must be filled with the awe of the moment.

Gedrhar dipped his chin solemnly, "The Prince has returned."

Catrian could barely hear his words over the din of the screaming people. They swarmed around Gralyre, reaching out to touch him and his sword for benediction, as though he were more than a mere man. He was the immortal Lost Prince.

Jord was speechless, as he pawed at the shoulder of an equally overcome Dotch. Knowing Gralyre to be the Lost Prince, and believing in his power, were two very different things.

Aneida's legs gave way, and she flopped back onto the driver's bench of the wagon. "By the Gods!" she whispered softly. Despite her skepticism regarding the prophecy, what she had just witnessed was as close to it as she could have imagined. She sheathed her sword, and reclaimed the tethers that Dajin had dropped.

Dajin, who had no snide comments to bandy, reclaimed his seat beside Aneida. He had spurned the friendship of the Lost Prince, the one man who could have made all of his dreams a reality. For once, he could find no one to blame but himself. He covered his eyes to hold back tears of frustration and self-pity.

The Rebels parted from Gralyre's path, as he strode back to his waiting horse, reclaiming his baldric along the way in order to sheath his blade. Once he was reseated upon the back of his steed, he proclaimed, "Spread the word to all you meet. Doaphin's days are spent!"

The din of the response echoed in rolling surges from the mountainside.

The column of Dream Weavers moved forward, and Gralyre nodded respectfully to Jacon, as he took his place at the head of the army.

People followed alongside, gathering more Northern Rebels to swell their numbers, as word spread of the return of the Lost Prince.

CHAPTER SEVEN

By the time that Vetroy had mustered his three thousand Eastern Rebels to defend the fortress, the invading army was already through the gates. Any advantage that the walls would have given his warriors in the fight ahead was already denied him. The man that Vetroy had sent to reconnoiter had returned with the stunning story of Gralyre's arrival with the Dragon Sword, and of how he had quelled the mob of Northern Rebels who were seeking Catrian's blood.

"I tell ye, 'twas the Lost Prince, Commander Vetroy! It was him!"

New to his position of higher authority, Vetroy did not want his men to sense his uncertainty. "Calm yourself. It was naught but Catrian, a witch's trick played upon the weak minded!" he disparaged. He turned his back and strode a few paces off, hoping that he struck a confident pose in the late rays of the setting sun. His face hidden, he indulged in a moment of alarm.

Rewn had spoken truthfully of at least one thing. The lowland spy, Gralyre, had claimed the Dragon Sword, and a foreign army of five thousand strong owed its allegiance to the pretender! How had Gralyre amassed such a force? Where had they come from? It was not possible that they were Dream Weavers, as Rewn had suggested. Was it?

After a moment to think, a slow smirk seeded itself upon

Vetroy's lips, and grew into a wide grin. There was no fight to be won in a head-to-head confrontation with an army that outnumbered his forces almost two to one. Only one battleground held the leverage that he needed.

Vetroy composed himself, and turned back to where his lieutenant awaited his orders. "Oren, tell the men we march on the centre square."

"What about him?" Oren smacked Rewn across the back of the skull.

Rewn almost went sprawling. His hands were still tied at his back, and by now he was only semi-conscious from blood loss and the sporadic gasps of air he was managing to draw down his damaged throat and into his lungs. Lieutenant Oren grasped his shoulder roughly, and pulled him back upright.

"Bring him!"

ଔଔ

Taken unawares, those Northern Rebels who had gathered for the promise of food and medicine marshaled only a token resistance when Vetroy and his men unexpectedly attacked. They had not the numbers to pose any real threat, and were quickly and efficiently overwhelmed and disarmed.

Vetroy had no desire to kill more of the Northerners than he had to. His fight had never been with them. Instead, he herded the able-bodied Northerners together, and posted a guard to keep them from interfering. Once the invaders were defeated, the

Sorceress and the sword were in hand, and Gralyre was dead, Vetroy would assimilate the surviving Northern Rebels into his ranks, and send word to Doaphin that he wished to bargain. 'Twas the only sane path.

Kierdenan, more than any of the other Generals of the resistance, had been a realist who had recognized that the Rebels could do nothing to halt the oncoming genocide. Trying to save the Lowlanders was a futile gesture of a dying ideology. Far from quenching the fires of war, Boris would have given the last of their men as fodder for its flames. The Lowlands were lost, and Vetroy, like Kierdenan, would not see one more Rebel life spent in their defense.

The din from the approaching army grew louder, and resolved into cheers of jubilation. The scout that Vetroy had charged with monitoring their advance sprinted from a side street into the central square of the fortress with his arms pumping for speed to stay ahead of the front lines. "They are here!" he yelled, as he dove for cover behind a pile of rubble.

"Take your positions!" Vetroy roared at his warriors. He had set his ambush, and baited his trap as well as he could on short notice, using a strategy that favoured the Eastern Rebels' strengths. He vowed that by day's end he would have all of the bargaining power he needed to safeguard his people.

Vetroy firmed his grasp upon the tongue of the belt strap encircling Rewn's neck, and kicked the backs of his knees to force him to drop.

With his hands bound behind his back, Rewn was unable to

soften the painful impact of his shins with the rocky ground. His gaze rolled weakly, as he gulped at the air, doing everything in his power to keep his breath flowing. Each time Rewn coughed, bloody spume sprayed the ground from the wound in his throat.

Restrained like Rewn, with a belt around her neck and her hands tied in front of her, Saliana screamed his name, as Oren shoved her to her knees. She watched with horror, as Rewn struggled to pass air into his starving lungs. Listening to his wheezing gasps, she knew he would not survive much longer.

Vetroy and Oren crouched down behind their prisoners, using them as shields. Knowing them to be friends of Gralyre, Vetroy had cleared a space in the centre of the square where they would be seen immediately, in order to lure the Lowlander into a crossfire.

His archers were spaced amongst the rows of wounded. The approaching army would be unable to return fire without raining death upon their own injured. Here and there, drawn steel glinted in the setting rays of the sun, where some of the Eastern Rebels held swords poised over the hearts of the stronger invalids to keep them from sounding a warning. Gralyre's army might outnumber him, but Vetroy's command of hostages gave him all the leverage that he needed to avenge himself upon the lowland spy and win the day.

Once Gralyre's forces had completely entered the centre square, the bulk of Vetroy's warriors, hidden in the debris to either side of the lane down which Gralyre's army marched, would close ranks behind them, boxing them in and leaving no retreat from the killing field.

The noise was deafening, as Gralyre's army neared. Behind the cover of limp blond hair, Vetroy's cold blue eyes gleamed with anticipation for the fight. "Stand ready!" he bellowed at his hidden men. Vetroy caught Oren's worried glance, and his lip curled into a sneer.

Oren faced forward, and licked his lips nervously.

"End this now, and Gralyre may allow ye t' live," Rewn burbled before another racking, bloody cough choked him.

"Shut up!" Vetroy jerked on Rewn's tether. For extra measure, he drew his dagger, and positioned the lethal tip at the nape of Rewn's neck, ready to thrust should he try to resist.

On his knees, a human shield, Rewn had no more fight left within him. He hacked and coughed, as the belt tightened painfully across the wound on his throat. His face began to purple.

"Stop it! Ye are killing him!" Saliana cried out, lunging to be free.

Oren clouted the side of her head to end her struggling, and Saliana sagged. He jerked her upright, his arm clutching across her chest to ensure that she was positioned for his protection.

The Dream Weaver army spilled from the side street into the centre square. Cheering Northerners paraded in ragged formations around the ordered lines of mounted warriors, clearing debris from their path to aid their march.

The sun dipped beneath a mountain peak, and cast a long shadow upon the ground below, though the sky above was still alight. For a moment, an iconic figure was silhouetted against the azure sky - that of a mounted, powerful warrior with the unmistakable outline of the Dragon Sword of Lyre strapped to his back. In a trick of the light, the dragon on the guard, like a living creature made of blazing Maolar silver, seemed to hover over the man's shoulder.

Vetroy gasped, and felt, rather than heard, his unsettlement echoed from his men. Every story, every imagining for three hundred years, was posed before them; it was unmistakably the image of the Lost Prince.

Then the powerful illusion resolved back into Gralyre, travel stained, weary and ragged from his journey to and from Fennick's Island. Vetroy flicked his long, blond hair back from his face, disgusted that he had allowed himself, even for the briefest of moments, to be caught up in the hysteria gripping the Northerners.

Gralyre was the first to notice Saliana and Rewn on their knees in the ash-blackened dirt of the square, and the crouching men shielded behind them. He held up a fist, and behind him the Dream Weaver army halted. The celebration hushed, as people craned to see what was occurring.

Catrian, weakened and exhausted, fought to rise up high enough to cushion her chin upon her folded arms atop the side board of the cart bed. When at last she could peer over, she sucked in a deep gasp of dismay for the tableau of horror that Vetroy had orchestrated.

Saliana gathered the courage to scream into the stillness,

"Gralyre! Run! 'Tis a trap!"

"Fire!" Vetroy screamed in concert, nearly drowning out her warning.

From their hidden positions, Eastern archers loosed a rain of whistling death.

Gralyre glanced upward to calmly watch the waves of arrows falling towards him, and the ruby pommel stone of the sword glowed red. Every bolt evaporated to nothing, all of them simply vanishing in flight.

"No!" Gedrhar yelled. "Che-li-ak! Che-li-ak!" The Dream Weaver's voice was filled with anguish.

છાલ

Within the Wizard Stone

The ancient sorcerer is exuberant, as every theory that he holds about the nature of Dream Weaver magic is proven. Gralyre is claiming the Godsmagic of the arrows!

He can feel the surges of power gained with each reaping, and slyly syphons this strength off into his own reserves. *'More! More!'* The red facets within the Wizard Stone pulse with each draw upon the fount of Gralyre's power.

His long patience has born fruit at last! The vessel is everything that he was bred to be. More! Such potential! With gifts such as these at his disposal he will become a God!

ജ്ഞ

The mob of Northern Rebel survivors, newly dubbed the Warriors of Lyre, roared defiantly, jeering and heckling the Eastern Rebels' inability to strike the Prince with their arrows. After the devastation caused by Kierdenan's invasion, it was empowering to see the Easterners failing before their champion.

Gralyre dismounted with as much seeming concern as if suffering a gentle rain, while the torrent of arrows continued to vanish from overhead. He strode purposefully towards Vetroy, with Little Wolf at his side.

From within the Dream Weaver ranks, Gedrhar stared upward, watching the spectacle with despair. His hands rose to grip his hair. "Che-li-ak!" he muttered softly. "He must not! No! No! This is forbidden!"

Vetroy signaled, and one of his Easterners blared a battle horn. As planned, Eastern warriors sprang from the rubble to either side of the lane's exit into the square. They closed ranks behind Gralyre's army, cutting off their avenue of retreat. In moments, the square was a melee of hand-to-hand combat.

In his hubris and inexperience with battlefields, having spent most of his life ambushing small 'Rider patrols from the shadows with quick vicious attacks, Vetroy could not conceive of the totality of the Dream Weaver forces that had been bolstered by the Northern survivors. The five thousand warriors he had expected had swelled to twice that number, too many to enter the square. The bulk of Gralyre's warriors were still standing in the lane down which they had marched. Far from closing a fist about the enemy's throat with his flanking maneuver, Vetroy had unthinkingly thrust his men into the midst of a superior force.

Gralyre's army easily shattered the bottleneck that the Eastern Rebels had sought to create at the head of the lane. Outflanked and outnumbered, Vetroy's men threw down their arms and surrendered.

From where he crouched behind Rewn's back, Vetroy gaped as his stratagems failed. Even his archers ceased to fire when they recognized that they would never strike a hit. The battle stuttered to a halt, having lasted mere minutes.

Gralyre's attention returned to Vetroy, who still crouched behind Rewn's tortured, bloodied body. The Prince's face blanked of all expression, though his eyes ignited with a terrible rage. Despite his ragged clothing, Gralyre's regal bearing commanded the attention of every eye.

Utterly terrified, as Gralyre advanced upon them, Oren abandoned Saliana to try to run.

Saliana sagged forward onto her bound hands, as the pressure of the belt around her throat was relieved.

Gralyre's lethal glare followed after Oren, allowing him to run for a few steps, before Vetroy's Lieutenant abruptly exploded in a rain of pink mist.

"Gods!" Catrian expelled on a breath of surprise. This was a spell that she had never taught him, that she had not known existed! Where had Gralyre learned such a thing?

The Northerners roared approval, as an enemy fell before their Prince.

Gathering the strength to rear up, Saliana ripped the belt from around her neck. She coughed, as she massaged the bruises that the leather had left. No longer under threat of death from Oren, she used her teeth to start pulling apart the rope knotted about her wrists.

"No further! No further, or Rewn dies!" Vetroy yelled at Gralyre, making sure that he saw the dagger tip at Rewn's spine, though his hand quivered from panic. Oren's abrupt death had shaken him to his core. "Then every wounded Rebel in yonder infirmary!" he dared to add.

"No!" Saliana cried out. "They are defenseless!"

Gralyre halted.

Little Wolf sat at his heel, a massive, dark presence blending perfectly with the lengthening shadows. Reflecting the lighter sky above, his canine eyes shone like twin coins of Maolar, glowing eerily.

"Ye would murder injured allies in their sickbeds?" Gralyre condemned the appalling threat. As before, he augmented his volume with a bit of magic, so that his deep baritone voice rolled out over the assembly.

Vetroy jerked Rewn's tether as a threat, proving that he was still in control.

Gralyre could clearly see that the life of his dear friend was fading. Rewn's face was rapidly progressing from purple to blue, as he fought the tight belt around his neck for one more breath.

Blood saturated the front of his shirt from a deep gash in the hollow of his throat. The right side of his face bore a massive contusion, swollen and painful.

From where she sat in the dirt, Saliana's hands covered her mouth with dread. Her eyes welled with tears to witness Rewn's last, strangling breaths.

Gralyre quickly scanned the rows of injured, seeking the veracity of Vetroy's threats, and spotted the vulnerable wounded with daggers hovering over their hearts. Off to the right, Dotch's wife Ella hugged her children from where she huddled amongst a small group of other survivors, guarded by a contingent of Vetroy's Easterners who were poised to attack.

The outraged Prince within Gralyre clamored to tear every last one of the Eastern Rebels apart for their betrayal! But there were too many hostages to protect, too many to reach before a heartbreaking loss. Forced to negotiate, Gralyre's voice was guttural with rage, as he demanded, "What do you want, Lieutenant Vetroy?"

"Ye will address me as Commander!"

"You will address me as Highness!" Gralyre snapped back. He breathed deeply, seeking the coldness of the sword dance to calm his rage and clear his mind so that he could think of a way to save the hostages and his friends. "Commander over what, exactly?"

"Boris and Matik are both dead! And so is Kierdenan! This fortress is mine by right o' conquest! That makes me the Commander o' the Resistance!"

Catrian gasped, as her heart contracted with pain. Vetroy had just coldly announced the deaths of her entire family. Her uncle was dead! "Ah, Gods!" she gritted. And Matik! She began to weep bitter tears of sorrow, remembering the last, harsh words that had passed between her and Boris.

Aneida passed her reins to Dajin once more. "Hang onto them this time," she growled, before she clambered into the back of the cart to rub Catrian's heaving back. "Bloody bastards!" Aneida whispered, as she comforted the Sorceress. "Gralyre will see t' them!"

Gralyre had turned his head slightly to address the masses of Northern Rebels arrayed behind him, though his hard gaze remained on Vetroy's. "Warriors of Lyre! Is this man your Commander?"

The "NO!" was immediate and thunderous, with no room for misinterpretation.

Vetroy shivered. Only that morning the Northern Rebels had been defeated and cowed! This was not the easy victory that he had envisioned. "Give me the Sword and the Witch, and I will let your friends and the wounded live!"

"Give to you our Lady Catrian?" Gralyre emphasized the respectful title, to correct Vetroy's rude address. "To what end? As Kierdenan did, do you foolishly mean to bargain her life to Doaphin to gain safety for the Eastern Rebels?"

Hisses and catcalls arose out of the ranks of the Prince's army in response to the accusation, although only minutes before most of the warriors present had been set on drawing Catrian's blood.

Gralyre noted that the irony of the moment seemed lost to them.

Vetroy jerked Rewn's leash again, needing to feel the control it gave him over Gralyre. "No' just the Easterners! All Rebels!" he cried out to the Prince's army in an attempt to move them to his side. "'Tis better than fighting a war we canno' win! The strength o' the resistance is spent, and Boris was too stubborn t' admit it!"

"And when you have relinquished your greatest weapons to Doaphin, and he knows that you are defenseless, do you truly believe that he will act with honour and not kill you all?" Gralyre paused to evaluate the fear that was crumbling Vetroy's men, a fracture into which he could hammer a wedge. "If you give Doaphin your sword, he will stab you through the heart with it!"

Vetroy sneered dismissively. "Ye are a pretender not a prince! Ye have no authority over us. Ye would blind us with superstition, and sacrifice us all t' the impossible!"

"What know you of sacrifice?" Gralyre taunted softly, though his contemptuous question was still clearly heard by all in the square. His iron features contorted with grief, as he fixed upon the horror of his remembrances. "I stood on the field of battle with an army of Heroes at my back, each and every one of them ready to lay down their lives to save this realm! In Centaur Pass we held back a horde of evil that outnumbered us fifty-to-one."

The silence was absolute, as the amassed people in the square strained to hear Gralyre's account of a famous battle that, to them, was only a legend from a long-gone age.

"I watched each of my men die, as they were struck down by Doaphin's foul magics. They turned into black stone before my eyes! They would not abandon me. Not one of them ran, though I ordered them to flee over the landslide." Gralyre's voice thickened with emotion. "Not a one!" he emphasized through clenched teeth.

Gralyre's gaze lifted and stabbed into Vetroy like twin daggers of midnight-blue ice. "What know you of sacrifice?" He demanded once more, as his upper lip curled with scorn, "You, who would sell your own for a place at the destroyer's table?"

Vetroy's face flamed with shame and rage, but Gralyre gave him no opening to respond.

"You ask by what right I have to lead my people? I am your Prince by divine right, for it was the Gods who threw the bones of fortune, and chose my birth and my fate." The sword at Gralyre's back began to glow with an icy blue light, and the ambient temperature in the square dropped until breath fogged the air. "I am your Prince through right of blood and war! I am your Prince through might of fire and power! I am your Prince through covenant with time itself!" Gralyre roared.

Rewn succumbed to his injuries at last, and pitched forward into the ash-laden dirt. Vetroy was suddenly unprotected.

In a swift, smooth motion, Gralyre drew his dagger from his belt and threw it. The long knife flipped end-over-end, a silver blur that buzzed through the air, and buried itself to the hilt in Vetroy's neck, in the same place as the injury dealt to Rewn.

The Eastern Rebel lifted a shaking hand to his throat, unable to fathom what had just occurred, before he fell forward into the dirt beside Rewn's prone body.

So quickly had the end come, that the Eastern Warriors had not carried out Vetroy's vile threat against the injured. Most were relieved that, with Vetroy's death, they were no longer compelled to follow through with the heinous order.

The Northerners roared in victory, as Saliana rushed to Rewn's side, and worked the tight leather belt from around his throat. "Be alive, Rewn!" she begged.

A bit of bloodied burble came from his lips, and she looked to the Dream Weaver ranks in desperation. "Ninrhar!" she screamed for help. Breath fogged the air about her face, for the chill of Gralyre's rage still iced the fortress square.

The Dream Weaver healer jogged out of the company, and reached her in moments. Together they began to work at saving Rewn's life. Little Wolf drifted over to stand guard against any further aggression from the Easterners.

Gralyre held up his hands for silence from his army, before addressing the Eastern Rebels directly. "The traitors Kierdenan and Vetroy are dead, and their plot has died with them! Gather your honour, throw down your weapons, and come forth to be judged!"

From the ranks of the Dream Weavers, the Easterners who had surrendered in battle were shoved forward to stand before the Prince. Calls to, "Kill them! Kill them!" began to erupt out of the army at Gralyre's back, as other Eastern Rebels cautiously started to comply, leaving cover to step into the open.

With Oren's blood staining the ground before them, none dared to run nor sought to resist the Prince's edict. The clang of their falling swords, as they made a small mountain of their weapons, rang throughout the square, a counterpart to the jeers of the Northern survivors.

As more and more Eastern Rebels came out of hiding, Gralyre realized that there would not be enough room for all of the people in the fortress square. "To the western field!" Gralyre roared the order, using magic so that his voice would overcome the clamor.

Herding the prisoners before them, a surge of people began leaving the square like water from a basin when the stopper has been pulled. Following the flow of the current, Gralyre paused by the sick cart to lay a gentle hand upon Catrian's heaving shoulders. She did not acknowledge him. So he directed his words to Aneida, who still held Catrian in a comforting embrace. "Stay here. Keep her safe."

Aneida nodded. "O' course."

With clouts and sticks, rocks and offal, the Eastern Rebels were harried through the fortress to West Gate, and ushered through onto the enormous practice field.

When last Gralyre had been here, it had been the happy, sunny day of Commander Boris' tournament, a celebration of kinship and allegiances. Now it would be the site of a tribunal for the betrayal of those very values.

Arrayed to all sides, Dream Weaver warriors and Northern Rebels stood shoulder to shoulder, guarding against any attempts by the prisoners to flee their fate.

After the three thousand Eastern Rebels had assembled before him, Gralyre shrugged out of his baldric, and drew the Dragon Sword once more. The blade glimmered brilliantly, bringing light back into the gloaming that had crept down upon them in the last moments of the day.

Gralyre stood alone in the narrow space separating the Warriors of Lyre from the disgraced Eastern Rebels. "Kneel!" Gralyre commanded with thunderous intensity. He watched on with majestic hauteur as he was obeyed.

The blade whispered to Gralyre of ultimate power, enticing him to release his regal ire upon his enemies, to take revenge for the innocent slain. His nostrils flared and his chest expanded, as he breathed deeply, combatting his burgeoning desire to wield the magic until it burned everyone before him to cinders. He sought the coldness of the sword dance to quell his urges, that he might pass sound judgment upon the three thousand Rebel Warriors, abased and awaiting his decree.

"You have all participated in treasonous acts against Commander Boris and the Lady Catrian. Your actions have resulted in the deaths of men, women and children who were your allies!" Gralyre's voice thickened with disgust.

Many of the Eastern warriors hunched shamefully, and not a few of them wept with terror.

Silence held the field, as all present awaited the Prince's final edict. Among the onlooking Northerners, many drew swords and cudgels, and fingered the edges of axes in anticipation of unleashing their vengeance.

Gralyre turned his back on the condemned, and addressed his next words into the ranks of the Northern survivors. "Will any among you plead clemency for these prisoners?"

The condemning silence stretched, unbreached. Gralyre counted out the seconds before nodding his head once with acceptance. "So be it."

His face iced over, as he regarded the warriors kneeling before him. Iron filled his heart so that he might do what he must. So many men. It was a senseless waste upon the eve of the war to end all wars. Damn Kierdenan and Vetroy for leading their men into this plight. "Rebels of the East," Gralyre began. "You cannot dispute your crimes…"

"We were just following our orders!" an Easterner shouted in their defense before Gralyre could ratify their sentences. "Kierdenan would have killed anyone who had tried t' stop him!"

"So you were honourable men, following the orders of your General?" Gralyre asked smoothly.

A chorus of *'Aye'* pattered out of the assembly of prisoners.

"Honourable men," Gralyre trailed thoughtfully, considering their alibi. "I would put that to the test! I will spare you all, if but one among you will shoulder the sentence for these crimes." There was a restless stirring, as the prisoners looked to each other. "Just one," Gralyre reiterated softly, "who will sacrifice his or her life, so that the rest of you may live."

After a long, tense moment, a man stood up at the back of the throng of prisoners. "Here!" he shouted boldly over the heads of the kneeling. "I will die for my people."

"Come forward," Gralyre ordered.

Prisoners shuffled to the side, as the warrior strode through the kneeling host. His boot steps were overloud in the silence, crunching purposefully through the dirt and gravel of the field. Prisoners reached out to touch him as he neared, and a babble of gratitude followed after he passed. He stopped at the front of the crowd, and stood bravely before the Prince.

Gralyre eyed him grimly. "Give me your name."

He was a man of middle years, who still stood tall and strong. His short auburn hair was greying at the temples, and had receded to show a bald pate. His eyes were at a level with Gralyre's. An empty scabbard, designed to hold a long sword, hung at his hip. His heavily muscled arms were bare under a sleeveless tunic of fawn brown. He crossed them, as he answered, "My name is Tobias Illian."

"What is your rank within the Eastern Rebel forces?"

"Me?" Illian's chin dipped, and he shrugged a shoulder. "I am no one, just a soldier. I have fought for the resistance my entire life. So did my da, and his da afore him."

"You would trade your life for the lives of these men? These Eastern warriors?" Gralyre probed. "You will take their crimes upon your shoulders?"

Tobias nodded once, though waves of fear emanated from his brave front. "Aye," he vowed quietly, "I will." His jaw flexed, as he gritted his teeth in terror, having sealed his fate with his words. A slight tremor began in his body. "Kierdenan would have killed any o' us that had tried t' resist his order." He swept out an arm to indicate the amassed Eastern warriors at his back. "They do no' deserve t' die for obeying. 'Twould just be more ills atop that which has already happened here."

Gralyre closed the distance between them, and placed a heavy hand upon the Easterner's shoulder. "You are the bravest of men," he commended sorrowfully. "Kneel."

As Tobias Illian dropped to his knees, Gralyre's gaze seared over the thousands of prisoners genuflecting before him. "Let it be known that your lives are now owed to this man, Tobias Illian. May you discover in yourselves a thimbleful of his honour and courage, and not let his sacrifice be in vain."

Absolute stillness gripped the thousands of gathered people, as Gralyre stepped back, and raised his glowing blade for the blow that would take Illian's head. "By Tobias Illian's sacrifice and atonement, let the Northern Rebels be appeased of their losses. Upon this act, I declare an end of this conflict."

The brightness of the Dragon Sword became too intense to gaze upon, and the Prince and the condemned Rebel were engulfed in its radiance. It lasted for the count of ten, before dimming enough that the watchers could see two men again, one standing, one still kneeling.

A murmur of confusion broke the silence, as the light within the sword vanished, and Illian was revealed to still be alive. The flat of the Dragon Sword now rested upon his right shoulder.

"Arise, General Illian," Gralyre bade, as he dubbed his

opposite shoulder. "Arise and show your men what courage and honour is."

Tobias looked upward in confusion. "What? I do no' understand, Prince Gralyre."

"Your men have suffered under the leadership of those who were not worthy of them, those who would set brother against brother, and friend against friend. Your men need a General who will walk the righteous path, no matter the consequence, and inspire them to the same. You, General Illian, have proven yourself that man! Arise, Warrior of Lyre! I hereby pardon the lives of the Eastern Rebels for their part in Kierdenan and Vetroy's treason against the resistance, betrayal of their allies, and invasion of this fortress."

The Easterners wept and cheered at the realization that they were to be spared, and were well content with the man that the Prince had chosen to be their new General. The Northern survivors milled restlessly, confused and angered by what they considered an abrupt turn from justice.

As the din erupted around them, the new General hesitantly gained his feet, and his face shattered with emotion at the Prince's mercy. "Thank-ye, your Highness." He bowed low. "Thank-ye for my life... for the lives o' us all!"

Gralyre eyed him coldly. "Do not thank me, General. You have sworn to accept all responsibility for the transgressions of your men. Be warned. Their sins are now yours to carry."

"Kill him!" someone yelled contentiously from the onlookers, and it seemed to draw forth the venom from the coiling snake of their rage. Chants of "Death, Death, Death" spat from the crowd on all sides, leaving the disarmed Eastern Rebels craning their necks in fear.

Gralyre raised a brow, and pointed an admonishing finger at Illian. "Your sins, General," he reminded darkly.

Tobias stepped a couple of paces away from the Prince, and knelt once more, bowing his head humbly before the amassed survivors of the Northern Fortress. A path had opened where none had existed before, a way out of the dark betrayal that they had been forced to participate in, and he now needed to begin the hard atonement that would bring his people to forgiveness.

"Let him speak!" Gralyre roared, and the Northern Rebels obeyed, quieting to hear Tobias Illian's words.

"I ask your forgiveness, on behalf o' my men. Kierdenan's actions were his own, but I make no excuses for what we did here, for we followed him." The new General's words were overshadowed by screams of rage.

Gralyre cocked his head. Who would have thought the man to be so eloquent?

"We still believe in our just and worthy cause," Illian shouted to be heard. "We are allies o' old. For generations we have shared in the hardships o' war against the Usurper. Let such history no' be discarded!" He remained upon his knees, as the Northern Rebels bellowed loudly of their discontent. Words did little to heal the horrors they had suffered. They wanted blood.

"I said that I would spare their lives this day, not that there would be no punishment!" Gralyre roared. The survivors settled back in expectant silence.

"General Illian, I sentence you and your men to be in the forefront of all of the battles ahead. You will undertake the most dangerous of missions. You will be the shields we wear when we go to war, that you may repay the lives that you took, and redeem your honour."

The new General stood and bowed deeply to the Prince, and then to the amassed Northerners. It would seem that their sentence was to be death after all, but in honourable battle. At least it would not be an ignoble execution.

Some Northern Rebels clapped and cheered the Prince's justice while others booed loudly. Gralyre cared naught. It was a compromise that they would live with.

The sword whispered to him seductively. *'You are their Prince! How dare they jeer you? Your power will remind them of their station!'*

Gralyre gasped, as the desire to lay waste to all who would question his edict punched the wind from his lungs. The discontent of the crowds seemed louder, shriller. Tempted beyond reason, he raised the Dragon Sword, and compelled fire to erupt in a thick, twisting column that reached high into the darkening sky.

It was gratifying to hear screams and cries of terror. If he could not lead them to accept his right to lead, then by the Gods he would drive them! If that meant killing the lot of them, then so be it!

Some small corner of his soul retained the clarity to be

horrified by his intent. Would he really kill his own people for such a capricious reason? His hands trembled, as he fought for, and won back control over his burst of tyranny. He shivered, as he allowed his magic to ebb, and lowered the blade.

"Let it be known!" he roared into the stunned hush that followed. "We are no longer Eastern Rebels nor Northern Rebels, for I have returned, and we have been reborn as Warriors of Lyre! Let the past be finished, for your enemy is not the man standing beside you! Together let us march into Dreisenheld and kill Doaphin!" Gralyre pumped his fist into the air, not trusting himself to raise the sword again. "For Lyre!"

Slowly, they took up the call until the oaths of all echoed off the mountainside. *"For Lyre! For Lyre! For Lyre!"* The army had found its battle cry.

CHAPTER EIGHT

It was a tremulous beginning, but for the moment, peace ruled the night. Gralyre had provided scapegoats in the persons of General Kierdenan and Lieutenant Vetroy, so that the Northern Rebels could be appeased of their losses, and the Eastern Rebels could be forgiven for following the orders of their leaders against their allies. Though noticeably tense to be in each other's company, the bloodletting had ended, and all present keenly felt the release of their fears.

Resentments held by the Northern survivors eased further when the Eastern Rebels returned their pilfered supplies. Bedding and tents were welcomed, though it was the food that softened their adversity further. To this, the Dream Weavers added some of their own staples, and a small celebration ensued.

This uneasy truce had to be nurtured until it had matured enough to protect itself. Gralyre charged the Dream Weavers to patrol the fortress to dampen any sparks that might reignite the war. Legends walked amongst the Rebels, and their world would never be the same.

Gralyre claimed a clearing in the centre of the fortress square, from where he watched over the celebrations from his place of honour under a tarp. Visible to all, he provided a further deterrent to more fighting. Flanking Gralyre's fire were his most trusted people, save for Rewn and Trifyn.

Rewn had not yet awakened from his ordeal. Ninrhar, the Dream Weaver Healer, had repaired his damaged throat using his magic, and Rewn was now recovering in Saliana's healer's tent. Gralyre missed his friend's presence but took comfort that he would survive. Rewn and Saliana with knives to their throats was not a sight that Gralyre would ever forget.

Dara was pale with worry, her eyes travelling repeatedly to the sick tent where her brother convalesced. In an odd dance, she continuously stood and shifted the stump she sat upon further from Jacon's and then closer, as though unable to find a place of comfort.

Trifyn had been borne off to rest after the Easterners had surrendered. The trip up the mountainside to the fortress had caused his fever to spike, but Ninrhar and Saliana both seemed confident that he would recover.

Catrian should have joined Trifyn, but she had refused to seek her sick bed. She now drooped with weariness upon a small stool at Gralyre's side, as a show of power and support. Unforgiving of their fight that morning, Catrian maintained a condemning silence towards Gralyre. She stared into the flickering flames of the fire with morose intensity, shivering periodically, though a thick fur draped her shoulders for added warmth against the cooling of the night.

Gralyre's people smiled and laughed as they ate their dinners, as though it were a grand feast instead of meager rations. Gralyre brooded quietly, as he peered closely at his companions; the firelight painted faces both dear and familiar. Each and every one of them was now in danger, though they knew it not, simply because of their relationship to him. Most especially, Catrian.

Gralyre remained alert for attacks, as the newly formed Warriors of Lyre paraded past in a steady stream, paying homage. Northerner and Easterner both witnessed the Lost Prince in good company with the Sorceress, which helped reorder their opinion of Catrian as an ally, and not as an enemy to be traded away to Doaphin.

No matter her coldness, Gralyre was secretly glad Catrian was beside him, for were she to be out of his sight he would be stewing over her welfare. Her safety was still not assured until she had recovered sufficiently to protect herself.

After a time, Catrian listed on her stool, almost falling, and Gralyre leaned forward to steady her on her seat.

"Leave me! I am fine!" she snapped.

"You are not well! You have over-taxed yourself. You prove nothing further with your show of stubbornness. Go rest," Gralyre bade quietly, so that the passing people would not hear. He wished that he could wrap his arms around her to soothe her grief over Boris and Matik, and to keep her warm against his side. But he had relinquished that right.

"Aneida?" Gralyre beckoned her to come assist the Sorceress.

"Jacon, post a guard on Catrian's tent…" he began to order the Dream Weaver.

"No." Catrian did not elaborate beyond the glare she shot Gralyre's way.

Aneida and Jacon both subsided back into their seats. They

recognized when not to step into the tangled crossfire between two strong-willed and powerful beings.

"Make way! Let us through!" Across the square, the call went up, and people jostled each other to part for four men holding a blanket drawn taut between them with a body suspended within its folds. "Call for the Healer! He yet lives!" One of the men yelled, as they sped towards them.

Saliana was up in a flash, and running to meet the stretcher. "Gods!" she breathed, as she recognized who they had found. "'Tis Matik!" she yelled over to Gralyre and Catrian.

Gralyre, Dotch and Jord rushed to Saliana's side at the news, adding their muscle to those already carrying the injured man towards the healer's tent. Jacon and Aneida stayed back to safeguard the Sorceress at the fire.

"Matik!" Catrian cried out in wild joy. She struggled to her feet, though she teetered unsteadily.

Aneida was there to sling an arm around Catrian's waist for support before she fell. "I have ye," Aneida promised.

This time Catrian welcomed her assistance. "Aneida, I must get t' him! Help me!"

"Come then, 'tis only a small distance." She braced her shoulder under Catrian's arm to keep her upright, and helped her to hobble weakly after the stretcher.

Jacon kept his hand near to his sword, as he followed closely behind them. His eyes played over all who passed, alert to any aggression.

Within steps, Catrian's quivering legs were failing, and

Aneida was hefting more and more of her slight weight to drag her onwards.

More than one Rebel witnessed Catrian's feebleness, and recognized that if she had not the strength to walk, then rumours of her illness had been true. She had not had the potency to summon a Stalker. Their certainty of her treachery was further eroded.

Still, there were others who viewed her vulnerability as an opportunity, and made their plans from the shadows.

Within the healer's tent, an unconscious Rewn was quickly transferred from the examination table onto a cot, to leave his spot vacant for Matik's more critical injuries. Saliana had placed the table there earlier in the day to ease the strain on her back from an afternoon spent bending to tend wounds.

"Put him on the table," Saliana ordered the men who had found Matik. "Gently!" she cautioned, as they lifted the blanket-suspended General up onto the hard surface. "Well done," she praised, "now go get some food."

"Aye, miss."

"Thank-ye, miss."

"How bad is he?" Catrian demanded, as she and Aneida crowded into the tent. "Will he live?" Dire hope lived in her eyes. How much worse it would be to have him snatched from her again after already grieving his death this day!

Saliana scarcely acknowledged Catrian. "Fetch lamps."

As the stretcher-bearers left, Jacon took up position outside the entrance to the tent, an intimidation to hold back the curious.

Within moments, two more of his Dream Weaver warriors had flanked him.

More lanterns were sparked to chase the shadows away from the corners. By the increased light, the General's flesh appeared tinged with blue. Saliana hovered over Matik, her hands sure, as she parted the blood-matted hair of his thick brown beard to reveal a gaping wound at his throat that stretched from ear to ear. The shallow rise and fall of Matik's chest, and the whistling breaths flowing in and out of the gash, bespoke the presence of life. Tendons and ragged flesh, impossibly, still seeped blood even though the material of his shirt and trousers was stiff and crusted.

"His throat is cut," Aneida rasped, her hand rising unconsciously to brush against the old scar upon her own neck.

Saliana's attention was momentarily caught by Rewn's moan of pain, from where he had been placed upon a cot across the tent. His neck was still welted red and swollen from his garrotting. A newly healed scar at the hollow of his throat was still ringed by dried blood. She shuddered from the thought that were it not for the Gods own luck, he would have suffered Matik's fate.

Gralyre shook his head in grim amazement. "Only Matik would survive having his throat slit."

He wished back his thoughtless comment when Catrian flinched. Matik was Catrian's loyal friend and protector. For that, and no other reason, if the cantankerous whoreson lived, Gralyre would make his peace.

Saliana regarded Gralyre with grave concern. "This is t' much for me. I need Ninrhar."

"I have come," the Dream Weaver healer announced, as he entered into the tent unexpectedly. "Gedrhar sensed your need," he explained.

Jacon arrived in the healer's wake, and sought Gralyre immediately. "My father would have a word with you, Prince Gralyre," he requested quietly. "'Tis a matter of much urgency."

Gralyre nodded. "In a moment."

Dotch fetched Catrian a stool so that she could sit at the tableside, and Aneida helped her to the seat. Catrian picked up Matik's cold hand, and pressed it to her cheek to warm it. Her eyes were rimmed red from exhaustion and the tears she had shed earlier over his and her uncle's deaths. That Matik had survived seemed a miracle sent from the Gods of Fortune. She clenched his hand tighter, her face fiercely determined, as though she could will him to live.

Sorry for causing her distress, Gralyre placed a hand on Catrian's shoulder. He squeezed tenderly in support, but she shrugged out from under its weight.

Gralyre's hand clenched into a fist, and he backed away, perversely relieved to be escaping her resentment. "Catrian, go nowhere without an escort, and eat nothing unless it has been brought to you by my people." In his displeasure, his words emerged with an autocratic overtone. "Trust no other, unless they are Dream Weavers."

Catrian's eyes narrowed at his lecture. "Do ye think me

witless? I am no' blind t' my danger."

Gralyre nodded tightly, uncertain of the new dynamic between them. He caught Aneida's eye. "Stay with Catrian."

"Aye," Aneida nodded. "I will keep her safe."

"Gralyre, I do no' need a minder!" Catrian snapped.

"Until you are fully recovered, and can use your magic, you are vulnerable. This is not open for negotiation, Catrian!" Gralyre commanded imperiously, every inch the Prince. "I will return soon." He escaped her scornful glare by following Jacon from the tent.

Of no further use, Dotch and Jord also left, rejoining Dara and Dotch's family who awaited their return at their fire.

୫୦ଓ

Within the Wizard Stone

The ancient sorcerer draws back into his Wizard Stone, a spider in its lair, lest Gedrhar note his presence when Gralyre meets with him.

To prepare the vessel, the Prince must be isolated from all those he cares for and who care for him. Alone, bereft, he will be less able to resist possession.

The Sorceress must be dealt with.

୫୦ଓ

Jacon and Gralyre spoke little, as they walked towards the East Sector of the ruined fortress, which had been claimed by the Dream Weaver army for their encampment. Debris had been cleared away, and supplanted by neat rows of cone shaped tents.

The pavilions were uniformly alike in their anonymity, yet Jacon approached one of the tents with confidence. He held the flap back so that Gralyre could precede him within.

As Gralyre entered Gedrhar's tent, the elder, his face contorted with outrage, confronted him. "What have you done, *unticol?*"

Gralyre halted in surprise at the unexpected reception, and his brows shot upward. The Prince in him reared his head proudly, as he glared at the old man. No matter what he had caused to happen, who was Gedrhar to demand he answer for it?

"To what do you refer?" Gralyre challenged icily. From the sheath against his back, his shoulder blades itched from the prickling presence of the sword's magic awakening at the first whiff of conflict.

Gedrhar's hands thrust out, and he was suddenly a supplicant begging an explanation while tears threatened his eyes. "You claimed the Godsmagic of those arrows! You took from them *all*! They are *no longer* because of you!" his voice grew more emotional as he spoke, and he stumbled backwards to a small, three-legged stool, collapsing onto it with a fretful sigh.

"I stopped those arrows from killing us!" Gralyre snapped, his regal ire leaching into his voice.

"What you did is forbidden! A corruption! Did your mother

teach you nothing of the Thewr 'ap Noir?"

Gralyre waved his hand dismissively. "My mother died when I was very young. What is the Thewr 'ap Noir? It means "sharing of dreams", does it not?"

"A literal translation," Gedrhar agreed sorrowfully. He motioned Gralyre towards the empty stool that sat opposite to his.

The sword's powerful draw subsided, and Gralyre's anger abated with it. He frowned at the elder's obvious aguish. Gedrhar was genuinely disturbed, but by what? As he settled onto the indicated stool, Gralyre shrugged helplessly towards Jacon who had taken up a position near the exit.

Jacon cleared his throat, and crossed his arms across his chest. "Father, he does not understand. You must explain it to him, as to an outsider."

Gedrhar mumbled into his trimmed white beard, as he stroked it urgently. "Yes, of course he needs a context so that he will grasp it…" He cleared his throat as, with a voice full of wisdom and age, he began to school Gralyre on the hereditary magic of the Dream Weavers.

"The Thewr 'ap Noir is the Deep Dreaming, a realm as real as this waking world. It shapes the destiny of our people. We see far into the future or into the past because its magic is beyond time, and every Dream Weaver who has ever been, or ever will be is heir to its power. It is within you, and you are within it."

Gralyre leaned forward, as curiosity overcame him, and rested his elbows along his thighs. "So… 'tis like a Wizard

Stone that everyone shares in?"

Gedrhar shook his head. "No. We hold no artificial link to the Dreaming."

Gralyre grew excited, imagining a Dream Weaver army of sorcerers. Together they would be able to crush Doaphin and restore the realm of Lyre! "Do all Dream Weavers have the ability to harness its power? Are you all sorcerers?"

"Not all, only some, just as with the people of your kingdom. You truly do not know this?" Gedrhar quizzed sceptically. "You do not remember? Your mother would have taught this to you."

Gralyre suffered the small disappointment, as he rubbed his brow. "My remembrance of my mother is vague. I was only six years old when she died."

Gedrhar stabbed a finger in Gralyre's direction. "The Thewr 'ap Noir is your birthright, *unticol*. Your mother was a Dream Weaver. So you are an heir to its power."

"My Godsmagic never seems to ebb. Is this because I am tapping the power within the Thewr 'ap Noir? Catrian wondered at my strength in magic, and once sought for my link to a Wizard Stone. Yet she found nothing."

Gedrhar sighed, and frowned. "Yes, though you have been using it unwisely. The Godsmagic of the Thewr 'ap Noir should never be spent that it is not then reclaimed."

Gralyre shrugged. "That is not possible. Power flows out. It never returns. If you pour from a cup it is gone." What he knew of the different energies wielded by sorcery had been learned of within the pages of Catrian's limited library. The practice of sorcery was the manipulation of the Godsmagic within to connect to and alter the Godsmagic of the world without. "If one uses too much at once it leaves one weakened. It is finite, and can be exhausted to the point of death," Gralyre recited from memory. "'Tis what happened to Catrian when she made her storm. It sapped her strength."

Gedrhar tsked under his breath. "The way you and that woman spend Godsmagic, aye, it will drain quickly enough."

Gralyre glared at the criticism. "It does us well enough if we are careful."

Gedrhar steepled his hands before his mouth, and watched Gralyre closely. "The energies of Godsmagic cannot be destroyed…"

"…only altered," Gralyre finished the first rule of sorcery.

Gedrhar nodded, and his hands dropped away. "I dreamed of a wagon in the Thewr 'ap Noir for your injured companions to ride in, and caused it to be birthed into the world. Now the wagon is no more, for I reclaimed its Godsmagic, and returned it to the Dreaming."

"As I reclaimed the arrows?" Gralyre frowned, momentarily setting aside all questions about the act of creation that Gedrhar was describing. It flew in the face of all his knowledge of sorcery.

"No! Not like that!" Gedrhar snapped. "I reclaimed only that which has always been ours! You reclaimed that to which you had no right!"

The light of understanding entered Gralyre's eyes. "Ah… I

did not create those arrows, so by reclaiming them…"

"You stole the magic that belongs only to the Gods! For the Gods dreamed the arrows into existence, as they dreamed us all! Every tree, grass, rock and mountain, every tear from an eye, every bird on the wing!"

Gralyre motioned that he understood, lest Gedrhar list all of creation. All of creation; those words now held new meaning. Gralyre bowed his head in thought, considering the time when Catrian had dissolved his beard from his face.

They had been saying their farewells, so many months ago, before the journey to Fennick's Island. Matik had interrupted their tender moment with harsh condemnations. In a petty, but gratifying, act of retaliation, Gralyre had replicated her sorcery to divest Matik of his clothes, before commanding a horse to drag his naked body through the snow and slush.

Inexperienced, and trying to reproduce Catrian's sorcery, he now realized that he had stumbled upon his first claiming of Godsmagic. Within Gedrhar's explanation, he now recognized the difference. Catrian had not claimed Godsmagic, she had only altered his beard's energies into another form - that of air.

"But why is this forbidden?" Gralyre was still confused over Gedrhar's distress. "Would not adding Godsmagic to the Thewr 'ap Noir increase its power tenfold?"

"How powerful must it be? When would it be enough? When would you stop, *unticol*? With the claiming of a tree? A stone? A mountain? A life? The lives of an entire kingdom?" Gedrhar's lips pulled back from his teeth in feral warning. "Drunk on power would you claim the entire world? Would you seek a throne beside the Gods?"

Gralyre drew back in alarm at the rapid-fire condemnations. He thought of the insane power held within the Dragon Sword that sought to corrupt his best intentions with each use. Unlimited strength demanded a terrible price.

Gedrhar quieted, and his voice became pleading once more. "The Thewr 'ap Noir is pure! Its power is the Godsmagic given of freely by every man, woman and child who dreams the Deep Dream. The magic of the Dream Weavers is never diminished or destroyed, it simply is!

"This is why Doaphin has never been able to conquer our lands. He is not of Dream Weaver heritage. He has no way of tapping our power. However," Gedrhar warned, "if corruption were to enter the Thewr 'ap Noir, by one of us reclaiming a Godsmagic that is not our own, like a sickness entering a healthy body it would destroy our people, in the past, the present and the future!"

Gralyre grew alarmed at the consequences he had skirted when he had claimed the Godsmagic of the arrows. "I am sorry Gedrhar, I did not understand. I do now. It will never happen again," he promised humbly.

"I must teach you, *unticol*. I see that now. Your mistake was one of ignorance, a child's first stumbling steps. I should not have been so harsh with you."

Unticol, Gedrhar had called him again. Uncle. Gralyre's mother's sister's great, great, great, grandson, so many generations removed that it scarcely mattered. Yet still, it filled an empty, yawning hole in Gralyre's centre, present since he had awakened with no memories almost a year ago. He was not alone. He had a family, and somehow, against all odds, they had found him.

"You speak of being able to see the future of things in the Thewr 'ap Noir. Can you tell me... is Doaphin defeated?" Gralyre asked hesitantly.

Gedrhar's gaze dropped, and he hummed under his breath for a moment. "It is unclear."

Gralyre sat upright with a harsh breath of exasperation. "Then tell me of my own future, seer!"

Gedrhar's brows snapped together at the royal demand. "As I have said, it is unclear." When Gralyre opened his mouth to comment further, Gedrhar forestalled him with a raised palm. "Allow me to clarify. When you were a boy, your presence within the Thewr 'ap Noir was sharp and bright. Even then, you were showing promise of possessing extraordinary gifts. Then, inexplicably," Gedrhar snapped his fingers, "you vanished. Such a thing has never happened before."

"When Fennick sent me forward in time..."

"No, this occurred well before that event. Your presence in the Dreaming ceased to exist soon after your mother died."

Gralyre shivered from the whiff of a memory that he could not quite capture, like an ember on a breeze that collapsed to naught but a smear of soot within one's grasp. "As though I had never been born?" he mused quietly.

"Yes," Gedrhar agreed, "as though you had never existed. There was no trace of you in the past, present or future. Had there not been tales of your deeds and bravery in the waking world, and had your mother's memories not been filled with thoughts of you, not one Dream Weaver could have confirmed that you had ever been."

Gralyre's throat tightened, and his eyes stung. "You speak of my mother," he was overwhelmed by the idea of the continuance of her existence.

"Of course, for is she not Dream Weaver? Her soul is safe within the realm of the Thewr 'ap Noir," Gedrhar assured. "We do not know what happened to you. It has been a question of some debate for centuries. It is as though everything that made you an heir to the Thewr ap' Noir was sundered from your soul."

"That would be why the legends never mention my sorcery?" Gralyre nodded in answer to his own question.

"For three hundred years, there was nothing," Gedrhar continued, as though he had not been interrupted, "until almost a year ago, when you suddenly reappeared in the Thewr ap' Noir; grown to manhood as though you had sprung from the womb in that state. Your power was impressive and unmistakable. The promise of the child had grown to fruition in the man. It was then that the Dream Weavers mobilized to come to your aid."

"And in the future? What of my presence in the Dreaming, Gedrhar?"

"You vanish once more. You experience sacrifice, and pain. Then there is nothing."

"When?"

"Not long now."

"Dead then? Or missing, as when I was a child?"

Gedrhar regarded him with deep compassion. "I cannot say. You are a man who does not belong in this time. Perhaps the Gods will reclaim you when your task for them is complete."

Gralyre shuddered at Gedrhar's dire prediction. "Can you teach me to see the future for myself?"

Gedrhar smiled, lightening the dark turn of their conversation. "Of course! It is easy enough to do." He spoke casually of this great magic, as though it were a mere trivia. "You need only ask the Dreamers, and they will tell you what they know to be true."

"How do I do that?"

"Within you is a lake of silver power..."

"Aye, my Godsmagic. As I mentioned earlier, Catrian has looked there before but seen no tie to a Wizard Stone, or to any other place."

"The Thewr 'ap Noir is not in another place," Gedrhar chided gently. "You will not find it somewhere," he gestured to the air, "out there." He pressed his hands to his heart. "It is within. Seek within your Godsmagic pool. Dive deep, deep, deep! Deeper than you have ever gone, and then..." He paused and his face assumed a sublime glow, "you will see them."

Gralyre was fascinated by Gedrhar's bliss. "Who?"

Gedrhar smiled beatifically. "The Godwombs of the Dream Weavers. All of them. Every Dreamer who has ever been. Every

Dreamer who will ever be. They are all within you, and you are within all of them. This is your birthright, *unticol*. This is what it is to be Dream Weaver. This is what it is to dream the Deep Dream."

Intrigued, Gralyre closed his eyes, and sought his place of power, the spreading pool of Godsmagic deep in the core of his soul where the massive tree of his consciousness rooted within its silver waters.

He paused in wonderment when he arrived. His Tree of Life was so verdant now, so lush, much changed from his last experience of this idealized place. Its spreading branches held his entire life on display, each leaf shimmering with a different memory. Though it drew him to explore and revel in his emergent past, this was not what he had come to experience.

His consciousness dove into his lake of silver, the pure light of his Godsmagic. Down he swam, or flew perhaps, for it was not as liquid, and his body breathed with no distress.

"Gedrhar, how far do I go?" Gralyre asked, and heard his words from a great distance.

"Seek the far away bottom of your lake, *unticol*," Gedrhar encouraged, and his voice sounded like an echo of a dream.

Gralyre continued to dive, or was he swimming upwards? It seemed the same. He spied a flash of gold deeper within the silver light of his Godsmagic. Like a fish after a lure, he pursued it. He broke the surface, and the might of the Thewr 'ap Noir was revealed to his awestruck gaze.

Billions of golden orbs, some small as a hand, others large as a man, bobbed in amber light. It was as though a universe of suns had been placed within his soul. The orbs floated like bubbles in a tankard of ale, an inadequate comparison, but Gralyre had no words for what he was seeing.

He approached one of the larger orbs, and peered within. Bathed in golden light lay the body of a man, curled like a baby in sleep. Gralyre brushed against the surface, and found it warm and soft, like the skin of an infant, a golden womb. A Godwomb, just as Gedrhar had called it, Gralyre thought with wonderment.

Memories flooded his awareness, momentarily supplanting his own identity. Gralyre became Horvod, and he was a wheelwright, and he lived a hundred and thirty-two years from now. His wife's name, the names of his children, his neighbours, his aspirations, even what he had eaten that day for breakfast, all became as Gralyre's memories, as real as if he were living them himself. When Gralyre withdrew his hand from the surface of the Godwomb, Horvod's presence faded.

Stunned by the experience, Gralyre hovered within the universe of the Thewr 'ap Noir, gaping at the vast glory of its power. Within each Godwomb, lay the curled soul of a Dream Weaver: some old, some young, some only now growing beneath their mother's hearts. Some were living in the present, some were living in the far past, and some, like Horvod, were alive in the future. All of it was happening at the same time. Time. It was meaningless here.

There were as many Godwombs as there were stars in the sky, and each orb radiated power that was feeding the silver pool of Gralyre's Godsmagic. Now he understood why he never tired, as Catrian did, after great expenditures of magic.

In the near distance, Gralyre's attention was caught by an orb of a deeper, richer hue of gold that flashed with overtones of magenta. "Gedrhar, I see a different Dreamer." He drifted nearer, and spied a familiar soul curled within. "'Tis Ninrhar!" He brushed his fingers against the skin of the orb, and for the moment became the Dream Weaver healer, heir to all of his experiences and knowledge.

Gedrhar's words drifted to him over the distance. "These are the Dreamers with the ability to tap the Godsmagic of the Thewr 'ap Noir. What you call Sorcerers."

Gralyre left the world of the Deep Dreaming behind, and opened his eyes to the mundane world of the tent. He was overcome by what he had experienced. "I did not see myself there."

Gedrhar smiled. "It is not possible to see oneself among the other Dreamers. Within me, I can see your golden light, and it blazes like a star, brighter than any I have ever seen."

"There are so many. Endless golden orbs. How do you find the ones that hold the answers you seek?"

"Practice and patience. The Godwombs tend to drift together into clusters of shared experiences. Families will often group, for example, or people within a village, lovers, or armies."

Gralyre now fully understood the danger of what he had done with the arrows. Were evil ever to gain a foothold within the universe of the Thewr 'ap Noir it would have the ultimate power to destroy the Dream Weaver people. "Gedrhar, what would happen if too much Godsmagic were drawn from the Thewr 'ap Noir?" Gralyre asked though he already suspected the truth.

"Just as your Sorceress was drained of her powers to the point of death, the lights of the Dreamers would extinguish. All of them. All Dream Weavers who have been, who are, and who ever shall be would perish."

෨෬

Saliana held a lantern high to spread its light, and memorized all that Ninrhar did, as he tended to Matik's wounds.

"Will he live?" Catrian asked with a catch in her voice. Aneida stood close to her shoulder, offering silent support.

"If he is strong," the Dream Weaver healer, Ninrhar, pronounced kindly in the strangely accented tones of his people.

"Here," he pointed, speaking to Saliana now, "must be kept clean and clear. See how he breathes through this place. We will leave it open until more swelling leaves the flesh of his throat."

"Why no' just use your magic t' heal him fully?" Saliana asked. "Like ye did with Rewn?"

Ninrhar smiled. "Magic is not the answer to everything, just the easy way. Take yourself, young miss. If someone had waved a magic stick at you, and all problems had vanished, you would not be so strong as you are now."

Saliana smiled shyly. "Me? I am no' strong."

Ninrhar shook his head at her obtuse avowal.

"How does your healing magic work?" Catrian asked. All that she knew of sorcery was self-taught after reading from less than a dozen books that had been recovered over the years during foraging expeditions into the lowlands. Being with the Dream Weavers presented her with an unforeseen opportunity to learn more of the nature of her gifts. Save for Gralyre, with whom she had shared her library of knowledge, Catrian had never had the opportunity to study another's sorcery at work. Battling Demon Lords did not count for much.

"I do not heal them, as such, I merely realign a patient's Godsmagic to encourage their body to heal itself," Ninrhar answered. "Had Matik been brought to me immediately after his assault, before his Godsmagic had depleted from keeping him alive, I could have healed him in full, as I did with Rewn. For this," he indicated Matik's torn throat, "the patient must heal in stages, as his body strengthens and restores its Godsmagic. Else I will be making a corpse, not a hale warrior. You know the dangers of which I speak."

Catrian nodded and shivered. Her full strength was still many weeks away. Had Gralyre not arrived when he had to replenish some of her Godsmagic, she would not have survived. She had lain as one dead for a fortnight. Breath had barely stirred, her heartbeat had slowed, and her soul had fled to her Wizard Stone. Death was the cost of exhausting a body's Godsmagic, even for one who did not practice Sorcery.

"For now, I will stop the bleeding and encourage him to make more blood," Ninrhar continued, "but the rest must await his return of strength."

Ninrhar bent to his work, describing for Saliana how the arteries circulated the body's blood, how the tendons moved muscle, and the tools that could be used to repair the damage seen before them.

Saliana absorbed all of the knowledge, watching the surgery closely. It was truly amazing. Everything fit together, like a puzzle. It made sense.

Catrian tried to observe the subtle play of Godsmagic between Ninrhar and Matik, yet she never once sensed the use of the Dream Weaver's power. It was as Ninrhar had described to her, yet he spent none of his own magic to accomplish his task. The healer realigned Matik's Godsmagic in a certain pattern, nothing more, yet when he was done, Matik's neck had ceased to bleed, and his breath was steadier. Though she had paid close attention, Catrian was left unsure of how Ninrhar had accomplished the feat. She had never seen such a thing, nor read of it in her books.

"Ah, pardon me," Rewn spoke up from his bed in the corner, his voice raspy from the contusion that spanned his throat. "I hate t' interrupt but it sounds as though ye have done what ye can for Matik. Could ye…?" Rewn waggled his fingers at the massive bruise on the side of his head.

"Rewn! Ye are awake!" Saliana rushed to his bedside, her face alight with relief.

"Welcome back, Rewn!" Aneida grinned, forgetting her grief for Mayvin in her happiness at his survival.

Rewn lifted his hand to touch the pink scar tissue at his throat. "I thought that I had died."

"No' quite all the way dead," Saliana smiled blurrily at him.

Leaving Catrian to watch closely over General Matik, Ninrhar crouched down at Rewn's bedside. "Young miss, the lantern please."

Saliana lifted her light high again, and Rewn winced away from the brightness.

"I shall describe to you what happens to a man when his head is struck," Ninrhar advised, as his fingers probed gently against the swelling on Rewn's face.

"Owe!" Rewn flinched back.

"Did the blow send you into blackness, Master Rewn?"

"Aye. Hurts like a herd o' Deathren are gnawing on me!"

"When one is hit hard enough in the head," Ninrhar explained to Saliana, "it is similar to what occurs when breaking an egg upon the edge of a skillet. If the shell cracks in the wrong way, or too much force is used to shatter it, the yolk emerges scrambled. It is the same when a head is struck. The brain slams into the inside of the skull, to bruise or to bleed. It can cause unconsciousness, and be quite dangerous, especially if the skull is broken with jagged edges."

Rewn gagged.

"Nausea is one of the first minor symptoms of a larger problem you must watch for," Ninrhar's lecture continued without pause or excitement, though he reached back for a leather pail, and dropped it into Rewn's lap as a precaution. "It does not seem to me that your skull has cracked, young warrior. With rest you will be fine in a few days."

Saliana's eyes were bright with interest.

Rewn was left feeling sorry that he had ever drawn their attention, as he bent his head into the bucket.

ℰℭ

Returned from his audience with Gedrhar, Gralyre reclaimed his previous spot in the centre square, under the tarp next to the crackling fire. His troubled gaze rested upon the brightly lighted healer's tent where, cast against the oiled canvas sides, multiple shadows could be seen working over their patient.

Gralyre would have checked on Rewn and Matik's wellbeing, but Catrian's anger made him leery of being in the same space with her again. He did not wish to cause her more pain.

She was protected for now. Two Dream Weaver sentries had taken position to either side of the entrance to the healer's tent, and Aneida stood sentinel at her side. It was the safest Gralyre could make Catrian without keeping her under lock and key until she was fully recovered.

Gralyre's spirits lifted slightly, as his attention crossed the flickering fire towards Dotch, who was swapping adventurous stories with his wife and sons. A crowd of Rebels, Eastern and Northern both, had gathered around the fringes of their firelight to hear the tale of their quest to Fennick's Island for the Dragon Sword of Lyre, and the subsequent return of the Lost Prince.

Dotch was a born storyteller, and his vivid and entertaining account held his audience rapt. His cheeks were reddened from a combination of drink and the cool wind. One arm was draped loosely around Ella, snugging her into his side. His boys sat at his feet, watching his every movement and heeding every word with awestruck joy, as Dotch described Gralyre's instructions in weaponry during their journey south.

Gralyre's mouth curled with humour, as he watched Dotch miming the search for his lost sword in the brambles alongside Aneida and Mayvin.

Jord laughed heartily, before drinking deeply from his tankard. The audience, sitting at the fringes of the firelight, chuckled in appreciation of the portrayal.

Despite the entertaining account, Gralyre was oddly detached from Dotch's storytelling, as though he had not played an integral role in the events. He felt isolated from the people around him, and sought the source of his ennui.

It was not just his fight with Catrian. It was the sword. Even without touching it, the magic reached out to him, beckoned to him, and whispered seductively of its powers.

He remembered when last he had worn this sword, less than a year ago to his memory of it, yet in reality three hundred years past, in battle against Doaphin's army. It had been just a weapon then, one that he had trained himself to wield as a master. But now it held magical dangers more terrible than Doaphin himself.

He now knew that it was the battle of Centaur Pass that haunted him: the crushing defeat he had suffered, the deaths of his men, his beheading. This one catastrophic event had held the power to seep through the black wall that had hidden away his past, even if only in his nightmares. Gralyre shivered, and pulled his cloak closer. Knowing them to be genuine, and not the fevered conjurings of madness, did not lessen their power, as he shied away from the vivid horror of the memory.

He should never have trusted Fennick or the letter that he had delivered from the King. Though the message contained the last words of his father, words that Gralyre had long since memorized, words that indeed seemed seared into his very soul, he cursed them violently for they formed an unbreakable chain of honour that bound him inexorably to the past.

My dearest son,

By the time Lord Fennick reaches you with this message, your father and King will be dead. Long live the King.

We are betrayed from within, though by whom, we know naught. We have retreated to the Keep, and will surely be overrun by first light. Our garrison is crushed, and we have been forced to collapse all but our personal escape tunnel to keep the sappers at bay. We have taken a grievous wound, and shall make our last stand within our stronghold. We send to you what troops we can spare, and our friend Lord Fennick. He brings to you the seal of our house lest it become a trophy for the cursed usurper.

Lord Fennick carries vital knowledge that we dare not

state in this missive lest it fall into enemy hands. He will tell you all. We pray to the Gods of Fortune that he can help you turn the tide of this war. It is too late for Dreisenheld, but perhaps you may yet live to avenge us.

Forgive an old fool who would not heed your words of warning until it was too late. Your affianced Lady keeps a vigil by our deathbed and tends the wounded. She would not leave with the other innocents. Though we both know that when Doaphin's horde enters the keep all within will die, she refuses to use the escape tunnel to save herself.

She sends her deepest respect and love, and hopes you will keep yourself safe in these dangerous times. Be not aggrieved by her choice, my son, for she does us all a great honour. Her beauty and courage has rallied the men's spirits, and perhaps given us the strength to keep Doaphin at bay long enough for Lord Fennick to make good his escape.

What a Queen she would have made you!

Long live the King!

Gralyre sighed heavily, rubbing a tired hand over his face. *Your affianced Lady...* Those three words destroyed all of his hopes for the future he had woven around Catrian.

Princess Genevieve, trapped in a crystal pillar in the palace of Dreisenheld. Trapped for all time by Doaphin. The woman that his father had pledged him to marry. His obligation.

Gralyre recalled their first meeting...

ՑՕՑՉ

Gralyre's Past

...The lights of a thousand tapers flood the ballroom. Glittering prisms reflect from the crystals adorning the barge sized chandeliers floating from golden chains anchored into the soaring, coved ceilings. Mirrors along the walls reflect back the brilliance, intensifying it to the point of pain. It is not helping my headache.

I stand against the wall, dressed in black, in subtle defiance to my father's command that I attend the revelries. I have ensured that the King has noted his son's compliance. I calculate that I need only stand here for an hour longer before I can flee without consequence.

How I hate these state affairs. And this one is more onerous than most.

The delegation from the Southern Kingdoms has arrived, and father has been extravagant with his imperial welcome. Whirling, drunken nobles in overdone costumes flow over the dance floor, to the trumpets and strings of the royal orchestra hidden in an alcove above.

The vapid, blond Southern Princess swans past on the arm of a duke of something or other that I had not bothered to learn. What is her name? Something similar to Geese? It definitely starts with a 'G'.

She simpers at me, and hides her smile behind a painted fan with coquettish flair, a well-practiced motion. Excellent of pedigree, excruciating of personality.

I am polite. I nod regally to her. Why must I attend these affairs? Surely, I can slip away soon?

"Silence!" roars the King, and the orchestra ends their latest tune with a flourish. Father arises from the throne, and the assembly drops into deep bows of respect. "Where is the Prince? Where is Gralyre? Step forward." His words are slurred and his stance wobbles. He is already deep into his cups. I cannot recall ever seeing my father sober.

Fennick stands to the left of the King's throne. As always. There to discipline should the Prince show defiance. I supress a shudder of hatred, as the Sorcerer's gaze settles upon me like a cat spotting a rat in the wainscoting.

With everyone genuflecting, there is no hiding, so I sigh heavily and push away from the wall. The crowds part, as I approach the dais from where the King commands the room. "Father," I bow deeply. "Majesty, I am here."

The King's mouth tightens, as he regards the sombre black dress that his son is wearing.

Inside, I smile, though I dare not let the King suspect my defiance. The night is not a complete waste after all…

Jord's attention was diverted from Dotch's story when he noted a strange red glow painting the side of Gralyre's face. The light emanated from the large ruby on the sword strapped to his back. Jord shrugged away the phenomena, assuming that the gem was somehow reflecting back the light of the campfire.

Gralyre was not participating in the revelry. The Prince sat alone across the flames, deeply ensnared by his own thoughts. His eyes were fixed and staring.

Jord felt a momentary pang of compassion. He did not envy Gralyre's new status and resultant cares that weighed so heavily upon his shoulders.

Dotch reached the part of their journey where they had battled the Deathren army in the Bleak, drawing Jord's attention back to the epic tale of their journey to Fennick's Island.

೫∞೪

A droning hum in Gralyre's head softened and reshaped the memories of his first meeting with the Princess. There was a brief sensation of falling, or of a shifting of a landscape, but his momentary alarm was quickly soothed, his attention recaptured by his recollections of an angel.

೫∞೪

Within the Wizard Stone

... Fennick stands to the left of his father's throne. As always. There is much approval and pride in his gaze, as Gralyre walks

through the genuflecting nobles.

The crowds part, as Gralyre approaches the dais from where his father commands the room. "Father," he bows respectably.

The King smiles lovingly at his son, and his arms spread wide. "My people, it is time that my son should marry."

Gasps and smiles abound, and a pattering of applause results.

Gralyre straightens, knowing what is to come, and excitement blooms in his chest, as he watches the King beckon to a petite, blond lady in the front of the throng.

The beautiful creature he had previously noted, the Southern Princess, Genevieve, steps gracefully up to his side. Her skin is like cream, and her eyes are blue sapphires, shimmering in the lights of the crystal chandeliers.

Gralyre smiles and bows over her hand, placing a warm kiss upon her palm. When he straightens, he looks to the King. "Father, I am well content…"

೮೧೮೩

A slight ringing in his ears drew Gralyre back to his present, and he shook his head to clear the cobwebs of the past. His brow began a dull ache that quickly escalated to a sharp knocking behind his eyes. He must have nodded off. He kept losing track of Dotch's adventurous tale. When had the companions reached the Labyrinth? Gralyre pinched the bridge of his nose in pain.

"Gralyre, are ye alright?" Jord asked from across the

campfire. The ruby had ceased to glow, he noted in passing. Gralyre must have shifted in his seat so that the firelight no longer reflected through the gem, as it had before.

Gralyre shook his head. "I think I am but exhausted. I bid you good ev'en," he said politely as he stood. As the others made to stand in respect, he motioned them to remain seated. Calling Little Wolf to his side, he stepped away from the light into the darkness. The night suited his mood much better, he decided, as he sought his tent, and its lonely bed.

He lay in the dark for a long time, waiting out the moments for his head to cease pounding. Listening to the sounds of celebration in the square, he again suffered the strange sensation of isolation. Now that he had retired, he found that he was still awake, and consumed by thoughts of the future, and of the past, and of how the two inexorably twined.

Gralyre perceived a prickling of magic exuding from the blade, shivering across his flesh like pins and needles. A soft, red glow painted the inside of the tent, emanating from the ruby pommel. What sorcery was it weaving?

His hand sought the sword where he had placed it alongside his low pallet. He rolled so that he could reach out to caress the silver head of the Dragon, much as Dotch's son, Demin, had done earlier that evening.

Little Wolf grumbled from the foot of the bed, as he was forced to readjust to the new angle of Gralyre's legs.

Gralyre was distracted from his curiosity about the sword's intent by thoughts of his poor Princess, Genevieve.

'How could I have forsaken her?' Like a butterfly caught in amber, his beautiful Princess was now merely a jewel adorning the throne room of the Usurper in Dreisenheld. Churning, blistering guilt ate at his stomach. His heart ached, and his eyes burned with unspent tears at the tragedy of it all.

Gralyre's hand lifted from the sword to rub his eyes, and the sensation of grief vanished. He blinked his confusion and sat up, thrusting his coverings away.

What was this? What was happening? He loved Catrian, not Genevieve. He rubbed at the back of his neck in confusion. His exhaustion was breeding crazed thoughts.

His decision to not rescue Genevieve had been an easy one to make. He had chosen his people over her, and would do so a thousand times over! Genevieve was the future queen of his father's choosing, not of his!

If Catrian had been his affianced so long ago, the choice would not have been so easily made. But then he loved Catrian. The Princess was an object of vapid beauty with little else to recommend her beyond her royal pedigree.

Gralyre had never cared for Genevieve. She had been a spoiled, thoughtless girl, a pampered princess born of privilege who held no regard for anything but her own comforts. Yet, if there was a chance that she lived, that she was in truth suspended in a crystal pillar in the throne room of Dreisenheld as the legends told, then he had to rescue her. His conscience could not leave her in her prison. He had failed in his duty to her once before, and could not do so again.

Frustration made him want to lash out and break something. Even after centuries had passed, he was still faced with the same dilemma. Rescue the Princess or save his kingdom. Only now, that choice had been complicated further, for rescuing the Princess meant losing Catrian.

His mind and heart warred violently, struggling with the decision that he had already made that morning. Love or duty. His heart's desire or his obligation.

Unable to help himself, Gralyre reached out with his magic to touch Catrian's thoughts where she still sat at Matik's bedside in the healer's tent. She slept now, for the journey back to the Rebel fortress had tired her healing body. Gralyre could easily sense her dreams from where she rested her head upon her arms alongside Matik's cot.

She dreamed of their tryst in her Wizard Stone, and Gralyre groaned from the memory of their shared passion. For the sake of his sanity, he broke away and returned to his own head.

Foul rage washed over him at his helplessness in the face of his destiny. Catrian or Genevieve. No choice to be made. None.

Seeking calm, Gralyre caressed Little Wolf's head soothingly. His mind was not yet ready to release all cares and find sleep.

Little Wolf stretched luxuriously, and began to snore lightly, as Gralyre's touch eased him into a happy dream of chasing rabbits.

ଚ୍ଛଔ

Within the Wizard Stone

The ancient sorcerer is uncertain if he has overstepped his manipulations of Gralyre's memories and emotions. He has distracted the Prince with thoughts of Princess Genevieve, and Gralyre has begun to sever his union with Catrian. Soon, he will set Catrian aside completely, and the danger that the Sorceress poses will be at an end.

But the Prince has always been wilful! Somehow, he is still clinging to his truth, despite all that has been blurred, altered and hidden from his sight.

He must be more careful, lest he alert Gralyre to his influence.

The thralls jeer at his schemes. Damn them. One day, he will have the power to silence them forever! When he has possessed his new vessel, and escaped his Wizard Stone once more.

₧₨

"Lady Catrian." Saliana shook her shoulder gently to rouse the Sorceress from her bedside vigil. "Matik will no' awaken tonight. I have had a cot brought for ye, so that ye might sleep, and be near t' him."

Catrian looked up at the healer with drowsy confusion. Gralyre had come to her, in her dreams, and she was uncertain if it were true or only her wishful yearning. Recognizing the wisdom of Saliana's suggestion, she allowed the healer to shift her onto the cot.

Catrian sighed deeply in appreciation for the comforting warmth, as Saliana snugged a heavy fur around her. "Thank-ye," was all she managed before she drifted back to sleep, hoping that Gralyre would come to her again.

ഇന്ദ്ര

"Master, this one seeks an audience." Sethreat kneels in the leaves and rocks of the forest floor to await the Master's terrifying touch. It is quick to arrive; a dark note of corruption enters the glade, and the cold of a grave taints the air.

'Sethreat, have you the Prince and the sword?'

"Master, this one hast secrets to tell thee." Sethreat equivocates, and nimbly sidesteps an admittance of failure.

The Master's ire smites It to the ground. Sethreat keens, as Its chin smacks upon stones. *'We weary of your excuses! 'Tis a simple enough task! BRING US THE PRINCE AND THE SWORD!'*

It pushes the Master's sufferance too far. Sethreat yowls, as Its head twists to an angle that will soon break Its thick neck. "My life is yours, my Master," It bellows in agony, "but kill this one, and who then will remain to do thy bidding?"

The weight upon Its neck eases, but still holds Sethreat's reptilian face mashed into the earth. *'SPEAK!'*

Death awaits if Its words please the Master naught! "Master, this one hast discovered the identity of the Rebel Sorcerer, returned from the south. It is thy Prince."

'He has awakened at last!' There is a sense of satisfaction and glee within the dark presence of the Master, and the heavy magical hand vanishes from Sethreat's head.

"Master, this one hast more to share."

'Tell us! We will crush you like a beetle should your words displease us or you seek to hold anything back.'

"Thy will is all, my Master. Glory be to thy mighty darkness!" Afraid to move lest It cause offence, Sethreat stays on the ground, humble before the glorious might of the Master. "Thy Prince hast taken the Rebel Sorceress as a lover. This one did observe their nesting in the yestereve. Together they did twine in the same tent."

Sethreat mewls, as the infection of the Master's fury withers new grown leaves on trees encircling the glade. Blighted beyond recovery the trees blacken and shrivel. Terrified, Sethreat cannot prevent Its tail from lashing like a hatchling's. On Its belly, It awaits Its death, as the Master's rage builds intensity.

'KILL HER! KILL HER NOW!' The scream cannot be heard by other than Sethreat's own mind, yet it grates upon Its ears, a sympathetic stab of pain from the force of the command within Its skull.

"Yes Master!" Sethreat is overjoyed. Its fear of execution is groundless. The Master has not taken away the kill! *A magic wielder to feast upon! So weak, so sick, she is unable to defend herself!* For a pleasurable moment, Sethreat revels in visions of murder.

'Wait... No! 'Tis too easy a death for her! Take her! Take her, and give the Prince the same choice as before. His kingdom or his lover! Let her feel the burn of his abandonment and betrayal when he leaves her to die in the Towers!'

"Master, thou didst promise!" Sethreat whines accusingly. "She is to be mine!"

'And so she shall be, my pet. After she has suffered for daring to rise above her station. Then shall you take your pleasure. Slowly. At leisure. In the Towers. For us.'

Sethreat preens at being named the Master's Executioner. "The desecration of the Sorceress will draw madness from all who hear of it, my Master!" Sethreat croons. "This one is thine. Thy most devoted of slaves."

'We send our servant, Fanghorn, to assist the capture of the Sorceress, as replacement for the Stalkers who were slain.'

No! Another comes! The safety of Sethreat's monopoly is gone!

A few feet in front of Sethreat's scaly snout, a captured bolt of lightning grows up from the ground like a bright sapling. It buzzes with the sound of a thousand bees, as it hovers before Sethreat's prone body. Flashes of blue light strobe the dead trees surrounding the clearing.

A clawed, reptilian hand reaches through the crackling energy, and widens the jagged thunderbolt into a gap. The world bends around the fiery slit, as though it is merely a pretty pattern upon the fabric of a curtain that is being shifted to the side. Seen through the rift are the mouldering ancient stones of the Towers.

A Stalker steps through into the glade.

Sethreat grinds Its double rows of serrated teeth. Only the Master's presence stops It from ripping the newcomer apart for daring to infringe upon Its Hunt!

The new arrival stretches to full height, and glares down upon Sethreat, who is still abased before the Master's presence. The gap snaps closed with a shallow clap, but the sizzling bolt remains, a rip in the fabric of the universe.

'We will tolerate no further inadequacies. This passage will remain open for three days only, yours to use to bring the Sorceress to the Towers. Be assured, Sethreat, that upon your failure, your life ends with its closing. Fanghorn will then assume your place in the Hunt!'

"Thy will be done, my Master."

'Use your three days wisely, Sethreat.' The Master's presence is gone, but as promised the flickering crack remains, awaiting Sethreat's success. A captured bolt of lightning, it strobes and snaps, ambushing the darkness with flashes of light.

Sethreat stands to confront the interloper, Fanghorn. They hiss and growl, circling warily, testing the limits of each other's dominance and power. Fanghorn is an old beast, at least as long in years as Sethreat and as powerful.

"Keep thee far from my Hunt, and perhaps this one will spare thy life!" Sethreat's warning ends on a deep sibilance of fury.

Fanghorn's armour snaps down protectively, in preparation of a fight. "I fear thee naught. Thy skills are pitiable," it taunts. "Accept thy failure, and step aside that this one might serve our

Master's will!"

"Our Master did not gift the Kill to thee!" Sethreat roars. Strings of spittle flay from Its teeth with Its words. The need to rend and destroy almost overcomes Its obedience to the Master's will. "Away with thee! Lest this one proves Its mastery upon thy flesh!" Sethreat rips great furrows into the ground with powerful hind claws, kicking clumps of turf into the underbrush of the dark forest.

Fanghorn swipes Its talons at a dead sapling, snapping it off to crash onto the forest floor in its own display of dominance. "Thou art weak, Sethreat!" Fanghorn leans closer and sniffs. "Thou hast allowed Maolar to injure thee." Its muzzle curls in scorn. "Thou hast less skill in the Hunt than a hatchling. This one needs do nothing. In three days time, our Master will kill thee for thy failure. I will abide until thy downfall is complete." Fanghorn turns insultingly and kicks dirt upon Sethreat's legs. "The sun arises soon, and this one must build a nest."

Sethreat glares darkly, hissing and spitting ineffectually after Fanghorn, as the new Stalker departs the glade. The Master's edict prevents Sethreat from killing Fanghorn, but there are other ways to gain victory. It conceives a plan to eliminate Its rival.

It follows. It watches, downwind and from shadows, as Fanghorn digs a daytime burrow.

There is still time to enact Its plot ere the sun arises.

₭⌒

Late that night, Saliana collapsed in exhaustion onto her own cot that was set in a corner of the healer's tent so that she would be close at hand should any of her patients need her. She marvelled at what she had done and learned that day. People were alive because of her. It felt good. It felt right.

Ninrhar's encouragement and praise had gone a long way in bolstering her confidence. He had been very impressed at what she had managed to accomplish with her limited resources and knowledge.

Deep within Saliana something profound had changed. Though she was tired, she was also exhilarated. She was not certain of who she was becoming, but she knew that it would be someone that she liked very much, someone who mattered.

CHAPTER NINE

Though the Prince had been provided a pavilion, those hale enough to do so had slept in the open. Luxuries, such as tents and tarps, had been ceded to the frailest of the injured. Gralyre's friends had camped on the ground, near to the fire they had sat at the evening before.

At dawn's first blush, Gralyre shook Aneida, Jord and Dotch awake, and invited them to leave the fortress for a hunt. He had noted that his friends were being culled by tragedy and injury, and felt an urgent need to tend to them. His disquieting thoughts of the night before had much to do with this desire. Today would be their last opportunity to steal a bit of pleasure away from the dark deeds of the future war.

Already wakeful, Aneida merely rolled to her feet. Sleep was a shy visitor since Mayvin had perished. Gralyre caught his breath at the change in her. Her cheeks were sunken, and dark circles rounded her eyes. Her fiery braid hung limply, the plaits rough and uneven, as though they had been made without benefit of a comb. Her lips were chapped and raw from her chewing upon them.

"Aneida…"

"I am fine." She leaned down to gather her weapons, inviting Gralyre to leave the matter alone.

The two men proved more difficult to rouse. Jord and Dotch

had been late at their revels, and Gralyre did not begrudge them of it. Having escaped from Fennick's Island into the teeth of a Rebel civil war, the previous night had been the first moment to snatch a bit of carefree diversion in far too long. Dotch's storytelling expertise had been in high demand, and payment had involved many tankards of ale.

Dotch lay with his arms securely bound around his wife's shoulders, spooned against her back. Their two boys sprawled across them both in a glorious, sonorous pile. At Gralyre's quiet summons, Dotch slowly uncurled from around his wife, and dislodged his children, who slept on.

He crawled away from them before standing stiffly amidst audible pops of joints. His balance was suspect, and he danced sideways to fetch up against the stump that he had sat upon the evening before. After waiting a moment to regain his equilibrium, Dotch slumped to the seat, hung his head, and shook it ruefully with a soft chuckle. His mood was unsinkable since reuniting with his family.

Jord glared at everyone as he arose. His eyes were bloodshot, and his ragged, black hair stood in clumps. His mouth worked as he cleared the fuzz from off his teeth with his tongue. He pulled a grimace at the sour flavour of the last night's ale. "I am up," he announced to no one in particular, and spat on the ground.

Aneida glared haughtily at them both, as she strapped her sword about her hips. "The two o' ye are a disgrace."

"Ye are a disgrace," Jord sniped under his breath, not quite willing to challenge her overtly with his head swollen to thrice its size.

Dotch grinned, and saluted them all with a flask that he had pulled from within his pocket. "Spirit o' the Beast," he toasted, and consumed a healthy swig.

Jord paled to a sickly green, as he stepped back from wafting scent of alcoholic fumes. "Ye bastard," he accused weakly, before reeling aside to retch.

"No," Dotch lost his smile, "do no'," he burped alarmingly, "do no' do that."

Aneida shook her head in exasperation. "Are ye sure ye want them along?" she asked Gralyre.

Gralyre nodded with a grin, anticipating the outing. "They will be upright once we get into the forest."

୫୦୯

Little Wolf caught the scent of a buck in a clearing ahead, and signalled to Gralyre.

With the ease of familiarity, Gralyre motioned to Jord and Aneida to flank him to the right, and Dotch to his left. Silently, the four stalked their prey with lances held at the ready. Little Wolf padded forward at Gralyre's side.

"Gralyre." Jord's grim summons broke the stillness.

Ahead, there was a crashing and snapping of branches, as the deer took flight. Little Wolf made an almost human groan of exasperation.

Aneida crouched over something large and black on the

ground, while Jord beckoned Gralyre and Dotch with a curl of his hand. Their faces were set and serious.

Gralyre's nostrils flared to the smell of dead flesh, as he approached. Aneida was kneeling over the desiccated remains of a bear. It was a fresh kill, only hours old, but already bloated flies and wasps buzzed the carcass, made ecstatic by their good fortune.

Little Wolf, trotting up beside Gralyre, gave a soft woof, and bent a shoulder in eager preparation of a good roll in the stench.

Gralyre growled at him, and the wolfdog fell back with a disgruntled warble. Little Wolf usually slept at the foot of his bed, and Gralyre would prefer not breathing in death whilst trying to sleep.

"Thanks for that. Last time he rolled in something he stank for a week," Dotch grouched, unknowingly echoing Gralyre's sentiments. His attention returned to the bear carcass, and he poked at it with the tip of his spear, near a series of five parallel gashes that had laid the neck of the massive predator open to the bone.

Aneida glanced up at her friends. "No blood upon the ground," she announced. "It was killed elsewhere and dumped here."

"Stalker," Jord confirmed the thought that lay unspoken between them.

Gralyre's memory of his first encounter with a Stalker arose like a flood to drown him. The beginning. Before they had known the extent of the evil that they faced, or the war that was to come.

Something had been killing villagers and livestock in the village of Foxbane near to Dreisenheld. Gralyre had put together a hunting party to search for a wolf pack, or perhaps a bear. Then, as now, it had been an enjoyable outing, a chance to escape the pressures of the castle, and his father's unrelenting oppression...

₭⌒

Gralyre's Past

...My men are in good spirits. Food is plentiful and wine flows sweetly, as we rest from our exertions of the day. The pavilions are erected in a loose circle within the clearing, and servants shuttle between the men and the tents, preparing all for our comforts. Several large boars, killed during the hunt, hang as trophies from the trees. One of the animals turns over a fire, on a spit worked tirelessly by two scullions.

Firelight glints off the minstrel's lute, as the clever musician sings of the deeds of the day. Reclining upon soft cushions and pillows, we laugh and join the chorus, mocking each other. It is a rare and pleasant frivolity.

A challenging roar echoes in the night, and we fall silent. I have never heard such a sound. What beast is this?

The creature bursts from the underbrush, and kills three men afore weapons can be grasped. Swords bounce uselessly from its hide. Spears splinter and slide off its tough, plated scales without causing so much as a scratch. The minstrel is silenced forever in a spray of blood.

The only metal sharp enough to pierce the beast's scales is the Maolar of my Dragon Sword. My men hold Dreisenheld forged steel. Left alone to battle the creature, I swing my blade, and neatly decapitate the beast. It is no match for my skill.

I have fought the creature and won, but the cost of victory has been paid in blood. Six of my nobles are dead, and with them are the bodies of ten servants.

Come daybreak, the corpse of the beast flames to dust in the morning light, and I have nothing to show for the bloody fight but the bodies of the slain...

ഇരു

Gralyre sighed heavily.

They had returned to the castle, a grim party much changed from the band of young nobles who had sought the excitement of a hunt.

That very day, he had sent word to the King to kit their troops with Maolar weapons, but as was usual, his father had ignored his advice. With no proof of the beast to show, the cost of Maolar had been too high to be justified. Gralyre had been left to use his own allowance to outfit his personal guard with as many Maolar weapons, as he could locate and afford.

It had not been enough. Not nearly enough. Perhaps if his

father had heeded his warnings sooner, the outcome of the war would have been different.

"Stalker?" Aneida's hands worked upon the staff of her lance. "Is it near? We should take it now, before nightfall."

Gralyre closed his eyes, and stretched forth with his magic, searching for a hint of evil sentience in the thoughts of the creatures stirring in the leafy bowers of spring. "I sense nothing."

Dotch scanned the forest for drag marks but there was no sign of the Stalker's trail. "If 'tis smart, then it has left its kill far from its den so that we canno' track it."

Aneida flicked back her long, red braid, as she stood. "It must be the one that escaped the Dream Weavers, the partner t' the one that Dara killed."

"This could be good," Gralyre mused after a moment of consideration. "It may have valuable knowledge of Doaphin's troop movements that we can use."

"Ye mean to capture it? Question it?" Dotch's eyebrows shot high. Though the Rebels killed a Stalker now and then, when they happened upon its daylight lair, by dragging it into the sun to allow the cleansing rays to reduce it to dust, to his knowledge no one had ever sought to capture one. There was no way to contain so powerful a beast. "Do ye think that wise, Highness?" Dotch asked carefully, mindful of Gralyre's new acute reactiveness to questioning.

Gralyre snorted, lifting a brow. "Every time you think that I may not like what you have to say, you invoke my title."

Dotch grimaced ruefully and shrugged.

"I have interrogated Stalkers before with the aid of Dream Weaver magic. Say nothing of this for now. I have a plan."

"Yes, Highness." Dotch, Aneida and Jord replied in unison.

₧₧

The morning dulled, and rain clouds threatened from horizon to horizon by the time they returned from their hunt. They had been successful, and bore two deer for the hungry people. Shared among so many, it was not as much as they had hoped for.

A hearty venison stew was soon bubbling upon the many smoking cookfires in the fortress square. The able bodied moved through the rows of injured, spooning steaming broth from wooden bowls into those unable to feed themselves, and providing what comfort that they could.

The day darkened further. Threatening rumbles of distant thunder echoed between the furthest mountain peaks until it was an unceasing roll that built upon itself, intensifying with each forked tongue of lightning, as the storm front approached. Almost as though wrung free of the clouds by the vibrations of the booming thunder, a thick deluge suddenly pounded the earth, so hard that the rain ricocheted up into a thick mist that smeared and softened the blighted appearance of the fortress.

The spring downpour cleansed the air of smoke, and extinguished the last of the smouldering embers from the fires that had ravaged the fortress. Lingering pockets of snow soon dissolved to nothing. Rivulets carved deep channels along slopes, and pooled into the low areas, forming frothy, ash-choked lakes in which charred wooden debris bobbed in the churning currents. Everywhere the ground grew slick with mud.

For those injured who were still without shelter, or even a barrier betwixt their bodies and the ground, it became yet another trial to endure. The Dream Weavers had lent to the Rebels what tents and tarps that they could spare, doubling and tripling the number of their warriors housed within each remaining pavilion, but it was not enough to spare all of the injured. Fevers spiked, and the dread spectre of disease and death began to haunt them again.

People cycled between the suspended tarps, pushing sticks up into the rainwater pooling in the fabric to drain it away before it could collapse the structures onto the wounded.

Ninrhar and Saliana moved unceasingly from patient to patient, doing all that they could to bolster strength, and prevent fever from finding a foothold in the weak. Though Ninrhar used his magic to heal where he could, he was but one man, and the wounded were legion. Fires were lit at intervals amongst the rows of injured to provide heat, but it did little to alleviate the unrelenting damp that wicked up from the ground, or fell violently from the roiling sky.

Sitting under the cover of his tarp by his smoking fire, Gralyre brooded, as he stared at the healer's tent through the curtains of water that slicked off of the wet canvas overhead.

Only the cracking thunder was loud enough to drown out the rattle of the rain upon the covering. Catrian still sat a vigil next to Matik. In the twilight of the storm, Gralyre could clearly see her shadow cast against the tent by the light of a lantern.

Gods, he missed her! He had not seen Catrian since Matik had been found. Gralyre's frustration spiked, as he considered her coldness of the evening before. Their strife could not exist, and still allow them to fight the war ahead. They had to come to an understanding.

As a peace offering, he ladled two wooden bowls from the succulent stew bubbling over his fire, and set them on a plank, under a cloth to keep the rain from watering them down during his walk to the sick tent.

Gralyre hunched his shoulders, as he stepped into the deluge, grudgingly enduring the streams of water that bypassed the collar of his cloak to trickle down his back. He was quickly drenched.

As he approached the healer's tent, Gralyre noted a small band of warriors milling a few feet away. There was no reason for them to be there, standing without shelter or fire to warm them.

The two Dream Weaver sentries posted at the entrance to the healer's tent were alert to the men, watching them closely, as was their duty. When Gralyre passed the group, the snatches of conversation he heard ceased, and the men sauntered away. He did not recognize them, and thought them to be Eastern Rebels.

Tray in hand, Gralyre paused his steps to wipe dripping water from his eyes, covertly spying several such clumps of warriors now that he was looking for them. Closed, tight groups, their aspects were markedly different from those people clustering for warmth, food and camaraderie. Covert glances in Gralyre's direction were quickly averted, breeding even more furtive exchanges.

Exerting his sorcery, Gralyre conscripted a crow to flap low overhead. Using the bird's senses, he eavesdropped upon several of the secretive conversations. What he heard made a muscle tic in his cheek.

No doubt they used the curtains of water to conceal their talk of sedition. The intent of the whispers echoed the fearful, dark mutterings of the storm above, and brought Gedrhar's warning of the day before to mind. *'Mutinous words hidden within the storm,'* Gralyre thought uneasily, as he released the bird from his service, and it gratefully flew back to its sheltered roost.

The Northerners still talked of revenge. Even though Gralyre had accepted the Easterners back into the fold, evidence of Kierdenan's treachery lay dying at the Northern Rebels' feet, making forgiveness a rare beast indeed. Despite the rains, it would take only a small spark to enflame the conflict again.

Less forgivable, were the Easterners who still plotted to use Catrian in a deal with Doaphin to buy their way clear of the war. An overwhelming urge to destroy these conspirators, before they could harm Catrian, swept Gralyre in a wave of protective rage.

The sword rejoiced, painting vivid images of the destructive powers available for his use to smite the traitors.

Gralyre breathed deeply, blinking his eyes to clear them of the spattering rain. He wanted to surrender to his rage! He shook with the intensity of his need to do so! *'I must not! 'Tis madness! There are other ways, better ways!'*

He lifted his face to the storm, and used the clammy wetness as a touchstone, seeking the discipline of his sword dance, the cold rhythm that calmed his bloodlust, and allowed him to reason in the thick of battle. The Dragon Sword's urgency faded to a background itch.

A violent reaction would do nothing to repair the damaged trust between the two groups. Another way had to be found. Quickly. Before he sent the Northern refugees to dubious safety at the Eastern Fortress, and marched to war with an army at odds with itself!

His gaze focussed upon the passing, rain-blurred image of a familiar friend. "Aneida!" Gralyre called out.

Rain sheeted off her skin and saturated her clothes, for she had not bothered to don a cloak. She shivered roughly, yet did nothing to seek the warmth of one of the many smoking campfires for either heat or companionship.

Gralyre's mouth tightened in compassion, but he had greater worries than their shared grief for Mayvin. "Fetch everyone to meet with me in the healer's tent."

"The Dream Weavers too?" she asked listlessly.

Gralyre nodded. "Gedrhar and Jacon," he confirmed. "And Aneida," he paused, as she looked at him expectantly, "Ensure you include our new General, Illian."

Inviting Illian was no guarantee of drawing the venom from the snake, but it was time Tobias donned the mantle of leadership, and gained control of his men.

Aneida set off on her errand, and Gralyre paused at the threshold of the healer's tent. His breath hitched with anticipation despite the cold welcome he was likely to receive.

"Good morn to you, Highness," one of the Dream Weaver sentries bowed, and politely held back the flap of the tent for his passage within.

Catrian glanced up from Matik to discover who had entered, and her jaw flexed, the only sign of her disquiet.

Despite the brazier set alight in the corner, Catrian's breath fogged in the cold damp. Her face was very white, and Gralyre worried that she was overtaxing her strength.

"How is he?" Gralyre asked quietly, feeling wretched that he was partly to blame for her hurt.

Shorn of his usual luxurious, brown beard, so that Ninrhar and Saliana could treat his throat wound, Matik seemed years younger than Gralyre had always thought him to be.

"Better," she said tersely. "Ninrhar, closed the wound in his neck today, and Matik is breathing easier. He has no' awakened." Despite her assertion, Matik's breath still held a wheezing quality that spoke to his dire injury.

Gralyre was uncertain of his footing, knowing it could turn to quicksand at any moment, and her cool, polite façade could be ripped away. "Where is Rewn?" he noted the empty cot where his injured friend had been resting.

"He is almost recovered. He went out for food. He will return soon."

Reminded, Gralyre drew the cloth from over the wooden bowls he held, releasing steam, and the succulent scent of the stew into the air. "I thought we could eat together, and talk."

After a short pause, Catrian nodded, and reached out for one of the bowls.

They sat in uneasy silence, listening to the constant drumming of rain upon the canvas above them, and the rhythmic, rasping inhales and exhales of Matik upon the table.

As they supped, Gralyre searched for a way to bridge their tension. He grieved the loss of the easy friendship that they had developed over the months while she had taught him to control his magic, as he had travelled towards Fennick's Island. He mourned the promise of love and passion that they had been forced to abandon after only a taste. "Better to have never had our night, than to miss it so fiercely," he growled softly.

She dropped her wooden spoon into her bowl with a clatter of impatience, and glared. "Your choice, no' mine!" She thumped her dish onto a side table.

"I know." Gralyre set his empty bowl back on the plank he had used, and placed the whole next to her abandoned bowl.

Her shoulders eased their stiffness, and she sighed. "Gralyre, we are going t' war. We have t' move past this. We have no' the luxury o' hurt." Her thoughts had obviously been following the same pathways as his.

"How? What do you propose we do?"

Catrian brushed back a stray lock of her golden brown hair, her face intent with thought. "If ye will no' change your mind, then we must no' speak o' this again. If we just pretend our time in the stone ne'er happened then maybe…"

"Never happened?" Gralyre snapped, struggling with an animalistic desire to lay claim.

Catrian's breath suspended, as she read his reaction clearly. A light blush tinted her cheekbones. "Well, clearly that will no' do," she murmured with a wry wit.

Gralyre glanced down at his clenched fists, and huffed out a soft laugh at his own expense. "No. I do not suppose it will."

"I think ye know what I want." She leaned forward, and hesitantly covered his large fist with her soft touch, as though fearful of rejection, but Gralyre's hand relaxed and turned so that their fingers entwined. "Your morals are o' the ancient past," she accused gently, "In a time o' upheaval and war, such useless trappings have long been discarded. No one would judge our love harshly. Let us be together," she implored.

"Sorceress, do not tempt me! It would never be enough! In the end, I would never let you go, and I cannot turn my back on Genevieve. You would come to hate me for having to be with her, for not being able to give you everything you deserve. I could stand anything but that," he finished hoarsely.

As he spoke, Catrian's hands abandoned his to grip her elbows for comfort. Gralyre made a point that she had not previously considered. He was right; she would come to hate him if she had to share him with another. Their feelings were too powerful. It was all or nothing between them.

"Alright," she ceded, the soft word masking her intentions. Catrian had learned the art of strategy at the knee of a master, her Uncle Boris. Alienating the Prince with her anger and hurt would not win her the prize. Genevieve would not take Gralyre from her. All or nothing, she vowed.

Catrian forced a wistful smile. "We will love each other, though we will no' be lovers, until the time comes that we must part. The best o' friends, as we were before."

Gralyre captured her hand, lifted it to his lips, and pressed a kiss to her palm, overwhelmed by her generosity. "Thank-you," he said simply, and his eyes closed with a yearning he could not act upon.

Catrian sagged back in her chair in response to the heat that his touch forced into her chilled skin, and Gralyre never saw the possessive flash that narrowed her grey-green eyes.

Gralyre still held her hand tightly, as the others gathered in the tent. They did not question the newfound closeness that marked the two. It was a hard life, and happiness was a fleeting thing not to be begrudged.

Present were those who had quested with Gralyre to Fennick's Island: Dotch, Aneida, Rewn and Jord. Trifyn was still too ill from his wounds to join them, and Saliana was with Ninrhar, tending to the wounded. These were the people that Gralyre trusted most, their exceptional loyalties proven in battle.

Welcomed, as new allies, were the Dream Weavers - Gedrhar and his son, Jacon.

And then there was General Illian, whose value was still an unknown, though Gralyre knew him to be a man of honour and integrity. It was enough for now.

It was to them all that Gralyre now turned for counsel, as he described what he had seen and heard of the disposition of the people of fortress.

"Catrian is definitely still in danger," Dotch agreed. "I had t' quell a small mob that was beating a young man who had stated his loyalty t' the Sorceress."

General Illian spoke up in defence of his men. "What o' the other side o' the coin? The Northerners are no' making it any easier t' abandon the bloodshed. We did no' come here t' conquer ye but t' find a way t' make peace with Doaphin. For all. No' just the Eastern Rebels. Kierdenan felt that the fighting was a necessary evil t' reach the Sorceress."

Catrian huffed angrily, and Gralyre shot her a warning look, calming her. "General, we appreciate your position, but as you know, General Kierdenan's plan would not have worked. It would have left us defenceless."

Tobias inclined his head. "O' course, Highness. But I was no' present at Commander Boris' war summit, and did no' hear nor see what transpired there. I only know what Kierdenan shared with us afterwards." He set his feet under his chair, and slid his palms along his thighs in a nervous gesture. "I feel he was right in one thing. With only Lady Catrian's assurances that Doaphin is moving against us, I need verification before I will commit my forces. I owe my men that much."

"Your forces?" Rewn questioned coolly. His voice was raspy from the injury done to his throat, though the pink scar, with the aid of Ninrhar's magic, was quickly fading. "Northern Rebels... Eastern, ... are we all no' Warriors o' Lyre now?"

Gedrhar shattered the sudden tension of the room with the clearing of his throat. "The Dream Weavers have also foreseen the genocide of the people of Lyre by Doaphin's hand this summer, General Illian," he confirmed sadly. "Because of this, we have opened our borders for the first time in over three hundred years to accept refugees."

Gedrhar steepled his hands in front of his lips in preparation to explaining further. "Prince Gralyre's mother was sister to my ancestor. Three hundred years ago, our people pledged to help the Kingdom of Lyre in its fight against the Usurper. Together with the Prince's armies, we would have had the strength with which to defeat Doaphin."

"What happened?" Rewn asked with avid curiosity.

"Due to our family allegiance, Doaphin anticipated our involvement. He forced us into border skirmishes along all our mountain passes. By dividing our forces, he made it impossible for us to lend our full might to Lyre's war.

"After Lyre fell, we sealed the mountain passes to protect our lands. Ever since, we have been repelling Doaphin's attempts at invasion. Do not believe that we ever abandoned you." There was deep regret in Gedrhar's voice. "We were unable to come to your aid. We could scarcely help ourselves.

"When the Lost Prince returned, and began to fulfil the

prophecy," Gedrhar smiled at Gralyre, "we realized that we were being given a second chance to redeem our honour. We have acted quickly this time, before Doaphin could trap us, as he did to our forefathers. Our forces stand ready, ranged in strategic passes along the Heathren foothills. This time, the Usurper will face the entire might of the Dream Weaver nation!" Gedrhar shook his fist in emphasis.

Catrian had been mulling over a comment made by the Eastern General. "Illian has made a valid point. He was no' present at the summit, nor were any o' ye, save Matik, and he is…" Catrian waved at her General, whose constant, steady wheezes had become a background for their talks. "Ye should be made aware o' what was decided, for we are set t' this course. The other Generals will already be moving into place. If we deviate from our agreed strategy, we will place the bulk o' our forces in danger!

"Before Kierdenan's attack, we were t' leave on the Solstice for Hondors Pass, southwest o' here, t' join with him and the Eastern Rebels. We must keep with this plan, and leave as soon as possible! We canno' afford t' delay much longer!"

She looked at Gralyre, who nodded for her to continue.

"Our mission is to save the people, not the land. We will advance southwest out o' the Heathren's, and into the lowlands where we will scatter our forces t' warn as many villages and crofts as possible o' the oncoming danger. Our lowland refugees will evacuate into the mountains. There, General Ryes o' the Southern Rebels is already fighting for control o' the southern passes, t' hold them open for our people's retreat into the lands o' the Dream Weavers."

"What o' the northern passes?" Aneida asked.

Jacon grinned. "Doaphin no longer controls them." The Dream Weaver army had left no enemy at their backs.

Catrian inclined her head to Jacon and Gedrhar. "Thank ye! That frees up a large portion o' our forces t' journey with us t' the lowlands.

"As Generals Chartrin and Laurazon return t' their fortresses in the west," she continued to outline Boris' plan, "they are spreading word o' the purge. Fleeing Lowlanders will gather at Verdalan, where General Baldric will relay them onwards into the Heathrens towards the Northern and Eastern Fortresses. We will leave a small contingent behind t' guide the refugees through the passes t' the Dream Weavers."

"I like not the idea of splitting my forces," Gralyre frowned.

"Throughout the summer, General Baldric's spy network will be providing us with updates on Doaphin's troop movements so that we can avoid open battle for as long as possible," Catrian replied.

"This evacuates barely half of our realm," Gralyre was still not convinced of the soundness o the plan. "What of the people in the west?"

"Once they cross the midline o' Lyre, Chartrin and Laurazon will begin herding refugees northwest towards the coastal town o' Ghent, where Chartrin's ships will be waiting t' ferry them off the mainland t' the safety o' his island fortress."

"Is that wise? How will they live?"

"General Chartrin's base is located on several islands off the coast beyond Dreisenheld. They grow their own food, and are independent o' Lyre. From there, he can survive a siege for years, barring magical attacks from Doaphin's Demon Lords. Everything south o' Dreisenheld is deserted o' humanity, so we need no' concern ourselves with it. Southeast, west and north. Boris thought this the only way t' cover as much territory as possible in the time that remains t' us."

Gralyre nodded. He mourned the loss of his lands, but his people could still be saved.

"By the first day o' summer," Catrian continued, "we must rendezvous with Laurazon and Baldric at Dapochar, north o' Verdalan. From Dapochar, we will begin a fighting, controlled retreat back into the mountains t' cover the escape o' the last Lowlanders. We will make our stand in these same mountain passes, where Doaphin's numbers will no' count so hard against us, and the cold may slow the Stalkers and Deathren."

Dotch and Rewn exchanged a speaking glance, but it was Jord who voiced their concerns. "I do no' understand why we have t' fight them at all. We have a superior defensive position here, and an escape route through the passes t' the lands of the Dream Weavers. Let the winter do our fighting for us."

Gralyre shook his head. "Only think of the numbers arrayed against us. If Doaphin reaches this deep into the mountains, and if we are huddled within our fortresses, he need not fight us. He need only lay siege, trap us behind these walls, and we will be dead of starvation afore the first snows. The bulk of his horde could pass us by, and still be large enough to invade the Dream Weavers." Gralyre eyed his people grimly. "There will be no retreat for us."

"Gralyre is right." Catrian sighed. "Doaphin will allow no middle ground. His horde will pursue our people through the passes. We canno' allow this t' happen. We must fight his advance at every turn, and make him pay dearly in blood for every foot of ground he takes. We are unlikely t' survive the war until the first snowfalls. And if we do, ye all know how dependent we are upon the lowland crops t' make it through the winter months. Our supplies are already depleted, and there is no hope o' replenishing them this year."

"What o' the Dream Weavers?" Dotch asked. "Could they no' resupply us?"

Gedrhar sought to make them understand the magnitude of the deadly evil that they faced. "We will do what we can, while we hold the passes. But if Doaphin gets past our armies, and attacks my country, it will be all we can do to keep him from destroying our lands, let alone to break a siege and bring food to your people."

Dark fear stretched its fingers into the hearts of them all. For a moment their thoughts were rife with the futility of their defiance against such a power.

Catrian shattered the stillness. "If we depart within the next two days, we can travel directly towards the Lowlands. With the Eastern Rebels already with us, we need delay no longer, and may even gain back our lost time."

"No' all o' us were part o' the attack upon the fortress, Highness," Illian explained. "There is a reserve o' three thousand waiting back home. If ye permit, I will lead the northern refugees t' safety at the Eastern Fortress, and collect the last o' our warriors. I will then meet with ye at Hondors Pass, as originally planned."

Illian switched tactics, trying his hand at politics. "It will be difficult t' convince the Eastern Fortress o' my new rank. No' t' give offence, Highness, but my men are no' used t' magical ways like the Northern Rebels are. They will no' be won o'er just because ye claim t' be the Lost Prince, and wave a magic sword at them. There must be more proof o' who ye claim t' be? Proof that I can give t' them?"

Aneida launched herself to her feet, making General Illian rock back in surprise. "Ye are offensive, ye black hearted demon lover! Gralyre is the Prince!"

Gralyre smiled coldly, unruffled by Illian's questioning, yet also not censoring Aneida's volatile outburst. "You speak candidly of your men and their beliefs," he gave a regal nod, "and I agree. It will take much more to gain their trust."

Aneida's mouth snapped shut in surprise, and she dropped back onto her stool.

"We must bring our forces together, and remind them of the common evil that we face, one that cannot be overcome if our purposes are divided."

Dotch crossed his arms, as he grasped Gralyre's intent.

"While hunting today, we discovered evidence of a Stalker. 'Tis likely the one that survived Gedrhar's Dream Weavers, and Rewn's sister. I propose a hunt."

General Illian shrugged. "We have killed Stalkers before. We all have. I think it will take more than this t'…"

He trailed off as Gralyre shook his head. "Think larger. I do not seek its head. We capture it alive."

Jacon grinned hugely at the idea. "I wonder if Dara would like to come?"

Rewn shuddered at the idea of his little sister facing such danger ever again. "No' bloody likely!"

The General jumped into the pregnant pause, his fear strengthening his voice to a near shout of aggression. "What purpose could catching a Stalker serve, if it can even be done? They are pure evil! Better just t' find its daytime lair and kill it!"

Gralyre smiled at Catrian while his thumb idly caressed the back of her hand. He could see from her expression that she had fully divined his intent, and his fingers tightened upon hers, grateful that the connection they shared was still intact.

"Firstly, we remind our people of their common enemy, and start spanning the rift between them. Secondly, we put the Stalker to the question for information," Gralyre decreed with no sympathy for the beast. "The Stalker may know when and where Doaphin's armies will strike. If we can get ahead of his battlefront, we can safely evacuate more Lowlanders through the mountains, without engaging in a face-to-face confrontation with an enemy who outnumbers us. Lastly, you, General Illian, will carry the beast back with you to the Eastern Fortress, as a trophy to convince the men who were left behind of your new rank, and of my return. After that you may kill it."

"Catch a Stalker!" Jord cursed incredulously.

Aneida sniffed at him. "Scared?" she mocked.

"Only a fool would no' be!" Jord snarled at her while daggers swirled in silver ripples through his fingertips.

"How will we do it?" Rewn asked.

"Carefully!" Dotch quipped. The flippant answer caused a mirthful ease of the tension.

Jacon smiled. "If I may, the Dream Weavers have done this many times. Doaphin has been trying to find a way into our lands for generations." He sighed mockingly. "Unfortunately, he never hears back from his emissaries."

Gralyre nodded to Jacon in thanks for his support. "We can do this," Gralyre declared.

Dotch thrust his hand through his salt and pepper hair. "Well it canno' be worse than traversing the Bleak or surviving Fennick's Island." He heaved a sigh of exasperation. "Fine!"

"Aye!" Rewn decided.

Aneida shrugged. "It sounds like fun." She displayed a hint of her manic grin of old.

Jord snorted through his large nose. "Ye have an odd sense o' fun," he groused. "When will this madness commence?" He tapped the tip of one of his blades against the dimple in his chin.

Illian's senses reeled at the casual courage displayed by those around him. He did not like how small he suddenly felt in their mighty presence, as they stared at him expectantly. "Aye. When?" he licked dry lips. "When shall we do this?"

Gralyre looked right at him, a challenge. "Tonight. At full dark."

Illian's only previous examples of leadership had come at the less than exemplary hands of Kierdenan and Vetroy. Still, he was smart and ambitious, and these people would not catch him off guard again. He nodded, without further comment.

They spent the next two hours creating a strategy for the coming hunt. In that time, the rain finally relented, leaving the atmosphere clammy with damp.

When all was in place, Gralyre watched his advisors file from the tent, intending to stay behind, and speak further with Catrian of the conversation that had been cut short by the arrival of the others. However, Gedrhar motioned to Gralyre to follow, before he stepped outside.

Gralyre nodded that he would join him in a moment, and waited until they were alone before leaning over and kissing Catrian on the cheek. "Do not worry. Everything will work out." He had correctly read the unease in her face.

Catrian smiled wanly. The doings of the afternoon had sapped her limited strength. "See that it does," she commanded imperiously, then spoiled it with a yawn.

Gralyre grinned, and forgetting himself, swept her up in his arms. Her hands were hot against the cool skin of his neck, where she grasped him for balance. In two strides he placed her upon her cot. As his body hovered above hers, an awkwardness gripped them both.

Catrian's face softened. Her gaze dipped to his mouth, and she drew a short, quiet gasp.

"Catrian..." For a moment Gralyre did battle with his intentions, unable to straighten.

"Ye should go."

"Aye." In his wild imaginings, he lifted Catrian's willing body to his, claiming her lips, taking and giving pleasure. His sanity howled at him to stand, to leave. He froze in place.

Catrian destroyed the moment when she yawned again, lowering her arms from around his neck to cover her mouth.

"Rest!" he growled, and fled while he still had the will to do so.

Gedrhar awaited him outside. "Come with me to my tent. We must talk," the old man commanded.

Curious as to what the Dream Weaver had to say that he would not in front of the council, Gralyre followed Gedrhar to the section of the fortress that the Dream Weavers had assumed possession of.

They halted outside Gedrhar's tent, and the elder waved Gralyre to a stump next to a cleared space. "It is time for your first lesson in the Thewr 'ap Noir, *unticol*," Gedrhar announced.

Gralyre's interest quickened. "What would you have me do?"

"Not do, not yet. Only watch. Learn," Gedrhar advised, as he set his staff to the side.

The old Dream Weaver closed his eyes, and breathed deeply for a moment. Slowly, his hands rose, and a grey mist collected around them, drawn from the air and his palms in equal measure.

Gralyre's gaze widened as he watched, for he could feel nothing. Always, if another wielded Godsmagic in his presence, he felt the vibrations of the power like a swarm of stinging insects upon his skin.

The mist flowed steadily away from Gedrhar's hands, as though blown by a wind. It collected in the empty space before him, forming a large cube, at least eight feet to a side. The undulating image grew thicker, heavier, and materialized bars. As the mist solidified, the shape became more concrete. Seconds later, the last of Gedrhar's Godsmagic vanished into the object, and a cage made of purest Maolar coalesced into being where nothing had existed before.

Gralyre wore an expression of pure astonishment. "This is incredible! How is it done?"

"This cage is but my dream, made manifest. No Godsmagic has been lost to the world around us. When the cage has served its purpose, I will reclaim its Godsmagic for the Dreaming."

It was the ultimate expression of conservation of power. With such a skill, one would never lose strength, and what had befallen Catrian would never happen again.

"Catrian taught me of fire and water, air and earth, and manipulating those energies. But to actually draw a thought into reality!" Gralyre walked around the cage, reaching out to test its strength and solidity. "How is this possible?"

Gedrhar smiled, "You have answered your own question, *unticol*. Hold the idea of what you wish to create. See it with your mind's eyes. Feel its shape and heft as reality. Feel its essence. Feel the energies that must be present in order to bind it together. Now exert your will, your Godsmagic, and draw your image out of the Thewr 'ap Noir to appear before us."

"What shall I create?"

"Best to start with an object you know well. A stone. The more detailed your vision, the better."

Gralyre closed his eyes, and envisioned an amber rock, large enough to fit into his palm. It was smooth, round and polished, as though it had come from a riverbed or seashore. When held to the sun, light could shine through it. "I have the vision."

"Now, feel its weight in your hand. How do your magical senses perceive it? What energies imbue it, to make it a stone, and not a stick? Reach out to that stone in your hand, and give of your Godsmagic that it might appear. Use the energies of the world around you as material for its creation."

Gralyre stared intently at the palm of his hand, imagining his stone sitting there, feeling the weight of it, as though it already existed. Grey mist wicked out of Gralyre's palm, swirling and coalescing until suddenly, where before there had been nothing, a round, amber stone now rested. Gralyre laughed, and held the newly created rock between finger and thumb that he might lift it to the light and see through it. It was real!

"Well done!" Gedrhar grinned, sharing his pride in Gralyre's success. "Especially for a first attempt. The ability to use the Deep Dreaming usually takes years of practice. Your ability is unprecedented!"

Gralyre's hand dropped, his fist clenching around the stone he had made. He frowned, as a wisp of memory tickled his mind. "I do not think this is the first time." A trace of nostalgia and grief sobered him. "I feel that my mother did teach some of this to me... before she died... I think, maybe...."

ഇര

Inside the Wizard Stone

The ancient sorcerer chaffs lest Gralyre remember the truth of it. He dares not interfere with the Prince's memories of his Dream Weaver mother in the presence of the Gedrhar, who might sense the influences exerted upon the Prince.

All could be lost!

He will act if necessary, he decides. He has waited too long for his new vessel! The old Dream Weaver can be easily killed, and an alibi created.

ഇര

Gralyre rubbed his brow, distressed by a dark memory that he could not quite bring into the light. "I remember very little of her, just impressions." His hand dropped away, as his mind shied away from the remembrance, a wild horse unwilling to take the rider to its haunted destination.

He cleared his throat, and sought to devote his full attention back to his lessons. "What else can the Thewr 'ap Noir do? Can it be used to create a living creature?"

"Yes," Gedrhar nodded. His face showed compassion for the Prince's sadness over the lack of memories of his mother. "But such a thing has not been done for an age. There are few who have ever possessed this power. It is a rare gift indeed. The essence of even the smallest of insects is still filled with more complex energies than one can hold in one's mind long enough to create in the outer world. A rock, a stick, a cage of Maolar," Gedrhar indicated the large construct using most of the space in front of his tent, "these have no bones, skin, hair, hearts, tendons, minds. They are simple."

Gralyre stared at the cage, lost in thought, as he fingered the amber stone. "Gedrhar?" he asked finally. "I need to make something special. Will you help me?"

"Of course, *unticol*."

∞⚇

Despite the weather that had made a muck of the ground of the practice field, Gralyre called an assembly of all the Warriors of Lyre, Northern and Eastern Rebels both. He left them standing in the cold for several minutes, before making his way through the throng towards a wagon bed, the makeshift stage that he had set at the forefront of the gathering.

He nodded a greeting to his council, who formed a loose semi-circle around the front of the wagon, already in place and awaiting him. Beyond them, a double line of Dream Weaver warriors served as honour guards.

The waiting, milling people began to cheer, as Gralyre jumped up onto the wagon bed so that all could see and hear him. The applause rose to challenge the thunderheads above.

The adoration that roared through the crowd was a force that could be felt, yet from his vantage point, Gralyre could clearly see that the Rebels were obvious in their polarization. The Northern Rebels clustered in the front, and the Eastern Rebels grouped at the fringes, as though uncertain of their welcome. Dream Weavers, spaced strategically throughout the Rebels, were on alert to immediately separate any fighting.

Unbeknownst to Gralyre, the dull afternoon light flared off the dragon wings on the sword of Lyre, and off the gleaming Maolar chain mail in which he was clad. His radiance was the only brightness in the dour day. Standing tall in the wagon bed placed at the edge of the high plateau, with a backdrop of craggy mountains, and with the wind teasing and tangling his ragged, overlong black hair, he looked every inch of what he was, a dangerous legend come to life to save them all.

Gralyre raised his hands for silence, and when he finally had it, he again used the trick of magic that amplified the strength of his voice so that his words boomed out, and could be easily heard to the far reaches of the throng.

"Warriors of Lyre! You are the chosen!" Gralyre declared, and had to await the cessation of cheers. "After generations of oppression, you are the men and women who will bear witness to the fulfilment of prophecy! Honour your sacrifices, and those of your forbearers, for your vengeance is nigh! There will be no quarter! There will be no truce! Doaphin seeks to end us, but it will be *his* end that he finds! Warriors of Lyre, we march to war!"

The people erupted with their approval. It was long minutes before he could speak again.

"Standing together, my people, we are strong! We are equal to the trials ahead, and we will prevail! The Gods of Fortune have already won the wager of our victory! Look to our powerful allies!" Gralyre extended an arm to indicate each as he named them. "The Slayer of Demon Lords, Catrian Kinsel, your Sorceress, stands as your shield against Doaphin's foul magics! The Dream Weavers have returned, bearing Maolar weapons, so that Doaphin's evil spawn will fall to your blades! The Dragon Sword of Lyre has been reclaimed…"

Gralyre awaited the screams and cheers, whistles and applause to abate slightly before shouting out, "and the Lost Prince has returned! Fell Usurper rule no more!" Gralyre pumped his fist into the air. "Death to Doaphin!"

The crowds screamed back at him, "Death, Death, Death!"

There was no holding back the army's wild exuberance. They rushed the wagon, reaching out to try to touch Gralyre. The Dream Weaver honour guard locked arms to strengthen the barrier between the Council and the surging people.

Solemn of bearing, Gralyre looked out over the sea of reverent, chanting people, and raised his arms open, as though to embrace them all. He noted that the Rebel groups had started to mix, forgetting their enmity in the exhilaration of the moment.

While the crowd settled, Gralyre motioned for Dara to join him, holding out a hand to boost her up onto the platform.

From his place within the inner circle, Rewn glanced up at Gralyre with a smile of pride. His face was misshapen from bruising, and he was newly arisen from his sickbed, but he had insisted on being present to see his sister honoured.

"Today, we celebrate the bravery of our people, the People of Lyre! This is Dara Wilson. Harken, to her battle with a Stalker." Gralyre gave her an encouraging smile, as she stepped forward.

Dara looked out over the heads of the assembly, and her mouth went dry with fear, as the crowd went quiet with expectation. Briefly she thought of the irony of recounting a story of bravery while standing terrified before them. She dropped her gaze to the wood of the wagon bed, pretending that she was anywhere but where she was.

"My brother and I carried the Sorceress, as far as we were able..." she began softly. Rewn had coached her not to mention the battle at the fortress, in order to keep the reminder of the civil war from souring the significance of her heroic deed.

"Speak up!" yelled someone from the back of the throng. Even with the help of Gralyre's magic to augment it, her voice was too soft to be easily heard.

Her panicked gaze flew to the sound, and she froze. Then she saw movement in the crowd, and spotted Jacon. He stood amidst the crowd near to the front. He smiled at her with pride. The encouragement rolling from him made her straighten her spine and lift her chin.

Dara began anew, this time in a strong voice that reached to the far edges of the gathering. Throughout her speech, her gaze remained locked on Jacon's, feeding her courage with his approval. She decided that if she just looked at him she would get through this.

She spoke of the Stalker's attack, and of how Dajin had been knocked unconscious, though she tactfully omitted that he had practically soiled himself with fear. She recounted taunting the Stalker to distract it away from feeding upon the comatose Sorceress. Finally, she finished her narrative with the beast's last charge, of the arrows that had skewered its horned hide unexpectedly, and then of her lucky blow with the dagger, into its eye to kill it.

"Show us the blade!" someone yelled, and others adopted the request throughout the crowd.

Dara drew her dagger from the sheath at her waist, a knife of no more than five inches long, and held it up above her head for all to see. The crowd's acclaim redoubled at the illustration of how close Dara had come to falling to the talons of one of Doaphin's most dangerous minions.

Gralyre was not yet through with Dara Wilson. From within his pocket he drew forth a shining medallion of pure Maolar, etched with Dara's name on one side, and the embossed emblem of Lyre upon its face; the swooping dragon with a sword in one talon and a crown in the other. Made earlier that afternoon during his first awkward attempts wielding the Thewr ap' Noir under Gedrhar's supervision, the one-inch medal hung upon a delicate golden chain.

"This medal is yours to bear, that all will know the metal of which you are made!" Gralyre intoned ceremoniously, as he passed the links of the chain over Dara's head, and kissed her cheek.

"I am so proud of you, Dara," he whispered into her ear, as they embraced. "Thank-you for your bravery. Thank-you for saving Catrian."

Rewn hooted and clapped, as the assemblage broke into cheers. Dara blushed, and smiled back at her brother, her dimples flashing in her cheeks. She jumped down off the wagon, and lifted the medallion so Rewn could peer at the design.

Gralyre turned back to the throng, and unsheathed the Dragon Sword. The blade whispered of ultimate power and of magic surrendered willingly. A tickle in the back of Gralyre's mind warned that such power would never be laid at his feet, save as a trap beckoning an unwise step into a snare. The pleasure gained with the fulfilment of his growing addiction made such considerations of no consequence.

The noise of the crowd quickly abated, and the eyes of the people followed the tip of the gleaming blade, as the Prince panned it slowly over their heads. "The Stalker that escaped is still alive in the vale. If a woman, armed with nothing more than a dagger, can *kill* a Stalker, perhaps the Warriors of Lyre will honour us by *trapping* the one the defiles our forest!"

There was stunned silence from the masses, as they considered the Prince's challenge, looking to one another to see who would show the bravery demanded of them.

"I will go with you!" Rewn stepped forward with a shout, as they had prearranged. Gralyre nodded in assent, as his friend joined him upon the wagon bed.

"Me!" Jacon yelled, moving through the parting crowds, and stepping up onto the wagon. Two more Dream Weaver warriors moved to stand next to their leader, and Jacon clapped them on the back, trading smiles. It would be a good hunt.

Other warriors in the crowd saw the jocularity of the Dream Weavers, and their pride prickled. A tall, blond man, his beard braded into his hair, made a stir, as he pushed his way through the gathering to reach the wagon. He had a crusted gash across one cheek, and his clothing was still soiled with soot and gore. "I have already fought a Stalker. I hurt it. I did no' kill it, but here I stand t' tell you o' it!" he boasted. "I vow t' finish the job I have started!"

The crowd began to get into the bravado. Choruses of, "Yeah, Ivor!" followed the blond giant, as he moved to position himself with the others.

General Illian stepped up to the group, and crossed his arms to show he stood with the Prince. "If there is a Stalker t' capture, I am your shield, my Prince." His Easterners roared their approval.

Aneida moved forward, with Jord and Dotch only steps behind. Jord noticed the blond Ivor leering at Aneida, and his vicious daggers appeared, flipped hypnotically, and vanished without a trace. Jord bared his teeth in the facsimile of a smile, his eyes narrowed warningly at the warrior.

Ivor stepped back, and looked elsewhere.

Two Easterners emerged from the crowd, strutting proudly though their clothes were heavily stained. "We two are with ye!" stated one boldly, speaking for them both. They stood next to General Illian.

Gralyre nodded his assent. After a moment of restless shifting by the crowd, it could be seen that there would be no further volunteers.

"We brave few will capture the beast, but the rest of you will also play a role," Gralyre announced, "by beating the brush to drive it into our trap!" Standing shoulder to shoulder in their first battle against their foe, the Northern and Eastern Rebels would begin to mend their trust in one another. It was a small, but important beginning.

"Three hundred years ago, my men and I fought the Stalkers, and killed them. We captured them, and used them to gain knowledge of enemy movements. I will show you the way. You will see first-hand that a Stalker is vulnerable, and that Doaphin is not all seeing, and all powerful. Trust in me. I am your Prince. I will not let you falter in your fight against evil! We will be free from Doaphin's tyranny!" he finished with a dramatic flourish, and pointed the Dragon Sword skyward.

He drew upon its magic, indulging his addiction for its power, and sent a fireball streaming upwards to burst with a thunderous boom amongst the clouds. Moments later, coloured lights trickled down like tiny stars, evaporating ere they reached the heads of the people.

The crowd was silent for the space of a heartbeat before a roar of approval broke from their throats. After witnessing their Prince's power, the people had more than enough confidence to fall in with his plans.

Gralyre watched them for a moment, their excitement and celebration. They were his. Utterly devoted to his will, they would do anything he asked. Sheep to the slaughter. His smile was scornful, as he released his hold upon the sword's power, and sheathed the blade.

The instant his flesh was no longer in contact with the weapon, a dull ringing headache began behind his eyes. The sensation of utter supremacy faded, leaving him slightly sickened and dizzy.

'What was I just thinking?' he shook his head, confused, and rubbed at his brow.

"Gralyre? Are ye alright?" Rewn asked with concern, as he noticed Gralyre's sudden affliction.

"Yes, of course," Gralyre answered quickly. There were bigger concerns afoot than his exhaustion. He leapt down from the wagon, and was joined by those who had volunteered for the trapping of the beast. Gralyre was content that there were representatives from all units of his army, North, East and Dream Weaver.

The Prince's ceremony now at an end, the Rebels drifted in

groups from the practice field, talking animatedly about the Prince's magic and the night to come.

Gralyre glanced around the small group of warriors who had volunteered to trap the Stalker. "I know all but a few of you." They introduced themselves to each other, their names passing around the loose circle.

"Rewn."

"Aneida."

"Ivor."

"Jacon." And here Jacon was obliged to introduce his men. "Patryd, Ulyde," he motioned to each in turn.

"Jord."

"Illian. These are my men, Vossen and Keyan."

Gralyre nodded to each one in turn then outlined their roles in the capture of the Stalker. "We will leave when the moon is up."

Keyan checked the butt of the sword that sat on his hip, a nervous gesture that had all the warriors tensing. "Why do we hunt it in the dark?" he asked contentiously.

"Because that is when it comes out of its hole," Gralyre smiled darkly.

Keyan swallowed uneasily, glancing at his compatriot, but Vossen was suddenly consumed with removing the dirt from under his fingernails. Keyan flushed red, as his hand slid limply off his sword, and back to his side.

"Aneida, a word," Gralyre bade, and drew her from the rest of the group that they might speak privately.

"I do not wish for you to come tonight."

"Why no'?" Aneida frowned darkly, chaffing at the feeling that Gralyre did not think her worthy.

Gralyre's gaze wandered beyond Aneida, to where the Sorceress still sat in her chair surrounded by six heavily armed Dream Weavers, awaiting an escort back to Matik's sickbed. "Catrian is still too weak to protect herself, and until I am certain that the Eastern Rebels no longer pose a threat to her, she must be guarded against attacks."

"What o' the Dream Weavers standing outside her tent?"

"Exactly. They are outside the tent. I want you at her side."

"Why me?"

"Because of your skills with your blade. Because I know that I can trust you."

Aneida was appeased by the Prince's simple faith in her. "Alright. I will keep her safe."

CHAPTER TEN

Rewn entered the sick tent in time to witness Dajin fetching a cup of water for the bedridden Trifyn. The two men had been billeted together, a privilege granted by their connection to the Prince. All other such tents were stacked wall-to-wall and head-to-foot with the most grievously injured. Sharing a space with only one other was a rare luxury, especially being one of the large Rebel tents that had once housed an entire family.

Rewn glanced from one man to the other, only now realizing that Dajin and Trifyn were of an age. *'Strange,'* he thought. *'I could have sworn that Trifyn was older!'*

"Dajin," Rewn said tersely, by way of greeting. Dajin had yet to apologize for the terrible things he had said and done, and Rewn, for once, was not going to play peacemaker. Not this time. He had come to visit Trifyn.

"Rewn." Dajin was just as curt in his reply. He flushed guiltily, though Rewn could not have known that Trifyn had been asking for the water for some time, nor that Dajin had finally complied only because he had heard footsteps approaching in the gravel outside.

"Here ye are, Trifyn. I am sorry I took so long. My injuries make it difficult t' move." Dajin pressed the tankard into Trifyn's shaking hands.

'And my arrows are made o' limp rhubarb!' Trifyn snarled to

himself, as he accepted the water. He had not had contact with Dajin prior to the journey to Fennick's Island, and wished that situation had never been remedied.

The water was accompanied by a threatening glare that Rewn could not see with Dajin's back turned. Dajin need not have worried. Trifyn was not one to carry tales though it was obvious that Dajin was drawing out his recovery. The moment that he was judged hale, Rewn's brother would be evicted to live outside with the rest of the army. His bed was awaited by one of the many injured still exposed to the elements.

Trifyn winced, as he shifted to a sitting position, his wounded leg held stiffly before him, and some of the water slopped over the rim of his tankard to soak into his bedding. His fever had finally broken but he was still very weak.

Rewn was immediately at his side, helping him to sit upright, and plumping his pillow to support his back. After he was settled, Trifyn gulped at the water, thankful for Rewn's care.

"How are you feeling?" Rewn asked, watching as Trifyn drained the cup thirstily.

"He is fine. So am I, by the way." Dajin flounced onto his pallet on the opposite side of the tent, and settled with much dramatics. His snit was born as much from jealousy over the care Rewn was showing to the other man, as for being ignored, a state that he had always found intolerable.

Neither Trifyn nor Rewn paid Dajin heed.

"They saved my leg!" Trifyn carefully patted the mound under the bedding that delineated his infected limb. "I must stay abed for a day or two longer, t' be certain the fever is gone for good, but Ninrhar says I can start putting weight on it after that."

"That is the best o' news!" Rewn smiled in relief. "We will miss your bow tonight. We are set t' trap a Stalker. The Prince thinks that we can interrogate it for information on Doaphin's troop movements."

Trifyn huffed out a weak laugh. "Catch a Stalker? How? Never mind. Ye be careful, Rewn. And tell the others t' be safe."

"Aye, I will."

Trifyn nodded, and a slight smile lifted his mouth, as his eyes drifted closed. "The Prince has returned. Can ye believe it, Rewn?" He sagged back against the bedding, his strength spent.

Rewn was immediately contrite. "I should no' be tiring ye like this." He leaned down, and helped the bowman to settle more comfortably upon his pallet. "If ye want, I will stop in later tonight, and tell ye how it went?"

"Aye, I would like that," Trifyn trailed off, and was asleep once more.

Before he left the tent, Rewn remembered something that he had meant to ask of Dajin, important enough for him to linger and exchange a few more words. "What has become o' the family heirlooms? The chain and seal that I gave t' ye afore I left for Fennick's Island?"

Dajin stiffened and sat up, as Rewn's visit suddenly made sense. "How should I know? I did no' have time t' retrieve it. I was too busy saving our sister and the Sorceress," he reminded snidely. His pride was still smarting that Gralyre had overlooked his valiance at the medal ceremony. As was usual, his family had eclipsed his deeds and stolen his tributes!

Rewn sighed, staring into the far distance, thinking about the loss of this last link with their ancestors. "I guess we do no' need a hunk o' metal t' remind us o' Da. I had thought that I might show it t' Prince Gralyre t' see if he could tell us aught o' our family's history." He missed Dajin's smug expression, as he left the tent.

Dajin reclined back onto his pallet, stacked his hands behind his head, and smirked. He knew exactly where the chain was, and he would never give it back! His gaze travelled to the rucksack in the corner that held his possessions, and his smile grew. This was the beginning of the reparations he would seek against Rewn, and everyone else who had ever slighted him!

∞∞

Matik opened his eyes, and stared in confusion at the muted daylight glowing through the ceiling of the dim tent. The soothing sounds of rain rattled upon the fabric. His throat was on fire, and he was weak, so weak that he could barely lift his hand, but the slight movement was seen.

Catrian appeared in his line of sight, leaning over him. She gasped once, and left his view, yelling for someone called "Ninrhar".

His brief flirtation with wakefulness over, Matik slipped back into a deep slumber.

When next he awoke, there was a woman bathing his forehead with a soothing, cool cloth. There was something familiar about her, but he could not quite place her face. She halted her ministrations when she saw that his eyes were open.

"So ye have decided t' live after all. I am glad. We were no' certain that ye would." She quickly placed a hand over his mouth when he attempted to respond. "No. Do no' speak. Your throat was cut. Ye must allow it t' heal. Ye are safe."

Now he remembered her. Saliana. She had been part of Gralyre's group, travelling with them into the mountains from Verdalan. *Where*, he mouthed at her.

"Ye are still in the fortress. Lie back and rest. I will fetch someone who can tell ye more o' what has happened." As quickly as that, she was gone.

Matik closed his eyes, only for a moment, he thought, but it was night when he awoke again. His head was clearer, and he could feel the ebb of his life flowing back into him.

Flashes of the battle assailed his memory. A vision of Boris, ambushed upon his own ramparts, caused tears to trickle from his eyes. Dead! He had failed to protect his oldest friend!

Kierdenan was drawing his last breaths! He would see the whoreson dead before the night was out!

With great effort, struggling against his infirmity, Matik rolled to his side. His head swam sickeningly, when he summoned the strength to swing his feet to the floor, hanging half off the bed. It suddenly occurred to him that he could not yet stand.

"If I were you, I would rest a few more days afore I started devising my escape," Gralyre interrupted Matik's plans.

Matik stiffened when he recognized Gralyre. *You*, he mouthed, the snarl in the word apparent in the expression on his face. Matik's gaze widened when he noticed the wings of the dragon on the Sword of Lyre thrusting up behind Gralyre's head. *Sword?*

"Yes it is me, and yes I retrieved my sword. I have also regained my memories. You may call me Prince Gralyre."

Prince?

"And lucky for you that we were successful and returned when we did, otherwise you would be dead."

Gralyre's brows knit in exasperation when Matik made a rude gesture. "No need to thank me," he muttered. It took only one hand to resettle the General onto the sick bed.

Catrian?

Hooking a stool with his foot, Gralyre pulled it near, and sat. "Catrian is safe. I used the power in the sword to heal her. She is still recovering, but she grows stronger daily. I have only just sent her to get some dinner, and she will return soon. Matik, there are things you should know."

Gralyre told Matik of the journey to the island, reclaiming the sword, and remembering his royal heritage. He spoke of the battle at the fortress, Kierdenan's death, and the arrival of the Dream Weavers.

Throughout, Matik mouthed one word questions and invectives, but was unable to argue any points. All in all, Gralyre believed it was the most productive conversation that he had ever had with the General.

"Saliana, my Healer, says that you are recovering rapidly," Gralyre said in conclusion, as he stood to leave. "I do not expect trust overnight, but I will not allow anyone to jeopardize the lives of my people. We need you, Catrian needs you, but if you find that you cannot follow me, then you must leave," Gralyre stated baldly. He would brook no subversiveness within his ranks. If they did not stand together, then they would surely fall. "Think long and hard before you make your decision, Matik. Boris is dead, and we need our new Commander."

Gralyre walked away, aware of Matik's thoughtful stare upon his back.

෫෬

A wide grin stretched Matik's beardless face, as Catrian entered the healer's tent on the arm of a woman he did not recognize. His smile faded, as he noted the pinched whiteness of her features, and how her slender frame still bore testimony to the severity of her recent illness. Her clothes hung loosely upon her, and her collarbones stood out sharply.

He did not suppose that he looked much better. The termagant named Saliana the Healer would not allow him to do more than lay propped upon cushions. Matik grimaced, as he saw that Saliana had spotted the intruders, and had moved to intercept.

"How are ye, Catrian?" Saliana inquired kindly. "Aneida?" she smiled at the other woman.

"How is he?" Catrian asked, keeping her expression blank so that Matik would not see her pity. The size of the scab sealing the wound on his throat bespoke the violence of the injury.

Saliana glared down at her patient. She was not intimidated when Matik glared back. "He is still very weak, and canno' yet talk, but I think that a visit from ye will cheer him up."

Saliana pointed out a stool, and Aneida fetched it for Catrian to sit upon. "Catrian, ye may stay for only a while. Ye are still too weak t' be exerting yourself," she lectured. "Aneida and I will be just over there," Saliana pointed to the small table set in the corner. "Call for me if ye feel faint."

Catrian waved them away, and settled herself on the stool. For a moment, she just stared at Matik, and he stared back. Her feelings were clear in her eyes, as she watched his mist. The absence of his beard left his expressions unguarded and clear.

Gently, she stretched forth with her magic, and made contact with Matik's mind. She would be able to sustain the sorcery for only a short time, after which she would have to take to her bed for the rest of the night to recover.

'Lass, lass, I am glad ye are awake!'

'Thank-ye, Matik. How are ye feeling?'

'My throat has been cut, that healer needs a beating, and an upstart spy is claiming t' be the Lost Prince. But otherwise, I will live.'

Matik's sardonic answer surprised a grin from Catrian.

'Gralyre is truly the Lost Prince,' she held up a hand to forestall Matik's black opinion on the matter. *'I have read it from his memories. There is no doubt.'*

Matik stared at her searchingly for a long moment. *'You are in love with him,'* the thought popped out unthinkingly. The problem with this form of communication was that you could keep nothing to yourself!

Catrian blushed and regarded her fingers. *'He does no' want me, Matik.'*

Matik's teeth ground against the loud invective he wished he could make. He had known Catrian her entire life, and felt a paternal indignation over the pain the man had caused her. *'What? Now that he is a Prince, he believes himself too good t' give ye the time o' day?'* he half raised himself onto his elbows from the force of his ire. *'Lost Prince or nay, I will beat him bloody for the insult!'*

"No, ye will no'!" Catrian barked, scowling at him. The last thing she needed were the two most important men in her life fighting a bloody battle over her!

There was a loud harrumph from the table behind her, and Catrian peered guiltily over her shoulder to see Saliana frowning at them both. Catrian leaned forward and pressed Matik's shoulders back onto his pallet, her eyes warning him to relax or their conversation would be terminated.

With a glare, Matik slumped back against his bedding, and folded his arms to glare mulishly at the ceiling. *'A Stalker hunt! That would be something I would like t' see!'* he chose a more innocuous topic.

'If the hunt is successful, and only if ye are stronger and Saliana allows it,' Catrian qualified extensively, *'I will take ye t' see the beast.'*

'Boris would have loved this!'

Catrian's breath caught on the grief that suddenly constricted her chest. *'Our last words t' each other were so bitter, Matik! How I wish that we had found our forgiveness. I wish that I had been able t' tell him how I loved him, one last time.'*

'He knew, lass. He felt the same. Ye were his family.'

Catrian laid her had against his chest. *'Ye are all that is left of my family, Matik, now that Uncle Boris is dead!'*

Matik could feel the heartbreak in her words, as he covered her fingers with his. Together they shared their memories of the brave commander who had kept the resistance alive.

CHAPTER ELEVEN

There would be no moon this night, for clouds still dominated the sky, and rain still fell intermittently. As the able-bodied Warriors of Lyre filed out of the ruined southern gates of the Northern Fortress, foggy breath wreathed their lips from the dampness and the chill. In their hands they carried pots and pans, sticks and drums, with which to make noise. Every fifth person carried a torch or a lantern for light, and every third person was a Dream Weaver warrior armed with either a pike or a bow. The deadly Maolar tips on their weapons would protect the beaters from attack, and repel the Stalker if it attempted to break through the closing ring of noise, as they herded it towards the trap.

Though most of the people were tense and fearful of the coming night, they drew courage from the neighbours to their left and to their right. They cheered, as the Prince and his small band of trappers rode down the slope ahead of them, hauling a small cart upon which sat the Maolar cage. A mood of rousing defiance overtook them all when Gralyre turned and saluted before entering the shadowy treeline below.

When the beaters reached the forest in the Prince's wake, they dispersed in a large arc across the south-facing slope of the mountain's skirt. Over the course of the night, they would work their way down into the valley, and through the area in which the carcass of the dead bear had been discovered.

Though Gralyre, Aneida, Dotch and Jord had not located the Stalker's daylight lair, they thought its den to be nearby. The large animal could not have been carried for a great distance without drag marks, even by a creature as strong as a Stalker.

Meanwhile, the trappers, under Gralyre's direct command, assumed their ambush positions, with the Maolar cage that Gedrhar had created, at the narrow end of a long gully. If all went as planned, the beaters would drive the Stalker towards them, and it would not sense the trap until it was too late.

When all was in readiness, and the cage was in position, and the cart that had borne it was hidden in a thicket, Gralyre nodded to Dotch. "Signal them."

Dotch lifted a horn to his lips and blew a sustained note.

The night erupted with noise, as the Warriors of Lyre began to beat the brush, seeking the evil that skulked in the shadows.

∽∾

Sethreat spies gleefully upon the activity from the cover of rocks near the southern gates, as the humans leave their fortress with their noisemakers.

So cunning a plan! A carcass, uneaten – as though It would ever be so careless! – left to mark the territory of the interloper. By night's end, Fanghorn will no longer bedevil Its Hunt, and the Master will never suspect Its part in the other's death.

But even more fortunes bless the darkness! The humans leave their stronghold empty of warriors. The Rebel Sorceress is alone, undefended, and weak!

A low warble of delight shivers from Its throat sacks, a suppressed roar of victory. Sethreat's opportunity to take the first of Its prey is nigh.

⊱⊰

The Prince had split his team of trappers. On one side of the gulch, Gralyre hid with Little Wolf, Rewn, Jord, and Dotch. Lying in wait on the opposite side of the ambush were the Eastern Rebels - Illian, Vossen and Keyan, the Dream Weavers - Jacon, Patryd and Ulyde, and the giant Northerner, Ivor.

After miserable, dark hours of huddling in the cold, wet forest, with no shelter from the intermittent showers, Gralyre and his men finally heard a horn sound from the lines of distant beaters. Three, quick blasts. The Stalker had been spotted.

Boredom and fatigue vanished, as everyone came to attention. Slowly, the din of the beaters grew closer, heightening their suspense.

"This will ne'er work! 'Tis going t' kill us!" In the stillness of the bushes where they crouched, Keyan's harsh whisper to his friend, Vossen, was clearly heard by all. The distant sounding of the horn had released his terror from the secret place where he had held it penned throughout the night.

"Calm yourself, Easterner," Ivor grunted at Keyan. His blond braids swung, dripping, as he resettled himself restlessly. Though the overtones of his comment had been pure scorn,

Keyan's panic was infectious.

"Trust in the Prince. His plan is sound," General Illian reassured his men quietly. He cupped his hands, and puffed into them to warm his fingers, before flexing them vigorously to keep them limber in the cold.

"But no one has ever caught a Stalker alive! Ever! Why would ye want t'? 'Tis madness!" As his panic grew, Keyan began to pant loudly.

Patryd crossed his arms in disgust. Speaking in his native language to keep his words private, he muttered to Jacon and Ulyde, "These Rebels have not the spine for this."

"Give them a chance to prove themselves afore you pass your judgement," Jacon murmured back, also in the Dream Weaver tongue.

"Keyan, wait!" Vossen grabbed at and missed his friend, as Keyan broke cover.

"The rest o' ye can stay here and die," Keyan yelped shrilly, "but I will no'!" He turned to run, but came up short against the glinting tip of the Dragon Sword, as Gralyre stepped into his path from out of the darkness. Keyan gaped at the speed and stealth with which the Prince had moved. Only moments before, Gralyre had been far across the other side of the gulch, hidden behind his own rocky cover.

With great difficulty, Gralyre suppressed the urge to clout the Eastern Rebel for cowardice, even while he acknowledged that there came a time when only an iron fist would drive some men down the right path. Keyan was placing them all in jeopardy. If he ran, or failed to heed an order in the heat of battle, lives would be lost.

Ever at Gralyre's side, Little Wolf sensed the discordant urges flooding the Prince's mind. His ruff expanded upon his shoulders, adding false mass to his already impressive size. His head lowered aggressively, and his amber gaze fixed intently upon Keyan's rolling eyes.

"If you run, I will set him on you," Gralyre menaced. He allowed Keyan a few terrified moments to fantasize about having his throat ripped out by the wolfdog.

Keyan glanced from side to side, slow to realize that he was alone in his cowardice, and shame hung his head low.

"Get back to your position." Gralyre cared naught why the Easterner complied, so long as he did so. Everyone was needed to play their parts if they were to succeed in the capture.

Shuddering his defeat, Keyan heeded the Prince's order, and resumed his place in the bushes next to Vossen.

Little Wolf sat at Gralyre's heel, but remained tense and ready to attack should that be Gralyre's wish.

Jord, Dotch and Rewn watched the confrontation between Gralyre and Keyan from where they hid in the rocks across the gulch.

"Do ye think that he would have set Little Wolf on him?" Jord quizzed Rewn quietly.

Rewn shrugged, before realizing that Jord and Dotch could not see the action in the darkness of the rain-soaked night. "I do no' know. Before the sword, nay, but now?" The Prince was unpredictable. How much remained of the Gralyre he had known and loved like a brother?

From within their cover of bushes, Vossen jostled Keyan in rough camaraderie. "Follow the plan. Everything will be fine."

"We are all going t' die!" Keyan whispered shakily, blinking rapidly in soul-deep dread.

Gralyre turned his attention to all in the party, seeking to bolster their nerves after their long, cold wait in the darkness. "These beasts of Doaphin are not all powerful," he reminded them. "Hold your ground, attend your role in the capture, and we will all walk away this night with victory on our shoulders!"

A rustle sounded in the trees bordering the path they guarded. "Hey lads, look sharp!" Dotch hissed the warning.

Gralyre and Little Wolf sprinted back to the rocks that they had previously hidden within. Everyone tensed in anticipation, shifting into ready crouches, their legs coiled to spring forward from cover. They huffed in relief, as three deer burst into the clearing, dodging and running in fear away from the din that sounded behind them. In a flash they were gone, heading for the far end of the draw.

Little Wolf danced in place momentarily before settling once more, a predator's response to fleeing prey.

"Gods!" Rewn whispered harshly, rubbing the tense sweat away from his eyes. "I thought that was it!"

"Too bad we are no' hunting food. We could claim enough game t' last the fortress until the end o' summer!" Jord flipped and caught the two daggers that had leapt instinctively to his hands. He palmed them, and they vanished back into the secret places they had emerged from. He reclaimed his grip upon the long spear that he had dropped in a panic, firmly reminding himself that this was to be his weapon for the night.

The beaters drew nearer.

The false alarm had been useful in bleeding away some of their tension, so that they were more focussed and calm when the sound of crackling underbrush sounded again. With harsh, panting grunts, a black bear ran through, kicking up forest debris with the speed of its passage. Again the warriors forced tense muscles to relax.

Little Wolf scrabbled up from where he crouched beside Gralyre, and a dirty growl mumbled in his throat, as he sniffed into the breeze. *Bad scent on the wind. Something evil comes our way. The world is wrong.*

Gralyre's skin prickled from a sense of magic being wielded nearby. "Steady," he advised softly, so that his voice would not carry beyond the men lying in wait. His gaze was intent upon the trail. "It comes!"

The men snapped to attention, hands slick upon weapons from rain and nerves.

The beaters drew nearer, the glow of their many torches colouring the night with flickering hues of oranges and yellows against the tops of the trees at the throat of the gulch. Screams and cries of alarm lifted from the line, but the sounds turned to jeers, as the Maolar arrows and pikes of the Dream Weavers threw the Stalker back. The din continued towards the trappers.

The night chill grew harsher but it was a cold that seeped from within, not without. The evil contained within the approaching predator was a physical force easily felt by every human in its path.

The crash of fleeing animals increased down the draw as creatures, great and small, ran past the hidden men. There was something else in their wake that they feared more than the noisy humans and their torches. Something far worse.

And as suddenly as that, the Stalker pushed through the bushes into sight, favouring its bicep where an arrow had impaled it. The creature paused, smacking the fletching end of the shaft hard enough that the Maolar head erupted through the scales of the other side of its arm, smoking and spitting, as from acid. With a quiet snarl, it broke the arrowhead off, drew the wood from its wound, and threw it into the underbrush.

They awaiting men listened to the Stalker's harsh, panting breaths, as it shuffled forward, a cavernous, rasping inhalation punctuated with deep growls of ire. It moved past their hidden positions, drawn towards the small cairn of rocks that Gralyre had built as a marker, snuffling deeply of the scents clinging to the stones.

Gralyre had liberally spattered blood to encourage the Stalker to step into the trap, the net that was hidden by fallen leaves and dirt. One of the Northern wounded, having succumbed to his wounds that morning, had unwittingly donated his essence for the lure.

"Blood? From whence?" The Stalker peered into the darkness

with a raptor's fixation, directly at the rocks where Gralyre hid. "Didst thou think to hide, Prince? Darkness is mine to command! I see thee!"

"NOW!" Gralyre roared.

With yells of effort, Illian, Jacon and Ivor hauled on the rope that held the trap in place. The Stalker was caught up in the thick, hemp webbing of the net, and hoisted off the ground to suspend from the thick branch of a sturdy pine tree. It bellowed and struggled, throwing the three men off balance, and making it difficult to hold the wet rope in a deadly game of tug-of-war.

From either side of the draw, Rewn, Jord and Dotch, and the two Dream Weavers, Ulyde and Patryd, leapt from cover with their Maolar tipped spears held at the fore, surrounding the beast like a deadly sunburst, lest it try to sever the strands of the net with its teeth and razor sharp talons. The men were breathing heavily in fear, though their weapons never wavered.

"Attempt any magic, and I will kill you afore the spell has left you!" Gralyre challenged, and the Dragon Sword burst into radiance. The Stalker roared defiantly, as the brilliance seared its eyes.

Little Wolf jumped and snapped, trying to reach the slowly twisting body of the suspended beast. The sword's harsh blue radiance cast their stark shadows against the backdrop of the surrounding trees and rocky hillside of the gulch.

"Little Wolf," Gralyre called the wolfdog back to his side.

Pinned in the netting, the Stalker stopped struggling, and turned its baleful, reptilian gaze upon Gralyre. "Thou hast not the strength to pit against this one's sorcery, Prince!"

The men holding the spears cried out, contorting with pain, as they fell to their knees and dropped their weapons. Their mouths foamed, as they seized, flailing roughly upon the ground.

Gralyre wove a cudgel from currents of air, and bludgeoned the Stalker hard enough to stun it. The cudgel became a collar about its throat, tightening until the creature gagged and choked, forced to release its spell. Recognizing the greater threat, the Stalker attacked the Prince, seeking to enter Gralyre's mind to dominate his thoughts.

Gralyre was familiar with this tactic, having endured just such an assault at the hands of the Demon Lord, Mallach, when he had been a prisoner in a Tithe Wagon a year ago. Having endured the unspeakable once, he had vowed never to be a victim of such a mind rape ever again, and had made a special point of practicing a defence against it.

He deftly captured the Stalker's consciousness, encapsulating it with his Sorcery, and compressing. He did not relent until the Stalker's eyes rolled back, and blood flowed from its snout.

Restrained by Gralyre's magic, It sagged in the netting, keening softly with pain.

Jord was the first to recover from the Stalker's magical attack. He arose back to his knees, and shouted in rage, as he stabbed upwards.

The Stalker howled from the wound, as the knifeman twisted the head of his spear in its flank. The Stalker's blood hissed and smoked from the tip of Jord's spear.

"Easy, lad," Dotch gasped, as he sought his footing and joined him. "We need it alive!"

Jord relented, drawing back to guard his friends, as they reclaimed dropped weapons.

While the five men continued to hold their spears upon the subdued Stalker, and Jacon, Illian and Ivor held the weight of the beast suspended, Vossen and Keyan struggled to haul the heavy Maolar cage out from the concealing brush, and manoeuvre it to rest beneath the slowly swinging net. Once within the confining bars of Maolar, the beast would be unable to work any spells. The danger came in lowering it into the cage.

"Thy flimsy metal wilt not hold. Wouldst thou be devoured first little human?" the weakened Stalker taunted Keyan. The stench of fear clung strongest to him, and drew its attention.

The cage banged onto the rocks, as Keyan dropped his corner, and backed away, shivering violently. "No-no-no!" he babbled, his gaze rapt upon the Stalker's baleful, reptilian glare, hypnotised like a small field mouse confronting a snake.

"Keyan," Vossen shouted, "come back! We are no' done!" The creature could not be lowered into the cage, until the opening of the pen was centred under the netting.

With Gralyre's magical bindings upon it, the Stalker could not wield sorcery, but it still had its claws and teeth. Biting at the hemp, it opened a hole that grew wider by the second.

The spearmen stabbed up at it, but had to be careful, lest they kill it. Though it screamed and struggled to escape the burn of the Maolar tips, the Stalker continued to attack the netting. It would soon win its freedom.

"Hold it a moment longer!" Vossen yelled, as he struggled to pull the heavy cage into position on his own.

Dotch growled in disgust, and threw down his spear. Taking up the corner of the cage that Keyan had abandoned, he added his muscle to Vossen's to centre the trap.

Putting their backs into it, Ivor, Illian and Jacon began to lower the Stalker into the open cage, one shuffling step forward at a time, careful to keep the rope taut, and the netting tight.

Keyan continued to back away, his face white with terror in the blue light of the Dragon Sword. The Stalker roared, making him flinch, turn and run.

"Keyan! No! Come back!" Vossen chased after his friend. He tackled Keyan to the ground. "Ye have the padlock! Give it t' me!"

"I… I do no' know where I put it," Keyan patted fitfully at his pockets.

The Stalker thrust its head through the hole in the netting it had created. It roared in frustration, for its arm was tangled, keeping it from pulling free. Sensing the true nature of the Maolar prison at last, it began to panic and thrash, throwing the three men hauling the rope off balance by its unexpected resurgence of energy.

The rope slithered through their wet hands with a whistling burn, and the creature slammed down into the Maolar cage. The freed end of the rope now dangled, swinging far from the ground up the tree, and well out of reach. Without the tension to keep it tight, the net slackened around the Stalker, granting it freedom of movement once more.

Though still tangled in the loosened net, the Stalker attempted to leap up and out, but Jord, Rewn, Ulyde and Patryd were still there to stick it with their spears through the bars. The tips of the Maolar blades sliced smoothly through the Stalker's scales with flashes of fire and bursts of smoke. With a shriek of pain, it fell back.

"Vossen! Keyan! The gate!" Gralyre barked, but when his urgent order went unheeded, he removed his attention from countering the magic of the Stalker for a split second, to find that the two Eastern Rebels were out of position. They were to have retrieved stepladders from the hidden cart while the Stalker was being lowered, so that they could climb up to shut the heavy hatch at the top of the cage. The metal gate required the muscles of two men to swing it closed. Instead, Vossen was struggling to remove the large padlock from the tangle of Keyan's shirt.

Sensing Gralyre's momentary distraction, the Stalker's sorcery slammed the Prince with a heavy blow of pure force.

The abrupt strike wrenched the Dragon Sword from Gralyre's grasp, as he flew backwards. The light from the sword flickered and died, as it clanged against the rocks. Gralyre hit the ground hard, ten feet away, his body digging a furrow up to the rock that finally stopped his slide. The breath knocked from his chest, Gralyre gasped, fighting to remain conscious.

The Stalker leapt again, high enough this time to clear the opening in the top of the cage. Fortuitously, the loose netting snagged upon the bars, jerking it shy of its freedom. Its roars of rage were so deep and loud that they vibrated in the men's chests, playing a demonic resonance upon their ribs.

The spearmen stabbed at it, trying to force it back down into the trap, but the Stalker had a firm grip upon the outside bars now. Despite the burning pain it experienced from contact with the Maolar, it was slowly pulling itself out to freedom.

"Gralyre!" Rewn shouted for assistance.

With a curse at the disaster, yet still unable to stand, Gralyre used his sorcery to drag the Stalker back inside the pen. Another burst of his magic threw the heavy gate up and over the top to slam closed, the job that had been Keyan and Vossen's to do.

"Vossen! Keyan! Who has the lock?" Rewn hollered, assuming command, as Gralyre fell back with a moan of pain.

"Give it t' me!" Jord approached the two Easterners at a run, and snatched the large iron padlock from Vossen's hand. Not breaking stride, he sprinted back towards the cage.

Dotch was already crouched, waiting, so that when Jord's booted foot met his back, he boosted him high.

Jord's concentration narrowed, as he flew upwards. The Stalker had jumped at the same moment as he had. Eye-to-eye, they arose together towards the top of the cage. Jord had but one chance to set the lock before the creature escaped.

Jord reached the top of his arc, and slapped the metal tongue of the gate down over the ring, just before the Stalker hit the secured lid of the cage. The knifeman's quick, dextrous fingers were equal to the task of attaching the padlock and snapping it closed as he began to fall.

The Stalker reached out to snag Jord with its powerful talons, as it also descended from its jump.

With a shout of effort, Jord arched back as he dropped, and felt the cold rush of wind upon his face and chest from the near miss of the Stalker's swipe. His shoulders hit the ground painfully, and he lay stunned, as the cage rocked from the impact of the creature into the bars.

Then it was the Stalker's turn to cry out. A meshwork pattern branded its torso from contact with the Maolar. Surrounded by the searing, magical metal, the Stalker vented its fury by trying to shake the cage apart. But the scaly palms of its hands were already raw from its previous attempt to climb to freedom, and it could not maintain a grip upon the bars.

Ivor, Jacon and Illian stepped out of the bushes. Ivor was spitting on his hands to cool them from the burn of the ropes when they had lost their grip.

Still recovering, Gralyre motioned weakly to Rewn, who raised his horn to his lips, blowing one long, sustained note. It was the signal that the beast was captured. In the distance, a spontaneous cheer erupted from the beaters, filling the night with their defiance against the darkness.

General Illian advanced with rage upon Keyan and Vossen. "By your actions did ye place us all in jeopardy! If this was no' the job for your courage, ye should no' have stepped forward!"

Keyan hung his head, utterly crushed by his cowardice. "I am sorry, General."

Vossen moved closer to his friend to plead clemency. "Please, General. He would have come back!"

Illian glanced over his shoulder at Gralyre, who had recovered sufficiently to sit up.

"He is your man, General," Gralyre reminded coldly, wiping blood from his nose, and breathing heavily after withstanding the Stalker's magical attack. He chose not to interfere in whatever judgement that Illian passed. The new General was responsible for his men, and needed to exercise his authority.

Rewn offered Gralyre a hand, and hauled him upright. "Are ye hurt?" he asked over the din of the Stalker's tantrum.

"I will recover." Limping slightly, Gralyre walked back to pick up the fallen Dragon Sword. He scowled as he hefted its weight. His eyes travelled up the silvery length to where the General confronted his men.

Illian struggled to rein in his anger, and temper it with reason. What he did in this moment would define the respect of his men forever. A violent act would lead to fear, a just response to respect. Had he been Kierdenan or Vetroy, both men would already be dead. But Tobias was his own man. "Twenty lashes for ye both for risking the lives o' us all by deserting your positions! Keyan, ye will return t' the Eastern Fortress with the women and children. Ye now work for the honey man!"

Keyan staggered a bit, and Vossen gripped his friend's arm, as Illian motioned them to proceed him up the trail. It may have been kinder to kill Keyan, to spare him his humiliation. After the whipping, he would no longer be a venerable warrior, but owner of the lowest job in their society, the menial apprentice to the cleaner of the latrines.

"Wait!" Gralyre roared, as he shrugged the sheathed sword into place against his back. "We are not yet finished, General."

Illian swung around to regard the Prince, questioningly. Had the Prince not just told him to discipline his warriors?

"The sins of your men, Illian, are yours to atone for," Gralyre gritted out the reminder, and beckoned.

Illian bowed his head with a sharp twinge of fearful acceptance. It was the covenant that he had agreed to in order to spare the lives of the Eastern Rebels. "Aye, your Highness." He strode forward with admirable bravery to stand before the Prince, and accept punishment on behalf of his men. His arms remained loosely held at his sides, as he braced for the worst.

Gralyre did not make him wait, but clouted Illian in the ear with enough force to tumble him to the ground.

Tobias wobbled as he regained his feet.

Gralyre waited until he was erect before he slammed a fist into his belly, deep enough to seek the General's spine.

"I am sorry, General!" Keyan cried out, flinching as Illian coughed in pain, and dropped once more.

Illian pushed up to hands and knees, shaking his head to clear the ringing in his ears. "Both o' ye! Get ye from my sight," Illian roared at the orchestrators of his humiliation.

Gralyre kicked Illian in the side, rolling him several feet from the force of the blow. He followed after, and his fists rose and fell, as though he would never stop. Illian did nothing to protect himself, as blood began to flow.

"Gralyre!" Rewn finally gasped an objection, as the Prince lifted Illian up by the front of his shirt, and punched the General in the face, knocking him back to the ground.

Illian groaned and coughed. His face was swollen and misshapen from the beating, and he was only barely conscious.

Gralyre glared at Rewn, his breathing harsh, his eyes wild with rage, daring him to utter another word of sanction. But he did not proceed further with the punishment. It was over.

Vossen quickly drew Keyan away, hustling him down the trail back to the fortress for their appointment with the whipping post.

"Vossen! I did no' know that the Prince would punish Illian."

"What did ye think that the Prince meant when he spared us the other day? From now on, the General is t' be blamed for all that we do!"

CHAPTER TWELVE

Once they had carted the caged Stalker back to the fortress, a tent was erected over top of it to shield it from the daylight that was only a few hours off. A four-man guard was posted to watch each corner of the pen, containing one each of Eastern and Northern Rebels, plus two Dream Weavers to discourage them from fighting.

An excited population filed past the Stalker, eager for a view of the caged nightmare. Initially, the Stalker hissed and spat curses while violently shaking the bars, but it was unable to escape or perform magic against the people, and contact with the Maolar burned it. The Rebels pointed and laughed, as the creature hopped comically to escape the sear of the bars underfoot. Eventually, it stood still, and curled into itself, whimpering and pathetic with pain, and afterwards ignored the humans who threw sticks and dirt in an effort to make it move.

A rapacious killer seen only in darkness, igniting if exposed to sunlight, few alive could have described a Stalker with any accuracy before now. The creature was nothing like the lore had portrayed it.

The Stalker was the size of an overlarge man, no more, and certainly not the giant of legend. Like a man, it turned out to have two arms and two legs, not eight like a spider. Its thick tail swished angrily back and forth, but it did not end in a toothed mouth, as the legends told, only a whip-like taper. Its spiteful reptilian eyes, faced forward like all predators, but were not, as one child pointed out, on stalks that could shoot burning fire.

As many characteristics as it shared with humanity it did also share with different animals. Naked of clothing, its genitalia were hidden, tucked from sight like a reptile. Its back legs were powerfully curved like a wolf's, built for speed and leaping. Its scaly hands were modelled similarly to that of a raptor's talon, each of five fingers tipped with wicked black claws that curved in towards its palms, designed for grasping and slashing.

The Stalker's body was covered in overlapping, shiny black scales, an armour strong enough to repel every weapon of man, save for Dream Weaver Maolar. Upon its shoulders were rectangular plates tipped with bony spines that flared upwards and quivered, as punctuation to its roars of aggression, a fearsome sight. Beneath these mobile scales, showed soft, black skin, the only place where an iron weapon might strike and do harm.

More than one person shuddered at the hideousness of its face. Its head was overlarge upon its thick neck, disproportionate to the size of its squat, powerful torso. Its powerful jaws dominated its features. Massive muscles controlled the strength of a bite that could easily shear through bone. Its scaled snout ended in two slits for nostrils. Double rows of serrated teeth curved inward, rotted and foul, but dagger sharp all the same. It did not appear to own ears like a human's, only openings on either side of its head where ears might be placed.

It was bleeding thick, black blood from several deep wounds, where spears had stabbed it during its capture. Each droplet of blood sparked a flame as it hit the Maolar. Every Rebel could now see that it was vulnerable after all, and not the invincible beast of legend. For was it not in the cage, and had they not put it there?

After conquering their fears this night, the Warriors of Lyre decided to celebrate. Some old-timers took out their musical instruments, and a space was cleared, as the people broke into song and dance. Northerner and Easterner rubbed shoulders, saluting each other with tankards of ale while retelling their part in the heroic capture.

Gralyre stood at the fringes of the celebration, holding apart from the revellers. The shadows hid his face, as he considered the punishment that he had meted out to General Illian. He had lost control. Had Rewn not stopped him, he would have murdered Illian. He had wanted to. He wanted it still. What was wrong with him? Deep shame shivered across his skin.

Red light glowed against the ground, cast from the Dragon Sword hilt behind his head. *'Your response was just. The Rebel deserved all of it and more!'*

Gralyre scowled at the ground. How dare Rewn interfere with his princely justice? The Rebels were a fractious lot. If he was to maintain control, he had to hold their fear. Gralyre should have made a greater example of Illian. Next time, he would have the man publicly flogged, drawn and quartered! And Rewn along with him!

A dull throb of pain erupted behind Gralyre's eyes, as he suffered yet another migraine. Gralyre did not notice the red glow fade from the darkness around him, as he rubbed at his brow, and the pain of his headache gradually eased.

His thoughts were mad with exhaustion. Rewn had been right to stop him. He was tired, and the hour grew late.

The giant, blond warrior, Ivor, strutted past with a cooing woman on each arm. He winked at Gralyre before he staggered into the darkness. His deep laughter, and the squeals from the women drifted back, making Gralyre grin at the spectacle, distracting him from his cares of moments ago.

଼ଓଔ

At first light, Gralyre entered the Stalker's pavilion, eager to confront the beast. He had left the creature enough time to ruminate upon exactly what would occur come daybreak.

Doaphin's Stalker uncurled when Gralyre entered the tent, standing fully erect to face him. The muted glow of sunlight through the oiled canvas had started its flesh smoking, so that it appeared clad in mists, an otherworldly creature indeed. Gralyre dismissed the four men who were standing guard, and waited until they had exited the tent before addressing the Stalker.

"What is your name?" Gralyre asked mildly, walking slowly around the cage, forcing the Stalker to twist awkwardly within the confining space to keep him in view.

"This one's name is Fanghorn. Learn it well, Prince, for it is the sound of thy doom!" Its jaws and tongue were oddly shaped, and formed words with difficulty. The quality of its voice was deep and raspy, a boulder being dragged through loose shale.

Gralyre's mouth tightened at the threat. The Stalker needed to be reminded of its situation. Jerking his dagger from the sheath at his waist, Gralyre jabbed upwards and punctured a small hole in the roof of the tent. A single ray of light fell upon the cage, and where it touched the Stalker, its scales burst into flame.

Roaring at the onset of agony, frantically patting at the coin sized ember to snuff it, Fanghorn squeezed to one side to avoid the deadly sunbeam. At its back, the Maolar bars branded it, and Fanghorn leapt away to a darker corner where it had space away from the thin ray of light, and the burning metal both. Panting harshly at the reek of its own seared flesh, it rolled its reptilian eyes towards Gralyre, in real fear for the first time.

"Now that we understand each other," Gralyre snarled, "I will ask. You will answer. If you say or do anything that displeases me, I will open another hole." Instead of sheathing the dagger, Gralyre drove the blade into a tent post, where Fanghorn could clearly view the implicit threat.

"Tell me of Doaphin's battle plans. Where is he? What does he intend."

"Thou wilt not perish at my hand when I escape! My Master hast long sought thee, and thy sword. It is my Master who wilt destroy thee!"

Gralyre considered the beast for a long moment, watching closely, as its gaze flicked between his stoic face, and the hilt of the dagger. In one smooth motion, Gralyre wrenched the blade free, and created another slit in the fabric of the roof.

The Stalker howled, as another ray ignited its flesh. It rebounded off of the Maolar bars for another few moments, twisting to fit into a place that was still in shadow. Watching the spectacle dispassionately, Gralyre repeated his question.

"Doaphin hast mustered at Dreisenheld! That is all that this one knows!"

"What is the strength of Doaphin's army?"

"Many there are! Many under his command. Many!"

"Foot? Horse? Demon Lords?"

"Ye-s-s-s!"

"Numbers!" Gralyre thundered, and opened another hole overhead.

"Millions!" Fanghorn bellowed, as it contorted, desperately seeking a remaining, dark space in which to shield itself. "Millions upon Millions. Who can say? Our numbers blacken leagues upon leagues. When we march to war the Gods themselves tremble in fear of our Master's might!"

"Ask it about the Tithe," Rewn's quiet voice interrupted the sudden hush.

Gralyre glanced over in time to watch him sit upon a stool that he had brought inside the tent with him, that he might enjoy the spectacle. "Ask it," Rewn demanded again, as he settled himself. "What happens t' the women?"

Gralyre turned back to the cage. "Answer him."

"None may say. The Master's will is all. The Master must be

obeyed!"

"What does that mean?" Gralyre flipped the dagger, and raised it up so that the pointed tip created a small peak in the canvas yet did not yet pierce it.

"The Master would not want this one to speak of this!" Fanghorn's arms covered its head as it cowered.

"I am your Master now! Tell me! Tell me the purpose of the Tithe or you will burn!" Gralyre was relentless.

Fanghorn's head reappeared slowly from its folded arms, its reptilian gaze fixated on Gralyre's face. It blinked once, its inner eyelids moistening its reptilian eyes. "Yes-s-s. Thou art my Master. Always and forever, my Master. Always and forever!" the Stalker crooned sickeningly.

Gralyre stepped back, lowering his blade. "The truth Demon!" His voice had roughened with his sudden disquiet at the Stalker's sinister assertion. "What becomes of the Lowland women?"

Fanghorn, sensing how its words had disturbed its tormenter, began to chuckle. "Thou art my Master." It goaded again in lieu of answering Gralyre's question.

Gralyre punched the dagger point through the material, and the Stalker's laughter turned into screams, as its flesh ignited in the thin ray.

"The women! I will not ask again."

"Thou hast thine answer already, my Master!"

"What do you mean by…" Gralyre suddenly stiffened, and his face blanked of emotion.

"Yes-s-s, my Master, yes-s-s. Thou knowest the truth! The Master is all-seeing, all-knowing!"

"What?" Rewn demanded, still ignorant. "Gralyre? What is it saying?"

Slowly, ever so slowly, Gralyre turned his back to the Stalker that he might look at Rewn, that he might hide his disquiet from his prisoner. His hard, emotionless shell rippled, and the torment that streaked across his face in that moment made Rewn suck in his breath. "Tell me."

"Millions, upon millions," Gralyre whispered softly. "Millions, upon millions of 'Riders, walking in daylight."

Rewn gaped, when understanding roared like a wildfire through his soul. Doaphin's army was bred from the women who were taken in the Tithe! "Gods!"

Just knowing the true purpose of the Tithe altered their war strategy. If they could prevent reinforcements from being spawned, Gralyre could force the extinction of the race of Demon Riders through attrition in only a few short years, severely limiting Doaphin's ability to attack in daylight. The Stalker had handed him the key to the Usurper's downfall!

"This is it, Rewn, we can stop him. We can defeat Doaphin!"

⊰⊱

Matik made his escape. Stealthily, he stuck his head through the flaps of the sick tent, checking the whereabouts of the healer.

Saliana was seated with her back to the tent at a small table, enjoying the reprieve from the drizzling rain in the afternoon sunshine. Bundles of dried vegetation surrounded her, and she appeared engrossed in grinding medicinal herbs. She had a distracted expression on her face, her mind far away, as she worked the mortar and pestle. Her white blond hair had come loose from its braid, sticking to the fine sheen of sweat that shined on her face.

A gleeful grin stretched Matik's mouth, as he inched outside, leaning heavily upon a walking stick that he had discovered lying next to his bed that morning. Another glance at his jailer showed her still grinding. She had not noticed his exit, he determined triumphantly.

He took his first unassisted steps towards freedom. He could feel the sunshine!

"If ye are no' back in a quarter hour, I will have ye found, brought back, and tied t' the bed," Saliana called out sweetly.

Matik froze, chills racing up his spine, as the thrill of escape seeped away. Slowly, he shifted his body so that he could glare at her. His neck was still too injured to just turn his head.

She was exactly as he had left her, seemingly paying him no mind, as she mixed her medicines. Until he noticed the small smile that lurked around her lips.

All of his sneakiness had been for naught, when he could have just strolled boldly from his sick tent. The walking stick by his bed had been no accident. He made the only sound left to him - a snarl. "Grrmph!" Still, she was allowing him some freedom, and he was not about to lose the opportunity. As rapidly as he dared, he began to walk away, fearing to hear her calling him back. The ground was slick with the saturation of the rainfall but the bright sunlight cheered him, as did the ongoing preparations for departure surrounding him.

Many of the Rebels who rushed past paused to wish him well, some even going so far as to clasp his hand. Matik stood taller, leaning only lightly upon his stick now. He felt like a conquering hero returned. He paused to decide upon a destination for his first outing.

Catrian had been noticeably absent today. Even though not well herself, she had been steadfastly at his side since he had been found alive. Matik hoped she had not suffered a relapse of her strength. Perhaps he would check on her wellbeing for a change?

"General Matik!" hailed a youthful voice.

Matik shuffled around to see Dajin Wilson jogging towards him. He rolled his eyes in vexation, and his outing soured a little. Matik had no desire to deal with Dajin today. Before the battle with Kierdenan, the younger Wilson had rapidly been becoming a nuisance. Matik regretted the necessity of having used the lad to torment Gralyre, not because he was sorry to have harassed the Lost Prince, but because he had inadvertently created a devotee. Matik tried to flee in the opposite direction but he was too slow to outpace the younger man.

"General Matik!" Dajin called again. "Wait!"

Ceding to the inevitable, Matik wheeled to face Dajin again, as the younger man skidded to a halt beside him.

"How are ye sir? Ye look well!" Dajin gushed, as he took Matik by the arm.

Matik's snarling reply was only heard inside of his own thoughts, as he shook his arm free of Dajin's grasp. *'How am I doing? I canno' utter more than a grunt, and I have no' eaten solid food since I had my throat cut. Now let go o' my arm, pup, before I decide t' cut yours!'* Despite his inner diatribe, Matik's face remained impassive.

Dajin ignored the less than enthusiastic greeting from his mentor. "I am on my way t' see the Stalker!"

'Stalker? Now that sounds interesting!' The day began to brighten anew. Gralyre and Catrian had both mentioned the hunt. It had obviously been successful!

"Last night, they captured one alive," Dajin shared redundantly. "I was no' able t' be there, as I am still recovering from the Stalker that I rescued the Sorceress from."

Matik's brows rose sceptically, for the lad seemed plenty hale to him. He had no need to hear Dajin's overblown version of Catrian's rescue, having already had the true tale from Gralyre and Catrian both, so he interrupted, making a sweeping gesture with his free arm to indicate that they should walk onwards.

Dajin patted Matik on the shoulder condescendingly. "I canno' walk with ye now. Some other time, maybe. Ye should go rest."

'He patted me! He actually dared t' pat me!' It was an insult not to be borne. Matik cracked Dajin in the shin with his walking stick. "Grrrmph," Matik snarled, his face alive with aggravation.

Dajin hopped back out of range with a howl, his hands wrapped tightly around his injured leg. He cursed, and glanced up at the grim-faced Matik. "What did ye do that for?" he demanded sulkily.

With exaggerated gesturing, Matik indicated himself, then Dajin, and then walking. *'Take me t' the Stalker. Take me t' the blasted Stalker, ye idiot!'*

Dajin watched in confusion, as Matik repeated the gestures. "I do no' underst.... Oh! I get it! Ye want t' see the Stalker?"

Matik gave an exaggerated nod. Once more he indicated that they should proceed.

"'Tis this way," Dajin paced his steps to match Matik's slower progress.

They had to walk a short distance across the fortress square to reach the isolated tent that sheltered the Stalker, but Matik did not stop to rest, nor ask Dajin for an arm to lean upon. It was tiring but it felt good to stretch his legs after being abed. The sun was shining, and if he could tune out Dajin's incessant chatter, he could almost hear the birds. Besides, his quarter hour would soon be up. He had no doubt that Saliana would follow through with her threat, and see him tied to the bed if he disobeyed her.

"This is it," Dajin announced in a hushed, nervous voice. "This is where they are keeping it." His jaw firmed, and for a brief moment, he looked more like Rewn. Perhaps it was Matik's silence that encouraged the younger man to over share.

"I need t' prove t' everyone that I am no' afraid o' it. Even after all I did, rescuing the Sorceress, Rewn still thinks I am a coward." Dajin's face twisted with malcontent, and all resemblance to his brother vanished. "Gralyre did no' even give me a medal. Rescuing Catrian was all my idea, and Dara got one instead o' me. My sister, can ye credit the insult o' it? Ye are the only one who has ever believed in me, General Matik," Dajin asserted dramatically.

Before he could stop himself, Matik snorted. He had forgotten how whiny Dajin could be. Dara had killed a Stalker with naught but a dagger. If ever someone deserved the recognition of valour it was she. *'No matter. The Stalker awaits,'* Matik faked a smile for the lad, and gestured them inside.

Four hardened warriors glanced up, as Dajin and Matik entered the tent. "Make way! General Matik wishes t' view the Stalker," Dajin announced officiously. The tent was filled with oily, rank smoke that boiled violently off the Stalker whenever the clouds revealed the brighter sun.

The men saluted. "*Commander* Matik, 'tis good t' see ye hale again, sir," one of the warriors stressed meaningfully, with a glare at Dajin for his pomposity.

Matik nodded in greeting but his eyes were already drawn through the smoky discharge to the cage.

"*Commander* Matik? No one told me that ye had been promoted!" Dajin sounded disgruntled, as though all decisions should pass through his hands. "Congratulations, sir," he added belatedly.

Matik realized that the lad had been well and truly cut from the Prince's inner circle. Perhaps Matik owned some of the responsibility for that. Certainly, he had encouraged the enmity between Gralyre and Dajin.

A guard moved to stand at Matik's side. "Do no' get too close, sir," he warned. "We had a near miss last night. It canno' use its magic in that cage, but it still has its claws and teeth. Do ye see the holes up there?" the guard continued, pointing. "The Prince came early this morning, and put the Stalker t' the question. He had it screaming right and proper. I suppose we should patch the roof, so it does no' die afore the Prince can question it again."

Matik halted as close to the bars as seemed prudent. The Stalker was burned, and black blood oozed from several wounds. It huddled to the far side of its cage to avoid the thin rays of sunshine that fell from the holes in the canvas ceiling of the tent. The black scales that covered its body glistened with flashes of metallic green. Matik had found a beetle once that had owned such colouring. The beast was so still that it did not even seem alive. Then it shifted, making Matik jump.

"Thou lookest as this one feels, human," whispered the Stalker morosely.

Matik took full advantage of the opportunity to study his enemy. Except for the injured Stalker that he had killed with his axe before it could finish Catrian, and that one had been burned beyond recognition by Catrian's sorcery and almost dead already, he had rarely seen them, and then only from a distance. If one saw a Stalker up close, one did not survive to tell of it.

Matik was surprised that the Stalker was little bigger than a man. He had always thought that they were giants. Certainly it was a deadly beast, but he could see that it breathed and lived, and so could die.

With the sun beating down, the temperature was high within the tent. The Stalker had raised the bony plates along the back of its shoulders to alleviate some of the heat. Matik could see that beneath the scales was tough leathery flesh, proving it as vulnerable to a sword thrust as any other animal would be, if one could get past its defences.

"Draw closer, human," the Stalker invited. "I will finish for thee what thine enemy hast begun." It thrust its arm through the bars, though its swipe fell short of reaching Matik. It clacked its talons together sharply at throat level, and then squealed painfully, snatching back its arm, for it had accidently brushed one of the beams of light falling through the punctured ceiling.

A puff of smoke arose from the newly singed scales. Matik had seen enough. He turned his back, and began to shuffle towards the door.

Dajin intercepted him. "Do ye no' want t' stay for a little while longer, Commander Matik?" he asked nervously, glancing over his shoulder.

Matik followed Dajin's line of sight, and met the irritated eyes of the four guards. *'Pissed them off already, have ye?'* He was amused by the thought that they had been holding back from schooling Dajin because of the connections the lad claimed.

Matik saluted the guards in farewell, and cut his eyes suggestively towards Dajin with a permissive nod. He was answered by sly grins, as the men returned the gesture. Sometimes words were not necessary.

'That will teach him no' t' pat me!' Matik smiled righteously. He left the tent without a backward glance, and had taken only a few steps, when his arm was unexpectedly taken in a firm grasp.

A young warrior blushed, as he looked into Matik's offended face. "Commander, Mistress Saliana sent me after ye, sir," he explained deferentially.

"Grrmph!" Matik snarled, but allowed the younger man to help him back to the sick tent. Little though he wanted to admit it, he was exhausted, and the man's help was welcome.

Saliana was waiting, her arms crossed, and her foot tapping menacingly. Her face was set in stern lines.

Matik was glad that he could not speak otherwise he feared he would be babbling excuses to the woman for his tardiness.

"Matik!" Saliana began, finger wagging. "Look at ye! Ye have gone and overtired yourself..."

The young man supporting him grinned at her, a smitten look upon his face. "Do no' be mad at the Commander for being late, miss. I found him already on his way back. He had walked too far, and had stopped t' rest," he winked at Matik.

Matik wondered if the boy was too old to adopt.

Saliana sighed, her face suspicious. "Help him t' bed then," she ordered with an impatient gesture.

The young man complied, doing Matik more harm than good, as he could not keep his attention off of the healer.

CHAPTER THIRTEEN

Later that afternoon, Gralyre called a council meeting. He needed to share the new information that he had gathered from his interrogation of the Stalker, and then decide how far it would impact their war plans.

He ensured that Dream Weaver guards were posted in a large circle surrounding his tent, facing outwards to prevent the curious from drawing near enough to eavesdrop through the thin canvas walls. The allegiance of the Dream Weavers was not in question, but the former Rebels had yet to prove themselves to the Prince's satisfaction.

He and his council would be strategizing long into the night, so he had moved a sagging, charred table into the space, set with what chairs could be salvaged from the burned rubble. Ale, bread and roasted venison landed in front of them as his advisors took their places. They would dine, as they talked.

Gralyre immediately noted a significant absence, as they settled themselves. "Where are Catrian and Aneida?"

Jord frowned. "I sent a runner t' fetch them from Catrian's tent. They should be here by now."

Gralyre exerted his magic, and sought the special bond that he and Catrian shared. Oddly, he was unable to sense her presence. It was possible that the wound between them was still so raw that Catrian had barred him from entering her thoughts, though he had thought their discord resolved. Even so, she would never miss so important a meeting.

General Illian arose from the table, responding to Gralyre's uneasiness. "I will seek them, your Highness." His face was blackened with bruises from the beating Gralyre had delivered to him, though Ninrhar had healed his fractures.

"Thank-you, General." Gralyre was ashamed upon witnessing the results of his punishment. Thank the Gods that Rewn had stopped him before he had caused worse damage! "Check with Saliana at the healer's tent. Catrian is likely at Commander Matik's side." He watched Illian limp towards the exit.

A prince is never wrong…

"Tobias," Gralyre called out before the General departed. Gralyre stood and cleared his throat. "I regret what passed between us last evening." Gralyre gestured awkwardly at his cheek in empathy for what Illian was suffering. "I took it too far."

General Illian regarded the Prince in surprise before bowing low. "Highness, I accept my punishment without complaint. 'Twas our pact, and 'tis a small price t' pay for the lives o' my men."

Gralyre nodded, yet was uncomfortable with being absolved. Illian's punishment had been delivered in a frenzied rage. There had been no forethought or restraint on Gralyre's part.

An uneasy hush had descended in the tent, and Gralyre's face flushed red with embarrassment. "Thank-you, General," he dismissed stiffly. He resumed his seat at the head of the table, as

Illian departed in search of Catrian and Aneida.

Gralyre began their meeting, as they supped. He would inform the women and Illian of what they had missed when they returned. "Rewn, how goes the muster?"

"Those who would depart for the Eastern Fortress are ready t' leave in the morn out South Gate under General Illian's command," Rewn informed. "As ordered, these will include the women and children, elderly, and any injured who have no' yet recovered sufficiently t' be o' aid in the battles ahead. Saliana and Ninrhar are working tirelessly t' bolster the wounded for the journey."

"Jacon, Gedrhar?"

Gedrhar answered for his son. "The Dream Weavers stand ready with five thousand horse and bowmen."

"Dotch?"

"Highness," Dotch reported, "prior t' the battle with Kierdenan, the muster had already been set in motion by General Matik and Commander Boris. We lost some o' our supplies, but the Dream Weavers have supplemented our lack. The Warriors of Lyre are ready t' depart through West Gate tomorrow."

"Jord?"

"I sent riders t' the outer defences. The Southern Outpost was deserted, the men all killed. Kierdenan's handiwork. It was strange that he stopped to burry them."

"It was us who did so when we entered the valley," Jacon spoke sadly. "To leave them in such a state would have been disrespectful of their bravery."

Jord regarded Jacon, as he sopped up a bit of gravy with a hunk of bread. After a moment spent evaluating the Dream Weaver's sincerity, he continued his report. "All of the outer defences have now been abandoned for the Western Outpost. The sentries are waiting to join with our army when we arrive." He popped the bite of food into his mouth.

"Numbers?" Gralyre asked.

"A hundred warriors," Jord spoke around his mouthful.

"Well done," Gralyre complimented all his people. He knew that it had been no easy feat to organize so much in so little time, especially with the acute tension between the two Rebel factions. "Illian will return home and gather the last of his warriors, around three thousand strong, and meet with us at Hondors Pass in four weeks time.

"Remember that when we reach the Lowlands, we will split our forces again, and again, as we move west and north, spreading thin to warn as many Lowlanders as possible. This will leave us vulnerable to attack, so we must move with stealth and speed. Our mission is to evacuate as many people as possible from the path of annihilation, while avoiding open battle for as long as possible."

Gralyre quieted, and his attention seemed to stray from the discussion.

Everyone was confused by the lull, save for Rewn, who hunched in upon himself, shoulders sagging, as he stared down at his plate. He knew what was to come.

"Gralyre?" Dotch finally prompted. It was not like the Prince to be so distracted. "What is it?" So far, everything was as had been decided upon at the other council meeting.

"Keep confidential what I am about to reveal." Gralyre finally looked up, and confronted their concerned gazes. "The people must not know of this, not yet." His grim demeanour garnered their full compliance.

In an act of frustrated rage, Gralyre stabbed his knife into the tabletop with a violence that made everyone jump. "The Stalker said that it is because of my return that Doaphin is mobilizing. Doaphin wants the sword, and he wants my head. To possess both is the only way to break Fennick's curse. Doaphin conceived the genocide to draw me into a battle that I cannot win. He will kill every living soul in this realm just to get to me and the sword."

Gralyre's hands fisted on the tabletop to either side of his plate. His proud head dipped in anguish. "All this death. It is all happening because of my return!"

Stillness ruled the people clustered around the table, as the shocking knowledge was digested.

"You dare not surrender yourself, *unticol*," Gedrhar urged, shattering the silence. "There is no guarantee that by sparing your people in the short term, Doaphin will not then wield the magic in the blade to a more bitter end for us all."

"'Tis my fault that my people are under attack, Gedrhar! Should I not consider this?"

"No!" Rewn burst out in denial. "'Tis o' no fault o' yours, Gralyre! Their deaths would have come anyway," Rewn asserted. "There are fewer o' us with each generation. Your return only hastened a journey that was already well underway."

The others nodded and voiced their agreement.

"Aye, the Tithe." Gralyre's voice roughened, and he stared fixedly at the tabletop.

The others, reading Gralyre's strain, grew uneasy. What news could be so terrible that this great warrior would falter at the telling? What was worse than what he had already divulged?

"The Demon Riders are half human," Gralyre began. "'Tis why they must be twice killed. Upon the death of their human side, their evil is freed, and they become the Deathren."

Jord made a face of disgust, "What woman would birth such vile…" The tortured look Gralyre shot him made him trail off, as he realized the full truth. "The Tithe! No!" He looked sickened.

Gralyre continued to reveal the full horror of it. "The women are driven to the north, taken to a hidden city in the wilds beyond the city of Tarangria. They do not survive the births," his words were clinical and cold, so alien in nature to his normal tones that none there doubted his torment. Only by supressing all emotion could he continue to function.

"Are…are they raped?" Jacon asked hesitantly.

Gralyre shook his head. "The Stalker did not say, but I had the sense that it is through the dark magic of Demon Lords that the women are quickened. The infants gain adulthood within four or five years. Their growth is made unnatural by their tainted blood."

Gralyre's control slipped, and deep wrath flushed his face,

making his midnight-blue eyes glitter so, that few there could meet his piercing gaze. "Doaphin has been using the heart of my people to breed the very weapons of their destruction!"

"There is more," Rewn rasped and cleared his throat.

"What could make this worse?" Dotch asked, his chair creaking, as he slumped back from the table.

Gralyre rubbed his hand past his brow. He felt fevered from the steaming cauldron of emotions that stewed within his chest. "Doaphin knew that one day the Tithe would falter. You cannot take generations of women, and not see mankind doomed to extinction. To bolster the dwindling numbers from the Tithe, he has been breeding human slaves for many generations. They have no language, and are like unto caged animals," Gralyre's voice trembled. "When they are of no more use, they are slaughtered like cattle, and used as sustenance for Doaphin's hordes." Gralyre regarded the congealing food on his plate, and his face twisted with disgust, as he pushed it away.

Dotch's hands had covered his mouth, as though he would be ill. Jord breathed harshly, his eyes round and shifting, afflicted by the mental images that Gralyre had painted. Rewn brushed covertly at moistness in his eyes.

Gralyre straightened his shoulders, despite his desperate sorrow. To show his people weakness was to invite them to be weak as well. Only strength of leadership would keep them alive in the coming conflict. His confidence would give them the courage they needed to stand strong against the evil they faced.

"All is not lost!" Gralyre reminded, his eyes burning

fervently. "The Stalker betrayed the location of the secret city! 'Tis from there that Doaphin gains his reinforcements. We can destroy it. Without a daylight army he is finished!"

"If it can be believed," Jord interjected pessimistically.

"What did the Stalker say o' Doaphin's armies?" Dotch asked despondently, rolling his pewter tankard, and watching how the light caught in the depths of the foaming, amber ale. "They will seek t' stop us. How many do we face?" He sounded old beyond his years.

"Doaphin deployed from Dreisenheld on the Spring Solstice; foot and horse, Stalkers, Deathren and Demon Lords." Gralyre's gaze met Rewn's warningly, to keep him from revealing the Stalker's assertion of *millions and millions*. There was no proof, and Gralyre would not perpetuate false information.

"The Stalker is from Doaphin's Towers, and was not present at the muster. It was vague with exact numbers, but we are surely heavily outnumbered. Doaphin's horde is marching west. If it is as large as we suspect, then it will be slow moving and unwieldy, making little more than six leagues each day. Our small, nimble groups will easily avoid it. Let Doaphin march on our towns and villages. They will be empty. We will evacuate our people ahead of him, and burn it all behind us! His army will rip itself apart as it starves, and do our work for us."

General Illian's return to the war council interrupted their discussion. He hesitated at the threshold of the tent to bow respectfully. Saliana stood in his shadow, having followed him through the flap. "Highness, the Lady Catrian canno' be found."

He had more to say, but Gralyre forestalled him.

"Saliana, did you see her with Matik?" Gralyre asked, as fingers of concern began to fist around his heart.

Saliana shook her head. "For certain, she was no' there earlier, but Ninrhar and I have been very busy. I do no' think so, but then I was no' looking for her."

Gralyre stood so abruptly that his chair spun away to fetch up against the fabric of the tent's wall. "Who saw her last?"

"She was at the gathering," Dotch reminded.

Rewn had also arisen from his chair. "Aye. She left no' long after. With Aneida."

Saliana snapped her fingers with remembrance. "She visited Matik last evening, just before the hunt. She did no' stay long. Aneida was there t' help her return t' her tent."

"Illian," Gralyre barked, "Did you talk to her sentries?"

"Aye, they are still at their posts. The Sorceress had no' yet emerged. They thought nothing o' it, as she has been so ill. They thought she but rested throughout the day. I spared a glance within, and... and I found... it was Aneida."

Jord paled. "Is she alive?"

Illian nodded. "She will no' waken. There is no mark upon her. I canno' understand it."

"Ninrhar is with her now," Saliana reassured.

All of Gralyre's fears settled upon Illian. "If your Easterners have aught to do with this, General, I will have you flogged bloody, and left to the crows!" he roared.

Saliana touched General Illian's elbow in a show of support.

Though Gralyre had always acted with honour in the past, and would be unlikely to follow through with such a terrible threat, the General's bruised face made her unsure of the unpredictable Prince, and what he was capable of.

"O' course, Highness." Illian stood taller, accepting his fate.

"Gedrhar, speak with the men who were standing guard last night and today!" Gralyre ordered. "Find out how Catrian may have slipped past them!"

"She is a Sorceress, Highness," Dotch reminded.

"One who is too weakened to walk far on her own!" Gralyre snapped back at him. "Gedrhar?" he prompted for action.

"At once, Prince Gralyre." Gedrhar and his son, Jacon, stood up from the table, and pushed past General Illian and Saliana who were still hovering at the entrance.

"Search the fortress!" Gralyre was frantic. "Pull it apart! Every tent, every rock! Find her!" He could not feel Catrian's presence, but refused to consider that she might be dead.

As the others took their leave to begin their searches, Gralyre called Rewn back. "Stay with me! We will examine Catrian's pavilion! I need to see Aneida!"

Using his magic, he called Little Wolf to his side. If Catrian had been taken, then the wolfdog's senses might be Gralyre's only chance to find her.

CHAPTER FOURTEEN

Doaphin's Towers

Catrian awoke slowly, wincing at the pain thrumming in her skull. She must have overused her magic while talking with Matik.

Her bedding smelled musty, dense with the aroma of mildew, and she wrinkled her nose with distaste. '*The rains o' the day before,*' she reasoned the damp away. Perhaps later she would presume upon Aneida to help her with her laundry.

She shifted, and her eyes sprang open in surprise at the heaviness in her limbs, and the clank of chains. Mild panic strengthened the speed of her heartbeat. '*What is this? Where am I?*' It was not the soft, daytime glow of a tent that had played against her closed eyelids, but the weak light of a flickering flame. The dancing shadows made the walls and low ceiling undulate, as though they would cave in to crush her.

A smoking oil lamp rested within a niche set into the damp, aged-blackened stones of a wall. Dripping water pooled into the recess, making the flame sputter weakly for continued life. The water overflowed the shelf, and trickled to the floor to meet its journey's end into a rusted, iron grate set into the filthy flagstones. Black mold marked its ancient flow across the stones.

Confused and alarmed, Catrian pushed up from the rotted

ticking of the straw-filled mattress, the rasp of her chains accompanying her every laborious movement. The extra weight upon her recovering body was immense, and made it difficult to coordinate her limbs enough to stand. Thick, iron manacles ringed her ankles, wrists, and neck from which hung short chains. These were welded together to merge into a sixth, longer link that was anchored with rivets into the wall. The soiled stone floor bore centuries of sculpting from the drag of these very chains by other occupants.

Along with the rotting bed that she had been flung onto, there was a three-legged stool next to a small, battered table. A dented tin bucket stood ready in the far corner for use as a chamber pot.

Tarnished, iron bars spanned the entire front wall of the ten-foot square room.

She was a prisoner.

As the thought ravished her courage, the gate of her cell rattled. Catrian whirled with a scrape of chains, and grew faint with fear at the sight of the Demon Lord who leaned there, outside her prison, smiling now that he had gained her attention. His clothing was ornate blue silk, decorated at lapels and cuffs with gold braids and lace. His light blond hair flowed to his shoulders in casual disarray, as though he had been enjoying a walk, and wind had ruffled through the length. He was beautiful. And corrupt.

"Welcome to Doaphin's Towers, Lady Catrian!"

Catrian tried to attack, to shatter the offensive chains, but nothing happened! Her worst nightmares were manifesting.

Uncle Boris had warned her repeatedly of the consequences should Doaphin's minions ever take her.

The Demon Lord's smile grew smug, as he witnessed Catrian's dawning realization of her complete helplessness. His angelic face did nothing to mask the taint of evil that lurked beneath, but only accented it further because of the contrast between the beautiful and the foul. "Your magic has been taken from you. You are as impotent now, as any other slave."

Catrian panted, as she searched deep within her soul for her connection with her lake of Godsmagic, or even her Wizard Stone. The Demon Lord had spoken truly, for she could not reach them. It was as though sheep's wool had been packed into her head. She perceived nothing of the world beyond her five common senses, and they too felt dulled and useless. "What have ye done t' me?" she demanded, reduced to yanking weakly upon the irons, to try to separate the links of the chains.

"A simple procedure to make you compliant to our will."

"How am I here?"

"This one didst take thee from thy bed," rasped a sinister voice.

What Catrian had assumed to be a darker shadow in the hall outside her cell, shifted and stepped into the flickering light of the smoking lamp. A Stalker! She could not contain her gasp of terror, as she reflexively sought her missing powers again. As before, they were denied her. She was helpless. Blood drained from her head to her feet, and she swayed unsteadily.

"This one didst use the Master's portal to bear thee hence."

The Stalker's tongue pattered in and out, forked like a snake's. "So easily mastered. So helpless. So easily taken," It crooned.

"Where is Aneida? What have ye done t' her!"

The Stalker bared its teeth. "The noise of thy vassal's death would have drawn thy guards with poisonous metal! She sleeps, just as thee did. Soon, Sorceress, wilt thou scream and beg for thy death. Thy suffering wilt be endless! Glorious! Thy torment wilt be this one's offering to the Master!"

Catrian backed away, with a heavy drag of chains, as far as the confines of the small cell would allow. Her shoulders fetched up against the mildew slick of the cold, stone wall, and damp wicked through her shirt and iced her skin.

"Not yet, Sethreat," the Demon Lord forestalled. "It has been long since we have held such a powerful prisoner. We would not harm the mother of a new generation of Demon Lords. Not yet."

Catrian shuddered, as she followed where her horrified thoughts were leading her.

The Demon Lord grinned wider, noting her shiver, feeding upon her terror. "Just as 'Riders are bred of the common stock of the land, Demon Lord's require a more rarefied gestation." He chuckled softly. "We have not captured one such as you in an age!"

Catrian shook her head in denial, and her weight rocked from foot to foot, as her chains refused her need to run. She had sensed it a year ago! She had told Boris that the key to the Usurper's destruction lay in abolishing the Tithe. Now she understood why Doaphin had guarded its purpose so closely.

Extinguishing both the Demon Rider race and the Demon Lord Sorcerers would essentially end the Usurper's stranglehold upon Lyre. The Demon Lord must have been confident that she would never escape this place alive to have revealed this most vital of secrets.

"Gralyre!" Catrian spat, desperate to remind herself that she had hope. "The Prince will come for me!" If she thought to intimidate the creatures she failed miserably.

"Will he?" The Demon Lord sneered. "He left his own fiancé, a queen in the making, to her fate at the hands of Doaphin. Why would he bestir himself for the likes of you?"

The Stalker thrust its powerful snout through the iron bars. At the aggressive gesture, Catrian yelped and flinched back harder against the wall, though she was already well out of reach of the creature's dagger-sharp talons. She could hear the Stalker scenting the air, snuffling loudly. Its mouth rippled into a snarl, displaying its double rows of serrated teeth. It was then that Catrian noticed the puckered scars that adorned each cheek. She gasped in recognition. It had to be the creature from the legend of the Lost Prince! The Stalker that had delivered the shorn tresses of the Princess to Gralyre!

"When thy usefulness hast passed, thine flesh will be mine to despoil!" The Stalker followed its threat with a warble of need and a snapping of teeth.

Catrian gagged upon a short scream, so that it emerged as a fearful gurgle.

"You have been ill. Rest and recover your strength for what is to come," the Demon Lord menaced. "Soon enough, you will be put to the purpose that the Master decrees."

As the Demon Lord and Stalker left, Catrian sagged weakly onto the three-legged stool, and braced her hands upon her knees, fighting to calm her shivers, tears and sickness.

'Gralyre will come! He will!' But deep within, she knew it was not so. The Demon Lord was correct. Gralyre would never sacrifice his kingdom for her. Her spine stiffened in defiance to her circumstances, and Catrian's breathing steadied. *'And I would never ask such a choice from him!'*

She traced her fingers over the fine network of blue veins that showed through the skin of her left inner wrist. It was already scraped, raw and bleeding, from the bite of the iron manacle. When the time came, she vowed she would release all of her blood rather than submit to evil.

But before that final end, she would try everything she could to escape. She had to get word to the rebellion about the true nature of the Tithe. Mankind's survival depended upon it.

₧₨

Gralyre, Rewn and Little Wolf burst into Catrian's tent.

Ninrhar glanced up from where he crouched over Aneida.

"How is she?" Gralyre demanded.

Ninrhar smiled. "Quite recovered," he leaned back to show Aneida with her eyes fluttering open.

"What is happening?" she demanded in alarm as she noted

the men standing over her bed.

"Catrian is missing," Rewn explained.

"Impossible! We only just retired..." Aneida squinted with alarm at the lateness of the light shining through the canvas.

"You have been attacked with a bit of Sorcery that forced you to sleep, young lady," Ninrhar explained. "If I had not been able to awaken you, there you would have stayed unto your death."

"Sorcery?" Gralyre demanded. "Why would Catrian do such a thing?" A quick scan showed nothing out of place, save that the covers upon her cot had been flung back, as though she was newly arisen.

Ninrhar frowned. "I do not believe she did."

With a gesture, Gralyre sent Little Wolf to sniff at the scents clinging to the bedding. Immediately, Little Wolf growled. *Evil took her.* For once his words failed him, and instead, Gralyre received images of a Stalker.

Gralyre swayed, and sank into a scorched, rickety, ladder-back chair, one of two that Catrian had placed in front of an unlit brazier. His face froze, and his fingers developed a fine tremor.

"Gralyre? What is it? What has happened?" Rewn knelt in front of him. His reaction was terrifying to behold.

Gralyre wet his dry lips, and his midnight-blue eyes blinked heavily with despair. "Stalker!" he announced hoarsely. "Doaphin has her!" He shook his head in denial. "Rewn, she has not recovered the strength to defend herself! She is still so vulnerable..." He reached out to clasp Rewn's hand.

જીભ

Inside the Wizard Stone

The Sorceress is gone! Eliminated without having to bestir himself to do it. She was too close to the Prince, making her the only one who might have stopped his plans. Now, nothing impeded his possession of his new vessel. Soon, he will walk and breathe life again, and break the world to his will!

જીભ

Little Wolf continued to circle the interior of the tent, until he halted at a place on the back wall, and looked back at Gralyre. *It entered through here.*

Gralyre shook off Rewn's touch, and hastened to Little Wolf's side. This close to the fabric, the Stalker's way in and out of the tent was now obvious. Gralyre and Little Wolf erupted through the slit in the oiled canvas into the lane behind Catrian's tent. Rewn followed closely, with Aneida and Ninrhar.

It has fled this way with your mate, Little Wolf announced. Nose to the ground, he began to run.

"Where...?" Ancida began, as she watched the wolfdog deserting them.

"He has its scent!" Gralyre's face was crazed, and he was already moving at speed to keep up with Little Wolf.

"Gralyre, wait for me!" Rewn yelled and set out after him.

Aneida turned to the healer. "Find Jord and Dotch! Tell them South Gate!" She guessed Gralyre's destination based upon his direction of travel. "Go!" she yelled, and gave him a push to get him moving. "And tell him t' bring the others! And horses!" she added, before sprinting away to maintain sight of Gralyre, Rewn and Little Wolf.

A Stalker could travel vast distances during a night, and they would have a lot of ground to cover if they were going to unearth the creature to the killing rays of the sun, and rescue the Sorceress before nightfall. If she yet lived.

ഇരു

Jord, Dotch, Jacon and Gedrhar rode down the switchback trail into the treeline below the south gate. Last in line, Illian dragged the reins of three additional horses, as Aneida had requested in her hurried message.

"Where t' now?" Dotch asked, as they entered the thick forest, and halted upon the road. He scanned the surface of the forest path and the thick bushes to either side of it, seeking Gralyre, Rewn and Aneida's trail.

"Look!" Jord pointed deep into the trees where Little Wolf stood highlighted within a single beam of sunlight that had penetrated down through the dense canopy.

Seeing that he had been spotted, Little Wolf turned away, and took two steps, before glancing back at them over his shoulder.

"He wants us t' follow him," Dotch declared with certainty,

having witnessed such behaviour from the wolfdog before.

"We will have to lead our horses. That brush is too dense for us to ride through," Jacon advised.

After a half-hour of pushing through the thickets, the company emerged into a larger clearing, where Gralyre, Rewn and Aneida awaited their arrival.

The trees surrounding this glade were blighted and dead. The soft spring grasses, that should have been lush in this oasis of daylight within the dark forest, were withered and scorched. The horses shied, fearful of the concentrated scents of corruption.

"Catrian was taken by a Stalker," Aneida announced in lieu of greeting. Dread had paled her face, and her red hair seemed brighter in contrast.

"Gods no!" Jord sputtered.

"No! Ah, lad, I am so sorry," Dotch grimaced at Gralyre.

General Illian frowned. "I do no' understand. We caught the Stalker."

Gralyre waved a hand, negating Illian's assertion. "'Twas another we knew nothing of." His gaze was tortured; his expression was bleak.

"Highness, Lady Catrian must surely be dead. Stalkers do no' take prisoners," General Illian reminded sadly. His breath hitched in his throat, as Gralyre took a threatening step in his direction. Tobias was slow to realize that the Prince's distress held far more depth than could be accounted for by mere fear for the life of a comrade. Rewn held Gralyre back with a hand on his arm.

"Silence about things o' which ye know nothing!" Aneida hissed on Gralyre's behalf. "We know she reached this glade alive. Little Wolf scented it."

Little Wolf hugged Gralyre's hip, and teethed at his loose held hand, as he had done as a pup. He sensed Gralyre's desolation, and for the first time in his young life felt helpless to offer comfort.

"Gralyre, it must still be nearby," Jord encouraged. "Still in the valley at least. It canno' have travelled much further before the sun arose this morn!" Jord was confused when Gralyre shook his head.

"The trail ends here," Gralyre confessed, on a deep sigh of despair.

Dotch glanced uneasily into the thick forest. "Then where did they go?"

Jord's daggers flipped and spun. Though he remained silent, his ragged breath and grim face said all, as he carefully eyed the blighted glade, seeking the continuance of the beast's trail.

Jacon crouched to examine the ground, where even insects were no longer present to rustle through the forest detritus. He pushed aside leaves and rocks, but found nothing alive. "What has occurred here?" the Dream Weaver mused.

"Even the birds have perished," Dotch announced, as he spotted several chickadees that had fallen dead beneath their nests.

Gedrhar bypassed Gralyre to examine a darker patch of scorched earth in the centre of the glade, his staff tapping in time to his steps. "Perhaps the Stalker used a portal," he mused, as he scuffed his boot against a faintly delineated line of soot. "I have read of such things. Yes," he decided. "A Sorcerer has created a rip in the fabric of the world, that they might step through into a far place, like you or I would step through a doorway."

Rewn nodded his understanding, "Like the doorways o' the Labyrinth," he referenced for his companions.

Gedrhar frowned in thought. "Perhaps."

Dotch thrust his hand through his hair, and scratched at the back of his neck, as he considered the condition of the forest glade. "'Twould explain the burns. There was always lightning at the opening o' those."

Gralyre's hand arose to cover his eyes. "I cannot sense Catrian. Even from as far away as the Bleak, I was still able to touch her thoughts. Even as she faded away into her Wizard Stone, I still found her." Gralyre's words strangled. "I am too late." His hand dropped to rub across his mouth, as though to muffle the finality of his thought. "She is dead." He staggered a step back, and reeled around to give his back to his friends. His head hung low; his hands fisted helplessly.

Gralyre's shoulders heaved, and Rewn's heart shattered in response to the Prince's extreme pain. Through every trial that they had endured for a year, Rewn had never seen Gralyre defeated. Until now.

Tears stood in Gedrhar's eyes. "I am sorry, *unticol*."

Jord's daggers snapped to a halt, clasped aggressively, but with nothing with which to do battle but his own demons, they vanished back into his loose clothing. "We do no' know that she is dead, Gralyre. No' for sure. It did no' stop t' kill Aneida. And If it did no' kill Catrian before it got here, then she is alive for a purpose!" He dragged Gralyre back around to face them. "Open the way! Let us go after her!"

Gralyre's face contorted, his eyes glistening with tears. "Do you think I would not if I could? I do not know how!" he roared, and shoved the smaller man away. "I do not know how," Gralyre choked on his inadequacy.

Aneida touched Gralyre's shoulder gently. "Gralyre, ye may no' know how t' open a magical door, but I reckon our Stalker in the cage does!"

Gralyre's head lifted, and his nostrils flared.

Rewn nodded, encouraged, as Gralyre grasped at the thread of hope along with a semblance of purpose. "It might know if she yet lives! It might know where she was taken and why! There should be just enough time before sunset to compel some answers!"

෨෬

"Out!" Gralyre curtly ordered the four guards, as he strode purposefully into the Stalker's tent with his councillors at this back. The warriors hastened to obey.

Smoke wafted off the beast from the burn of muted daylight, as it shifted weakly to face Gralyre fully. It did not look well. A grid of burns seared the Stalker's palms, feet and various places on its torso from its collisions with the Maolar bars. Pink, seeping wounds showed at the bottom of pits drilled into its black scales, where sunlight had touched it during Gralyre's interrogation earlier in the day. The holes in the oiled canvas of the tent's ceiling had been patched over with tar and bits of fabric, to spare the beast for further questioning.

"Master, my Master," the Stalker crooned tauntingly, before it noticed Gralyre's agitation, and began a gravelly rumble that was its version of laughter. "Hast thou misplaced aught, my Prince?"

Gralyre jerked his dagger from the sheath at his waist, and Fanghorn flinched. Gralyre's face blanked of emotion, as he pulled together the tattered remnants of his control. The pulse of the sword dance steadied his heartbeat, giving him the ability to speak through his rage and pain. "You have lied to me Fanghorn."

"Master, my Master, never!"

Gralyre punctured the roof, as he demanded, "Tell me of the other Stalker!"

Fanghorn roared, scrabbling to escape the burning beam of sunlight. "Master, my Master, thy anger is misplaced. This one wilt tell thee all." It affected a mewl of hurt that Gralyre would immediately seek to cause it pain when it was complying.

"Then tell me!" The thrice-damned beast had held him distracted throughout the day, knowing all the while that its partner had abducted Catrian!

"But thou knowest this Stalker. Thou hast marked it!"

Fanghorn traced a line down each of its cheeks with a sharp, black talon.

There was a moment of confusion, until Dotch shifted in recognition. "Gralyre, it speaks o' the Stalker from the story, from the legend o' the Lost Prince," Dotch looked to Rewn, snapping his fingers for inspiration. "Has it a name?"

"None that I ever heard," Rewn frowned.

Gralyre drew a steadying breath. If his dread overwhelmed him again, he would be useless to aid Catrian. "Sethreat. Its name is Sethreat." The Gods were mocking him. Gralyre had dreamed of this very beast only a few days past, as he had lain in Catrian's arms for the last time. His breath hitched.

"Yes-s-s," confirmed the Stalker. "Its name. Sethreat. It betrayed this one to be trapped, but now this one sees the Master's design!" The Stalker began the sickening singsong once more. "Master, my Master."

"Silence!" Gralyre roared. "Where has Sethreat taken the Sorceress? Where is she?" Waves of undiluted terror pounded the shores of his heart, eroding the control he had gained using the pulse of the sword dance, as he awaited the Stalker's confirmation of her death.

The spines on the Stalker's back flared with its excitement. "To the Towers hast thy Sorceress been borne. And for thee, my glorious Master hast rewarded this one with a message to give."

"She lives?"

"Yes-s-s!"

Gralyre's knees weakened in relief, making him stumble for

balance. His dagger dropped from his nerveless fingers. Catrian was alive! Rewn's hand on his shoulder steadied him. "What is this message," Gralyre gritted out over the sound of blood roaring through his ears.

"Deliver unto Dreisenheld thy Dragon Sword, and bend thee a knee, or she wilt perish. Choose thy love or thy kingdom, my Prince! Choose!"

Gralyre reeled from a crushing sense of déjà vu. All control fled his tenuous grasp. "Curse you!" he roared, shaking off Rewn's supporting touch.

Fanghorn chortled from the dark corner of its cage.

Gralyre reached up and ripped a patch from the ceiling. The Stalker's laughter turned into eerie howls of agony, as a thin ray of light found its chest and ignited its scales, drilling through to the pink under-flesh in seconds.

Rewn had never seen Gralyre in such a state, and feared he would kill the Stalker ere it could answer all their questions. Rewn stepped forward, taking charge of the interrogation while Gralyre recovered from the crushing blow he had just been dealt. "Share with us the secret t' creating a door to elsewhere, that we can make the journey t' Dreisenheld this day," he bargained with Fanghorn reasonably. "So that your Master may receive the sword, and the Prince may kneel."

Fanghorn threw back its head and roared victoriously. "Release me, and this one shalt make for thee a portal to Dreisenheld!"

"Not good enough!" Gralyre growled. "Tell me how to make

my own." When the Stalker only hissed threateningly from the corner of its pen, Gralyre snatched another patch off the ceiling.

The Stalker flipped and screamed until finding the smaller space of remaining darkness in its cage. "The sorcery is beyond this one's strength!" It admitted finally. "Only the Master can create what thou seeks! Only the Master! I must beseech the Master to open the portal!"

⛭

Gedrhar dropped into the chair opposite to Gralyre's at the table within the Prince's tent. It still bore the cold food from their earlier, aborted meal. The other members of the Prince's council were already seated. "Allowing the Stalker to contact Doaphin would be a mistake, *unticol*."

"I agree," Dotch said. "Its nature canno' be trusted. 'Tis treacherous. What further traps have been set that we know nothing o'?"

"Gedrhar," Gralyre asked carefully, fingering a knife he had used to cut his meat, and left abandoned upon the tabletop when they had gone in search of Catrian. "Did you feel the use of another's magic other than mine over the past few days?"

"No, *unticol*."

"Nor did I."

"Gralyre, what does that mean?" Aneida asked.

"When magic is used it affects the energies of the world around it. It feels like a shiver across your skin, a vibration in your skull. Yet, I never once felt the creation of the Stalker's portal. I know of only one type of magic that cannot be sensed when 'tis wielded." Gralyre glanced up at Gedrhar from beneath hooded eyes, and suspicions lived in his glare. His hand firmed around the handle of the knife.

Gedrhar blinked. "Oh. Of course you are correct. It must have been made of the Thewr 'ap Noir." The silence stretched, and Gedrhar's face tightened with the understanding that he was being accused. Before he could speak, Jacon leapt to his father's defence.

"Highness, I know that you are new to us and our ways, but place your trust in my father's honour! We would never betray you."

Gedrhar patted his son's arm to sooth him, and addressed Gralyre in his own language. "Uncle, you need only seek within the Deep Dreaming and touch my orb to know that I speak truly."

Regret stole across Gralyre's face. He released the knife back to the table with a clatter. Speaking for the benefit of all, he took back his veiled accusation of moments before. "Of course 'twas not you, Gedrhar, but ye must agree that only someone of Dream Weaver heritage could have wielded this magic."

Gedrhar nodded his acceptance of Gralyre's apology and logic. "That is true."

Jord leaned forward in his chair to peer around the others, and glare at Gedrhar and Jacon. "Ye have a traitor in your ranks."

Gedrhar shook his head, as he stated with certainty, "No. We do not." He looked to Gralyre. "You know that a sorcerer could not hide themselves, nor a traitor."

"We have only your word on this," Aneida snapped.

Gralyre was heartsick. "No, Aneida. Gedrhar is correct. The nature of the Dream Weaver magic would make it impossible for such a person to hide."

"Then how was it done?" Aneida demanded.

"Gedrhar?" Gralyre asked, leaving it to the older man to decide how much of the secrets of the Dream Weavers he was willing to share with the others.

"I know naught. To have the ability to wield the Thewr 'ap Noir, but not be a part of its magic? It is beyond my wisdom to say how this was accomplished, Highness. This magic is something that we have ne'er seen."

Gralyre blew out a sigh. He clung stubbornly to his last bit of hope - the Stalker's word that Catrian yet lived. "Let us leave the matter of blame for the moment. I must rescue Catrian from Doaphin's Towers."

Illian's mouth set mulishly. "Highness, this is folly! Ye canno' be considering this! 'Tis the tale o' the Lost Prince played out anew. Ye knew it was a trap the first time, with Princess Genevieve. Ye know it t' be a trap now. Highness, ye must leave Lady Catrian t' her fate."

"No!" Rewn censored, "Catrian is a powerful ally. We need her! If there is a chance that we can rescue her, then we must try!" Rewn sighed heavily, as he threw the General a sop. "But Illian is partly right. Ye canno' go, Gralyre! Ye canno' risk yourself or the sword. Open a passage to the Towers, however ye can, and I will rescue the Sorceress for ye."

"No, Rewn. It must be me."

Rewn raised his chin. "Why? Why must it be ye?"

"Because I am the only one at this table who knows the secret ways in and out of Doaphin's Towers. Once, it was my home," Gralyre's voice grew wistful, nostalgic for days long passed. "When I came of age, I bargained with my father for ownership of the citadel of Wealdeld, north of Tarangria, what you know today as Doaphin's Towers. In return, I agreed to marry."

"Princess Genevieve?"

"Aye."

"But I thought that ye loved the Princess?" Illian blurted, and then looked abashed when he recalled the purpose of their strategizing.

Gralyre was caught up in a stray mental image.

...Pain lashes against my back.
'So ye remember, boy!'
The cold. The darkness. Rats crawling over my legs...

Gralyre shifted uneasily, as the nebulous recollection slipped away. "Not everything is as pretty, as the histories and fables paint it, General," he advised. He frowned. He did not know why he had said that.

Under the table, Aneida's hand toyed with the pommel of her sword. "If ye are set t' this course then ye will need help. I will come with ye," she stated. Her eyes held a maddened gleam. Catrian's life had been hers to protect.

Jord also put his name forward. "Count me in. Ye will need someone who can slip in and out o' unseen places."

"A thief!" Aneida sneered.

"A spy," Jord corrected haughtily.

Gralyre halted their burgeoning spat by agreeing to their inclusion.

Rewn was not done with his arguments. "We have only just brokered peace between Northerners and Easterners. If they discover that ye have left them it will shatter their truce. We canno' afford t' loose control o'er our army."

"Gralyre," Dotch warned alongside Rewn. "With both ye, the sword, and the Sorceress gone that may be inevitable."

"Does anyone else here no' realize this is madness?" Illian sputtered, and threw up his hands.

Gralyre ignored him. "I will stay with the march until we clear the western pass, that far but no further. After that, you must hide my absence."

"How do ye propose we do that?" Rewn demanded. "Your army's courage hangs by a thread that will snap should ye no' be there t' give them heart!"

Gedrhar cleared his throat. "I may have a solution. Using the Thewr 'ap Noir, I can create the illusion that the Prince still marches with his army."

"Will that work?" Gralyre frowned. Gedrhar had told him that the creation of life was beyond his abilities.

"Yes. But one of your men will need to volunteer to wear the mask and play the part."

"Ah," Gralyre nodded his understanding.

"Do no' look t' me," Dotch advised.

Gralyre raised an eyebrow.

"I am too short."

"It must be ye, Rewn," Gralyre tasked.

"My own face will be returned when this is over?" Rewn asked Gedrhar.

Gedrhar nodded gravely.

Rewn sighed and rubbed a hand over the back of his neck. "Fine. I will do as ye ask."

"Rewn," Gralyre delegated, "Gedrhar and Jacon will advise you in my absence. They are experienced campaigners who will help keep our warriors in check, and help you to maintain the illusion. When Matik is hale enough, he will assume command."

"Gralyre," Rewn reminded quietly. "Ye have still no' said how ye will open a portal."

Gralyre fell silent for a long time, until Rewn heaved a sigh. "Ye mean t' use the sword. How do ye know it will even work?"

"I know that Fennick has the knowledge that I need. He created the portals of the Labyrinth." Gralyre's gaze pled for understanding. "'Tis my only option, Rewn,"

"Ye risk us all! Ye are gambling with the lives o' every man, woman and child o' Lyre! Ye are bringing Doaphin everything his heart desires!"

"I know the dangers! If ye see another way…"

"Ye could abandon Catrian, as ye did Genevieve," Illian submitted again. "Ye made that sacrifice once, for the good o' your kingdom. It was the correct decision, then and now."

No one would make eye contact with each other or with Gralyre.

"Was it?" Gralyre snarled. "My kingdom still fell, and Genevieve paid for my defiance with her life. For all that I know she is paying still! Do not ask me to do the same to Catrian. I could not! I will not!"

Gralyre could not believe the ill luck that had placed this very scenario before him again. Only a few days past, he had acknowledged that he would not have been able to make so simple a choice between Catrian and his kingdom, as he had with the spoiled fiancé of his father's choosing. His previous speculation was now proved true.

Rewn traced his finger across the grain in the wood of the table. "Then the solution is simple," he suggested carefully. "Open the portal, but leave the sword behind."

Gralyre stiffened in rejection.

"How do we make good our escape from the Towers?" Aneida denounced. "And how will we return t' the army after?"

Rewn's glare challenged hers. "On horseback, as would any other traveller."

"I will not leave the Dragon Sword behind!" Gralyre slammed his hand upon the tabletop, rattling the half-finished dishes of food. He could not tolerate being apart from the powerful talisman! "I need it! It is of no use to you!"

Rewn's eyes widened at the Prince's violent assertion. "O' course, Gralyre. We would no' make use o' it, only keep it safe against capture!"

Gralyre shook his head, a vehement no.

Rewn was thrown by Gralyre's uncharacteristic stubbornness in the face of good reason. Frustrated, Rewn gestured violently towards the Eastern General. "Then do what Illian suggests, and abandon Catrian," Rewn's hand returned to thump upon his chest, "or trust me, and leave the sword behind. There is no third option, Gralyre, and ye know it!"

Gralyre struggled with his decision, amazed that it was so difficult. He loved Catrian! He could not abandon her! What Rewn proposed was the only sane course. The sword had to be left behind lest it fall into the hands of the enemy.

Even now, it whispered to him, cajoling his allegiance away from his council's wisdom. *'Leave the Sorceress. You do not need her,'* the sword whispered insidiously.

"I need the sword," Gralyre blurted petulantly.

'You need me. We are one. We will win this war without her. Stay. Abide with me...'

"What is happening?" Aneida cried, pointing. In the darkening tent, a red glow emanating from the ruby on the sword painted eerie highlights within Gralyre's black hair, and upon the canvas wall behind him.

Her exclamation snapped Gralyre's attention back from his thrall. "What?"

"Gralyre, the sword's ruby was alight," Dotch explained

nervously.

"I saw this once before," Jord recalled their first night at the Northern Fortress, when he had assumed firelight to be reflecting through the gem.

"'Tis nothing," Gralyre assured dismissively. "It talks to me sometimes."

"The Dragon Sword is Fennick's Wizard Stone," Gedrhar reminded. "Fennick's soul dwells within."

"What did it say t' ye?" Illian asked with wonder.

Gralyre felt a need to keep the sword's secrets. "Nothing of import." He looked upon his council, and wondered at his previous hesitation when there was a chance that Catrian was still alive, and that he could save her! "You are right, Rewn. After I open the passage, I will leave the sword in your care, as I must. Guard it well for my return."

Icy fingers of rage danced upon Gralyre's nerves, as the sword expressed its displeasure.

෨෬

It was a subdued group who exited Gralyre's tent with a quiet "Good ev'en" for each other, as they went their separate ways. Though the sweet aroma of approaching rain invigorated the senses, they were too heartsick to appreciate the crisp evening air. The wind had picked up, and Rewn paused his steps to turn his face into it, letting it erode his worry and sorrow for Catrian and Gralyre.

The Prince remained in his tent, alone save for Little Wolf. Rewn would have stayed, so that Gralyre would not have been so abandoned to his sorrow, but the Prince had not invited that closeness. Rewn was too unsure of Gralyre's new moods to push the issue, as he would have of old.

Saliana captured Rewn's attention, as she crossed the square. She had been tending to her duties as healer, and so knew nothing of the Stalker's involvement in Catrian's disappearance. Rewn sighed heavily. It would seem that telling her had fallen to him.

Saliana stopped to pour a cup of liquid from a steaming crock set near to a cookfire, using a small towel to protect her hand, as she lifted the pot. A young man stepped forward, and gallantly took over her chore. She smiled at him, touching his arm in gratitude.

Rewn watched, as the young Rebel blushed at what she had said, and slopped the liquid back onto the fire, yelping as he scalded himself from his distraction.

With consideration for her gallant's injury, Saliana quickly sat him down. She reclaimed the towel he had dropped, dipped it into a pail, and wrapped the warrior's hand in the cool, dampness. Rewn frowned at the attention she was lavishing. The fool had brought the injury upon himself.

He stared hard at the young woman who had caused the incident with naught but a casual smile. The face that Rewn had always considered nondescript, shone in the firelight, earnest with kindness, as she talked to the young warrior.

Rewn's frown turned to a scowl, as another warrior walked by, grinned at Saliana, and bowed deeply with respect. It made him feel strange, as if these men were seeing something that he could not. She seemed no different to him.

Rewn had been avoiding Saliana since the men had teased him about her infatuation. But his inattention had seen him miss her sudden blossoming of newfound confidence.

His feet started him moving when the warrior she was tending to put his free hand on her arm to bring her attention back to him. Rewn's hands clenched in a wave of protectiveness. The man should not be taking such liberties! Saliana was fragile, and timid! She did not have the fortitude to deal with an aggressive suitor.

"Saliana," Rewn greeted as he neared.

"Hello Rewn," she threw indifferently in his direction. "Now Fowyrt, ye must avoid using this for at least a day, until it heals," she held his wrapped hand cupped in hers.

Fowyrt grinned at her. "I am going into battle in a day, miss. Have ye no more t' offer me than this?" he asked cheekily, indicating his bandage.

Saliana blushed and smiled shyly, as she reached into her bag of medicines for a salve. "If ye only knew how often I have heard that clanger these past days." She chided humorously, and missed Fowyrt's blanch at the murderous expression that crossed Rewn's face.

"I need t' go, miss!" he yelped, jumping to his feet.

Saliana looked up in surprise. "Oh, all right," she cocked her head quizzically at him. "I will send ye this salve later then?" Her question had to chase him, as Fowyrt was striding rapidly away. She turned her head to look up into Rewn's bland face. "I wonder what got into him?"

Rewn shrugged. Saliana did not seem particularly saddened that her beau had decamped, or offended by Fowyrt's overtures. In fact she did not seem particularly happy to see him either. She just seemed impatient.

"What is it Rewn?" she asked, shoving the rejected jar of salve back into her medicine bag. "I must return t' my duties soon. Ninrhar told me that Aneida awakened, but little else. Has Catrian been found?"

Rewn took Fowyrt's spot on the stump facing Saliana's. "Catrian has been abducted. By a Stalker," he murmured for her ears alone. "Gralyre, Aneida and Jord will be leaving the army at the Western Pass t' go after her."

Saliana abandoned what she was doing, and clasped her hands over his. "No! Oh no! Rewn, this is terrible!" she keened quietly. "Poor Catrian! Poor Gralyre! Where did it take her?"

"Doaphin's Towers."

Saliana hung her head. "Will it ne'er end?"

"We need t' speak about the march tomorrow. Can we meet later?" he hedged, and then cursed his tongue at what he thought was a blatant opening to further encourage her affections. To his surprise she declined.

"That will no' be possible. I am too busy readying my patients for their trek t' the Eastern Fortress." She gusted a sigh, blowing a trailing strand of her white-blond hair from her eyes. "Can ye no' just talk with me now?"

Something odd unfurled within Rewn at her refusal. Surely he was glad that she no longer pined for him? Why then did he feel as if she had stolen away something that belonged to him?

"Let us walk and talk then," Rewn drew her from her seat, and took her arm in his. He leaned over and plucked her heavy medicine bag from her arms as they strolled. It did not take him long to begin lecturing.

"Ye may meet resistance at the Eastern Fortress. They are no' expecting refugees, so ye need t' be careful o' who ye trust until ye..." He was unexpectedly pulled to a halt, as she dug in her heels, and further surprised when she jerked the medicine bag away from him.

"I am no' going t' the Eastern Fortress. We are going into battle, and a healer will be needed." Saliana shouldered her medicine bag with casual strength.

Rewn's jaw dropped. Saliana never argued a decision. "Nay! Ye are no going t' war!" His face reddened, as she raised her brows.

"Rewn," she sighed, placing her hand on his arm in much the same way that she had talked to her injured beau only minutes before. "There are plenty o' healers at the Eastern Fortress. I will no longer be needed. I have as much right t' fight for my people as do ye, or Gralyre, or Aneida." Her grey eyes were the colour of warmed pewter, as she blinked earnestly up at him. "I am no' who I was. I do no' need protecting. For pity's sake, we travelled t' Fennick's Island and back, yet ye still see me as the scared girl ye rescued from Raindell."

"No! I... good," Rewn stuttered at her frank assertion. "But ye should no' be going towards danger," he tried on his sternest big brother voice. He lifted his hands to her shoulders, squeezing them lightly. "Ye are going t' retreat t' the Eastern Fortress with Dara, and the injured, and the rest o' the women and children. Where ye will be safe," he ordered gently, not wanting to frighten her.

Saliana laughed without amusement, and shrugged her shoulders free of his paternal intimidation. "No, I am no'," she tilted her head, regarding him seriously. "Ye have no authority over me, Rewn Wilson. Ye are no' my brother, nor my husband. You are no' even my lover."

Rewn scowled. "Lover?" What knew she of such things?

"I will go where I am *needed*," she finished, as though he had not interrupted her.

'Needed,' Rewn latched onto the word. "And if I said that I needed ye t' be safe?" He winced, realizing how his words could be misconstrued.

Saliana's eyes flared wide for a moment before she patted him lightly on the chest. "Rewn, I had no idea that ye had these feelings for me, but I canno' allow them t' affect my decision. I will be going with the army. My talents will be needed where battle is the worst."

They were standing far too close, and Rewn took a step back. "No! Ye do no' understand. I do no' have feelings for ye... I mean I have feelings for ye, but they are no' like *that*!" Rewn closed his eyes in frustrated embarrassment, wishing that he had left well enough alone. What had possessed him to even start this conversation with her?

Offended, Saliana's hands came to rest upon her hips. "I do no' think that ye know how ye feel, Rewn Wilson!" Exasperation peppered her words. "Why do ye no' think about it for a while! When ye finally decide what it is ye want, ye know where I will be." She spun, and flounced away from him.

"We are no' through speaking o' this!" Rewn yelled after her.

"Yes we are," she shouted, as she gained distance.

"Where are ye going?"

"I need t' check on Trifyn!"

"Ye are no' coming t' war!" Rewn yelled ineffectually.

"Try t' stop me!"

෨෬

Saliana tried to quiet her roaring heartbeat, as she approached Trifyn's sick tent. She hated to fight with anyone, but her days of subjugating her will to another were over! Rewn had never cared about her comings and goings in the past. Catrian's kidnapping must have rattled him, as it had them all.

"Hello?" she hailed from outside the tent shared by Trifyn and Dajin. "May I enter?"

"Aye," came the invitation, and Saliana pushed through the loosened flap.

Wearing a long nightshirt, Trifyn swayed in place, using the back of a chair for support. A grin overtook his face, as he welcomed her. "Saliana! Look! I am standing!" he crowed.

"I see," Saliana smiled shyly. "'Tis good, Trifyn. We march tomorrow. A couple more days o' riding in a wagon, and ye should be strong enough t' sit a horse!"

Dajin produced a small moan of pain from where he lay fully clothed upon his bed.

Saliana regarded him askance. "Why are ye still here, Dajin? Ninrhar declared ye fit days ago. Ye were t' have moved out t' leave this bed open t' someone in need."

"My ribs still hurt. They have no' healed properly. I am sure o' it!"

Though she had asserted herself to Rewn, Dajin had always frightened her, so she let his malingering stand unchallenged. However, she needed privacy to inform Trifyn of what had happened to Catrian. "Regardless, ye will be riding with the men tomorrow, Dajin. Perhaps if ye went for a walk, and stretched your side with the swing o' your sword..." She let it hang, waiting expectantly until Dajin rolled his eyes.

"Fine!" he griped. "I will do as ye say."

"How is your wound?" she asked Trifyn, after Dajin had stomped dramatically from the tent, and his footsteps had receded into the distance.

Trifyn raised his nightshirt high enough to reveal the thin pink line that was all that remained of his dire injury. "Ninrhar says that I am mostly recovered, in good time too, though I think that tomorrow's ride will be hard. It will take a few more days to get my muscles back from my illness, and then I will be hale enough to bend the horns again."

"Aye." Saliana glanced aside.

"Saliana? What has happened?" Trifyn intuited, taking a wobbling step forward.

Saliana was quick to lend him an arm to steady his weakened leg. "Catrian was captured by a Stalker," she murmured quietly, so that her words would not carry beyond the thin canvas walls. "It has taken her to Doaphin's Towers!" she sniffed once, and then her tears were flowing.

Trifyn hugged her into his side, and rested his cheek along the top of her head. "Ah, no. That is ill news!"

"Poor Gralyre! 'Tis just like the story of the Lost Prince all over again." Her voice was muffled from where she was pressed into his chest.

"And poor Catrian!" Trifyn added. "Do ye think that Doaphin will place her in amber, like he did t' the Princess from the story?"

"Trifyn, Gralyre is no' going t' abandon Catrian. He, Jord and Aneida are going t' leave the march at the Western Pass, and travel t' Doaphin's Towers t' rescue her."

"Would that I could help!" Trifyn released her, and slumped into the chair he had been leaning against when she had arrived. His face shone from the exertion of standing for as long as he had.

Saliana nodded. "Aye. It feels odd that we are going our

separate ways after all o' our trials."

"We all have a road t' travel. Theirs leads elsewhere." Trifyn was uncharacteristically philosophical.

"Rewn wants me t' go t' the Eastern Fortress with the wounded, and the women and children!"

"What do ye want, Saliana?"

Saliana sighed. "I want t' help. I canno' do that from the Eastern Fortress."

Trifyn smiled. "I, for one, am glad t' have ye. Ye are good in a fight!" He well remembered her bravery on Fennick's Island, during their last stand protecting the gates of the Labyrinth from the army of Demon Riders.

Saliana's chin dipped bashfully as she blushed. "Thank-ye." It felt good to know that not all of her friends viewed her as useless.

ഇറ

Late in the night, unable to sleep, Gralyre paced the creaking, wooden boardwalk that encircled the inside of the fortress wall, what remained of it after the fires. From there, he stared out over the darkened valley. Nothing stilled his grief over the loss of Catrian. The wind was cold in his face, fogging his breath as it left his lips.

Had he his way, he would have departed hours ago, but the others were right. The army needed to see him, to feel his presence, as they set out in the morning. Still, he chafed at the delay. What was Catrian enduring? Why could he no longer feel her? Was she already dead?

He walked onwards, trying to outpace his fear for the Sorceress. The wooden planks were scorched by flame in places, and eaten away enough that some cracked and fell the thirty feet to the ground, as he stepped down upon them. In these places he dreamed of hard oak to replace the boards, and exercised his Godsmagic to draw them from the Deep Dreaming into the world. Though they would be abandoning the fortress on the morrow, there were still guards on the walls, and the temporary repairs were necessary for their safety. Plus, the practice was useful, as he gained mastery over the magic of his heritage. Gralyre would reclaim his creations back into the Dreaming before their exodus in the morning.

The structure of the Thewr 'ap Noir was a constant amazement to him, a magical place of dreams where everything was possible. He shuddered now, as greatly as Gedrhar had, at the thought of Doaphin's taint befouling such a wondrous place. The death of dreams was not something that he could long contemplate.

As he passed them, the warriors who stood lookout greeted him warmly. Gralyre stopped and talked to some of them, thankful for the distraction from his woes, as he listened to their concerns, and provided reassurances before moving on. The people would follow him for they finally believed in the Lost Prince. The problem was that he did not fully believe in himself.

The Lowlanders were dying in scores, and he could do

nothing, just as he had failed to protect them three hundred years ago. This past year, he had witnessed first-hand the privation of generations of his people because of his defeat at Centaur Pass.

He had not been able to save his realm then. In fact, had it not been for Fennick's selfless act of swapping places at the battlefield execution, it would have been Gralyre who would have died under the sword, beheaded by Doaphin. Fennick had given him a second chance to avenge himself upon the Usurper.

Though Gralyre had regained his memories, those terrifying moments immediately before Fennick's magic had hurtled him through the void of time were still disjointed. What if he was forgetting something crucial?

೮೦೧೩

Within the Wizard Stone

The ancient sorcerer broods over Gralyre's decision to run after the Sorceress. It is unexpected. Who could have imagined that the boy had become so sentimental, he who had shown no mercy in abandoning his fiancé three hundred years ago? It could not stand. Catrian could not be allowed to resume her influence over the vessel. Not now. Not when Gralyre is almost his.

The thralls wail, each of them unable to change what is about to happen. Soon a new soul will join them.

CHAPTER FIFTEEN

The bustle outside the tent told Dara that it would soon be time to depart for the Eastern Fortress. She paused for a last look around her borrowed tent. There was nothing left to pack. Men waited outside to knock it down, as soon as she left. The tent would be going with the army to war.

She hefted her pack, and ducked outside. Though the sky was still clouded over, blocking the sun from warming the mountain, the rain had relented from the endless drizzle of the past days. The ground was still saturated, and in the cool of the spring morning, was misty and mysterious, muffling the din of the muster, shrouding the busy people loading supplies and packs onto the lines of horses.

Soon she would be quit of this place forever. Dara's shoulders sagged, as she remembered the horrors she had endured at the Northern Fortress. And now her brothers were deserting her again. What further bedevilment would she endure at the Eastern Fortress, as a woman on her own? What would become of her if they never returned from the war?

One shuddering breath after another escaped before she got control of her panic, and straightened her spine. What was past was past, and she could not undo it. Dara could only hope that as more time went by, the raw wounds would heal.

Unable to help herself, Dara's gaze roamed over the Dream

Weaver warriors who were efficiently packing their horses and equipment, seeking that one face. She did not see Jacon, and grew angry at her sense of disappointment.

She was glad that she would never see him again! She was relieved that she would never again suffer the prospect of watching his warm gaze turn cold should he ever discover how soiled she was. What man would ever want her should they discover her dishonour?

Dara froze, as she noticed a man eyeing her from across the lane. In a gesture that had become habit, she checked her waist where her dagger was sheathed, reassuring herself that she had not left it behind. She felt foolish, as the man glanced away indifferently. Had he even been looking at her?

"Dara!"

Her grim thoughts relented, and she turned with a smile to greet Rewn, as he jogged her way. "Hello, brother! Have ye come t' say good-bye?" she affected a cheerful tone. She knew how distressed he would be by her ongoing terrors, and she would not add to his burdens before he marched to war.

Rewn tugged upon her fat, brown braid that had slid over her shoulder, as he had when they had been children. "I have t' make sure ye get a proper send-off!"

Dara smiled blurrily. She was going to miss him so. He had only just returned, and now she was saying farewell again. "Ye will keep yourself safe, will ye no'? When this war is over I expect t' see ye again, Rewn!" she ordered him.

He hugged her to him, pack and all. Their brown hair, so

close in colour, mingled in the light morning breeze. Rewn pulled away, and gave her a little shake. "Nothing is going t' happen t' me."

She chuckled through her tears, knowing that his promise was a ridiculous assertion, but feeling better for the words all the same.

They kept their arms locked around each other's backs, matching steps, as they walked towards South Gate where the most vulnerable of the Northern Rebels were assembled in preparation for departure to safety.

Led by General Illian, the muster for the Eastern Fortress was a confusion of horses, people walking with bundles tied to their backs, and carts filled with the direly wounded. The Stalker cage rested upon a wagon, well shrouded in canvas against the weak light of the morning. People gave it a wide berth, as they bustled past it.

"Have ye seen Dajin?" Dara asked carefully. "I went by his tent earlier t' wish him farewell, but it was already packed and gone."

Rewn snorted scornfully. "He is back in the ranks, somewhere," he gestured with a wave towards the west where the bulk of the Prince's army was preparing for their own departure. With the tents gone, the thousands of milling warriors could be clearly seen in the distance across the emptying fortress.

"Rewn, do no' let what happened be the last words between ye. Make your peace with Dajin ere ye find battle. I know ye. Ye will ne'er forgive yourself if ye do no' and Dajin dies."

"Do no' say it. If Dajin would see me relent, 'tis he who must apologize for once, and accept the consequences o' his actions!"

Dara bit her lip. "Well, if ye see him, tell him I said farewell, and t' keep safe."

Rewn tightened his grasp around her shoulders. "I will tell him," he sighed heavily. Anger spiked at Dara's glum expression. Dajin could have seen her off had he wanted to.

As they sought a place in the forming lines of refugees, a light touch upon Dara's arm halted both siblings, and they turned to see Jacon. Her foolish heart leapt, and she was suddenly glad that she had not missed seeing him one last time.

"Dara, I came to wish you gentle journey," Jacon smiled. "Will you walk with me for a moment?" He held a hand out for her to take.

Rewn watched Dara's features freeze into their customary blankness whenever a man talked to her. She stared at Jacon's outstretched hand, as though it were a dangerous viper. Rewn placed a cautionary hand on the Dream Weaver's chest to keep him back from her.

Jacon's determined gaze met Rewn's. "I mean her no harm," he promised quietly, as his hand dropped away with regret.

Rewn did no doubt this; it was only his sister's distress that he was trying to ease.

Dara fought to slow her rapid pulse, as equal measures of excitement and trepidation blasted through her. "I am fine, Rewn," she said, as equitably as she could. After all, what could

Jacon do with Rewn standing watch? She shrugged out of her pack, and dropped it to the ground. "I will speak with ye, Jacon."

Jacon's mouth stretched into a pleased smile, and he reached for her hand again. Dara hid it behind her back before he could touch her, and strolled on ahead of him, a study in nonchalance. Undeterred, Jacon fell into step beside her.

Dara glanced up, searching his face for the pity she had convinced herself that he felt for her, or worse, for the disgust should he have discovered her terrible secret, but could detect signs of neither. The customary warmth he seemed to engender pinkened her cheeks. Gods! She wished she were normal, and could enjoy how he watched her!

Jacon halted her with a touch on her arm. She could not help when her body went rigid. Jacon frowned thoughtfully, and trailed his fingers down her wrist to take her hand. "When will you tell me what you fear?" he asked astutely.

'Never!' Dara thought hysterically. If he ever discovered her secret, even this small contact with him would be lost! That was her real dread, she suddenly realized, and her hand convulsed within his.

Jacon raised Dara's palm to his lips. His warm, brown eyes mesmerized her. "I would never hurt you, *belitar*. You are my most cherished," he murmured gently.

'What did he just say?' She was too stunned to even try to free herself, though his grasp was light. He had kissed her hand, and it had felt nice. Yet his words hurt too, for she knew them to be undeserved.

"I have brought you something for your journey, to remember me by." He released her to reach into his loosely laced shirt.

Charmed into momentarily forgetting her fears, she smiled. "A gift? For me? Truly?" Dara tried to act indifferent, but she could not. She loved presents of any kind.

Jacon drew out an ugly bundle of feathers. It made an urgent *peep* sound, as the sun awakened it. "Hold out your hands," he instructed in his deep, lightly accented voice.

Entranced, Dara did as she was asked, and he smoothly transferred the large chick.

"It is an eaglet," he said. "I found it knocked from its nest this morn, and knew that the Gods meant it for you." Jacon reached out and cupped her face, drawing her gaze back to his.

Her smile iced on her face but she could do nothing to evade him with her hands full of baby bird. She held her breath, as he bent towards her, doing everything in her power to stay in this tender moment, and block her memories of past violence. In the end, Dara was acutely relieved when Jacon did nothing more than kiss her brow.

"It is scared and unsure. But you will teach it to be fierce again." It was not a question, but a statement of fact.

Dara knew that he was not referring to the chick. "What if I canno'? What if it will always be this afraid?"

"It is young, and one day it will remember that it is an eagle, and it will fly without fear."

Dara fought tears, as she looked down at the little eaglet. Its plumage was soft grey, and its yellow beak seemed overly large and fierce, the promise of the raptor to come. "What does it eat?" It cocked its head at the sound of her voice and squawked.

"Any raw meat, worms, bugs," Jacon listed for her, as he lifted a finger to gently caress the soft down of the chick's breast. Its beak opened wide, and its neck stretched upwards. Its noise level increased, as it begged for food. "Dara, I wish to speak to your brother," Jacon announced, changing the subject abruptly.

"Speak to Rewn?" Dara asked in confusion, "About what?"

"I want his permission to court you after the war is over, but I want your permission first," his hands moved around to cup the backs of hers, supporting their sudden trembling so that she would not drop the chick. "Be fierce, my little eagle!" he urged.

Her breath rushed in and out, as she panicked, but she held herself still, her thoughts in chaos, and tried to consider what he was asking. Could she pretend, just for a moment, that she was normal?

"Alright," she breathed. Her head was light, dizzy.

Jacon had bent his head to hear her answer, and at her whispered reply, his lips swooped down, and he stole a kiss. He pulled back so fast, that Dara did not have time to react, only to feel the warm impression left by his mouth on hers.

"You have made me very happy. I could not allow you to leave my side without your promise to wait for me!" he grinned. "I shall talk to your brother at once!"

Dara's senses were overwrought, as though the volume and colours of the world had been intensified. It was fright and hope, and terror and anticipation. It was a soft baby cupped in her palms. It was Jacon's warm gaze upon her face, his lips touching hers. She nodded, stunned at what she had agreed to.

Jacon strode back to Rewn, and began to talk with him, his arms gesturing earnestly. Dara smiled sickly at Rewn, as his head popped around Jacon's broad shoulders to stare in amazement at her. He shrugged, and nodded his head in agreement.

Jacon turned back to look upon Dara, his gaze warm and his handsome face satisfied. He was tall, taller than her brother. Dara sighed quietly, as she considered the breadth of his shoulders. Larger than life, brave, muscles everywhere, he was every girl's dream. Only last year, she had been foolishly yearning for just such a match.

'Gods willing, we will both die in the war,' Dara thought grimly.

"Cheep," agreed the bird.

๛ณ

"General Illian," Dotch bade, gesturing the man over. "This is my family. This is Ella, my wife, and my sons, Kentle and Demin."

"Hello," Illian nodded. "General Dotch has asked that I keep a close watch o'er ye, and make sure ye have the best o' the food and shelter."

"Dotch, ye should no' have," Ella frowned at her husband.

"There are others in more need."

"Hush luv. I stand at the Lost Prince's side. 'Tis your due," Dotch decreed, and nodded to Illian. "Thank-ye for this." The two men clasped arms.

"Aye," Illian nodded. "Ma'am, I will see ye again upon the road," he promised before walking away to settle a dispute that was disrupting the lines.

"Ye lads heed your Ma," Dotch cautioned, as he went down upon a knee to hug his sons. "Promise me," he demanded fiercely. Would this be the last time he ever held them? It was very likely. The coming war would be brutal, as all wars must be, but surviving against the forces arrayed against them was a slim bet that even the Gods would not take.

"We promise," Kentle answered for his brother.

"I promise, Da," Demin spoke manfully.

"Good. Ye good boys." Dotch blinked back tears. "Now off ye go t' hold the horse while I say good-bye t' ye Ma." Dotch watched them scamper away.

Demin stooped to pick up a long stick along the way. "I am the Lost Prince. Ye be the Stalker!" he called out to his brother, as he waved it with a flourish. It had become a favourite game since the capture of the beast.

Kentle immediately turned, and rose up on tiptoes with his arms canted above his head, and his hands shaped into claws. "Rarrrrrr!" he yelled.

Demin giggled, and swatted at his brother with the stick. Kentle jumped back nimbly, and the stick swished past harmlessly, though he acted as if he had been mortally hit. He shuffled away, clutching his gut, and moaning dramatically, as Demin gleefully gave chase. The horse had been utterly forgotten in their play.

Dotch was brought back, as Ella slid her arm about his waist. "They are your sons," she quipped.

Dotch nuzzled his face into her neck, and gave her a buss on the cheek. "They better be," he chuckled. He tightened his hug until she laughed.

"They do no' believe that ye will come t' harm. Ye stand with the Lost Prince." Ella laid her head against his heart, growing serious. "I will no' mourn ye again, Dotch," she vowed fiercely. "Ye remember what ye are fighting for. Ye come back t' us," she ordered.

"Yes, ma'am."

Dotch held her until the column of refugees began leaving through the South Gate. He was loath to see her and his sons go, and waved until he lost sight of them.

ℰℭ

The Prince's army, the Warriors of Lyre, journeyed across the valley to the Western Outpost, making good time and arriving by nightfall. As ordered, the outer defences had been abandoned, and a hundred more Rebel warriors had gathered to join them. The army camped in the trees overnight, leaving the leaders the tents inside the earthen fortifications of the Western

Outpost.

The following morning, Gralyre made a grand appearance, ensuring that as many people saw him as possible. He rode at the head of the column with great fanfare, as the army began its march through the mountain pass out of the hidden valley.

Once they were well underway, Gralyre left Jacon guiding the army's journey towards Hondors Pass, where General Illian and his three thousand reserve Rebels from the Eastern Fortress would meet up with them in a fortnight. Gralyre faded back into the woods with the other members of his council, ensuring that his departure went unseen.

Jord and Aneida would accompany him to Doaphin's Towers to rescue Catrian, while the others would safeguard the Dragon Sword, and quell any rumours that the Lost Prince had deserted the army. When the Warriors of Lyre reached the Lowlands, and began to separate into their smaller units, it would be even less likely that Gralyre's absence would be noticed. Gods willing, he would meet back with them, Catrian in hand, before the rendezvous at Dapochar.

The small group found a small glade that suited their purposes, far from the sounds of the marching army. There they dismounted, and tied their horses to trees. Gralyre, Jord and Aneida would not be taking their mounts through the portal.

The clouds overhead were still a persistent menace, and the smell of ozone promised the resurgence of the thunder and lightning of the spring storms. The forest had quieted, as birds sought roosts away from the cold damp, puffing their feathers for warmth, as they huddled upon hidden branches. The hush seemed to await their departure.

"Rewn, Gedrhar, 'tis time," Gralyre beckoned.

The three men gathered together. Gedrhar peered closely at Gralyre's features, grasping the Prince's chin to turn his head to either side to study his profile. "I am ready," he announced.

"Will it hurt?" Still feeling the soreness of the bruising in his throat and head, Rewn was not eager for more injury.

"'Tis only a mask. Ye will feel no' pain," Gedrhar reassured. Mist swept out from his palms and settled over Rewn's head.

"'Tis sticky," Rewn commented, shifting uneasily.

"Hold still for a moment longer," Gedrhar replied. The mist coalesced, and the spell was done.

"Well? How do I look?" Rewn asked.

Gralyre was nodding. "It will do, so long as you do not speak." He clapped Gedrhar on the shoulder. "Well done."

"'Twould fool his own mother," Aneida declared, in amazement as she approached. She poked Rewn in the face. "Feels real."

Rewn rubbed at the new contours of his cheek. His brown hair was now black, his eyes a deep indigo blue. To anyone who did not know his voice, his every feature was now that of the Lost Prince. "How long will it last?"

"As long as I wish it to," Gedrhar replied.

Gralyre slipped from his baldric, and unsheathed the Dragon Sword of Lyre. It did not go unnoticed that his companions stepped back at the harsh whisper of the Maolar steel, as it left the sheath.

'Please, Gods, let this work!' Gralyre silently prayed. He could not imagine his life without Catrian. He cursed his stubborn, meaningless honour now, such a hollow posturing, that had stolen away their brief moment to be together. If the worst came to pass, and she was dead, he would live with that soul crushing regret for the rest of his empty days. His face was grim, as he handed his scabbard to Dotch.

"Good fortune, Highness." Dotch clasped his arm to Gralyre's.

"And to you and your family."

As Dotch stepped back to give him room, Gralyre called out to Fennick's soul in the sword, and braced for the powerful surge of magic that seemed more intense with each use. The base of his skull vibrated from the sense of another's sorcery, even as he drew upon the same fount for the slaking of his burgeoning addiction.

'What is your command, my Prince?' though the words were subservient, the Dragon Sword's insidious whisper tempted unrelentingly, to cede the fight, to submit to Fennick's will.

Gralyre struggled to gain supremacy over the magic. The task grew harder with each use, and he knew that it was because he was battling with himself, as well as with Fennick's soul. Gralyre's mind surged with ideas and emotions that were not his own but he still recognized the danger of embracing those foreign thoughts.

"Gralyre are ye certain o' this?" Rewn asked uneasily, as he eyed the bared blade that seemed to have collected a shimmer beyond the reflection of the dull pewter sky.

Gralyre nodded, unable to speak for the distraction was too great. He wrested enough control from the sword to make his will known. *'Make for me a safe passage to Wealdeld Castle,'* Gralyre used the ancient name for Doaphin's Towers that the soul of Fennick would be familiar with. *'I wish to arrive in the woods to the east of the citadel.'*

From there, Gralyre hoped to find an escape tunnel that he had built. It had been well hidden, opening into his private chambers behind a false wall, and it was possible that the invading forces had never discovered it. It was their best chance for entering into the Towers unseen.

"Stand back," he warned his companions, only just keeping his head above the watermark of power. Gralyre gripped the sword tighter, as it bucked in his hands, and sheets of lightning arced from the tip of the blade.

The powerful magic spat outwards, detonating against an invisible point in the space between two large pines. Brilliant light flared, growing brighter and larger with each impact of a lightning bolt. With a final cataclysmic boom of thunder that sent birds fleeing into the sky, the bark of the forest giants burst into twin towers of flame.

Held suspended between the two flaming tree trunks stood the familiar shimmering mirror of a portal, akin to the doors they had used in the Labyrinth of Fennick's Island. Its surface undulated like water, a bright bubble to elsewhere.

Dotch gave Jord a friendly little nudge upon his back. "I am glad 'tis ye going through, and no' me this time."

Jord nodded grimly. "As long as we do no' step into another graveyard I will be fine."

Gralyre motioned to Dotch to bring his scabbard. Then, having sheathed the Dragon Sword, Gralyre bent and placed it upon the ground. Mustering his discipline, he took a large step back, then another. Leaving it behind was harder than he had anticipated. Every muscle in his body urged him to reclaim the sword, and escape through the door afore anyone could stop him.

"Gedrhar!" Gralyre rasped, as he backed further away. He retained just enough resolution to leave it be. "Take it! But do not touch it with your hand. Remember what became of Doaphin." They all vividly recalled the tale of how the Dragon Sword had withered the hand of the Usurper, who had sought to steal the Prince's blade.

Gedrhar tossed his cloak over the scabbard, and it fluttered in the strengthening breeze, as he wrapped it securely. Being careful not to touch any portion of the sword, save where his hands were protected by the cloak, he picked it up and cradled it. "I will take great care of this until your return, *unticol*," he promised.

The whisper of the sword had become an angered roar in Gralyre's head. "Thank-you." Gralyre's skull pounded with pain, and he began to shiver, though the twin fires in the trees had spread warmth throughout the cool clearing.

"What does it feel like t' go through?" Aneida asked, as she eyed the shimmering magic. She had not taken any of the portals of the Labyrinth, having remained outside with Trifyn, Saliana and Mayvin to protect their retreat.

Rewn answered her. "It feels like jumping into a pool, but without getting wet."

Aneida reset the sword at her hip, and flung her fat, red braid back over her shoulder. "Let us get t' it, then!" she challenged with her old bravado.

Rewn passed Gralyre a common longsword. "Be careful," he cautioned while Gralyre buckled the scabbard around his hips, and settled the blade at his side, "I will no' be there t' watch your back!" he quipped, though his borrowed features were tense with worry.

It was the first time that they would be parted since they had met. It seemed strange to them both, as though they were hexing themselves somehow by separating.

Gralyre embraced Rewn, pounding his back roughly with affection. "Thank-you for accepting this burden. When I have found Catrian, I will meet with you at Dapochar."

"May the Gods favour ye, Gralyre. Stay safe," Rewn replied.

When Gralyre stepped back from Rewn his gaze was snared again by the long, wrapped bundle held by Gedrhar.

'Do not abandon me! Destroy anyone who seeks to come between us.' Violent images pulsed in Gralyre's mind; he no longer knew whether they were sent by the Dragon Sword or originated from within. Gralyre's breathing accelerated. *'Yes,*

take it!' His gaze held rapt before he broke free from the hypnotic, addictive summoning.

"Aneida, you go first," Gralyre rasped, motioning her over. It had to stay. He knew this. He passed his hand across his forehead, and found it wet with sweat.

Reaching the portal, Aneida hesitated before her reflection, for it seemed as though she were about to walk through a solid image, a wall of sorts. Cautiously, she pushed her arm into the shimmering mirror, watching the limb appear before her as normal though the rest of her was still reflected, as though she was surfacing from beneath the water of a still pool.

She jerked her arm back, and examined it for damage. Shuddering slightly at this magic, Aneida turned for a last look at her friends. "See ye on the other side," she quipped to Jord and Gralyre, before she boldly stepped through the mirror.

"Little Wolf," Gralyre gestured, and the wolfdog whined and held back, as he confronted both the fearful remembrance of a portal, and the flaming trees to either side of it.

"Come, Little Wolf," Jord walked past him, "there is nothing t' fear." Without hesitation, he stepped into the mirror and vanished.

Little Wolf danced at the edges for a moment longer before collecting his courage, and springing through his reflection.

Gralyre's last view of Dotch, Rewn and Gedrhar was of their hands raised in farewell, as he followed his friends into the unknown.

ഇൻ

Dreisenheld

Dreisenheld is almost empty, an uncommon occurrence in these last three hundred years. For a moment, as the floor is crossed, and the dais is ascended, and the seat of power is taken, the lone echo of footsteps among the stone columns of the throne room captures the imagination. One echo. Separate at last. The illusion is a compelling one.

Soon the severed will be made whole, and His coming will shatter the world, and autonomy, unfelt for centuries, will be restored. Love does not last, nor heartbreak, nor betrayal. Power though - that lasts forever. Side by side, they will rule the world eternally, as living Gods!

A thrum of magic tickles along nerve endings, an irritant when, for so long, the world has been silent of all sorcery save for Dreisenheld's.

Seeks… seeking…

High in the Heathrens, the Prince has used the power of the Sword. Another, closer epicentre of power appears in the lowlands.

A portal! He is coming!

But wait… NO!

Where? Where has he gone?

Not to Doaphin's Towers to rescue the whore, the Rebel Sorceress, whom he thinks himself in love with. That one moulders unrequited and ignored in the Towers. Has she yet realized that she has been abandoned? That he has left her to her fate? Jeering laughter echoes cruelly throughout the empty columns of the throne room. Now she too will learn the burn of his rejection!

But neither does the Prince journey to Dreisenheld, to atone for what was sundered: the sword, the flesh. The betrayal.

The laughter halts, but the echoes continue mockingly for several moments afterwards, competing now with a newer roar of rage. "NO!"

For a moment both glee and wrath shatter the stillness, a dissonance of madness.

∞∞

The Lowlands

When he stepped from the portal, Gralyre stumbled slightly at the change in the ground level, as though he had unexpectedly missed the tread of a stair. Spring was far further along in this forest. The lush, maturing foliage of the lowlands had replaced the newly budded bushes of the mountain glade. Down through the canopy of trees, the sun shone hot from a bright blue sky, though grey clouds were forming, and the humidity promised that rain was not far off.

Little Wolf leaned against Gralyre's legs in greeting, seeking a kind caress after overcoming his fear of the magical passage.

"Which way?" Aneida asked.

Gralyre considered the shadows on the ground. "I ordered the sword to dispatch us to the east of Doaphin's Towers."

"That is west," Jord announced with certainty, pointing with a dagger that then vanished up his sleeve as if it had never been.

Aneida sighed, and shook her head with exasperation. "Does that trick ne'er grow old t' ye?"

Jord grinned. "Never."

"Wait!" Aneida stopped the two men, as they began their hike. "What do we do with that?" She hooked a thumb back over her shoulder at the open portal.

Gralyre shrugged. "I do not know how to shut it. I thought it would close itself, like the ones in the Labyrinth had."

The mirror surface undulated, like a pebble had dropped into a pool. They all stepped back with alarm. Something else was coming through.

೧೦೧೩

The Heathren Mountains

"That is that, then," Dotch declared rhetorically. "We need t' get back t' the army afore we are missed."

"Aye," Rewn hesitated while his troubled gaze considered the portal. "What do we do with that? We should no' leave an open doorway t' Doaphin's Towers."

"Gods! Ye look just like him when ye frown like that!" Dotch exclaimed, squinting at Rewn's borrowed face. "'Tis uncanny!"

"This is foreign magic to the Dream Weavers," Gedrhar gestured at the shimmering mirror hovering between the two flaming trees. "I cannot say what is supposed to happen. But I can stop the forest from catching fire." The trees doused with sputtering *whomps*, leaving thick smoke rising in twin pillars to be lost against the grey sky.

"Ye think we should we leave the portal open, then?"

Dotch shrugged. "I do no' see as we have much choice, Highness." Dotch sketched a mocking bow.

With lagging steps the small group turned towards the horses.

"May I carry that for ye, Gedrhar?" Dotch asked politely, seeing Gedrhar's difficulty in wielding his walking stick while balancing the massive sword.

Gedrhar hesitated a moment before nodding. "Be careful to keep the cloak between you and the blade," he warned, as he passed the bundle carefully into Dotch's waiting arms. The moment that the Dream Weaver Sorcerer released it, the sword began to buck, twisting and jerking in an effort to be free.

"'Tis trying t' escape!" Dotch yelped, and clasped it tighter against his torso. The sword jerked forward, lifting Dotch off his feet and slamming his chest to the ground. He spat out rocks and dirt, as the strength of the pull dragged him towards the open portal to Doaphin's Towers, a precipice no less terrifying than a cliff's edge.

Rewn lunged forward, and tackled Dotch's legs, trying to halt his forward slide. "Do no' let go!"

Despite Dotch's best effort to hold it tight, the scabbard tore free of his arms, leaving him clasping nothing but Gedrhar's fluttering cloak.

The Dragon Sword shot towards the hovering mirror, and speared through the surface like a falcon diving through mist. With a deafening clap of thunder, the portal snapped closed behind it.

෫ාය

The Lowlands

The sword in its scabbard flew out of the mirrored surface of the portal, and slid to a halt at Gralyre's feet. Behind it, the magical door slammed shut with a clap of thunder.

"That should no' be here!" Aneida gasped, horrified. "Why would they throw it after us?"

Jord eyed the blade. "Maybe they did no'."

Little Wolf growled, pawing at the ground.

Aneida rested her fists on her hips. "Gralyre, did ye call it t' ye?" Her tone was faintly accusatory.

"No. It came of its own free will." Gralyre bent to retrieve it. The moment he laid hands upon the sword, the ruby cabochon pommel stone flared brightly.

Gralyre lost his breath in a whoosh. His vision went dark, and he was falling.

ഇൻൽ

Within Gralyre's Soul

Gralyre's consciousness was sucked inward. Confused and fearful, he gathered his tattered power, and scrabbled to halt this unwanted descent into the depths of his own mind. He tried to rise back up towards a far off light, but struck a barrier, invisible in the blackness to all but his touch. He pounded at the surface, producing a hollow tolling, like a hammer upon an anvil. He could not get beyond it! He was trapped!

The ringing that had begun with his blows against the barrier grew in volume. Discordant tones played off each other, producing an odd feedback that sounded like guttural chanting amidst terrified screaming.

"Sleep!" The decree came from without, and within, it would not be denied. "Sleep!" It reverberated, adding texture and purpose to the chaotic noise.

"No!" Gralyre yelled defiantly. The pressure to obey grew with intensity. The resonating echoes, the screams, the chanting, they entered him, aligning his will to theirs, pounding within his mind, and shattering his hold on his Sorcery.

"Sleep!" The edict overthrew his refusal. His eyes rolled back, and he fell again, powerless to resist this time.

Gralyre's spirit splashed down into his pool of Godsmagic, and there he remained, floating insensate.

ଛଠ

The Lowlands

Jord watched Gralyre's face blank of all emotion, as he arose with the sheathed sword clasped tightly in his fist. "Gralyre? What is wrong?"

The Prince ignored Jord's question, as he calmly settled the Dragon Sword's baldric over his shoulder. The ruby on the hilt dimmed, yet still caught a sparkle in the muted daylight that sifted down through the canopy of the forest.

Ears flattened to his head, Little Wolf trotted a wide circle away from Gralyre's side. His head canted watchfully, as if his beloved master were a danger.

"What are ye doing?" Jord stepped forward cautiously, leery of Gralyre's abrupt change. "Ye canno' bring the sword with us t' the Towers," he reminded, holding his hand out to receive the blade. "The danger is too great that it could be captured. Give it t' me, Gralyre. Aneida and I will draw straws t' decide who will remain behind t' guard it."

"It stays with me!" Gralyre snapped. He unbuckled the longsword that Rewn had gifted him, and let it clang to the ground uncaringly. "Henceforth you will address me as your Highness! You shall not use my name again!" The autocratic demand iced the small clearing with menace.

Jord's arm dropped back to his side, and he took a long step back, as his instincts screamed at him that this was no longer his friend, outward appearances to the contrary. The Gods voiced their agreement with a distant rumble of thunder. Grey clouds moved closer, slowly eroding the light of the day. A harsh, chill wind began to rustle the leaves, as the promised storm approached.

"Follow me," the Prince ordered, as though his waspish words to Jord of a moment before had never happened. He pushed into the surrounding bushes, but instead of heading west, the direction that they had decided upon, his steps led them in a northerly direction.

Aneida bent and retrieved the longsword that Gralyre had discarded. When she stood, her gaze went from the sword to the swinging branches that marked the passage of the Prince from their small glade. She opened her mouth, as though she would voice a protest, but Jord caught her eye, and shook his head at her. His concern was enough to caution her to silence.

No. Not where the Prince can hear. Jord made use of Mayvin's hand language.

What is wrong with him? Aneida signed back.

Little Wolf came to Aneida and Jord, staring up into their faces urgently, as though he would speak. But no words were needed. Something was terribly amiss.

"Come on," Jord said grimly, "We must no' lose him." Together they trailed after the Prince.

෪෬

Within Gralyre's Soul

'Dream on, my Prince,' Fennick whispered cunningly. *'All is well.'*

Gralyre succumbed to a pleasurable haze, drifting upon the surface of his lake of power, floating upon the peaceful currents of his Godsmagic.

ഇന്ദ

Dreisenheld

No! Not Possible! It is too well hidden. He could not have found it alone! The secret of the Tithe has been betrayed! Woe be unto the creature that has failed to remain silent!

Perhaps there is nothing to fear. After all, what can one man do against so many? There is still time to set the trap. It will work as well there, as at Dreisenheld or the Towers.

The Demon Lords of the Tithe respond quickly to a magical summons. *'Yes, my Master.'*

"The Prince comes to you. Make ready. It falls to you now. Take him alive. Return him with the sword to Dreisenheld. If he is harmed, you will suffer his same fate."

'You are the darkness and the power, my Master. Your will is our will.'

The rote words are angering. The Demon Lords must constantly be reminded that they exist only to obey! An example must be made.

Magic reaches out across the leagues to Doaphin's Towers. One dies in screaming pain, spraying blood, as arms and legs are ripped from its body. Delicious terror rises up in the four remaining creatures. "If you fail us, death will come to you all… after a time." The promise is not empty like the Demon Lord's faint praise.

'Yes, Master. We live to serve your glorious will!' The Demon Lord's fear now harbours the sincerity that was sought.

Satisfaction, as the connection is severed. But there is little trust in the competencies of minions. A contingency then? Yes.

"Doaphin, hear us!"

'Yes, my Master.'

"The Tithe is betrayed. The Prince has deceived us!"

'The sorcery from a moment ago was a portal?'

"Why do you ask questions to which you already know the answers? Why must we badger you? Make your own gateway!" The tantrum is gaining strength. "Bring Gralyre and the Sword to us now! Now! NOW! Do not make us wait longer!"

'And if Fennick has been resurrected?'

"Bring him, regardless. The Prince's flesh belongs only to us!" Always with problems and never solutions! Absolute power fears nothing!

'But, my Master, if Fennick has claimed his vessel he will be too powerful to defeat.'

"Fennick is ours to banish. You have already proven yourself unequal to that task!"

Waits to savour Doaphin's humiliation before leaving, while he rubs that disgusting, withered hand in remembrance of pain and failure. His compliance is as absolute as his ineptitude, but when he succeeds in taking the Prince and the sword both, then utter victory will be claimed this very night!

When the fleshless is at last possessed of the vessel, the Gods themselves will flee before Him in terror! There is much to make ready to receive His coming.

But not just yet. Excitement and anticipation breeds cravings. "Bring us a slave. We are hungry."

A darker gloom lurks nearby, hidden within the shadow of a pillar. It moves now, revealing itself. The shade wafts across the gold-veined, white marble floor, and slides out under the polished gold of the doors, existing to comply with all demands.

₧₨

The Lowlands

After a few minutes of hiking, the aroma of smoke teased their noses, yet the Prince's strides remained incautious and uncaring. He pushed through the forest underbrush, moving with determination and purpose.

"Highness!" Jord warned quietly. "It could be a 'Rider patrol!" When he was ignored, Jord grabbed hold of Aneida's hand to hold her back in safety.

Aneida shook him off. "We have t' protect him and the

sword!" she contested, whisper soft.

"And how do ye suggest we protect him *from* the sword?" Jord mouthed back as quietly.

Aneida grimaced and shrugged. She wheeled to follow after the Prince before he could outdistance them. Little Wolf was close on her heels.

Jord's daggers made their appearance, and stayed firmly held in his hands, as he scanned the thickets for danger. He crept forward with far more prudence than was being displayed by his companions.

"Stand there!" The loud demand hailed from ahead, and Jord broke into a sprint to catch up with his companions. He burst through the trees into a rude campsite within a small clearing, where about thirty ragged men and women were arrayed against the Prince, Aneida and Little Wolf.

The Prince stood at ease before the strangers, waiting with a smug little smile for them to recognize the iconic sword.

A man sidled forward, holding a branch that had been sharpened into a makeshift spear, his gaze avid upon the wings of the Dragon Sword's hilt that framed the Prince's head. "That... that is," he stuttered, "...impossible!" His weapon fell from his loosened fingers, and his hands rose to cover his mouth. "'Tis true? All true? The Dragon Sword has been found," he breathed. "The 'Riders kept repeating it, as they killed everyone but I ne'er imagined..." His head whipped back to look at his people, as a muttering of amazement began.

"Who are ye?" Jord demanded.

The man licked his dry lips, and sorrow pinched the skin at the corner of his eyes. "All that remains o' Tarangria. My name is Hektar."

Aneida rubbed the scar at her neck with a forefinger. "Tarangria is destroyed?"

"Aye. Since a day after the Solstice. The gates were barred, and the garrison emptied..." Hektar choked on his words, his breath heaving with sickness at the blood soaked memories, "...and the 'Riders butchered everyone."

"How did ye escape?" Jord challenged, taking a long step further into the glade, and setting his balance. These people might have been spared because they were collaborators. Jord catalogued his personal arsenal, deciding which knives he would throw, and which would be kept at hand to maim. There were few swords or daggers in the ragged mob arrayed before them, but a spear or a sling would still do the job, even against his steel. Jord singled out the ones holding blades. They would die first if it came to it.

Hektar indicated over his shoulder. "Us few knew all the secret ways in and out o' the city, and we managed t' save ourselves. It all happened too fast t' rescue many others, though we did get a few out with us."

Hektar's eyes assumed a desperate gleam, and he suddenly rushed at the Prince. "Give me the sword! I will take it t' the 'Riders! We can stop the killings! 'Tis all they want..."

Before Jord could respond to the danger, the Prince raised his hand, as though to signal a halt. "The Dragon Sword is not for the likes of you!" he dismissed imperiously. A snapping blue bolt of energy lashed out of his palm, striking Hektar in the chest.

Hektar flew backwards, landing amidst his group. His warriors rushed protectively to guard their fallen man. Though they yelled out and brandished their makeshift weapons, none there braved a retaliatory attack against a Sorcerer.

"'Tis alright, lads. I am alright," Hektar gasped to his hovering people. He sat up while rubbing at his breastbone where a round bit of charred fabric marked the spot where the Prince's magic had struck him. He glared up at the trio of interlopers, wiping blood from under his nose with the back of his fist, as he regained his wind. "Ye are a Sorcerer," he accused. He regarded them with more suspicion than before, and no small amount of caution.

"We are Rebels from the Northern Fortress in the Heathrens," Jord supplied, deciding that their clothing and goods marked them as too destitute to have been collaborators. At best, they were Rebels, and at least, merely refugees.

"Lady Catrian and Commander Boris? Ah," Hektar nodded sagely, as he slowly stood. "Ease your weapons!" he ordered his people, as some were still gripping their makeshift spears and slings. As they complied, Hektar turned back to the Prince, Aneida and Jord. "After all, we are among friends." His caustic tone and accompanying glare made a lie of his declaration.

"Ye serve the resistance?" Jord ventured.

The Prince spoke rudely over Jord's question. "Which

General holds your allegiance, peasant?"

Aneida and Jord gaped at each other, having never seen Gralyre assume so autocratic a manner.

After an uncomfortable moment of offence, the Rebel admitted grudgingly, "Baldric. We report t' the spymaster."

"Knifeman," the Prince motioned Jord forward. "Test his honesty."

Jord stiffened, resentful of the Prince's rude address, but complied with his order all the same, mindful of the magic that had so easily felled Hektar. Jord had once been of General Baldric's contingent at the Northern Fortress before being conscripted into the service of the quest for the Dragon Sword. "Where is your tribute?" he challenged obliquely.

Hektar snorted, relaxing for the first time, as he found familiar territory. He reached into his ragged shirt, and drew forth a small leather pouch that rattled, as though filled with pea gravel. He loosened the drawstring, and shook bloodied, uprooted teeth into his palm.

Jord nodded to the Prince, verifying Hektar's allegiances.

Aneida's brow knit in confusion. "How did ye get this far north in so short a time? And what possessed ye t' lead your people towards the Towers?"

Hektar shook his head, as he returned his gruesome purse back into his shirt. "What are ye on about? We are nowhere near the Towers."

"What?"

"We are about ten leagues west o' Tarangria."

Jord cursed. "Highness, the sword has taken us t' the wrong place!"

The Prince's answer was as emotionless as stone. "We are where I will us to be."

"Ye think yourself the Lost Prince Gralyre?" snapped Hektar, latching onto Rewn's words. "Ye think this is a game? People are dying!"

The Prince's face contorted with rage to be spoken to with such disrespect, and Hektar quickly silenced. His hand arose to cover the sore spot on his chest.

"But Catrian…?" Aneida sputtered.

"What of her?" the Prince snapped back at Aneida, now turning his ire upon her.

Jord edged a protective step closer to Aneida. "Ye have been distraught for her safety," he enunciated carefully, watching his friend minutely.

The Prince drew a deep, calming breath, and waved his hand dismissively. "She is no longer relevant. We are here to destroy the Tithe."

Aneida and Jord's gazes clashed in mutual concern. Little Wolf crowded against them, peering at the Prince with his ears flattened to his head. He whined so quietly that the sound was lost within the distance of a foot or two.

"The Tithe?" challenged Hektar. "What do ye know o' it? What was that ye were saying about Lady Catrian?"

The Prince shifted back around to face the Rebel, deigning to answer only his first question. "Not far from where we stand, to the north there is a compound where the women of Doaphin's Tithe are held prisoner until they birth the next generation of Demon Riders."

Hektar glanced uneasily into the darkness of the forest in the direction that the Prince had indicated. "Gods on their thrones!" His mouth pinched, as though to the taste of something foul. "This was the fate o' my mother! Argh!" His sound of disgust was accompanied by leaning over to spit.

"What ye say, canno' be true." A second Rebel stepped out from the gathering of people.

"Enog," Hektar cautioned his friend to be careful.

Enog's hand held a sling down low by his side. The strip of leather still contained the lump of a stone, swinging gently against his knee. "Ye forget, this is our protectorate, and we know every inch o' it," he challenged. "If there was a place such as ye describe, we would have known about it generations ago."

"You?" the Prince scorned. "You have been walking past it for three hundred years, and never suspected its existence."

"Impossible!"

The Prince smiled condescendingly. "What if I were to show it to you? Would that be proof enough?"

"Aye," Hektar nodded to Enog to ready their warriors, and then demanded of the Prince, "Show us!"

"It lies about three leagues," the Prince pointed north. Without waiting to see if the Rebels followed, he turned and vanished back into the trees.

Mindful of the strangers, Aneida used Mayvin's hand

language again to sign to Jord, *You saw what he was like afore we left. He was frantic! Catrian's safety meant all!*

Jord responded in kind. *Did you see the glow from the Dragon Sword's ruby when he picked it up?*

Aye

Something foul is afoot. I would bet all that the cursed thing is controlling him. Stay on your guard, Jord advised, *Look for an opportunity to get it away from him.* As Aneida made to follow after Gralyre, Jord stayed her with a hand upon her arm. *And be careful. Ye have seen how he is with it now?*

Aneida nodded.

Together they hastened to catch up with the Prince, unwilling to allow Gralyre far from their sight.

Enog and Hektar stared after the direction that the three strangers had taken, waiting until they could no longer hear receding footsteps before engaging in a quick conversation of their own.

"He may have the sword, but he is mad!" Enog decided. "There is nothing in that direction for hundreds o' leagues!"

Hektar nodded his agreement, "True, and he is no Lost Prince returned."

Enog shrugged. "Perhaps he intends t' surrender the sword t' Doaphin's forces himself?"

"The way he was guarding it?" Hektar sneered, as he fingered the charred fabric of his shirt. "He has claimed it for himself! And what was that bit about Catrian? I think that he is ignoring direct orders from the Rebel Commanders."

"Where does that leave us?"

"Enog, the Gods have given us the means t' stop the massacres! Ye remember the 'Riders' threats. We need only t' bring them the sword, and the one pretending t' be the Lost Prince. Here we have both, almost in hand!"

Enog smiled slyly, "Aye, 'tis a plan. What o' his sorcery?"

Hektar left off massaging his sore chest, as he snarled resentfully, "Knock him on the head, and he will fold as easily as the next man."

Hektar turned around to address his people, pointing in the direction taken by the Prince, Jord and Aneida. "That man carries our salvation upon his back! Upon my signal, we will wrest it away from him. Until then, we indulge his madness."

CHAPTER SIXTEEN

It took the small group a little over two hours to trek to the boundaries of Doaphin's hidden city. The hardened Rebel warriors slipped silently through the trees, their garb blending them into the bushes so well that they seemed only shadow and light as they passed. A soft drizzle began to fall, soaking deeply into the earth, saturating the forest floor so that not a rustle of leaves betrayed them.

The ancient sorcerer who had once been Fennick breathed deeply as he walked, glorying in the strength of young muscles, tireless. Gralyre's imprisonment was almost complete, but Fennick's possession could still come to an end if the Prince began to vie for control of his body again. The vessel would not be fully prepared for Fennick's permanent occupation until the Prince's soul had been banished into the Wizard Stone. But for now, Fennick enjoyed his temporary freedom after an eternal three hundred years restrained within his Wizard Stone.

A prickle of sorcery drew his attention, and Fennick used a gesture to quietly indicate that they had reached their destination. The warriors came to silent attention, readying their slings and sharpened sticks.

Fennick motioned Hektar to join him. "Walk a straight line forward."

"Why should I?" Hektar demanded suspiciously.

"Ignorant churl! Your proof awaits. Walk." These peasants had been too long without a true king. They knew nothing of respect for their betters. Fennick would kill Hektar for his insolence if he did not need his Rebels in the fight ahead.

Hektar locked gazes with Enog, and gave a subtle nod. *Watch my back.* If something was going to happen it would be soon, when the madman's phantom city was revealed for the lie it was. He crouched low, tense and ready, as he crept forward, heading away from his men.

Fennick smiled with satisfaction, as he watched the Rebel's progress. "Hektar!" he whispered softly after the man.

Hektar turned, and his mouth slackened with shock. He could have sworn he had travelled in a straight line away from his men. He had even kept his eyes locked to a single tree, as he walked, to maintain a bearing, yet he was as far to the side as if he had been striding steadily to the left. "What trickery is this?"

"The magic that protects this place will not allow unwanted visitors. Even if you were to follow the Tithe Wagons upon the road, you would soon arrive at a fork, and invariably travel to the right, never noticing the existence of a lane to the left that leads to a secret valley. You will never be able to reach it. Not without my help. Anyone who draws near is influenced to travel in a different direction."

Hektar brushed tree needles off his clothes, giving himself a moment to think. "Alright," he growled with resentment, "there is something here. How do we overcome it?"

"Gather around me," Fennick ordered. "Just the men!" he

admonished, as the female warriors also made to step forward. "Women have no business in a fight!" he disparaged, "They are too weak! A liability!"

"But...!" Aneida protested, startled by the hurt she felt. A resentful muttering began within the other female warriors.

"Heed me!" Fennick snarled. "We do not need to gift Doaphin with any more breeders!"

Aneida bared her teeth in aggressive reaction. She was thrice the warrior of any man here! Only Jord's hand on her arm restrained her from venting her rage at the snide discrimination. Little Wolf pressed tighter against Aneida's legs, shivering.

Jord leaned his chin close to her shoulder, as though they were embracing in farewell. He whispered into Aneida's ear, "'Tis no' him. I do no' know how, but it must be the sword."

"Be careful. Trust no one," Aneida breathed out in reply to Jord's allegations, before pushing from his embrace.

Meanwhile, Hektar nodded his concurrence to the madman's plan. If the pretender was leading his warriors into an ambush, then Hektar was content to have half his forces guarding his retreat. He had no problem trusting his safety to the martial skills of the women.

Hektar quickly organized his twelve female warriors to be under the command of their best fighter. "Guard our return, and keep hidden!" he admonished.

Aneida stalked over to join the other women. Chin lowered with resentment, she glared at the men, as they gathered around the Prince.

Fennick was excited to feed upon Gralyre's connection to the Thewr 'ap Noir for the first time. He had spied upon the lessons from Gedrhar, and thought that he knew how to make use of the power. The Dream Weaver magic was perfect for what he had in mind. Wielding it caused no disturbance within the Godsmagic of the world, and so it would not alert the Demon Lords in the secret city to his presence.

Fennick had wanted to try his hand at this since watching Gedrhar transform Rewn's appearance into that of the Prince earlier that morning. He studied the worn warriors arrayed before him, imagining them in crisp, red uniforms, with strong boots and short swords swinging at their hips. He imagined the pupils of their eyes elongated like those of a serpent. He imagined teeth that were sharply pointed, and tongues that were forked. He reached out to exert his will upon them and… nothing happened.

Fennick flushed red with embarrassment, as the Rebels grew restless, wondering. Frustration seethed at being curtailed from doing as he wished!

He had no natural connection to this magic within Gralyre. Until he had full possession of the host, he was forbidden the direct use of the hereditary Dream Weaver magic. But Gralyre's cooperation could be compelled. And Fennick would not be denied.

ଽଠଔ

Within Gralyre's Soul

The pool of Gralyre's Godsmagic heaved, as though from a
mighty storm, and he was flung shoreward. He fetched up
against the roots of his Tree of Life, the keeper of his memories
that grew from within the shallows of his silver lake of power.
Gralyre's calm serenity faded, as awareness flowed back. He
drew a deep breath, and felt it as his first in a long while.

He was weakened and crushed, his spirit no longer large
enough to occupy the space contained within his own flesh. He
could sense nothing of the outside world. He was a ghost trapped
within his own body.

A thick, black tentacle wrapped the trunk of Gralyre's Tree of
Life, strangling it. Supple and rubbery, it shifted and moved
constantly, as though alive and seeking a stronger grasp. At the
roots of his tree, its near end was anchored deeply into his silver
pool of Godsmagic, while its origin was lost to distance and
darkness far above. The black tube surged with amethyst pulses,
as it syphoned his Godsmagic away - black, because the soul on
the far end was no living entity but a parasite bent on stealing all
that he was! The silver of Gralyre's pool was tarnished and
dimmed in a large radius around his Tree of Life. The dark
blight grew by increments, as he watched on in horror.

Gralyre grabbed hold of the tentacle, and strained to uproot it
from his pool of Godsmagic. It took both hands to span its
circumference and pull. It was clammy and slippery, and burned
with icy fire, and time and again, his hands went numb and slid

away. He was too weakened to shift it!

Sensing Gralyre's tampering, the pulsing, black cord shifted upon the bole of the tree, tightening, wringing. Gralyre gasped at a sudden constriction in his chest, and pressed his hand over his heart to relieve the pain. Though within this place he was nothing more than a disembodied fragment of a thought, he could still feel it coiling within, as if he were made of flesh and bone.

'You have awakened, my Prince.' Fennick's voice boomed through the darkness, godlike and powerful, making Gralyre feel even more vulnerable than before.

The memory leafs upon Gralyre's verdant life-tree rustled from the unnatural disturbance. "Fennick! Why are you doing this? Release me at once!"

'Silence! I will kill them all, unless you do as I say!'

Across the blackness of the sky, an enormous image appeared, as though a giant's window had been unshuttered. A ragged group of Rebels clustered around him/Fennick. Jord was there, his face hard and cynical as of old. Perhaps he had guessed that Gralyre did not occupy the body before him?

"Jord!" Gralyre shouted frantically. "Jord can you hear me?"

Gralyre's brief vision of the outside world vanished before he could use it as a foothold for escape or to warn Jord and Aneida to run. He roared in thwarted frustration, "What do you want of me, Fennick?"

'Open a path to the power of the Thewr 'ap Noir! Draw upon it, that I might work my magic.'

The memory of Gedrhar's warning echoed fearfully through Gralyre's desperation. If evil ever gained a foothold in the Thewr 'ap Noir, the taint would destroy the Dream Weavers in the past, the present and the future. "Never!"

Fennick's intent lashed through Gralyre's consciousness. *'If you do not do as I ask, I will kill these men, and make you watch, as your hands commit the murders!'*

"Do as you will. I will not aid you!" Gralyre braced for the worst. He tried to console his grief with the knowledge that Jord and Aneida would have been the first to volunteer had they known what was at stake.

Needing a stronger incentive, Fennick pushed the extra distance. *'As for Catrian, I have special plans for your lover! She will think that I am you, as I taste of that sweet meat,'* he declared crudely. *'Then, you will see all, smell all, feel all, as I burn her to cinder! You will watch her face melt around the betrayal in her eyes!'*

Gralyre was utterly horrified by Fennick's threat. How he wished he could defy that snide voice, but in his heart he knew he could not risk Catrian. Fennick had discovered his most vulnerable underbelly, and had pressed a dagger to it.

Gralyre hung his head in defeat never noticing a thin, black tentacle descending out of the darkness. With lagging strides, he waded into his pool of Godsmagic.

Strength bolstered his soul, and clarity of purpose returned. He could protect the Thewr 'ap Noir! If he acted as a conduit, then Fennick would have no direct contact with the Dreaming.

The Godwombs would remain safe. For now.

But maybe he could do more?

With enough strength he could oust Fennick and retake control of his body! He would have to be cunning and quick! Fennick held far more experience and knowledge of magic than Gralyre could conceive of, but raw, brute force would do the job if he could take the ancient sorcerer by surprise.

He sought the vast, golden universe that lay beneath the undulating waves of silver light, opening up his soul to the potent magic of his birthright, and began amassing the power that he needed to fight.

It was then that Fennick's thin, black tentacle stabbed into his back, directly into his heart, hooking Gralyre like a fish. Gralyre roared from the unexpected pain of ice slicing into his soul. He swatted at the thin cord impaling him between his shoulders, but had not the flexibility to reach it. His escape plan crumbled to ruin, as Fennick began suckling upon the Godsmagic of the Thewr 'ap Noir that Gralyre had accumulated, weakening him.

He staggered, and fell to a knee. The pain followed him down, unabating. He rolled, trying to dislodge the tentacle, but it would not be moved. It felt like his soul were being sliced in two with a dull knife. His connection to the Deep Dreaming faltered, as he wavered on the edge of unconsciousness.

'Do not let go of the Thewr 'ap Noir. Remember what I will do to your Sorceress.'

"NO! Do not touch her!" Gralyre rose to hands and knees, screaming as Fennick stripped away Godsmagic, as quickly as he could collect it.

His quivering arms were submerged to the elbows, holding his face above the shallows of his Godsmagic. His pain-contorted features reflected back at him from the mirrored surface of his silver pool. He fought to withstand the searing agony of channelling between the triumphantly gloating Fennick, and the powerful Deep Dreaming, but his strength began to fail.

'Not yet, my Prince.'

Crying out against his torturous agony, Gralyre mustered all of his remaining willpower, and held his connection to the Thewr 'ap Noir open for Fennick's pillaging.

ଛେଙ୍କ

The Lowlands

A deep thrill of triumph shivered through Fennick's stolen flesh, as the Prince ceded the fight. The entire might of the Thewr 'ap Noir was there to use as he would! He gasped at the pleasurable surge of unlimited power, a preview of what would soon be forever his.

Fennick concentrated once more upon the appearances of the Rebels surrounding him. This time, a heavy mist flowed from his hands and settled over the group.

A cloying stickiness adhered to all, as though they were being coated with spider webs. The men wiped at their faces and hands, trying to brush free of the viscous fibres of magic. Clothing morphed into red uniforms, and faces distorted, as the Thewr 'ap Noir wove masks of new flesh over their true appearances.

The warriors murmured in shock, as they took in the changes. Some backed away, trying to avoid the magic, but the mist followed after, forming around each man, and leaving a Demon Rider in his place.

One of the Rebels brandished his sharpened stick, threatening his own comrades. "What have ye done? Ye have turned us into monsters!" he accused Fennick hysterically, and began to swipe at everyone in reach, driving them back.

Hektar approached him with hands held soothingly to the front. "Calm down, Pardel. Ye have changed as well." His brutish new Demon Rider features were not suited to expressions of compassion.

"No! No! No!" Pardel grew frantic, as he dropped his spear, and patted his altered features. "Change me back! Bring back my face!"

"Calm your men," Fennick disparaged. "'Tis not permanent."

Hektar clapped Pardel on the shoulder, and gave him a little shake. "Ye are the same beneath, are ye no'?"

Pardel nodded, shivering.

"As are we all. 'Tis a good disguise for entering their lair. Just think about the revenge we will have for all the lives lost in Tarangria."

Pardel's fearful gaze settled upon Hektar's. "And then we go back t' the way we were before, right?"

"Aye."

Pardel gasped heavily, as he visibly sought to calm. Finally, he bent and retrieved his spear from the ground. "I am ready." His hands worked the shaft nervously, but he no longer sought to kill his comrades.

"Good man," Hektar praised.

Little Wolf backed away from the group, growling, before tucking his tail, and trotting away into the depths of the forest.

"Little Wolf, come back!" Aneida called.

Jord walked to her side. "He will return once he has settled. How do I look?"

Aneida narrowed her gaze, as she examined him from crown to boot. "Terrible. Ye are even uglier as a 'Rider," she jeered. His smile was the same though, she noted with disgust, as he grinned at her.

"Be safe, Aneida," Jord bade, as the Prince led the men forward.

"And ye."

This time, the men did not veer from their course. About ten paces from where they had started there was a surge of stinging pain that grew sharply and then vanished, as they passed through the magical barrier protecting Doaphin's city from outside detection.

☼∽☙

Little Wolf watched from the cover of the dense foliage, quietly stalking the being that wore his master's flesh. Step-by-step, assessing, planning, the wolfdog crept through the thickets, shadowing the Rebels.

Gralyre had smelled wrong since their passage to the lowlands. Now he understood why. The wolfdog had heard Gralyre's screams of agony when Fennick had pillaged his magic, though his voice had been distant and weak.

Ahead lay a concentrated scent of evil, a wellspring of corruption. Little Wolf fought every instinct that told him to run, for Gralyre needed him.

Doaphin's barrier did nothing to halt Little Wolf, as he passed through. It did not see him, and so did not seek to confound his sense of direction. After all, what threat was an animal?

ഓരു

Within Gralyre's Soul

It was over.

"Uugh!" Gralyre moaned, as the thin, black tentacle jerked out of his heart, and reeled back up into the distant darkness. He coughed weakly in relief, as the acute agony faded to a dull ache.

His quivering arms barely supported his weight, as he crawled from his Godsmagic. He collapsed weakly beneath his

Tree of Life, resting and recovering from the sundering of his power.

He felt tainted in a fundamental way, as though what stained his Godsmagic now also polluted his spirit. He pressed his cheek against the smooth warmth of the tree's trunk, weeping, as the burning ice left by the touch of the parasite melted from around his heart.

His exhausted gaze traced the offensive black umbilical cord that strangled his Tree of Life. Only now, at the last, did he understand that Fennick was bent on steeling away everything that he was.

Why?

ಶೋಚ

The Citadel of the Tithe

The Master's portal manifests, a captured lightning bolt that grows upwards from the black stones of the citadel's main hall, until it is the height of a man, a tear in the fabric of the universe. The snapping electricity glitters off the sparkles of mica in the surface of the rough, black granite blocks of the chamber.

The surviving Demon Lords of the Tithe leave their thrones to greet the newcomer. Walking through the black, glistening room is like stepping through the night sky, and the powerful beings within know themselves as the Gods of this captured realm.

Wooden wheels of sconces suspend twenty feet overhead on thick iron chains from the citadel's ceilings. The smoking wicks of the oil lamps have soiled their glass globes with generations of soot, muting their glow. The dimness suits the creatures that dwell within the castle.

First to appear through the tear is a tall, black boot clasped in silver buckles from toe to shin, looking like the exposed spine of a small beast. The gash widens, bending the image of the world around it to reveal the leg that follows, clad in thick red cloth, loose and finely woven. Above this swings a long, red coat, with gold braids circling the hems. A short, silvery sword hangs from the scabbard fastened at the narrow waist with a wide black belt. Then the hands, one hidden by a black glove, grasp either side of the portal to widen it further, and the man finishes stepping through onto the stones of the hall of the Demon Lords of the Tithe.

"Doaphin," a Demon Lord draws out the syllables with a sneer, as the Supreme Commander exits from the snapping, buzzing fissure.

Doaphin is slight of stature; his blond hair is thin and wispy around his face where it escapes the severe binding at the nape of his neck. His chin is weak, and his blue eyes watery, but his aura of power makes up for all lacks in his appearance.

"Tell me your name, worm." The boom from the closing portal stresses Doaphin's demand. His withered hand, protected in a soft, black glove, crosses his chest to hide within a space between the golden buttons that fasten his coat. Each button is stamped with the imprint of the Master's coat of arms.

"I am Lord Harventhall. These are Lords Amitall, Jothall and Iontan." He names the other surviving Demon Lords.

"The Master has sent me to oversee the capture of the Prince and the Dragon Sword, to ensure that no further mistakes are made."

At the mention of the Master, Lord Harventhall's attitude changes significantly, and he bows deeply, as does the other three. "The Master is all knowing and seeing. We live to serve the Master's will!" The catechism is recited with zealotry.

Doaphin's knowing gaze traces a pool of gore that is being sopped and spread by slaves who are tasked with cleaning it. All that remains of a fifth Demon Lord, victim, it would seem, to the Master's ire.

"Yes. The Master is most powerful and terrible. And I speak with the Master's voice."

CHAPTER SEVENTEEN

City of the Tithe

The Rebels moved in silence, as they hiked through the forest. The rain-soaked trees showered droplets upon them, as they disturbed the branches in passing. The men crept stealthily, alert to their surroundings, and fearful of discovery despite their altered appearances. Gradually, the land to either side began to rise, and the forest began to thin, forming steep, grassy hillsides that funnelled them towards their destination.

Soon, they crossed a well-travelled road that snaked through the bluffs. As Fennick turned to take the easier path, Hektar jogged forward to confront him. "What are ye doing? Are ye mad? They will see us out here in the open!"

Fennick turned and jabbed the Rebel in the chest with Gralyre's index finger, insulting and arrogant. "Unless you are careless, Demon Rider, they will never know that we are here."

Hektar clenched his fists and glared. This man was no Prince! Even the pretender's companion, Jord, was distancing himself, lagging at the rear of the column of Rebels.

Fennick needed no magic to read the Rebel's thoughts. "Go ahead and try," he provoked, and shoved Hektar again, provokingly. The drizzle of rain had made muddy stew of the rutted, packed surface of the road, and Hektar slid off balance.

Fennick smiled. What a joy Gralyre's muscled strength was turning out to be, equal to the task of reminding this baseborn knave of his station! When the Rebel hesitated to retaliate, Fennick sneered disdainfully, and walked on ahead.

Breathing deeply to stave off his rage, Hektar subsided. It was not yet time. Only by catching the Sorcerer unawares would Hektar survive the encounter. Soon the sword would be his, and the sorcerer a prisoner, and Doaphin's massacres would end.

Hektar slowed his pace until his men had caught up. They were nervous, fingering weapons, and peering carefully at the grassy hilltops for enemy movement. The bluffs to either side of the road were so steep that there were only two directions of travel now, forward or back. It was the perfect place for an ambush. The Rebels did as all soldiers were trained to do, and strung their forces out in a ragged wedge shape to minimize casualties from any attack.

Fennick glanced back to ensure they followed, and glared with exasperation. The Rebels were acting like a paranoid, invading force instead of an arrogant platoon of Demon Riders returning from patrol. "Form up, ye louts!" Fennick yelled, making the Rebels jump in fear, as their clandestine silence was shattered. "If ye want yer warm beds and gruel tonight ye will step smartly!"

"Do as he says," Jord ordered quietly from the back of the pack, as the men hesitated indecisively. "If the Demon Riders have posted guards, we must act the part."

Hektar evaluated Jord's bland expression, seeking to discover where his allegiances lay.

"Do no' challenge him," Jord warned Hektar further, even quieter than before, so that his murmur would not reach the twenty feet separating the Prince from the rest of the group.

Hektar rubbed the soreness of his bruised chest, and nodded slowly in understanding of the deeper warning. "Ye heard him!" he shouted suddenly at his warriors, giving Enog a pretend kick to his arse for effect. "Ye are a disgrace t' 'Riders everywhere!"

The Rebels formed columns, snarling and pushing each other out of pecking order, doing credible impersonations of unruly Demon Riders.

Satisfied that they were now behaving in character, Fennick boldly led them at a quick march up the road.

Jord remained unobtrusive at the back of the group, watching and waiting. He did not want to arouse Fennick's suspicions while he figured out how to help Gralyre, for it could only be the ancient sorcerer who had possessed the Prince.

There was no certainty that taking the sword away would return Gralyre to normalcy, and once taken, how was Jord to keep the two separate? The magical weapon had already proved itself capable of remaining at the Prince's side. The urgency of the situation plagued Jord, as he discarded plan after plan.

They had proceeded only a short distance further when a rumbling of wagons sounded behind them. They were about to put their camouflage to the test. They stepped into the ditch and waited.

The Rebel, Pardel, tried to run up the steep bluff but his

comrades pulled him back into the ranks, restraining him, as the first of the Tithe wagons hurtled around the bend in the road.

Its wheels sprayed mud and water upon them as it trundled by. Cart upon cart followed, thundering past, their teams of horses lathered and spent, the women in the cages whimpering and beaten. Pardel gradually subsided, as the wagoners and outriders continued to pass without giving the disguised Rebels anything but passing attention.

The men glared sullenly at the 'Riders who were delivering up their human cargo to their heinous fates. Each of them silently pledged that these would be the last women to ever suffer this indignity.

When the last of the wagons had rolled onwards, the Rebels continued their march. Having passed this crucial first vetting, the men were more confident of their disguises.

Soon, the bluffs receded from the road, and an enormous valley opened up before them, revealing a city larger than any that remained in the land of Lyre. The wind changed direction, blowing into their faces, fetid and damp, infecting the air they breathed. There was not a man among them that did not shiver in primeval fear. They paused on the cusp of the last rise, hesitant to continue, as they took in the multitudes of the enemy that they faced.

The city spanned from hillside to hillside, covering the entire floor of the valley in grey, stone constructions and cobblestone streets. Dominating all, a large black citadel ruled from the valley's centre. Squat and ugly, it lurked in the mists. Soaring, square buttresses and ramparts guarded four vast wings that glared down at the surrounding buildings from narrow windows. Undoubtedly, it was the seat of power from which the Demon Lords presided. At this distance, the building's wings, jutting off from around the octagon tower, made it look like a spider, giant and poisonous, that might suddenly scuttle away across the web of roads in search of prey.

Multitudes of square parade grounds littered the valley at marked intervals. Ranks upon ranks of Demon Riders, the size of ants from this distance, could be seen training at arms.

Fennick tried to take an approximate count. It was futile. The misty downpour hid the far sides of the valley, concealing the total proportions of this nest of evil, and the light of the afternoon was fading prematurely, filtered and blocked by the thick clouds above.

"There are thousands o' them! Tens o' thousands," Hektar whispered in utter terror. In the near distance, the wagons that had passed them on the road were now parked outside one of thousands of barrack-like buildings. "We should leave now, while we still can! Your task is impossible! No' with the combined might o' the resistance could we attack this place!"

"Find your courage, cowards." Fennick eyed the men with disgust; his stolen lips twisted into a sneer. "You will follow me, or I will take back your masks. Then we will see how long you survive with thousands of the enemy hunting you!"

Confident of their compliance, he abandoned them, and stalked boldly down the hillside towards the first of the buildings. There were no gates, and no guards posted. The magical barrier was trusted to keep out any who sought the secret of the Tithe.

Unable to do otherwise, one-by-one, the Rebels followed after.

ಬಂಚ

Jord trailed the group further and further, hesitant to leave, yet knowing he must. This was not Gralyre. There was nothing he could do to fight a Sorcerer. Self-preservation dictated that he abandon the Prince as soon as possible.

The creature would have to sleep sometime. That was when he would try to liberate Gralyre from the sword. Drawing upon his spycraft, he faded into the space between two grey stone buildings, and watched Gralyre walk away. Not Gralyre. Not his friend. The Other.

Jord yelped and jumped, as his leg was pawed.

Little Wolf stood quietly in the shadows behind him, staring intently up into his face.

"Gods! Ye scared me! Where did ye come from?"

Little Wolf bypassed his legs to peer around the corner after the retreating troop of camouflaged men. A low growl huffed quietly from his chest.

Jord slicked a hand up over his 'Rider distorted features, and wiped the moisture of the rain back into his ragged black hair. "Ye feel it, do ye no'? No' Gralyre?" He dropped his dampened hand to stroke the wet fur of the beast's head. "Aye. Me too."

Little Wolf ducked Jord's touch, and led him back down the alley, away from the corner. The wolfdog halted at the edges of a stone-lined well, and pawed at the pavers, looking up at Jord once more.

Jord glanced into the hole, and his world-weary features tightened, the only sign of his distress. It was an ossuary, filled with the decaying bodies of thousands of women. "Gods! I knew it! Another demon-humping boneyard!" he muttered quietly.

ༀༀ

Within Gralyre's Soul

Gralyre lay feebly beneath his Tree of Life for a long time, until pride thrust purpose back into him. He had to oust Fennick! He had to fight for his right to live!

Fighting his flaccid strength, he levered upwards, and rolled awkwardly to place his aching back to the warm trunk. The black cord strangling his tree tightened and shifted, seemingly in response, and Gralyre rubbed limply at the echo of constricting pain in his chest. Every movement sapped him further. He was dying.

He was reminded of his first awakening after his journey through the vortex of time, a year ago in the King's Forest. Then, as now, he was weakened and shaken to his core by an experience beyond his ability to comprehend.

Fighting to remain conscious, though he quaked with fatigue and pain, Gralyre tried to understand why this was happening. All tales spoke of Fennick as a hero who had sacrificed his life to save the Prince. This vicious attack made no sense! These were not the actions of an ally!

More warmth crawled up his spine from the tree, comforting his pain, nourishing his thoughts so they cleared of the fog of hysteria. His Tree of Life was trying to show him something, a memory was being returned...

...Flashes of a tent. Catrian's tent. A large, heavy book, dusty, onerous. Sorcerer Aegon's History of Magics in the Kingdom of Lyre.

My hands trace text. My eyes are gritty. My shoulders ache after long hours hunched over the table. The archaic language is annoying to decipher. Enough!

I lay the leather bookmark on the page. I slam the tome in disgust. Blow out the lamp. She is not coming...

Wait! What was that passage he had been deciphering? Gralyre reversed the memory, back to the page of the book, focussing upon the words...

...Another's Godsmagic canst be safely wielded from a Wizard Stone until the other's word of binding, that magic that dost unite the soul to the object, is discovered, thus granting dominion o'er its powers. Else wilt the other,

from his kingdom within his stone, possess thee, and rip thy soul from thy body, and pour themselves into thy empty vessel like water from a cup. Thy soul will forever reside in servitude to his Wizard Stone. A soul for a soul, a life for a life...

How could he have been so careless? How had he failed to remember the danger of not possessing Fennick's Word of Binding?

Gralyre roared his rage, the tendons of his neck like ropes, as he threw back his head in abject madness. Fennick had been manipulating him from the first! The sword had freely gifted its sorcery, encouraging its use at every turn, encouraging Gralyre's burgeoning addiction for its power. And had slowly, insidiously, gained ownership of Gralyre's soul.

Each use of the sword's Godsmagic had brought Gralyre one step further into this cage. Now the trap was sprung, and there would be no escape, and he had nobody to blame except himself.

෨෬

City of the Tithe

Gangs of Demon Riders of various ages strode the streets, hissing their strange laughter, and talking in voices made sibilant by their forked tongues. Fennick and the Rebels mingled easily with the population, eavesdropping on conversations at will.

The 'Riders were mostly complaining about their extra weapons training. The rumours abounded that they would soon be joining Doaphin's horde to the south. They were inflamed with the blood lust with which their drill sergeants had been conditioning them all their lives. They anticipated the rape and murder that they would unleash upon the people of Lyre. They bemoaned the fact that the purge had already begun, and they were not yet a part of it.

The Rebels trailed Fennick, as he weaved through the crowds of 'Riders towards the castle. Periodically, they would skirt huge stinking pits where the smell of rot and death arose from the depths to choke their breath. The men were thankful that the falling darkness made it impossible to see the rotting corpses tossed into the mass graves. They were men of war, and knew well the scents of the slain.

As night fell, the rainy streets began to empty, and the group would soon be conspicuous, alone upon the byways. They had only travelled half the distance towards the Demon Lord castle.

Most of the barracks they passed were in complete darkness, but there was one, just ahead in their path, that showed signs of life. A glow of light illuminated one of the narrow slits that passed as windows in the low stone building, and dropped a rectangle of brightness upon the wet cobblestones outside the wall. The rain became visible as it fell through the beam, as though it were manifesting only there.

Curious over what the building housed, Fennick altered his course slightly so that he would pass by the window. Screams and cries for mercy drifted out to him as he neared. Fennick motioned the Rebels to block him from the view of passersby, as he paused to spy within.

Fennick pulled back with a pang of professional envy at what he had seen, before pressing his face more tightly to the opening in the thick wall.

"What is it? What do ye see?" Hektar demanded impatiently.

"A birth."

∞∞

"Cursed place!" Jord muttered, as he and Little Wolf paused in the alley at the corner of yet another stone building, staring out at a broad avenue, still busy with traffic despite the heavy rain and the approach of dusk. The wolfdog was too conspicuous to walk openly in the streets, so together, they skulked within shadows as they trailed the others.

Jord's gaze sharpened upon a group of 'Riders rolling east pushing carts full of foul smelling mash. Steam rose in the cooling air, and the rainy drizzle pounded down into the contents without care. "That is new."

He motioned to Little Wolf to stay put. "Keep following Gralyre and the others. I will return soon."

Jord had no doubt that the wolfdog understood his every word, and would remain undetected by the Demon Riders. The beast possessed an uncanny intelligence, well known to Jord after their travels together. The darkness now settling over the emptying streets would make following Gralyre and the Rebels that much easier for the black wolfdog.

Jord left Little Wolf, and hastened after the carts, glad for the opportunity to walk openly. He spied on them for a long time, hidden in the darkness just beyond the throw of light from the torch that one in the group carried above its head. It was apparent that the 'Riders were sullen and angry at performing this task.

Jord took a chance, and hailed them, adopting a similar stance of disgust, as he jogged into the circle of light thrown by the torch. "Wait! I am supposed t' help ye." Jord spat on the ground. "As punishment," he snarled resentfully, supplying a vague backstory. He set his feet to run if his magical disguise did not pass closer examination.

"Where were ye an hour past when we were cooking this slop?" demanded the torchbearer aggressively.

In lieu of explanation, Jord punched the creature in the face, vicious with the enjoyment he felt, as the 'Rider dropped. The light dimmed, as the torch bounced to a stop in a puddle, and the rain did its best to douse the heavy lards and oils that fuelled the sputtering tinder.

The other Demon Riders grinned, and hissed with laughter. One abandoned his slop wagon, and threw an arm around Jord's shoulders. "That will learn him," he lisped his approval. "He thought he was better than us because the sergeant said he could hold the torch."

Jord ducked away. "Do no' touch me!" But what the 'Rider

said had sparked an idea. Why were they carrying a torch? The city was dark, for Doaphin's forces did not need the light. *'Holding the torch must be a sign of privilege.'*

Before any of the others could do so, Jord bent and claimed the torch that the one he had assaulted had been carrying to light their way, assuming the easier job by right of might.

The group of 'Riders stilled threateningly, their faces cunning and covetous, as they evaluated the odds of wresting the torch from Jord's grasp.

Before they could make a move, Jord mumbled in a passible Demon Rider sibilancy, "What are ye waiting for? Pick 'im up so 'e can haul this mess!" he swept his arm to indicate the felled 'Rider, and the abandoned slop cart. He hissed Demon Rider laughter at the weak joke. The others joined in.

The Demon Rider who had been relieved of slop duty, assumed a position of power by Jord's side, cementing Jord's dominance of the group. The rest visibly relaxed, fully ceding Jord the torch, and accepting him as their new leader.

The felled 'Rider was dragged up, and forced between the handles of the abandoned cart. Jord grinned, as the creature threw him a rancorous glare before hefting the weight.

The 'Riders did not suspect Jord's subterfuge. It was almost too easy. He had never had cause to speak to a 'Rider before now, and was surprised to discover them to be of so little wit. They were bred to excel at only one thing – killing Humans. All other thoughts were atrophied by their aggression towards everything under the sun, including each other.

Less troops passed them in the darkness now, and those who did, kept their distance from the odorous mash in the carts. The group of 'Riders travelled east down the broad thoroughfare, pushing their carts across uneven pavers. The disgusting contents spilled as they went, the chunky stew slopping back and forth from the rough momentum. Jord did his best to avoid the splash, fearful that if the stuff touched him he would never remove the odour. The contents of the carts were cold and congealed by the time they finally reached their destination.

Enormous pens stretched as far as the eye could see, fading into the rainy distance and darkness. Far down the line, Jord could see other slop carts arriving by torchlight. Appalled, he realized that the thousands of undulating white tentacles that swarmed from between the bars of the pens were actually waving human arms. The reek wafting from between the iron bars was a horrid combination of sewage and unwashed bodies. The prisoners' moans were unintelligible, mindless whimpers of need and hunger.

The captured Stalker that Gralyre had put to the question at the Northern Fortress had spoken of humans kept for breeding and food, but the scope of Doaphin's madness beggared belief.

Jord hefted the torch that lighted their way, following closely, as their group of carts trundled along the perimeter of the nearest pen. Jord had witnessed evils while growing up in the slums of Dreisenheld that still gave him night terrors. This was worse.

As they passed by the iron bars, thousands of hands reached through to grab a handful of slop from the carts. It oozed between scabbed fingers, most of it ending up on the ground.

Others knelt there, cupping hands to catch drips or reaching out to scrape away handfuls of the wet, filthy dirt, and shoving it into open maws that contained rotten and broken teeth. Jord stared into the depths of the cage, just able to perceive individuals by the weak light of the torch he carried. They were all men. Their hair and beards were matted with filth, their bodies naked and smeared with a lifetime of muck. They were skeletal from starvation and disease, their arms and legs like matchsticks, their bellies rounded with malnutrition.

Jord made eye contact with one who had just stolen a handful of food from a weaker specimen. The man's age was indeterminate, but the madness in his eyes was not.

Jord fought back his disgust and pity, as the stronger pushed the weaker out of the way so that they could pace the carts and grab more handfuls of fetid food before it was spent.

The mindless grunts and brutal fighting that erupted over the inedible slop were not the actions of humans but the bestial responses of caged, maddened animals. Jord realized that this was the future of all mankind should the Rebels fail to defeat Doaphin. Despite the magical mask he wore, Jord had to work hard to keep his rage from showing upon his face.

In less time than Jord would have thought possible, the food was gone, and the 'Riders were wheeling the empty carts away. Jord hardened his heart to ignore the cries of anger and pathetic wailing of the caged men who had not received a share.

The 'Rider at Jord's side hissed angrily, and threw a loosened paver at the occupants of the pen in parting. "If we did no' need 'em t' breed us more females, we would no' 'ave t' put up with this!"

"I heard that the Demon Lords will let us kill them after we destroy the Prince!" another 'Rider crowed. "Kill them all! That will be a good day!"

Jord grunted his approval along with the others. He had learned more than enough. "Here, take this. I am sick o' carrying it." He passed the sputtering, smoking torch into the hands of the 'Rider whom he had rescued from slop duty.

The 'Rider growled victoriously and lifted it on high, as Jord bestowed the status of leadership upon him.

Though he continued on with the empty food carts, Jord gradually fell to the back of the group, slowing, until he disappeared into the dark shadows.

"Where did he go?" One of the 'Riders questioned, but the answer was not of sufficient interest to the others to pursue.

From within the shadows, Jord smiled grimly with triumph. His disguise had worked perfectly, leaving the group of 'Riders without suspicion.

He jogged back across the city towards the place where he had last seen Little Wolf trailing the others. There were few still out and about in the cold, wet night. He was alone in the darkness, noticeable, but the heavy rainfall masked the sounds of his boots pounding upon the pavers.

Should he tell Gralyre of the slaves? Not Gralyre. Fennick. Jord was unsure if the ancient sorcerer would care.

Even if the men in the cages gained their freedom, they would still be only feral animals. Their prison was never-ending. Pity filled Jord for their reduced state. One way or the other, he vowed that they would be released from their misery ere he quit this place.

෨෬

Within Gralyre's Soul

'Would you care to see what your failure has wrought, my Prince?'

Gralyre flinched back from Fennick's godlike voice, apprehensive of what he would be coerced to do next. Then his vision blinked, and opened, and he was *present* in his body, and could *see*.

Gralyre struggled for more, but Fennick was in complete control of his limbs, leaving Gralyre feeling like no more than a voyeur peeking through a keyhole. Fennick allowed Gralyre this spiteful glimpse of the outside world to taunt him with his powerlessness.

"Merciful Gods! Fennick! Help her!" Only his tormentor heard his plea for mercy. Gralyre had no control of his neck, and could not turn away nor shut his eyes against atrocity before him. Fennick's cruelty was unrelenting.

What Gralyre witnessed, obliterated his heart with terrible guilt. It unmanned him that the women of his kingdom were being used so foully. If only he had won the war hundreds of years ago, killing Doaphin at Centaur Pass, this atrocity would never have come to pass!

'I will kill them all!' the insidious thought worked its way into his mind, as he was forced to watch the birth. Gralyre was unsure if it came from Fennick in his Wizard Stone, or the blackest pit of his own soul's need for vengeance.

₧₨

City of the Tithe

Across from the window slit that Fennick spied through from outside, a single, flickering torch was set into a metal bracket above the bunk of a naked woman who was in labour. Her wrists and ankles were raw and bleeding from the burn of the rough ropes that bound her to her narrow cot. She loosed eerie screams of agony, as her grossly distended belly heaved and jumped, ridging from hands and feet kicking and pushing from within.

'Do you see it, my Prince? Do you see how your shortcomings have doomed your people? You have not the stomach for what must be done. I can make it all go away, if you will only surrender to me.' Fennick did not allow Gralyre to respond. It was enough to feel the Prince's torment, as Fennick forced him to watch.

To either side of the woman in labour, others were tied down in similar fashion upon their own beds, their bellies hideously bloated beyond what an ordinary pregnancy would account for. Most of the women lay quietly, staring into space, their minds fleeing what their bodies could not, while others sobbed and muttered with madness.

Their cots were lined up efficiently, side-by-side down the length of the long, stone building, disappearing beyond the reach of the sputtering torchlight in either direction. Fennick estimated that the structure housed over a hundred fecund women about to bring forth a new generation of Doaphin's soldiers.

The women lay in filth, untended and neglected. An overwhelming smell of faeces, urine and blood wafted through the window. At least one woman was already dead, and had been left to rot in her bunk. Her abdomen had been ripped open, as something had clawed its way to freedom from within.

The woman in labour thrashed and shrieked, as she tried to birth the monstrosity erupting from her womb. Her attendants were two Demon Riders who gossiped in the aisle at the foot of her metal cot while she screamed for mercy, and wrenched at the bonds that held her pinned to the filthy ticking. Her naked belly heaved and jumped, distending upwards until finally her skin split. She uttered a terrified gurgle, her eyes round and horrified by what was exiting her womb.

Black blood oozed from the tear in her flesh, as a small hand thrust its way from beneath her ruined skin. Another hand joined the first, pulling and tugging to widen the rift it had clawed into her abdomen.

Fennick smiled with satisfaction, as he felt Gralyre's despair and pity escalate. The memory of this ghastly birth would weaken the Prince's will further, making him more malleable when Fennick began the final subjugation. By the time Fennick was done torturing him, Gralyre would exile himself voluntarily into the Wizard Stone, leaving his vessel empty and ready for its new possessor.

All around the birthing bed, women were screaming in sympathetic horror, yanking against the bonds that kept them tied to their cots. Some of them cried out for the Gods to kill them now, for they knew that soon this poor woman's fate would be their own.

A head pushed out of the gash in the woman's belly, and the newborn pulled and kicked to free its shoulders. The atrocity that slowly drew itself from the woman's body was male, but was no baby. If it had been human, Fennick would have judged its age to be almost two years.

The woman contorted, arching high off the cot from the pain, before she fell silent, and dropped limply back to the bare, filthy ticking. If she was not yet dead, she soon would be. There could be no survival of such a wound.

The newborn was coated in black blood from its violent birth, and lay huddled upon its mother's cooling body for a long moment to gain its strength. A thick, red umbilical cord trailed from the newborn's navel into his mother's shattered belly.

Covetousness coiled like a snake around Fennick's corrupt heart. What magic was this? How had Doaphin managed these creations? They were the perfect melding of sorcery and man.

The Demon Riders had ceased their conversation, and were staring impatiently at the newborn. "Hurry it up!" one carped.

"It has t' do it on its own. If it canno' then we kill it."

Finally, the newborn rolled off the cot, and thumped to the floor. The attendants did nothing to assist it, waiting and watching, as it struggled to stand. The new Demon Rider was wobbly, as it got its legs under him, like a newborn colt. It swayed in place, its expression curious, as it reached out to touch the dead face of its mother.

Seemingly satisfied, one of the 'Riders drew his dagger and stepped forward. He pulled the newborn's bloody, slippery umbilical cord taut, and severed it with a quick cut of his knife.

The newborn yelped with pain and began to sob.

"Shut up, ye turd," the unsympathetic 'Rider snarled. "Come tie this," he told his companion, holding up the bleeding end of the umbilical cord.

The other 'Rider stomped forward, and tied off the spurting cord using a thin strip of rawhide. He lifted the torch from the bracket in the wall, and together with his partner, walked the newborn from the building. They left the screaming women without even the meagre comfort of light.

The Prince had seen enough. Fennick thrust Gralyre back into confinement, then turned from the window and sagged back against the wall of the building. Fennick had devoted his long years to the accumulation of knowledge and Godsmagic: learned, earned, bought and stolen. He searched through his vast lore of magic, gained over the seven centuries that he had walked this land, and knew of nothing that could account for what he had just witnessed. *'This power should be mine!'*

Hektar misinterpreted the sour expression upon Fennick's stolen face. "Was it bad?" He peered over Fennick's shoulder, but there was little to see through the window, now that the torchlight had vanished.

"This place is steeped in evil. It must be destroyed!" Fennick's pride could not stand that another's strength could challenge his own! The urge to quash Doaphin's power and destroy his work burned like wildfire in his envious, black soul.

"Come. We make for the castle!"

First, Fennick would rip the knowledge of this powerful magic from the minds of the Demon Lords. Then, he would shatter this city with all his godly powers, and send a clear message to the Usurper.

Doaphin was no longer the dominant power in this land!

What Godsmagic Fennick used this day would return to him tenfold when Gralyre was finally bound within the Wizard Stone, and the Thewr 'ap Noir was Fennick's to feed upon for eternity.

⊱⊰

Within Gralyre's Soul

Fennick allowed Gralyre to know his intent.

"No!" Gralyre shook his head in denial of the contemptible

plan. If Fennick destroyed the city he would destroy all of the imprisoned women along with it! Thousands of innocents would perish!

Gralyre scrabbled against the warm trunk of his Tree of Life, seeking the strength to rise and challenge what was about to occur. He wavered and fell.

'You always were a weak, pathetic boy!' Fennick derided. *'Even now, you lack the spine to challenge me! You will watch, as I destroy them all.'*

Unable to stand, Gralyre rolled to his knees instead, his hands raised in supplication. "Fennick! I beg of you," Gralyre was reduced to pleading. He had never been so desperate, so vulnerable. "Spare those who are human! There must be a way to destroy the demon seeds growing in their wombs, and yet save the women?"

Fennick did not deign to reply; he was done listening. The parasite wrapping the Tree of Life pulsed indigo, as it drew deeper upon Gralyre's Godsmagic. The trickle of loss became a river. Fennick was preparing a terrible sorcery, and was syphoning massive amounts of power into his Wizard Stone.

Gralyre reeled with an onslaught of intense weakness and collapsed. "Please, Fennick!" He breathed harshly, gathering the strength to bellow, "You will murder thousands!" His accusation reverberated throughout the recesses of the dark, where once his spirit had been large enough to reside.

The ancient Sorcerer's magic continued to build, the harbinger of the doom of thousands.

"Please! Please!" Gralyre whispered faintly, his ebbing strength spent after his shout. "I will do anything! Anything you ask of me!" He dug the heels of his hands into his eyes, sobbing at his inability to combat Fennick's intent. It was hopeless. He was a mere ghostly spectator to what was about to unfold. Moment by moment his life waned further.

'I am here.'

"Little Wolf!" Gralyre breathed, profoundly thankful to hear the disembodied voice. The wolfdog's thoughts had somehow found a chink to creep through and find Gralyre's crushed spirit.

'I heard your cry. Finally! I followed you home.'

Gralyre realized that when Fennick had forced him to watch the suffering woman giving birth, drawing his imprisoned soul closer to the surface of the world, it had left an opening for Little Wolf to reach him.

'You, not you. Attack. It wears your face!'

"I cannot," Gralyre confessed, trembling away from what was coming. Worse! So much worse than what he had survived at Centaur Pass! "I have tried. I have not the strength." He was terrifyingly exhausted. "Little Wolf, I am dying."

'Life is escape. Death is meat in another's belly,' Little Wolf urged with his wolfish logic.

"Fennick is too powerful. Even if I were to escape, he would only imprison me again. I do not know his Wizard Stone's word of binding, and without it I am doomed. It is too late for me. Soon I will be gone."

'Who will hear my voice if you depart?'

As Gralyre repressed his sadness, his guilt bubbled up in its place. "You will do better without me. All of this, everything that has happened. 'Tis my fault. 'Tis who I forgot I was. Fennick is right. I am weak. I am nothing."

'I have seen your nightmares. You are fierce. You never hesitated, one against many, protecting your pack so that they could live. The Other has made spoiled food of your memories. Do not eat of them, for they have made you ill. Eat of this.'

A small, shimmering silver leaf fell from out of the darkness, casting a bright halo around Gralyre's prone body as it neared, a gift from Little Wolf. It wafted gently into the palm of Gralyre's limp hand, and as the petal-soft surface of the silver leaf touched him, the wolfdog's memories merged with his own.

Gralyre saw himself through the eyes of his wolf-son. He was rendered mute by Little Wolf's simple faith and love, as a cacophony of images, memories and impressions assailed his consciousness.

Not an ignoble failure.

Not weak.

Not a Rebel.

Not a Sorcerer.

Not even a Prince.

Simply, himself. Simply, Gralyre.

'This is who you are. Safe. Father. Comfort. Fight!'

Warmth pulsed to life within Gralyre's defeated heart, and he gasped at the heat of it, the certainty of it. It was Love.

Little Wolf was correct. He was not dead yet! He could not

abandon his people to the brutal judgement of Fennick, nor the despotic rule of Doaphin!

The Godsmagic lapping the roots of Gralyre's Tree of Life was tainted black by Fennick's poison, but he spied a tiny puddle of pure silver light caught in a circle of its roots. Isolated from the rest of his lake of power, it had survived the taint. It was not much, but perhaps it contained the power Gralyre needed to recover.

He stretched forth feebly, flopping and clawing with his fingers to draw his arms straight, that he might reach his trembling hands into the silver Godsmagic. As he touched the glowing light, life surged back into his weakened soul, giving him the strength to stand.

He staggered down the shoreline beyond the spreading, oily contamination in his Godsmagic, and fell into the heart of his power. Surrounded by the pure light of magic that filled and warmed him, he grew slightly stronger, but soon despaired, for Fennick was sapping his strength away just as quickly. Gralyre needed to draw upon his Godsmagic to survive but in doing so he was only aiding Fennick's cause, and making his captor all the stronger.

Gralyre slogged ashore to limit the drain upon his remaining magic. Until he was able to sever the virulent black cord tying Fennick's soul to his body, he would remain a weakened captive. He considered his options, as he hobbled back to his besieged Tree of Life.

He had tried repeatedly to uproot it, but Fennick had planted his tap too deeply. Gralyre dared not dive into his Godsmagic to seek the Thewr 'ap Noir, to make an axe with which to sever the cord. He could not chance that Fennick might somehow ride his wake into the realm of the Deep Dreaming.

How? How was he to do this thing?

Fighting for his life, Gralyre attacked the parasite with animalistic growls, pulling and tugging to no avail. Finally, in a fit of frustration and panic, he lashed out and bit down hard. Ice of the grave filled his mouth. He spat it to the ground, and saw purple ichor flowing from the wound he had made in the black tube. Triumph made him loose a battle cry to challenge his prison. It would work!

But Fennick's parasite was not without its defences. It writhed upon the trunk of Gralyre's Tree of Life, wringing tightly. Gralyre clutched his chest, staggering from the pain, tripping and falling to his back. He could not do this alone.

"Little Wolf, help me!"

The wolfdog trotted out of the darkness of Gralyre's prison, a ghostly, shimmering wolf of brightest light. *'I have come.'*

"Bite! Chew! Destroy!" Gralyre snarled, so overcome that he was beyond the ability of complex thought.

Little Wolf unfolded with eagerness, pouncing. The flowing lupine grace of his predator spirit attacked the parasite that was sapping Gralyre's life force. His long, dagger-sharp teeth ripped and tore, the muscles in his powerful shoulders bunching, as he braced his paws and shook and yanked on the black cord. He yelped in pain from the icy flavour of death filling his mouth, but continued, unrelentingly.

Gralyre's screams answered when the black cord clenched aggressively upon his tree. It was killing him! As Little Wolf ruptured it further, Gralyre moaned and gritted his teeth against the blinding agony, steeling himself to endure. He would rather die fighting, than be slowly suckled to a dry husk!

His eyes rolled back, and he was… elsewhere.

෨෬

City of the Tithe

The Sorcerer stopped walking mid-step. He tripped sideways, and fetched up against the wall of a building. He began to chuckle quietly. "He is gone! I have won!"

"What is happening?" Hektar jogged forward to catch up to the Sorcerer who was always arrogantly strutting at least ten feet ahead of the rest of the Rebels. "What is so funny?" Hektar asked, watching closely, seeking for the opening to take this false Prince prisoner, and to gain the sword.

"'Tis nothing! I am fine!" the sorcerer chortled, as he steadied himself upon the stones. "'Tis always this way when the vessel empties. I have to learn to control it all now, you see? Toes, feet, legs, everything!"

"Ye make no sense. Are ye drunk?" Hektar had not seen the false Prince sneaking nips from a flask, but perhaps that was why he had taken point guard. "Just shut up and keep walking afore we get noticed!" Hektar's head swivelled to check, but they remained the only ones on the empty street.

"Aye, of course." The sorcerer took a wooden step forward, but his eyes rolled, and he toppled back towards the wall. "Something is wrong!" He did not look well. His head hung lower and lower, as his breath came in harsh pants. "How did he…?" Even though he was braced, his knees buckled suddenly so that he had to scrabble to catch himself. "Ah, there you are. Gods, he is strong!" He began to vomit with great heaves.

The fool *was* drunk, Hektar decided. All his hesitation fell away. There would never come a better opportunity to take the Dragon Sword.

"Now!" Hektar cried out to his men, and swung a cudgel towards the Pretender's skull.

ᏕᎧᏣ

Inside the Wizard Stone

The sky above and the ground below were facetted with red crystal shapes, diamond hard and glowing. Gralyre shivered when he realized what had happened. He was within the ruby of the Dragon Sword! He was within Fennick's Wizard Stone! Had he failed? Had Fennick utterly supplanted him?

Gralyre glanced down, and was relieved to see that his naked soul still retained the glowing cord that was his lifeline back to his body, a familiar sight after bringing Catrian back from her

Stone when she had become trapped. As long as his lifeline endured, he could return to his flesh. He was still weakened, but felt stronger than he had been. Fennick had drawn upon so much power in preparation of his spell, that residual Godsmagic was bleeding from the surfaces around Gralyre to bolster his flagging strength.

"Thou hast come to challenge the Stone for dominion?" It was a weak whisper, but startling when it broke the stillness.

Gralyre whirled to see six vaporous beings wafting towards him. They all bore a gaunt, ethereal appearance of unrelenting torture too long endured. Their naked souls were as insubstantial as ghosts, and Gralyre spied jagged facets of the harsh red landscape through their wispy bodies. He was unsure who had uttered the greeting until the entity spoke again.

"We once thought as thee. We once sought the power of the Stone for our own." His mode of speaking was deeply archaic. This entity seemed older than the others, more skeleton than man, as though he were almost starved from existence. "Now we are his slaves."

They were the tormented souls of Sorcerers whose Godsmagic Fennick had fed upon over the ages, Sorcerers trapped after failing to conquer the Wizard Stone. Gralyre was staring into the eyes of his haunted future if he did not find a way to defeat his enemy.

"No," corrected another wraith, while stroking a wispy beard that adorned his chin. "Do you not recognize him? He is the new vessel."

"Ah," chorused the others, nodding sagely to each other.

"Vessel? What do you mean?"

"He bred thee." The skeletal soul answered, brandishing a bony finger.

"He created you." Agreed the bearded spirit.

"Ye are made t' be his. Just as I was." A third entity now joined the conversation. His blue eyes retained cohesion, strangely large and solid within his soul's transparent, mournful face.

A chill of pure shock zinged through Gralyre's mind. "*Fennick*?" It was a distorted caricature of the man he had known as his father's Court Sorcerer, but recognizable all the same.

"That was once my name ere he took it and me, as he will take ye." The spirit droned morosely. "He has worn my face for longer than ever did I."

"How did he breed me?" Gralyre demanded. An evil thought bored through his mind.

"Be at ease. He is no' your sire." The blue-eyed sorcerer uprooted Gralyre's fear before it could grow.

"You heard my thoughts!" So not all magic was lost to them in this place, Gralyre mused.

"I am the youngest here. I still keep a piece o' myself." The spectre's blue eyes glowed. "But he will eat it all one day…" The ghostly spirit faded to the point that his blue eyes seemed alone in space, hovering at the height of a man's head.

"When he perishes, then dost he reside with us in the Stone

until a new vessel is found," the soul of the skeletal sorcerer whispered. "He is cruel. Our pain. It dost give him pleasure. Our Godsmagic is his sustenance. Thou escapement was our doom. For three hundred years didst thou elude him, and we did endure his tortures and appetites."

"How did he create me?" Gralyre asked again. He must know more! He needed to understand what was happening, and how to protect himself. The meandering musings of the spirits of the stone were of little help!

The owner of the wispy beard clarified. "In the beginning, he would be dead for an age, awaiting a fool seeking the power of the stone, whose soul he could corrupt and supplant. But there were no assurances that such a vessel would prove powerful enough to contain his Godsmagic for long. Is that not correct, Xalier?"

"Sixty-three days!" The thrall named Xalier vanished after the cryptic lament.

"In time," wispy beard continued, unsympathetic to the spirit that had fled, "he grew wiser, and realized that he need not leave his resurrection to the vulgarities of chance. He began to plan for his ends, influencing the breeding of his next host by carefully selecting the sires and dames of each."

"Each more powerful than the last. That his Godsmagic might grow," the faint-voiced skeletal being added. "Each one's spirit utterly crushed and his to control, so that they lacked the will or knowledge to fight his possession, making his triumph assured."

The five remaining thralls chorused their agreement again.

The blue-eyed soul, who had once been a sorcerer named Fennick, solidified back into the shape of a man. "With his new vessel at his side when he died, he could be resurrected within days instead o' awaiting years. The one ye know as Fennick created ye t' gain access t' the Thewr 'ap Noir, hitherto denied him because he was no' a born son o' Dream Weavers."

Gralyre was staggered by the scope of the monstrous scheme. His mother? His father? His birth had been carefully orchestrated!

"When thy power o'er the Thewr 'ap Noir dost become his, he will be as a god."

Wearing a grimace of terror, another thrall vanished back to wherever it had hidden before Gralyre had arrived.

"No! I will die before I allow him to corrupt the Deep Dreaming!" Gralyre cried defiantly.

"Then die thou must," the soul of the old sorcerer admonished, waving a long, bony finger. "But thy defiance wilt be in vain. He will merely await the next fool seeking power."

The four eerie souls of the remaining sorcerers floated away, their interest in Gralyre at an end.

"Wait! Please! Please, will you not help me?" Gralyre chased after the four wraiths. "There must be a way to destroy him?"

"Nothing to be done," the eerie whisper drifted back to Gralyre. "Nothing, without the Word."

"Do you know it? What is his Word of Binding?" Gralyre overtook the four souls, and blocked their path, halting their retreat, forcing them to stay and answer more of his questions.

"None can say. Never did he tell it t' us. Failed, we did. Taken, we were," intoned a sorcerer who had been silent up to this point. The spirit's face was misshapen, its features askew and misaligned so that it was difficult to maintain eye contact with the vaporous being.

"There must be something?"

"Why should we aid thee, when there was no one to aid us?" They ghostly group parted around Gralyre, and moved away once more.

"And that is the problem, is it not?" Gralyre censored harshly, pivoting to watch their retreating backs. "Every man for himself though the world burns? If you would only stand together, how could he defeat you?"

"We have tried."

"Nothing t' do."

"Bound to the Stone, we are. Our Godsmagic, his to feed upon."

Gralyre hung his head. "Is there no hope, then?"

"No"

"None"

"Prepare thee for thy doom."

"Wait." The misshapen wraith returned. The others halted their departure, hovering in place as they watched. "One chance only. A book, in a library, in the hall of kings."

"Dreisenheld?"

"Aye. Seek the journal. Within its pages… maybe… the Word can be found." The distracted being drifted away, as though lost in thought. "Maybe."

"He is coming!" The spectral skeleton alerted upon a whisper of breath. *"Flee! Flee!"* The misshapen soul remained, though the others heeded the warning and vanished, as though they had never been.

"The journal?" Gralyre prompted. He glanced upward with alarm, as the red sky darkened, crimson to vermillion and beyond, blackening.

"I must away!" The shade began to fade.

"Wait! Written by whom?" Gralyre asked, desperate for any knowledge that could save him. An eerie bellow was drawing nearer, growing louder.

"Penned in his true name, it was. The name of his birth." The being became more insubstantial by the moment.

"Tell me the name. Quickly! Before it is too late." Gralyre's soul had to leave the Wizard Stone before the ancient sorcerer arrived and trapped him! All would be lost!

"Aeges."

"Aeges? How do you know this?" Gralyre had to shout now to be heard over the approaching roar. That name! It was the author of the ponderous book of magic that Catrian had set him to read in her tent those long months before.

"I am Aegomon. I was his son… *his son… his son…*" drifted out of the air, as the being vanished entirely.

"His son!" Gralyre was horrified. The monster had supplanted his own son in his obsessive quest for life and power!

Howling with triumph, a twisted, misshapen gargoyle of a

man materialized in the Wizard Stone, and performed a caper of glee. Unlike the thralls, this soul was solid with power.

Gralyre gaped at the madness of the display. "*Fennick?*" This soul bore no resemblance to the staid man who had stood at the shoulder of the King throughout his life. This was the true face of the ancient sorcerer.

"Once, I bore that name. Henceforth, I shall be known as King Gralyre!"

"Never!" Gralyre snarled.

"You should not have come here to challenge me, boy! I am the god of this kingdom! This is my realm. Here, I rule supreme. Did you think you could thwart me? Did you think you could force my Word of Binding from my lips?" Aeges crowed. "You have nothing with which to coerce me!" Powerful magic wreathed the twisted Sorcerer's hands. "But I have only to cleave your soul's conduit back to your vessel to claim victory!"

Gralyre would have run, had he thought it would do any good. Instead, he readied for battle, and coalesced his limited Godsmagic into a defensive shield. Through the distorted shimmer of blue, protective power, he watched the sorcerer, Aeges, whom he had always known as Fennick, release a powerful blast of energy.

It lashed against Gralyre's shield, throwing him back several feet. Gralyre steadied his footing, and braced for another attack.

Aeges laughed heartily, as at a joke. "You cannot protect yourself!" He waved a hand, and Gralyre's shield vanished.

Gralyre collapsed, as his Godsmagic drained away along

with his borrowed strength. The glow of his lifeline dimmed.

"I am in your soul, boy. Your power is mine to control!"

Far away, alone at the centre of Gralyre's Godsmagic, Little Wolf finally severed the black tube that tethered the sorcerer's dead soul to Gralyre's body.

The ancient sorcerer screeched as the magic gathering within his hands sputtered and died. "What have you done?" He reached for Gralyre, grasping and clawing. "Impossible! You cannot escape me! You are mine! MINE!"

Gralyre's glowing lifeline snapped him free of the Wizard Stone. He spiralled back into his body, back into his own flesh, alone and free. For now.

He opened his eyes to the storm and the night, and drew a deep breath, tasting deeply of his freedom, though the air smelled fetid with death. His skin vibrated from the unspent Godsmagic gathered into the sword by Fennick, for the immoral spell that was, as yet, not released. He had done it! He had stopped Fennick, and saved the women! He was free!

Gralyre caught movement in the darkness, and instinctually ducked. A heavy cudgel hammered into the wall of the building where his head had been only moments before. A platoon of Demon Riders surrounded him.

He ran, bowling over the ones who stood in his path.

Hektar turned to the rest of his men. "Come on! We must no' lose him!"

Gralyre glanced back, saw that he was being pursued, and ducked around the corner of a barrack into an alley, hoping to lose the 'Riders in the darkness of the rain-soaked night.

He careened into a wall, losing his balance, as the sword on his back suddenly gained ten stone in weight. It was Fennick! The ancient sorcerer was trying to recapture him!

Gralyre grunted and braced his legs against the downward strain, fighting to take his next step, and then his next. The water drummed off the cobblestones, deadening his hearing beyond a few paces, so he checked the corner of the building in expectant dread, while he struggled to shrug out of the wet, leather baldric, and abandon the Dragon Sword. Any moment now, the 'Riders would be upon him! Gralyre had to get away from the magical blade before Fennick could take him again.

'My Prince, why do you fight me? Surrender all, and I will grant you eternal life by my side!'

"Never!" Gralyre snarled in response to the insidious whisper. He had met the six spectres haunting the Stone, and witnessed the consequences of ceding his soul to Fennick. Better to die here and now than to suffer their fate!

The storm above increased its assault, and the rain slammed down harder, bouncing high off the cobbles. Water cascaded from the peaked roofs to either side of the alley, joining the rivers flowing down the street. Multiple strobes of lightning pulsed blue light and black shadows, stark and harsh, that suspended raindrops in flight with the power of the flash, before thunderous darkness released them to fall again.

The weight of the sword increased further, and the baldric became too heavy to lift off his shoulders and over his head.

Overcome, Gralyre crashed painfully to his knees, sending up a spray of water from the puddles on the cobblestones. Gravity crushed him down until he was pinned helplessly to the ground like a turtle on its back, spitting and blinking the torrential rainfall from his face.

The 'Riders rounded the corner, and slowed, approaching cautiously.

Gralyre drew his dagger, the only weapon remaining to him. "Stay back!" he warned uselessly. Water flicked in wide arcs off of the glimmering, sharp edge, as he waved the knife threateningly. The first 'Rider to touch him would die, and perhaps the second as well, but then their numbers would overwhelm him. This was how he would meet his end. This was how he would defeat Fennick.

There were many regrets to consider as his death neared. The decimation of his people. The revenge he would never be granted against Doaphin. But there was only one that remained foremost in Gralyre's thoughts.

'Catrian,' he drew upon the memory of her warmth in his arms, the scent of her golden brown hair, and the passion of her lips upon his. *'I am sorry I failed you!'* With Gralyre's death, would come hers. His heart overflowed with sorrow and love for the woman who had been his match in every way.

CHAPTER EIGHTEEN

"Where do ye think ye are going?" Hektar shouted in order to be heard over the thrashing tempest roaring above their heads.

Gralyre gasped in belated recognition of his voice. "You are the Rebels?" His head fell back in relief, thumping against the pavers, as he stopped fighting the sword's weight, and went limp against the runnels of water flowing across the cobbles against his back. He had not recognized them from the brief glimpses of the outside world that Fennick had afforded him throughout the day. Gralyre raised his head, and frowned as he noted someone missing from the group arrayed before him. "Where is Jord?" Gralyre shouted to be heard over the din of the storm.

The dark shape that was Hektar shrugged. "Who knows?" he yelled back. "He abandoned us after we entered the city."

A frisson of unease prickled the nape of Gralyre's neck. Their body language was off, stiff like adversaries, not relaxed like allies. "Why did you try to club me?"

Hektar fingered his cudgel. "T' keep the Dragon Sword safe. I thought ye were a 'Rider."

Alarm swept Gralyre free of all other concerns. Hektar had made no mistake. He wanted the sword, and had just tried to kill him for it!

Gralyre squinted into the storm, as he considered his options. There was no danger of Hektar taking the blade. The Dragon

Sword would never leave Gralyre's side, despite the best efforts of the Rebel to take it, and he needed Hektar's help to get free of Fennick's trap. Better to seem to give it freely than to lie helpless before their knives. "The sword is pinning me! 'Tis yours if you but help me to lift it!" he hollered at the Rebel and made a show of sheathing his dagger at his waist.

Hektar could not believe the luck. The Lost Prince pretender wanted him to take the sword! He was surrendering it without a fight! His face settled into lines of satisfaction, as he dropped his club and strode forward to liberate the iconic weapon.

He reached past Gralyre's shoulder and grasped the hilt, straining to draw it from its sheath. It would not budge. The sword was as melded into the leather as if it were all one piece, and the whole of it as heavy as the stone buildings surrounding them.

Hektar abandoned the blade to try to unbuckle the straps across Gralyre's chest that held the scabbard tightly against his back. He tore a nail on his first attempt to slide a wet leather strap through a buckle, for the rain made it slippery and difficult to grasp, and the weight of the sword put too much strain on the leather, making it impossible to gain the slack necessary to release the baldric. "Enog," Hektar beckoned for help.

Lightning spat like the tongue of a dragon, and Gralyre was granted a clear view of the men hovering over him. "Gods!"

"What?" Enog asked, fumbling with a buckle, while Hektar tried to press slack into the leather.

"Your faces!" Gralyre roared over the crashing storm.

Hektar turned to Enog. "Enog, what is wrong with your face?" he demanded, squinting closer at his friend through the rain and the darkness.

Enog raised his hands, and quested along his wet cheeks. "What? Nothing!"

Hektar grabbed Enog's head, and angled it to catch what light could be found in the black, foul night. Lightning forked above them from one end of the valley to the other, briefly revealing the truth. "Your disguise is gone!" Thunder lashed the air, vibrating the ground with the force of the clap.

Hektar spun away and grabbed another of his men, and peered intently at his face. Human! Plain human features stared back at him!

Gralyre felt his face, and realized that his disguise had faltered as well. Within the sword, the spiteful Fennick was dissolving the spell that altered their appearances to that of Demon Riders. Gralyre watched with alarm, as the Rebels' clothing reverted into the tattered rags and remnants they had worn previously. They looked human again.

"Ye did this!" Hektar howled at Gralyre. He drew his dagger, and leapt upon the Prince's prone body. Hektar raised the weapon with both hands, high above his head, and brought the glinting point slamming down with all of his might towards Gralyre's vulnerable chest.

Gralyre caught Hektar's wrists, wrestling to prevent the blade from descending further. Pinned to the ground, and unable to roll to gain leverage, he fought to hold Hektar's bodyweight from forcing the blade downwards. As strong as Gralyre was, even he could not suspend a large man over his chest forever. The blade inched closer to its mark. Gralyre's arms shook with strain, as Hektar bore down upon the dagger, forcing it the final distance.

It stuck fast, as though it had hit a stone, just shy of Gralyre's skin. "Sorcery!" Hektar spat accusingly, rising to his feet with his reclaimed knife in hand.

"Fool! The Sword will not release me! Your disguises are gone! Run! Get free before sunrise! Save yourselves!" Gralyre ordered, as he strained to rise.

"No' without the sword!"

A wave of stinging pain swept Gralyre's body, and he cursed helplessly. Vaguely, he was aware that the Rebels were falling to the ground, rolling and crying out, as though they were afire.

The Demon Lords were aware of their presence! The Godsmagic of their arrival by portal earlier in the day must have incited the Demon Lords to high alert. The illusion that the Thewr 'ap Noir had woven over their bodies had been good enough to fool their seeking magic, until now.

From the nearby castle, a roar of triumph challenged the thunderous storm, the voice of thousands who had just been given the call to arms.

Gralyre growled and strained to escape the sword. If only it would let him rise! He closed his eyes and concentrated, trying to reach his Godsmagic in order to burn the straps of the baldric free, but the magics of the Demon Lords increased in intensity and pain, as they felt his attempts to work sorcery.

With the Demon Lords focussing their magic solely upon Gralyre, the Rebels were able to recover enough to crawl away from the pain.

Gralyre opened his eyes, and blinked away the spots of light that were flashing in his vision. Transmitted into his spine from the cobblestones upon which he lay, the ground shivered with the vibrations of pounding footsteps. The 'Riders were coming.

೮೦೧೪

By the time that Hektar and his Rebels reached the far end of the alley and turned the corner, the powerful sorcery that had attacked them had waned. The Rebels stumbled to a halt, pressing to the wall of the next building to hide their presence upon the empty street while they paused to recover.

Hektar slid over to the corner of the alley, looking back at the vulnerable figure of the pinned man who still struggled against the cobblestones of the wet street.

Enog grasped his arm tightly, halting him. "Where are ye going? Leave him!"

"The Dragon Sword! Enog! We must have it!"

"No, Hektar. We leave it and him. Our purpose is served! The sword and the Lost Prince pretender are delivered unto Doaphin! We have won! We have saved our people!"

Hektar's shoulders heaved, and tears of relief mingled with the rain slicking his face, as he recognized their triumph. "Ye are right! O' course! Aye!" he clapped a hand to Enog's shoulder, as he absorbed the truth that he had been too single minded to see.

The decision was instantaneous. "We leave him. Make for the barrier!" Hektar yelled. "Run like Doaphin is on your heels, because if he is no' yet, he soon will be!"

The night became a blur of movement, as the Rebels ran. Several men fell, stumbling in the blackness on slick, uneven cobblestones, but they quickly regained their footing, scrabbling fearfully to keep pace with their comrades. Their retreat was ragged and inelegant. Danger and death nipped at their heels, lending them the fleetness they needed to escape.

೫ೕ೪

Gralyre made a last attempt to reason with the cold soul of Fennick in his Wizard Stone.

Fennick responded with a surge of sullen resentment before vanishing from Gralyre's thoughts, refusing to answer further summons, and refusing to lighten the weight of the sword.

"Release me, you petty bastard!" Gralyre shouted in frustration. "They are coming!" The first Demon Riders rounded the far corner of the alleyway.

Gralyre had time to hide his dagger up his sleeve so that it would not be taken from him. And then it was too late. Multitudes of hands reached down and hauled him upright. Bitter rage coiled through his chest at the sudden lightness of the Dragon Sword.

As the 'Riders patted his clothing to find and discard his

weapons, they missed the dagger that Gralyre had secreted at his wrist. Little good that it did! Fennick had deceived him, and had betrayed humanity. And now all was lost. The Dragon Sword had fallen into the hands of the enemy. Mankind would be purged from the land. Evil had won the war. Gralyre felt the need to roar his disappointment loudly enough to challenge the thunderous storm overhead.

"Get the sword!" ordered the troop's Sergeant. He carried the only torch, lifting it high so that he could enjoy the triumphant capture of the Lost Prince.

One of the 'Riders grabbed the hilt of the blade at Gralyre's back, and a massive discharge of sorcery knocked the creature against the wall of a building. Smoking slightly, it fell dead into the rivers of water washing through the cobblestone alley.

Nor could the baldric be lifted up over Gralyre's head, despite the efforts of several of the enemy. Sparks flew from a 'Rider's knife, and it snapped in half when it tried to hack through the black leather straps. Fennick, it would seem, had decided to stay where he was.

"Leave it t' the Demon Lords!" the sergeant ordered, delegating the magical problem up the chain of authority.

Holding fast to Gralyre's arms, the 'Riders dragged him off towards the nearby castle. At first, Gralyre's boots skidded on the slick, wet cobblestones of the street, as he tried to resist the forward momentum. They meant to take him alive, and he resolved to make them pay for every foot gained.

In response, the swarm of 'Riders merely plucked him from

the ground, hefting his weight with many hands, as they toted him onwards. Gralyre kept still after that, conserving his strength for what was to come. A few blocks on, the Demon Riders shoved, beat and carried him through the gate, and across the lower bailey of the black castle. They passed through ranks of marching Demon Riders. There were thousands of them. The anthill had been kicked over, and the ants were swarming.

Gralyre's captors carried him through the inner portcullis, into the central bailey, and then into the keep that arose in three stories of towering black stone. As Gralyre looked up at the hulking building through the sheets of rain, the lightning spat blue light across the uneven black stones, a fittingly sinister last glimpse of his freedom.

Just across the threshold of the keep, the 'Riders tossed Gralyre down a short flight of wide, stone steps, and he rolled into the great hall. The din above him silenced, as his captors departed, slamming the heavy oaken door closed behind them, and muting the noise of the storm.

For a moment, Gralyre lay still to catch his breath, and assess his damages. His Maolar chain had protected his torso from the fall, but his chin had hit the bottom step, rattling his teeth. His skin shivered and arose with bumps from the feel of the potent Godsmagic that was shifting the energies throughout the room.

Gralyre arose to hands and knees, blinking to adjust his eyes to the muted light. The warm wetness of blood seeped heavily down the side of his face from another scrape. Mingling with rainwater, it dripped to the floor and seemed to vanish against the black stone.

He glanced back the way he had entered. Two 'Riders glared at him from the top of the short flight of stairs, their lips drawn back in a snarl of pointed teeth, as they flanked the closed doors. Their hands clenched threateningly on their long pikes.

Fifty feet across the hall, Gralyre spied four Demon Lords seated on elaborately carved chairs of stone, set on a dais that they might tower above all who stood before them. They were clad in rich velvets and satins, the colours bold with the clashing colours of precious gems. They were beautiful of feature, and utterly deficient of morals and mercy.

Their four thrones were arranged in a half circle, with Gralyre at the focal point of their disdainful gazes. The waves of Godsmagic were emanating from them, as they guarded Gralyre against the use of his sorcery.

The silence stretched unbroken. Their Godsmagic shivered through the hall. What were they awaiting? Why did they not just kill him and take the sword?

The breath stuttered in Gralyre's throat, as the occupant of a fifth chair arose lazily. Gralyre had not previously noted him, as his throne had been set apart from the others.

...A Demon face emerges from a boiling, red mist. His merciless eyes burn with triumph... He comes to take my head... The executioner's sword swings....

Gralyre passed his hand across his eyes to wipe away the last of the rainwater, trying to clear his vision of an apparition that could not be!

But the slight man clad in a long, red coat was no figment. He stepped unhurriedly down the staircase in front of the raised dais, and walked towards Gralyre. His booted footsteps sounded overloud in the hushed hall.

'Doaphin!'

སྣ

Jord found Little Wolf huddled in the corner between two buildings. In the blackness and rain, he would have walked right past if he had not been carefully searching for him up and down each street and alley in the area. The wolfdog had found a good place to hide, and to await Jord's return.

"There ye are! Come, Little Wolf! Let us rejoin Gralyre and the Rebels. Perhaps between the two o' us we can bring him back from the sword's... Little Wolf?"

Little Wolf did not stir as Jord approached. "Little Wolf?" he called again, softer, and his worst fears were realized when he crouched down and touched the cold, wet muzzle. "Ah, no! No' ye!"

Jord bowed his head, grieving, and patted sadly at Little Wolf's shoulder. "Ye do no' deserve this." He could not find a wound. The way the wolfdog was curled, it was as though he had simply drifted to sleep.

Never had there been so loyal a companion. If beasts were

afforded a place of honour beside the Gods, Little Wolf had more than earned the right to be in their mighty company. Jord let the rain wash his tears from his face, as he gently stroked the wolfdog's wet fur. Mayvin, and now Little Wolf. The weight of their loss was crushing for their friendships had been so preciously rare in his life.

Jord did not like this feeling, this grief. This was why he did not seek out the company of others. They either died and left, or betrayed you for their own gain and left. Either way, Jord was always alone. Companionship had been foreign to his solitary self-reliance. Yet at some point on the dangerous road south to Fennick's Island, Jord had forgotten this hard life lesson, and gained a family.

He raised his face to the heavens, blinking water from his eyes that he might glare at the Gods with a resentment that bordered upon hatred. They had made him care, and thus he had never had so much to lose. They had given to him, only so that they might take it all away upon the whims of their amusement!

Jord rubbed his dripping hair back off his face, and hesitated with alarm. He patted at his features, feeling the normalcy of human flesh under his questing fingers. Without him being aware, his Demon Rider disguise had vanished.

Movement past the mouth of the alley startled his attention, and Jord glanced over in time to see Hektar and his Rebels rushing past. They were fleeing, making for the barrier. Gralyre would be with them.

He stood and jogged a few steps to catch up to them, before

halting and glancing back at the lonely form of the wolfdog. Exposed to the storm and abandoned in the street of an enemy's lair was no fit resting place for so brave a friend.

Jord returned to Little Wolf's side. He grunted, as he hefted the hundred and twenty pound animal up over his shoulders to rest upon the back of his neck. Little Wolf's legs dangled limply down each side of his chest, and Jord took them in his hands to help steady the wolfdog's weight as he walked.

Once he was back through the barrier, he would help Gralyre find a nice place, perhaps upon a hilltop or near a stream, in which to usher Little Wolf to his eternal rest.

∞∞

Gralyre clenched his eyes in denial. What he feared above all else had come to pass! The Demon from his nightmares had finally run him to ground! Gales of terror and paranoia buffeted his shivering flesh, tempests born of recurring trauma from a year of nightly executions. He bowed his head to it, gritting his teeth to prevent their rattling, as a phantom sword struck his neck, over and over.

Finding a kernel of fortitude, Gralyre staved off his overwhelming remembrance of Centaur Pass by narrowing his focus to minutiae. He watched the bloodied rainwater drip from his chin to the floor, the pool slowly widening. He blinked his eyes heavily, concentrating upon his quivering arms, outstretched beneath his prostrate body, and his splayed hands, pressed against the glittering black granite of the hall's floor. *'This is no nightmare!'* His long fingers were filthy and wet, his nails chipped and uneven, his knuckles white with tension. *'This! This is real!'* The battle for Centaur Pass was no more than a terrifying memory.

One thought, then as now, suddenly cleared his mind of all chaos. *'I will not cower before him!'* Kill him, Doaphin would, but he would never see him grovel or beg! Gralyre owed it to his kingly forefathers to meet his death with bravery.

The steady pulse of the sword dance stilled Gralyre's shudders, slowed his heartbeat, and calmed his breathing. Disdaining the bruises from his tumble down the stairs, he pushed up to his feet.

Momentarily ignoring the disquieting nightmare striding towards him, he concentrated instead upon his peripheral vision, quickly evaluating his escape options. They were dismal.

Three archways opened up from this central hall, two on the right, and one on the left. All led into windowless rooms.

There was a staircase beyond the dais of the Demon Lords that hugged the wall, as it circled upwards to the next floor of the tower. Doaphin and his four Demon Lords stood between Gralyre and that avenue of escape.

To the rear, two Demon Riders stood guard at the locked oak door leading outside to the central bailey. Beyond them, there remained a gauntlet of thousands of Doaphin's troops in the lower bailey and the city to fight through to reach the magical barrier and freedom.

Gralyre assumed a relaxed stance, his level-eyed stare betraying no distress, though he knew himself to be doomed. He counted the pulses of his heartbeat, a measured throb that beckoned for the dance of war. Only one avenue was left to him.

The Dragon Sword still swung at his back, and his dagger was still hidden up his sleeve at his wrist. Overconfident, and certain of the supremacy of their sorcery, or perhaps fearful of Fennick's Wizard Stone, the Demon Lords had not yet disarmed him.

Fast as a striking snake, Gralyre palmed his knife, and threw it at Doaphin. Flipping through the air, a vengeful blur, it sought the heart of the Usurper.

Doaphin gestured with his fingers, as if shooing away a fly, and the dagger went wide, burying up to its brass hilt into the chest of one of the sitting Demon Lords.

The Demon Lord grunted quietly, and slumped forward, rolling out of its throne into a lifeless heap upon the floor. The surviving three Demon Lords surged from their seats. Snaking black mists whipped out from their hands towards Gralyre.

Gralyre erected a barrier of protection before their magic could strike him. The whips of mist pounded against the blue shield, sparking and snapping, as they tried to penetrate his defenses. They encircled him, and lofted him into the air.

He had no idea what the Demon Lord Sorcery would do if it touched him. He only hoped that it would not find a chink in his weakened sorcery. After battling Fennick all day, he had little Godsmagic remaining with which to defend himself.

"Enough," Doaphin roared. The smoky ropes evaporated, and the Demon Lords collapsed back onto their ornate seats, as if they had been clouted.

Gralyre hissed in pain, as his blue shield ruptured, and he dropped back to the hard, stone floor. That easily, the more experienced sorcerer had disarmed his magic.

Never losing his momentum, Gralyre shrugged from his baldric, and drew the Dragon Sword. The blade sang out as it was freed, a siren's call to war. Gralyre was somewhat surprised that Fennick allowed it to be unsheathed after his earlier impediment. It would seem that the ancient sorcerer had finally recognized the peril of the situation.

Doaphin's step hitched at the appearance of the Dragon Sword, and his hands gathered together at his waist. He rubbed his withered palm, hidden by its black glove, an unconscious gesture.

Amassed power still vibrated from the blade, the accumulation meant for the spell that had never been released. Gralyre doubted that the Demon Lords or Doaphin could sense it among all of the dissonant sources of Godsmagic playing havoc with their senses in the hall.

'Destroy Doaphin!' Gralyre ordered.

Fennick remained unresponsive within his Wizard Stone.

'Kill him!' Gralyre curbed his frustration, as the sword remained inert. Fennick's contemptible shunning of common sense would see Gralyre dead, and his Wizard Stone captured!

Fennick might have denied him the magic of the sword, but

as a weapon, the Maolar blade was second to none in the hands of a master. Gralyre held the Dragon Sword easily before him with a two-handed grip. He slashed a figure eight in the air, the silver blur of the massive sword under perfect control. Four lethal feet of shimmering silver metal awaited the first creature to draw too near.

Doaphin halted twenty paces away, well out of the reach of Gralyre's massive weapon, and bent a knee, sweeping his fingers to the floor in a courtly bow. "Here we are again, Highness, our lives made long enough to bear witness to history repeating." His voice held the smooth, velvet timber of a practiced seducer.

Gralyre could see that the years weighed heavily upon Doaphin despite his appearance of youth. It was there in his bitter, blue eyes, where networks of fine wrinkles, that should have been deep canyons, fanned out in patterns of strain and malcontent. The indulgent decrepitude about his mouth betrayed elements of unwholesomeness to leach through into the world.

Gralyre remained silent, and patient as a stone within a deep pool. Waiting for Doaphin to draw fatally closer. The weight of the sword in his hands, the pulse of the dance, Doaphin's death; nothing else was of any import.

"You still believe that you will win free of this?" Doaphin mocked Gralyre's warrior stance. "You are ridiculous. I will have the sword." He beckoned with a curl of his fingers. "Now."

"You will have to kill me to get it." Gralyre gritted out.

"My lord Doaphin! The Prince is to be taken alive! The Master commands it!" a Demon Lord reminded piously. Its voice was pitched high with disquiet, as it resettled upon its ornate seat upon the dais. It was obvious that the creature was unused to not being the supreme power within the room. Leery of how Doaphin had disciplined it, the Demon Lord did not dare to summon its sorcery again.

"Silence!' Doaphin snapped in a voice much different than the soothing tones he had reserved for speaking with Gralyre.

"The Master?" Gralyre came to attention. The Master was the title that the captured Stalker had taunted him with under torture. The Demon Lords were not referring to Doaphin. Something else was at play here.

Doaphin ignored them all. He extended his good hand covetously, and approached, step by deliberate step, as though taming a wild beast. "Give it to me. Give me the sword." His voice was rich and rounded, soothing Gralyre to his will, as though Doaphin was a dramatic actor playing a role upon a stage.

"Draw nearer," Gralyre encouraged icily, "that I may whither the rest of you."

Doaphin prudently halted his forward progress. "Why so contentious? It does not have to be this way between us, Highness." He sounded so calm, so reasonable. "Fennick is treacherous. If you keep the blade, he will take you. 'Tis only a matter of time. Frankly, I am surprised that he has not possessed you already."

Gralyre's face tightened in remembrance of the dark place within which he had been trapped all that day.

"Ah," Doaphin tsked knowingly, shaking his head in mock despair. "I can see that you know of what I speak. Allow me to rescue you from him."

"Why would you save me, when you clearly mean to kill me," Gralyre stated with certainty.

Doaphin smiled then, as though at a pleasant thought.

"My Lord Doaphin!" the Demon Lord interjected again.

Doaphin ignored the protest, his unwavering attention fixed upon the Prince. "If not of yourself, think of your kingdom."

Gralyre drew a steadying breath, as a spike of red-hot rage sought to disrupt his control. "You dare to speak of the safety of my kingdom, when evidence of your villainy surrounds us?"

"My wickedness is nothing when measured against yours, Highness."

A muscle jumped in Gralyre's jaw, as he clenched his teeth. "Aye, I will admit my sins, my failures and defeats that left my kingdom vulnerable to unspeakable hardships. If you will accept yours. I witnessed a birth this evening. There is no justification for what you have done to my people."

"Your people? They have been mine for far longer than ever they were yours."

Doaphin took a rash step closer, almost near enough now for Gralyre to reach with the sword. Almost. His mastery of the blade versus Doaphin's superior skills with Sorcery; Gralyre would never have a second chance should he miss with his first.

"You speak of your sins, but you omit one, Highness. The sin of abandonment." For the first time, Doaphin's velvet voice roughened with unguarded emotion. "The sin of betrayal."

"You speak of Genevieve."

"You chose your precious kingdom over her life."

"And would do so again."

"She awaited you. She never abandoned the hope that you would come for her."

Gralyre scowled, as Doaphin pressed upon one of his deepest regrets.

"You discarded the greatest gift in this world, like it was nothing!" Doaphin continued to scorn. "You proved yourself unworthy of her!"

Gralyre sucked in a breath of recognition. "You loved her." Past events, barely noted, now collected within his mind to paint a vivid picture. He recalled his brief, forced courtship of the Princess. Doaphin was there, the unwanted chaperone, always hovering in the background. Following. Watching.

"Aye! A chaste and pure love that a privileged man like you could never know!" Doaphin derided. "She needed only to ask, and I would suffer all to comply. I will do anything to save her from you and your evil. I have gone to any length, and, aye, participated in every depravity to do so." He looked down at his boots, and his voice lowered to a musing whisper, "Every depravity." It was not a confession of guilt, but of pride. This was how the twisted man measured his love.

"All this destruction and chaos and death, because you were spurned?" Gralyre disparaged.

"You understand nothing! She loves me, not you, but she

cannot see it! I need to save her. She is there, in Dreisenheld, trapped just beyond my reach because of your evil!"

"Like a butterfly in amber?" Gralyre thought of the legend of the Lost Prince, and the tragic fate of Princess Genevieve who was frozen in time by Sorcery. Not a story then. A truth of his past. She was still there, alive and awaiting his rescue. His obligation.

Doaphin's brow creased. "An apt analogy." He glanced up, and his face warped with hatred. "Only the sword contains the power that can save her. Give it to me, or I will take it by force."

Disgust churned acid in Gralyre's stomach. The man was obsessed with the Princess. Even after three hundred years, Doaphin still sought to thwart Genevieve's rescue in order to keep her imprisoned for his own twisted affections! Everything that had happened began to make perverse sense but for one detail. "You never answered me. Who is the Master?"

Doaphin's sly, spiteful smile returned in full force. "But you know who it is." Venom dripped from every syllable.

Gralyre shook his head once, an abrupt denial.

Doaphin's eyes narrowed with malicious joy, as he sensed Gralyre's uncertainty. "You really do not remember," he breathed in simulated astonishment. "Think back, Prince, seek into the dark hidden places of your memory. You know who the Master is."

"I do not."

"You do."

As Gralyre sifted his memories for the knowledge that

Doaphin alluded to, a spike of agony pierced his temple. He winced, and stepped back with one foot to keep his balance. Fennick had not been idle since Little Wolf had severed his connection to Gralyre's body. He had been planning his next campaign.

'Your useless resistance is at an end. 'Tis time to take your place in my Wizard Stone. You will not escape me again!'

"No! Never!" The piercing agony was intense, blinding his vision with flashes of light. He stumbled down to a knee, a palm clutched to his brow, as though it would keep his skull from splitting in two. For a brief, dizzying moment he was in two places at once, the hall of the Demon Lords and the red landscape of Fennick's Wizard Stone.

Gralyre erected every mental barrier that he could manage, to block the ancient Sorcerer before Fennick could reestablish dominion over his soul. The vision of the Wizard Stone vanished, and he was back in the hall, fighting a battle on two fronts.

Doaphin barked with laughter. "Ah. I sense that Fennick has decided to join us." He took a long step forward.

"Get back!" Gralyre roared, lifting the tip of his blade defensively. His legs quivered, as he stood to face his corporeal enemy. His headache ebbed to a dull pounding, and nausea pressed against his throat.

Doaphin beckoned towards one of the antechambers to his left. With a metallic skirl, a long, narrow, Maolar chest skidded out of the side room to slide to a rest at his feet. Doaphin had made the mistake of laying hands upon the Wizard Stone three hundred years ago. It was a not an error that he would repeat. Time and research had provided the solution for containing Fennick's powerful soul.

The lid of the chest swung up, revealing a soft bed of crushed blue velvet that waited to cushion the Dragon Sword's rest. Gralyre immediately recognized its purpose. Just as the Rebels had isolated the Stalker in a Maolar cage, rendering it unable to perform magic, so would this chest contain the Wizard Stone.

Gralyre's momentary distraction with Doaphin gave Fennick the opening he needed to increase the intensity of his attacks. Even if Gralyre had not been weakened by his daylong imprisonment, Fennick would have been the stronger, bolstered as he was by the Godsmagic seething through his Wizard Stone, and his years of experience and knowledge that Gralyre lacked.

Most of Gralyre's weak magical barriers collapsed like he had been hit with a bolt of lightning. The sword's magic coursed down through his body. Coldness followed the heat of the pain, a numbness that travelled rapidly upwards from Gralyre's toes, overtaking his ankles and legs, his hips, his chest, and freezing his spine, so that he was suddenly unable to move.

His breath stuttered with panic, and he lifted his chin, as though he were anchored to the bottom of a pool whose flood levels were rising. Only one magical barricade remained to protect his soul from Fennick's total possession. Gralyre pushed all of his power into bolstering that last defence, and was able to stop Fennick from claiming the last of him.

'You will never stop me, you weak boy! Cede yourself, for I will not aid you. I will let you die, and let Doaphin have my Wizard Stone. Surrender to me, and I will kill Doaphin and save your precious kingdom! I alone hold the power to defeat him!'

Gralyre was horrified by Fennick's strategy. Fennick had weighted the sword to ensure that Gralyre would be captured, just to maneuverer him into a situation where he would be forced to surrender his soul of his own volition, or give a weapon of terrible power to the enemy.

Doaphin also had an offer. "Release the sword, Highness, and I promise you a quick and painless end. If Fennick exiles you to his Wizard Stone, he will feed off your tormented soul for millennia, until you vanish from all existence."

"Traitor!" The Demon Lords had overheard Doaphin's words. "The Master will hear of your treachery!"

'My aid comes at a price, Highness! Choose.'

Gralyre's haunted gaze latched onto the salvation offered by Doaphin's open metal chest. A quick, painless death in place of eternal torture while Fennick ate of his Godsmagic, shaving slivers off his soul until he faded to nothing, until he joined the ranks of ghostly thralls haunting his Wizard Stone.

Perceiving Gralyre's wavering resolve, Doaphin's voice dripped with faux concern and urgency. "Fennick is taking you. I can sense it. Soon you will be gone. Place the sword in the chest! Hurry!"

Both choices ended with certain death, but if submitting to Fennick would save his people from Doaphin's despotic rule, then it was a worthy sacrifice. "May the Gods damn you both," Gralyre whispered, and allowed his last defence to fail.

Fennick pounced. Up past Gralyre's shoulders and his neck, the flowing ice finally encased his head, and all sensation vanished. Though the bargain had been struck, their souls did not immediately make the swap between flesh and stone. In his hubris, Fennick wanted Gralyre to bear witness to his supremacy.

Gralyre watched from afar, impotent against the restraints that bound him, as the Dragon Sword readied its spell. He had managed to stop this heinous sorcery once, but was without the resources to do so again. *'Fennick! No!'*

"You fool! What have you done?" Doaphin yelled and ducked, as the great hall detonated into an inferno.

The thralls in the Wizard Stone prison wailed, lamenting the pain, as Fennick fed their stolen Godsmagic into the explosion. He was immune to their torture; their powers were his to reap.

The Demon Lords on their thrones vanished in a curtain of flame. The magical explosion that Fennick conjured blasted free of the confines of the fortress, throwing large granite blocks outwards to smash buildings several streets away. The black towers toppled, as a column of fire stabbed skyward. The plume grew wider, killing everything in its path, as it rushed outwards from its epicentre. Nothing was spared.

೮ು೧ಜ

Hektar and his Rebels fled through the darkness. Past the outskirts of city, and the end of the paving stones, the road was deep with sucking mud and dangerous ruts left by the wheels of generations of wagons bearing human cargo. Forced to slow, the Rebels cursed and slid as they jogged on through the storm.

Instead of using the route taken that afternoon through the thick woods, they kept to the road instead, reasoning that they would make better time to the barrier that protected the valley from detection. Judging by how the city had fallen silent at nightfall, it seemed unlikely that there would be 'Riders about until morning when the Tithe wagons began to roll once more. It was a sound plan, and a more direct path than the one that they had taken earlier.

It was not long before they reached the barrier, coming upon it unexpectedly, and roughly. The men hit it at a run, rebounding off the invisible surface, and falling to their backs. Without their Demon Rider disguises to fool the sorcery, it was preventing them from leaving the confines of the valley. Apparently, it was also used to keep human prisoners from escaping.

A flash of light and crack of thunder sounded in the distance, as they moaned in pain and picked themselves up from the mud. Hektar wondered if the storm had produced a massive bolt of lightning, as he glanced back towards the city. A column of fire speared up into the stormy sky, a false sunrise that cast an orange glow upon them, even from afar.

"What is that?" Enog breathed in awe, as he pushed his dripping, muddy hair from his eyes.

Hektar just shook his head. "Ignore it! Keep your wits on getting through the barrier! Ye men, dig down and see if we can tunnel under it."

The rain had softened the ground enough that the Rebels were easily able to scoop earth away from the edges of the invisible wall. "There is no bottom! It keeps on going down!" one of the men grouched breathlessly, as he threw sloppy handfuls of mud to the side.

"Keep digging," Hektar ordered.

Enog pointed a shaking finger back at the plume of fire that bloomed larger and larger. "'Tis coming closer, Hektar!"

Hektar spared a glance, and his breath left him in a whoosh. In just the brief moments he had glanced away, the pillar of fire had grown to impossible heights, and widened to greater proportions, curling downwards like the cap of a mushroom as it hit the ceiling of the sky. Even as he watched he could see the walls of flame moving towards them at incredible speed, rippling outwards. Hektar tried to swallow past the lump in his throat, but found his spittle had vanished.

"We are going t' burn!" screamed Pardel. He stopped digging to scrabble mindlessly at the barrier, marking the invisible surface with his muddy handprints. The wall did not give way to his frightened pummelling but his actions provoked a panic in the rest of the men. As one, they surged against their trap.

From out of the trees, several Demon Riders ran towards them. They did not stop to fight, but passed effortlessly through the barrier, escaping the oncoming, fiery death. The 'Riders fled up the muddy road, glancing behind with fear contorted features. Through the deluging rain, their bestial eyes glowed orange in the approaching light of the firestorm as they vanished into the darkness of the stormy night.

To witness the escape of their enemies while they could not devolved the Rebels into a frenzy. The Demon Lord sorcery remained a solid presence that they could not push through.

ॐ

Through the pounding rain, Jord watched in awe as the fiery column blew through the city with the roar of a thousands demons. He could not look away. For the first time in his life, he could think of no clever escape.

He thought of trying to run back down the road into the city, into the streets to find an ossuary to dive into, but the speed at which the plume was bearing down upon him made that a fool's bet. And the heated wind already blowing his ragged hair back from his face told him that such a hiding place would be nothing but an oven set to roast him alive.

The others had outpaced him, burdened as he was with Little Wolf's limp body. As fast as they were moving they were probably at the barrier by now, whereas he had only just crested the ridge out of the hidden valley.

He would go no further; running would not save him. He lifted Little Wolf off his shoulders, and sat in the mud at the edge of the road, cradling the wolfdog's limp body close to his chest, as he watched his death approach.

Mostly, he was angry, raging at the betrayal of the very Gods that he had held up to Aneida as having saved them for a purpose. If they had wanted him dead, they could have left him to rot in the boneyard of the Labyrinth! Why allow him to live if there had been no greater design to it?

He would be sure to ask when he stood before them.

Jord's lips twisted into a sneer beneath his large nose. His knives emerged from hiding, and he idly swirled and juggled them, as the firestorm roared across the valley towards him, driving roiling debris before it, a tsunami of flame.

Aye, the Gods had much to answer for.

ಬಂಌ

Though the floors above were now gone, and the ruined hall was open to the storm, nary a drop of rainwater made it through the intense heat to dampen the clouds of roiling flames.

The Prince struggled within his prison, screaming for mercy for the women who were dying.

Fennick smiled. Gralyre's weak presence was like an annoying moth fluttering its wings against the brightness of the sun. Fennick gloated over his victory. His patience had won out at last! He was finally free of his Wizard Stone, Doaphin was dead, and Gralyre was his slave. Fennick was now the ultimate power in the Kingdom of Lyre! Sword in hand, he raised arms wreathed in flames, and threw back his head to shout triumphantly, basking in his transcendent rebirth, his immortality.

It was past the time to exile the Prince to the Wizard Stone, and complete the transposing of their souls. This was the most pleasurable part of the process for Fennick, when the tables turned, and the prisoner recognized that Fennick's supreme rule was merciless. The moment was made doubly sweet, for this time he abased a Prince of Lyre!

The stone slabs of the floor heaved upwards when Godsmagic suddenly stabbed out from within the billowing flames. Fennick catapulted high into the air, and landed on his side, losing the Dragon Sword. It clanged from his hands and skidded into the crevice of two dislodged stones.

Impossible! No one could have survived the explosion of fire!

Doaphin strode out of the churning flames, struggling against the tides of fire and stones, bodies and debris that rushed past him and around him. The shimmer of heat waves distorted his form, as though he too were made of flame. A bright nimbus of light, a shield that rendered him impervious to the heat, surrounded him. The Maolar chest that he had summoned from the antechamber hovered after him like a faithful pet on a leash.

Fennick was utterly caught off guard. His plan to kill the Usurper had failed dismally. Gralyre's lips formed curses, but it was Fennick's voice that emerged.

The Dragon Sword lay equal distance between the two formidable Sorcerers. Doaphin's covetous gaze found it through the distortion of heat and flame, and his Sorcery lashed out to claim it.

"NO!" Fennick roared. His magical response slammed molten rocks onto Doaphin, gathering more and more debris to pile down until the Usurper was pressed beneath a large mound.

Fennick wove his Godsmagic into a tether of air, and lassoed the shimmering blade with it. One quick draw, and it flew back towards his waiting hands.

At the same moment, Doaphin's open Maolar chest swooped to intercept it. Doaphin, though buried alive, was still protected within his magic shield. He retained the wit to direct his Maolar chest. The flying sword met the blue velvet interior of the box and stuck fast, the metal lid fell, and the clasp turned.

Fennick's scream of denial stopped abruptly, as he lost all connection with the outside world.

Suddenly free of Fennick's possession, Gralyre collapsed, retching and coughing at his abrupt return to dominion over his flesh. He recoiled from the searing heat of the roaring flames against his body, gathering what Godsmagic remained to him to erect a sputtering, blue shield. Fennick's magic, that had protected Gralyre's flesh from incineration, had vanished along with the ancient sorcerer.

'The sword!' Gralyre lunged out weakly in a bid to grab the Maolar box that was drifting away from his reach, but his body was numb and useless. He did little more than flop like a trout caught on a fisherman's line.

Doaphin exploded upwards from beneath the pile of rubble

that Fennick had buried him in. His sorcery had been strong enough to withstand the extreme weight and heat of the stones without injury.

Gralyre was caught within the radius of the concussion of Doaphin's magic, and was rolled across the molten stone floor, casting flaming slag and sparks from his path. He fetched up against a ruined wall. Doaphin dragged him upwards to hang there, pinioned limply. Gralyre's body began to prickle with needles of returning sensation, little good that it did him now.

"I have you in my grasp, Prince of Nothing! Prince of Worms!" Unable to control his limbs, Gralyre's head smacked into the wall, as Doaphin's sorcery shook him like a child's doll. Black spots danced in Gralyre's vision before Doaphin relented.

In the lull, Gralyre spotted movement beyond Doaphin's gloating face. A dark shape advanced along the glowing, red stones of the liquefying floor. It was a surviving Demon Lord dragging itself through the smoke and clouds of fire using the point of the dagger that Gralyre had thrown, recovered from the chest of its deceased counterpart. Repetitively, it spiked the knife tip into cracks, and dragged itself forward by inches.

Its one blackened limb was barely within its control, though its magic now protected it from the furnace heat. Its other arm was reduced to a bit of charred bone that stuck out from its shoulder. Its body ended at the waist with a bit of trailing remnants of legs. One eye was missing, burned away with the rest of the Demon Lord's face, but the other was fixed malevolently upon Doaphin's back.

'The Master wants me alive…' The Demon Lord was an unlikely ally, if only it could survive long enough and arrive soon enough to be of use.

"Now you will die, Highness!" Doaphin snarled. All pretence of civility was stripped away, and the Usurper's true evil was revealed at last. "Finally! I will be rid of you! Fennick's prophesy of doom is ended! I have been dreaming of this moment for centuries!" His face alight with gratification, he gestured roughly.

Gralyre's weakened shield against the inferno collapsed. He turned his head to the side, and clenched his eyes shut to protect his vision from the searing, red-hot air. His hair curled to ash, and his face blistered. His saturated clothing steamed free of rainwater, scalding his skin, as the liquid boiled away. Only his Maolar mail remained to protect his torso from incineration against the glowing stones at his back, and that would soon fail. He tried to get his shield back but, though he could reach his Godsmagic, he could not focus to wield it. Doaphin's spell was scattering his concentration. Gralyre screamed, as he burned.

The dagger that was clenched in the Demon Lord's charred fist adopted an intense green glow, ensorcelled to penetrate Doaphin's protective barrier. The creature crawled the final few inches.

"Burn, Gralyre! Die like you left her to die!" Doaphin crowed, revelling in every moment of the Prince's torturous death.

The Demon Lord drew back, and plunged Gralyre's knife

into the back of Doaphin's calf.

Doaphin cried out in pain, staggering, as the glowing blade impaled his leg. He reeled to see what had managed to pierce his shield.

No longer a creature of beauty, the Demon Lord cackled in its ruined voice, "Betrayer! I have summoned the Master…"

Doaphin yelled with rage, and punched his fist towards the injured Demon Lord. The creature exploded into ash.

Doaphin seemed harried now, as he wheeled back towards Gralyre. His hands glowed and crackled with energy, to finish him quickly, where before he had been content to revel in a prolonged and agonizing execution.

Gralyre braced for death, glad that it was to be quick.

A look of fear swept Doaphin's face, and he abruptly stifled all of his Godsmagic. He spun away from Gralyre, and bowed low, his gaze held to his boots as he genuflected. He froze in place, waiting.

Unexpectedly released from Doaphin's sorcery, Gralyre pulled the tattered remnants of his glowing, blue shield around him for protection, as he fell forward off the wall, and landed in the molten slag of the floor. Intense heat penetrated his sputtering barrier. He had no strength remaining to build a more robust protection.

Gralyre wobbled weakly up to his feet, and slapped at the flames licking at his clothes, as he reeled to seek an avenue of escape from the confusion of roaring, twisting fires. He did not understand how, but he was alive! Why had Doaphin relented his attack?

The cold of a grave swept through the ruined hall, felt even amidst the tides of flames. The fires seemed to dim, losing much of their yellow lustre and orange glow. Even through the smoke, Gralyre caught a whiff of the dank darkness of a dungeon. His flesh shrank from a horror that made him feel small and helpless as a child. Was this, at last, the Master that he had heard of?

"I have the sword, my Master," Doaphin declared resoundingly.

Gralyre flinched at the sound of Doaphin's voice, poised to repel an attack, but Doaphin was paying him no heed.

There was a pause, as of a conversation unheard.

"No. The Prince has eluded me, my Master. Fennick had already possessed him. Now he has destroyed the city. I could not reach him in time, and he has fled."

Doaphin cringed, his head snapping sideways, as though from a heavy blow. "I am sorry, my Master. There is no way through the flames. I can return with the sword, or seek the Prince and return with nothing."

Gralyre wondered why Doaphin was lying, but the answer was not as important as survival. Gralyre made Doaphin an honest man by running, taking the opportunity while the Usurper was distracted.

Gralyre found the remnants of the broad staircase rising up and out to the central bailey. Flames rippled in rivers down the buckled treads, a beautiful and deadly waterfall of heat that flowed around his shielded body, as he took the steps two at a time.

Gralyre came up against a field of tumbled blocks from the collapsed towers, and clambered over them to reach the outside. Here, the inferno met the pelting rain, producing clouds of scalding vapour and ash. He glanced back once to see if he was pursued before the fog and choking smoke engulfed him, hiding him as he fled.

A captured bolt of lightning twisted and snapped before Doaphin, crackling with energy against the walls of flame. The dark presence was fading from the air, and Doaphin was straightening from his bow.

"Until we meet again, Highness," Doaphin yelled after Gralyre over the noise of the firestorm, as the Prince disappeared over the mounds of stone. "If you survive!" Doaphin did not look back, as he stretched forth with a hand and parted the gash. The world of flame bent around the widening fissure. With the long metal chest containing the Dragon Sword tucked securely under his arm, Doaphin stepped through the portal. The magical doorway vanished behind him.

ೞೞ

Flaming debris blocked all avenues, confusing Gralyre as to which direction to flee. He gasped for life giving breath in the heated, thinning air, as the fire robbed more and more atmosphere to feed its power.

A building on Gralyre's right collapsed amidst the agonizing screams of its occupants. He yelled in fear, pushing his exhausted body for more speed to avoid being crushed. He was as a wild animal, dodging and jumping, seeking a safe pathway through the fires to the outside world. There was none.

He won through to a wider space, what had been a training ground perhaps, though now it was twisted and buckled from heat. Five 'Riders rushed past. Their bodies were engulfed in flames and smoke that trailed like flapping, bright cloaks from the speed of their passage.

Startled from his panic, Gralyre halted his mindless flight, and gasped hungrily at the depleted air, coughing until he grew dizzy and dropped to his knees, then fell to his side against the hot stones. He closed his eyes, listening to the roar of destruction. The air was clearer down lower, and he revived enough to realize that the explosion was still moving outwards in an ever-widening circle. If he could erect shields around the remaining buildings, he would be able to save some of the remaining women from incineration.

Lying amidst the maelstrom, Gralyre sought his Godsmagic, before realizing that Doaphin had depleted him to such an extent that he had barely enough left with which to protect himself.

Still, he would have sacrificed it all. He sought for the clear places outside the expanding ring of destruction, the barracks that had not yet been destroyed, but there were too many buildings to count. He could not split his exhausted magic in enough directions to save them all. Fennick's power would blast through his weakened conjurings, as though they did not exist.

And what of Jord and Little Wolf, and the Rebels? They too were in the path of the destruction, if not already dead.

Gralyre screamed his frustration, his cry lost to the roar of wind and flames, as he agonized over the decision he must make. Save a few, or none. The fire was moving too rapidly. He had the time and strength for only one try.

ഇൽ

With a hissing pop, the magic barrier vanished, and the Rebels fell forward onto the muddy ground. "We are free!" Pardel yelled.

The warriors stumbled away, as fast as their legs would carry them. Death was almost upon them.

The Rebels cursed and slid over the wagon ruts and mud, as they sprinted onwards through the rain, vainly trying to outpace the oncoming wall of flame.

"'Tis like a dream!" Enog whimpered breathlessly from his place beside Hektar. "My legs canno' move as fast as I try t' make them! The mud clings so heavily t' my feet, 'tis like t' stop my running altogether!"

A hot wind lapped against their backs. Hektar fought back an ominous shiver. "Faster! Do no' look back!" He wished he had heeded his own advice, as he glanced over his shoulder. The fire was rushing at them, less than fifty feet away now. It would reach them in moments. A scream of terror worked its way out of his throat, as he pumped his legs for more speed.

And then suddenly, they were engulfed in the twisting flames, and ash, and smoke.

Hektar threw his arms over his head and huddled into the ground, as his terror released the contents of his bladder. He heard his own screams echoed from the throats of his men.

A loud, horrific screech beside him made Hektar turn in time to witness a Demon Rider flash into flame, and vanish into the swirling reds, oranges and yellows of the firestorm. In the panic of their flight, Hektar had not been aware that the 'Rider had been running in their midst.

It was another moment before he realized that he could not feel heat. The fire bore no warmth; it did not burn. He burst into tears, unable to fathom the miracle. Within seconds the massive firestorm had rushed past.

Hektar arose hesitantly, and watched the wall of flame diminish into the distance, sputter and die away. His men were untouched. Some had lost consciousness from their fear, while others, like Hektar, were openly weeping in thankfulness that they had been spared.

He turned to face the distant valley that they had just fled from. A dark pall of smoke hovered over the basin, easily seen by the light of the fires that burned brightly despite the hissing rain. Doaphin's secret city was no more. After three hundred years, the Tithe was over.

෫ൠ

A particularly intense peal of thunder roared in the far distance, startling them all. The storm was worsening.

Aneida was crouched low to the ground next to the posted lookout. Being left behind by the Prince still burned at her pride. If she had been able to pass through the Demon Lord's barrier, she would have followed behind regardless. She snugged her cloak around her shoulders against the heavy rainfall, while lightning continued to paint bright cracks across the sky.

The Rebel women grew restless, as they waited out the remainder of the night for the return of the men at dawn. Now and then, Aneida could hear them over the patter of rain in the treetops, milling in the darkness with soft conversations, testing their weapons or stamping their feet for warmth.

The trees suddenly bent with a roar, their massive trunks and limbs dancing from a hot blast of air. The rain began to fall sideways, as the wind took the drops off course. As the heated gust blew into her face, Aneida closed her eyes and turned away, though the warmth was welcome after the cold, wet hours spent waiting for the return of the men.

Aneida had only experienced such a sensation once before. In the Bleak. When Gralyre had incinerated the horde of Deathren who were swarming them from out of the dark mists. She stood slowly, uneasy, as she caught a whiff of smoke. Stinging ash peppered her exposed skin, carried before the wind. An oncoming rumble grew louder over the noise of the rainstorm, and a red glow grew brighter in the sky. Foreboding swept panic through her.

"Run!" Aneida bellowed, and turned tail. She heard the other women following her in a ragged retreat, as they crashed through the wet underbrush.

A forest fire approached with the speed of a horse drawn chariot from the direction of the hidden city. Soon, sparkling motes of burning embers kept pace with their flight, driven before the hot gust. It was not long before treetops around them began to ignite. Just when it seemed they would be caught, the wind inexplicably changed direction, and the massive blaze rolled back upon itself, and began to diminish.

"What was that?" A Rebel demanded fearfully, leaning forward and gasping for a clean breath from the smoky air.

Aneida regarded her grimly, her sweating face painted with flickering red lights and shadows from the forest fire. "If I had t' bet," she panted, "I would say that the Prince has destroyed the Tithe."

Saved from burning alive, the Rebel women watched mutely over the next few hours, as the flames sputtered smaller, until they died away from lack of fuel. The wet forest and pounding rainfall soon had the forest fire contained to nothing but rolling clouds of smoke, and a few coals that glowed eerily from the pre-dawn darkness like the eyes of unhinged demons.

As soon as it was passable, Aneida began the long walk back through the scorched forest, to return to where they had been awaiting the men throughout the night.

"What are ye doing? Where are ye going? Come back here!" ordered a Rebel.

"No. If the Demon Lord barrier is gone, I am going t' find the others!" Aneida announced, as she vanished into the lingering clouds of smoke.

"They are all dead! Nothing could have survived the fire!" The Rebel woman called after her.

"Then I will find their bodies!" Aneida yelled back.

஧௸

Dreisenheld

"Where is it? Give it to us!"

Doaphin swallows his sickness at the avarice on display. "It is here, my Master." He walks ceremoniously up the steps of the dais, his eyes downcast lest the Master sense his lies. He places the metal chest containing the sword across the ermine clad lap, and backs away, bowing low, until he reaches the floor of the throne room once more. At his back, the open portal that he stepped from moments before snaps and pops with electrical discharges.

Doaphin had never intended to deliver up the Dragon Sword to Dreisenheld, but the interference of the Demon Lord made that inevitable when it summoned the Master to the hall. He had needed time with the Wizard Stone, to gain control over Fennick's powers, that he might challenge the creature sitting on Dreisenheld's throne. Without it, all he can do is obey.

But there is still time, so long as his lies go unnoticed. So long as he can keep the vessel from the Master's grasp, by killing Gralyre before the severed can be made whole. So long as the Master never discovers that it is Fennick, and not Gralyre, trapped within the box!

"Ah… Gralyre is ours at last! Fennick has prepared the vessel for us by exiling his soul into the Stone!"

"Yes, my Master."

Triumphant laughter answers, grating along every nerve ending that Doaphin owns.

"We reap the fruits of our labour, Doaphin! Return to the City of the Tithe! Find our vessel!"

Doaphin bows low. "My Master, the city has been destroyed," he reminds. "By now Fennick has spirited the vessel beyond our reach."

"Then raze Lyre to the ground! Find him, and bring him to us! Nothing else maters! Do not fail us, Doaphin. Not when we are so close to triumph!"

"Yes, my Master," Doaphin steps backwards into the awaiting portal, relieved to have escaped detection once more. He needs to rethink his strategy.

Moments later, he exits into the midst of his army. They have camped only about twenty leagues east of Dreisenheld. As he predicted, the enormous horde is ponderously slow moving.

The night is filled with the sounds of murder, as Stalkers and Deathren feed upon the 'Riders asleep in their tents. Food, it would seem, is already running short of supply.

"What news from Dreisenheld, Lord Commander?" The

flickering torchlight reveals the cabal of Demon Lord Generals who await his arrival. Standing in a half circle, they block him from entering his tent. It is possible that this is a trap set by the Master to test his loyalty. He has to be seen to be complying.

"I want a legion of Demon Riders ready to travel by morning. Fennick has claimed the vessel. He eluded us at the City of the Tithe."

"Eluded you," sneers one of the Master's pretty creatures. It picks at a bit of lint upon the pristine fabric of its green velvet cape. "You should cede your task to one who will succeed."

Doaphin stills at the insult. It galls him that the Master's fell creations are elevated to his company. He will not stand for their lack of respect! His Godsmagic whips forward, and slices the head from the body of the Demon Lord. The trunk geysers blood as it falls.

"I will command them myself," Doaphin continues, as though naught has occurred. The other Demon Lords make no comment. They shift restlessly, and are markedly more attentive. "The rest of you will continue onwards, but not with your full forces."

"We do not understand, Lord Commander." The Demon Lord's tone is decidedly more deferential than that of its dead colleague.

"Every night we are losing 'Riders to the appetites of the Stalkers and Deathren, and that attrition will continue until we have no daylight army left. We need no strategy to destroy peasants. Release the dark ones into land. Scatter them to the four corners. They are to destroy everything that stands before them, down to the last spring lamb."

"And the daylight army, Lord Commander."

"Each of you will assume the command of your legions and march on the Heathrens, to put a stop to the Rebels and the Dream Weaver incursions. You to the north," Doaphin directed, splitting the nineteen surviving Demon Lord Generals into three groups, "you central, and you to the south."

"And where will you be, Lord Commander?"

Doaphin smiles. "Fennick has lost his Wizard Stone, and will be seeking to reclaim power. He knows that we hold the Rebel Sorceress in the Towers. It makes sense that he will try take her." A lie and a truth, should the Master be testing him.

It was a gamble that Gralyre would seek to rescue the Sorceress, but having lost the Dragon Sword, he would be in more need than ever of his magical allies. If he had survived the destruction of the City of the Tithe.

CHAPTER NINETEEN

City of the Tithe

The torrential rains had finally relented, and the weak light of daybreak diffused through the lingering grey clouds above, and the twisting drifts of smoke and steam that occluded the burned wasteland below. It was twilight in the lands of the dead.

Gralyre stumbled onwards through the blackened slag, seeking survivors, though he knew it to be a fool's quest. Nobody could have lived through Fennick's explosion of fire without the protection of magic. The tumbled and smashed stones of buildings and streets had fused together, vitrified by the extreme temperatures. In places the ground underfoot had turned to glass, and it splintered with overloud *cracks* as he crossed it.

The odour of burnt flesh from the smouldering remains of tens of thousands assaulted Gralyre's senses. Demon Riders and the poor women who had suffered so in the birthing barracks - Fennick's firestorm had not favoured one above the other.

Gralyre staggered and almost fell, unable to see past the wetness in his eyes, unable to breathe past the ropes of dismay banding his chest. His lungs hurt, damaged from the breathing in of superheated air when Doaphin had momentarily stripped away his shield. He coughed, his throat raw from inhaling smoke. Residual heat radiated from every surface, raising salty sweat to his skin that stung the blisters and weeping burns of his face, neck, and hands. He knew that he was in shock, and that he should give up the search. Still he wandered through the devastation.

Gralyre paused at a large, rectangular barrack that was still more or less erect. Its long walls still stood, supporting a partial roof that had not fully caved inwards. Rows of twisted, blackened corpses, bodies curled from the extreme heat that had consumed them, lined the long length of the building, still chained to the metal frames of their birthing cots. Burned alive.

A low growl of grief rumbled in Gralyre's chest, and he fell forward onto his knees, weakened by the mercilessness before him. His shoulders shook with sobs, as he prostrated himself at the feet of the innocent dead. Begging for their forgiveness for failing to protect them.

He forced himself to gaze into their tortured faces, memorizing the ghastly evidence of his failure. He wondered morosely if some of them had been from Raindell, women who had travelled north with him in the wagons that fateful, long summer past.

'Curse you, Fennick!' Gralyre hissed in his mind. *'How many women? How many did you use me to kill?'*

How he wished he could leave Fennick to his just ends, locked inside Doaphin's metal box! But what the Usurper would do if he were to gain control of Fennick's Wizard Stone would make the horrors of the Tithe seem as nothing. Despite the dangers of allowing the sword near to him again, Gralyre would have to risk all to rescue his lesser enemy from the clutches of his greater one.

Gralyre forced himself upright, though he lurched with exhaustion, whipping himself forward to continue his search for survivors. Eventually, he happened upon the slave pens.

Thousands of charred corpses heaped the interiors of the vast cages. The only sound to break the grisly silence was the crackling of embers, the only movement was the settling of piles of bodies, as hot coals continued to feast upon the dead.

"Gods," Gralyre whispered, horrified, unable to fathom the number of bodies that he was gazing upon. "What was this place?"

"Slave pens."

Gralyre's head whipped around at the unexpected answer to his question. "Jord!" He overbalanced, and had to brace upon a warm stone block from a tumbled wall to keep his footing.

Jord sucked in a breath. "Your face!" he grimaced in sympathy for the blistered and melted skin.

"'Tis nothing. Who were they?"

"Human males that they kept for food and for breeding. Even had they escaped the fires, ye could no' have released them. They were no longer men. They were utterly deranged. Doaphin had reduced them t' no more than maddened animals! It was just as the Stalker at the fortress said."

He eyed Gralyre suspiciously. "Is it ye?" Jord seemed poised to flee. His face was blackened with filth and soot. Though his clothing was scorched, he seemed otherwise hale.

Gralyre was confused for a moment. "Of course 'tis me!" Then he realized that the last time they had seen each other Fennick had been wearing his skin. "Fennick is gone!" Gralyre reassured gruffly. "'Tis me, Jord. I promise, 'tis me!"

"Gralyre!" Jord declared with certainty, sensing the truth of his friend's soul behind the tortured midnight-blue eyes. The entity that had possessed Gralyre the day before would not have blanched so at the death that surrounded them. "Thank the Gods!"

Gralyre pulled the knifeman into a rough embrace and, for once, did not meet with Jord's usual resistance to being touched. "You survived!" Gralyre pounded his back with rough affection. "I was not sure that I had gotten a shield around you and the others in time."

"Just in time, though I do no' know about the others. I have no' seen them since last night." Jord stepped back, and a shadow of a smile crossed his lips. "Thank-ye for that. I thought that I was done for." He grimaced and glanced away, his hands falling empty to his sides.

Perceiving Jord's expression as condemnation, Gralyre blurted his confession of failure. "The women, Jord! So many. All of them burned alive! I tried to save them, all of them, but there were too many, and the firestorm was moving too fast! It was the sword…"

"It did all this? Where is that thrice damned thing?" Jord interjected. "I reckon we can find a hammer, and destroy it once and for all!"

Gralyre rubbed a hand across his mouth, and his shoulders sagged further from the weight of his defeat. "Doaphin took it."

"Doaphin was here? He took the sword?" Jord raised his face to the clouds, and lifted his fists to his temples. "Gods!" he shouted with disbelief. "Can this day become blacker?"

"I was not strong enough to fight Doaphin. Fennick said that he would defeat him if only I submitted to his will! Instead," Gralyre made a helpless gesture, indicating the destruction they stood amidst, "he spent his magic on this horror, and wasted our best chance to kill Doaphin."

Jord clapped a hand on the Prince's shoulder to ease his pointless shame. "Ye are bloody lucky t' have survived! I canno' believe that ye faced Doaphin alone!" His gaze narrowed, and his supportive touch fell away. "'Twas the sword that arranged that too, I suppose?"

"I am no longer a slave to it, Jord!" Gralyre reassured again. "Doaphin captured the Dragon Sword before Fennick had exiled my soul from my body. Really, 'twas Little Wolf who saved me! Earlier, he gave me the time I needed to resist. If not for him, I would be a mere ghost within the Wizard Stone by now, a prisoner forever, and Fennick would be wearing my flesh like a new cloak."

Jord's chin dipped sadly at the reminder, and his suspicions drained away. "There..." he huffed sadly, "...there is something ye need t' know."

"Jord? What?" Gralyre's chest expanded in icy dread. "Little

Wolf!" he intuited.

Jord glanced away again, uncomfortable with the frantic fear that filled Gralyre's face. "Last night, I found him in the streets." His voice was strained and dull. "I did no' want t' leave him in this cursed place, so I carried him out with me."

"What are you saying? Is he… he is… d... d…" Gralyre stuttered on the hard consonant for he could not force the word up past his throat. It caught in there with rough jagged edges.

Jord nodded. "I am so very sorry."

Gralyre's ears rang, tuned now to the ghostly silence that surrounded them. This was a grief that he was not strong enough to carry, not on top of all that had occurred in the last hours. Everything in him went numb, and he swayed. "Take me to him." His words felt foreign and wrong, as though his tongue had become swollen and misshapen.

Jord turned, beckoning. "This way. I left him up on the ridge."

෨෬

Gralyre followed Jord up out of the ruination, dreading each and every step that moved him towards the body of his pup. He was unaware of the tears rolling down his fire-blistered cheeks. The sting of salt against his burns was a small hurt, unfelt amidst the pain of the sword thrust through his heart.

Jord glanced back once, and could not bear to look more upon the grief-ravaged features of his friend. From then on, he kept his gaze forward, one foot in front of the other, steadily leading the way.

Just as with all else that the fires had touched, the ridge overlooking the devastated city was scorched black on all sides of the road, save for one pristine, grassy circle wherein Little Wolf lay, shrouded by Jord's cloak. It was the place where Gralyre's magic had shielded them from being charred by the firestorm of the night before. Jord's cloak fluttered lightly in the breeze, the press and pull of the wind hinting at Little Wolf's lonely outline within the immaculate circle of green.

Jord folded back the corner of his cloak to reveal Little Wolf's face. He stepped away so that Gralyre could approach his pup's side.

Gralyre knelt down, and gently drew Little Wolf's head onto his lap, careful of his limp neck. Though no breath stirred his chest, he seemed to be only asleep. His ears canted forward, as if he dreamed of something pleasant. His eyes were closed in gentle repose.

It was all the *'Last Times'* that played through Gralyre's thoughts in that moment.

The Last Time he saw Little Wolf run with pure joy, his lupine body arching and stretching with powerful freedom. His limp paws would not dance over the ground, ever again.

The Last Time Little Wolf had curled with him, soothing Gralyre from his nightmares. There would be no warm comfort for his terrors, ever again.

The Last Time Little Wolf had flipped Gralyre's hand up

over the back of his head to ask for a scratch. There would be no touch from his pup, ever again.

The Last Time Little Wolf was alive. Gralyre would never hear the thoughts of his pup and his wolfish poetry. Ever again.

Gralyre's shoulders heaved from a soul-deep sob. He pushed his burned hands into the thick, black ruff at the back of the wolfdog's neck, and kneaded gently, petting Little Wolf soothingly, as he had done all of his pup's life, steeling himself to say goodbye. "He saved me from the sword, Jord. Little Wolf sacrificed everything to save me. And Fennick killed him for it!"

Jord nodded sadly. "He was a good lad."

"Aye!" Gralyre lost his voice then, and curled his body down over Little Wolf, bent by the pain of his loss.

Jord glanced up at the sound of boots jogging towards them on the road. He drew his knives, standing guard over Gralyre, who was helpless in his grief. He relaxed, as Aneida loped from around the bend.

She slowed to a walk, panting lightly. "So, ye are alive then," she grinned saucily, as she sauntered up to them.

Jord did not return her smile, as he hid his blades. "No' all o' us," he indicated Gralyre and Little Wolf.

Aneida's face fell, as she perceived what had happened. "Oh! Oh no. Oh Gralyre, I am so sorry!"

Gralyre shook his head, unable to look up at her, unable to answer, as he continued to weep bitter tears over the loss of his pup. He rubbed his hands through Little Wolf's black fur, over and over, unable to say his final farewell.

Aneida crouched down across from Gralyre and Little Wolf, crying openly now as well, but not talking, just being present so that the Prince was not so alone.

Gralyre finally looked up at her; his eyes were a brilliant blue in his damaged face, their hue changed by the strength of his sadness.

She sucked in a breath of surprise as the extent of his burns was revealed fully.

"I raised him from a baby, little bigger than my hand. I taught him all. What shall I do without him, Aneida?"

She sniffed noisily. More than anyone else, she understood Gralyre's loss. Mayvin, and now Little Wolf. Once, she should have sneered to compare the death of a beast to that of her sister, but Little Wolf had been no mere animal. He had possessed a voice. He had been an equal companion in their adventures, and a courageous friend who had saved all of their lives on more than one occasion. Like Mayvin, he had died in sacrifice for the life of his treasured friends. That, if for no other reason, was enough to earn his tribute of honour.

Jord cleared his throat. "I will go find something t' dig with."

"I will go with ye," Aneida whispered, trailing after Jord, and leaving Gralyre to the privacy of his grief.

ഓരു

Aneida's eyes shifted back and forth, absorbing the destruction surrounding them, as they walked back down the hill into the devastated city. "'Tis finally done," she whispered.

Jord glanced over at her. Her voice had held an exhausted tone that he had never heard from her before. "What do ye mean, *'done'*?"

Aneida's jaw clenched, and lines of white appeared around her mouth. After a long tense moment wherein she seemed to be arguing with herself, she shot Jord a challenging glare. "Mayvin and I lived in the town o' Chesterson Mills."

Jord's expression stilled. "Chesterson Mills was destroyed."

"I know."

"'Twas no' the 'Riders that did it."

"No." Aneida's shoulders slumped, and she focused intently upon her footing.

"'Twas said t' have been vengeful spirits, if ye are prone t' believe such rubbish." Jord waited, watching Aneida closely, as she decided if she would share her story.

"We had a goat farm, a few miles south o' the town," she began.

Something in Jord eased at the trust she was showing in him.

"Mayvin was married t' a fine man, Shawan, and they had two handsome sons," Aneida's voice caught, "Aiden and Fig." Her hands clenched into fists. Her mouth twisted into a pained scowl, and her eyes blurred with tears. "They were six and four. So young. So filled with promise.

"I was no' but newly wed, myself," Aneida continued, "t' a sweet, gentle man named Raulf." A lone tear escaped her eye, and trickled down her cheek. She heaved a large sigh that was not quite a sob, as she dashed it away. "And then the Tithe came," she announced woodenly.

To witness the vulnerability of this bold creature made Jord's guts tighten with foreboding.

"We seldom left the farm, and were no' well known in the town, so we thought that we would be overlooked. T' be safe, Mayvin and I fled deep into the woods until well after the Tithe had moved on."

Their footsteps sounded artificially loud in the stillness, as they entered the ruined city. Neither bird nor insect remained to trill of spring's advent.

"I remember that 'twas raining, a dull day, when we returned home. We had been away for a fortnight, and were so eager t' reunite with our family." Her fingers arose to caress the scar on her throat, rubbing back and forth, back and forth, hypnotically. Her gaze was fixed, staring deep into her bleak past.

"But everyone was dead, our farm burned, and our stock stolen." Her mouth worked, and her face contorted. "We had been betrayed," she spat with loathing. "Our families had been tortured and killed by men who were trying t' find Mayvin and I for the Tithe, collaborators who would betray their own for the lure o' Doaphin's gold!"

Jord grimaced with compassion. "I did no' know…" He had witnessed firsthand such atrocities in the Lowlands at the hands of collaborators, and unfortunately, so far, Aneida shared a tale that was not uncommon under the oppression of Doaphin's rule.

Aneida's face blanked from an emotion that was too

enormous to feel, an emotion that could imprison in chains too hard to break. Her tears vanished, dried by the heat of her undiluted hatred. "They were still there, awaiting our return, the collaborators o' Chesterson Mills, and they ambushed Mayvin and I. They tried t' rape us. I was too wild for them t' control, so they slit my throat…"

Jord reached out with a hiss of shock, and grasped Aneida's fingers, lowering them from the scar at her neck. Aneida's face was sweating and frantic, and her breath strenuous in her throat. They stopped walking, facing each other. Her hands tensed and relaxed within his, as she relived her fight for survival that horrific night.

"After that, Mayvin bore their assaults alone, as I lay in the muck, discarded like a broken doll, no' ten feet away from them. They had no' cut my neck deeply enough," she sneered. "They saw all the blood, and thought that they had killed me but they had done little more than slice my skin." Remembrance hardened her face, a merciless goddess filled with righteous fury. "Still, I was badly hurt, and it took awhile t' come t' my senses.

"When I did, I saw Mayvin bound t' a tall post, and they were heaping brush and wood at her feet. I… I saw the bodies o' her two boys impaled on the stake above her. They were laughing… *laughing…* They were going t' burn us all, t' make an example o' us. I remember the thunder and lightening crashed, and the storm broke free, and the rain washed the blood o' her children o'er her head, like the Gods were baptizing her in death. Mayvin was screaming, cursing them for the murders o' her children and our family, and o' me, for she thought me dead as well. They did no' want t' hear her, so they forced hot coals into her mouth, and stole her voice."

Jord waited in helpless horror, gripping Aneida's hands, anchoring her to the present, as she relived her past. Her voice lowered to a monotone of pure rage.

"They were paying me no mind, for I was already dead t' them. I took up the knife they had dropped by my body, it was slick with my blood and with mud, and I killed each and every one o' the sodding demon-lovers!

"I freed Mayvin, and we unearthed our swords from where we used t' hide them, the ones that our father had taught us how t' use. That night, we walked the miles t' Chesterson Mills. We set fire t' every building, every home, every barrel and barstool. And killed everyone who sought t' hinder us. The rest we drove before us like the spineless sheep they were," she finished with a terrible satisfaction.

"When we were done, we buried our loved ones, and made our way t' the Heathrens t' join the Rebels."

Jord's jaw knotted at the appalling suffering that she had endured. Only snippets and rumours had ever circulated of the fate of Chesterson Mills, whispers of a night of fire and terror, vague and unsettling. A mystery no more. "How many people lived in the village?"

Aneida shook free of Jord's clasp, glaring at him for his perceived judgment, yet unapologetic for the vengeance that she and Mayvin had enacted. "Almost three hundred people lived in the village but most fled our wrath.

"Before we left, we swore upon the innocent, spilled blood of our families that we would see t' the end o' the Tithe! When Mayvin died, it fell t' me alone t' see it done."

A dark silence gripped them, as Aneida glanced slowly around at the melted stones of the buildings and streets they stood amidst, absorbing the truth of the Tithe's end, and of her oath's fulfillment. "Ye think me mad?" she whispered.

Jord breathed deeply of the chilling sadness that had overcome him, as Aneida had shared her tragic past. "No. Madness is the sane response."

The crackle of the still burning fires filled the stillness between them. Aneida broke first, and threw her arms around his neck, sobbing heavily against his shoulder.

Jord tensed, his arms held stiffly at his sides. Uncomfortable with being touched, yet wanting to offer comfort, he steeled himself to gently rub her shoulders. It was the second time that day that he had been obliged to hold a grieving friend.

Jord glared angrily up at the sky, at the capricious Gods who seemed determined to taunt him.

ഇന്ദ

Jord and Aneida returned from the destroyed city with a couple of warped and twisted spades.

When Gralyre made to pick one up, Jord stopped him. "No' with those wounds."

Gralyre finally noted his injuries. He turned his hands over and over before his eyes, as though mesmerized. He had not realized how badly he had been burned during his battle with Doaphin. His palms were scorched and red, and the skin had melted, as though he had plunged his hands into boiling oil. Large blisters had risen on his palms. Many of these had burst from his stumbles and falls, leaving filthy, weeping sores that began to pulse with pain now that he was looking at them. Infection would be upon him soon.

"Your face is blistered too." Jord described. "Just half, like ye had turned away."

Gralyre trailed his fingers across his cheeks, feeling the injuries that Jord spoke of. He remembered the plumes of fire roiling around him; he remembered Doaphin's magic pinning him in place as he burned.

"Stay with Little Wolf," Aneida said kindly. "Jord and I will see t' making his grave." She hesitated, not wanting to leave Gralyre's side. He seemed uncharacteristically confused, as if he could not decide what came next. "Maybe ye can do something t' heal yourself?" she suggested gently.

"Aye," Gralyre agreed morosely, but he wanted to hurt! He wanted his pain! He flinched when Jord and Aneida begin to dig. They speared the green sod and flipped it to the side in the spot that they had marked for Little Wolf's eternal rest.

Aneida was right. No good would come from succumbing to his wounds; it was the selfish wish of a defeated man. There was too much left undone. So many people were relying on him. He had to save Catrian. He had to find a way to liberate the Dragon Sword from Doaphin, and somehow save his kingdom. There was no one else who could do this. This burden fell upon his shoulders alone.

Gralyre did not know how to heal himself, but he knew where to go to gain the knowledge that he needed. He would find Ninrhar, the Dream Weaver Healer, floating amongst the other golden orbs of the Thewr 'ap Noir, and borrow his memories and expertise.

Gralyre closed his eyes, and sank his consciousness, down towards his core. What was once a place of wonder for him, now teemed with overtones of dread after his helpless imprisonment. *'I am no longer trapped. I can leave at any moment!'*

Arriving at his centre, Gralyre stood at the edges of his lapping pool of Godsmagic, and gazed out over the shimmering surface. His gleaming power had lost all traces of the black contamination of Fennick's possession.

He did not immediately seek the Thewr 'ap Noir, for his grief weighed even heavier upon him. This was the last place that he had seen Little Wolf alive.

Fleeing his sadness, Gralyre dove into his Godsmagic, drifting deeper and deeper until the golden Godwombs of the Dream Weaver nation appeared before him.

Millions upon millions of drifting souls surrounded him in the Thewr 'ap Noir, the collective consciousness of every Dream Weaver who had ever lived in the past, present and future. How was he to find Gedrhar and Ninrhar amongst them all?

Gedrhar had been vague about how to find individuals, and Gralyre was left with little guidance on how to begin. The Dream Weaver had mentioned that like attracted like. Families clustered near to each other. Villages and cities also. Sometimes comrades of like enterprise grouped together.

Gralyre scanned the orbs nearest to him, and did not spy the magenta flashes that bespoke those who were endowed with the ability to wield magic. Swimming aimlessly through the multitudes would be pointless. He had to reason a solution.

If he had been in the waking world, searching for Catrian or Little Wolf, he would have simply sent his consciousness winging outwards to seek the essence of who they were, finding them by way of their distinctive characteristics. Would this work in the Deep Dreaming?

Gralyre thought of the elder Dream Weaver. He concentrated on how it felt to be in Gedrhar's presence, the substance of the soul that he had connected with on several occasions. There was a pull towards the far distance, to the right. He followed the draw, flitting past thousands of floating sleepers in their golden orbs.

He soon spied magenta flashes that identified a cluster of sorcerers. Uncertain which one held Gedrhar, he peered within the first Godwomb, and saw a woman. She was young and beautiful, perhaps no more than his age, with long brown hair and a kindly face.

Gralyre gasped in recognition, and his dream body convulsed in shock. "Mother!"

One day he would have sought her out, but there had been no time to indulge in considering it. To encounter her so unexpectedly under these dire circumstances triggered a grief that he could scarce understand. She had died so long ago.

He should not have been surprised to have found her, for all Dream Weavers existed here; past, present and future were one.

Unable to resist the urge, he reached out and touched the warm, soft womb in which her soul drifted, and became… Alyssa V'tar, Queen of Lyre.

૪૦૦૪

"Momma!" My son reaches up to me with his sturdy little arms, as he runs to me. I swing him up with a laugh. Pure joy and love fills me.

"You grow so large, Gralyre! Soon I will be unable to hold you!" His beautiful face dances with happiness. Such a winsome boy! "What did you do today?"

"I made a cat with wings, and it flew up into a tree and would not come down! So I made a dog with wings, and he chased the cat into the kitchens, and I scared the cooks!"

Concern and worry choke me. The darkness of the realities of Dreisenheld give me nightmares about his safety. "Gralyre you must keep what I teach you a secret, and you must never, ever use your powers to harm others."

His little face crumples. I do not often chastise him, and I can see that I have hurt him. I make steel of my heart and hold firm. I must protect him.

My son is powerful yet so vulnerable. There has not been a sorcerer to match him in generations. He can use the Thewr 'ap Noir to create actual life! So far, I have been able to hide his full talent. Should Fennick discover his abilities...! I shiver. The court sorcerer is always watching. He is the true power behind the throne.

"*I will try to be good. I am sorry Momma. I will not do it again.*" *Gralyre does not like to disappoint me. He is such a good little boy. He cups my cheeks and grins, before pressing his forehead to mine. The lashes of his eyes flutter against my brow as he delivers up butterfly kisses.*

Little imp. How I love you!

"*You are damned right, it will not happen again!*"

The smile flees from our faces, as I whirl to face the chamber door of the nursery with Gralyre cradled in my arms. It is the King.

"*Bylyre! Husband!*" *I drop into an awkward curtsy, still clutching Gralyre tightly to my breast. He senses my unease and his lower lip is trembling.* "*My King. What is amiss?*"

"*I will not have the nobles gossiping about how my son is a freak! I will not have them ridiculing me behind my back!*"

"*Of course he is not a freak!*" *I cannot control my spike of rage, although I know it is not safe to contradict him.*

"*Silence!*" *Roars the King, and his heavy fist flies.*

He fells me to the floor. I twist to absorb the impact so that Gralyre is not harmed. My head cracks with some force against the flagstones.

The violence is so unexpected that Gralyre starts to cry. This is the first time he has seen his father strike me. Usually it is done in private, and never in the face where signs of the abuse can be noted amongst the nobles of court.

"Fennick has informed me of what you have done, witch! What you have been teaching my son! You are corrupting my Heir! He makes monsters that chase people! He creates horrors from nothing! Think ye that the nobles will follow such an abomination when I am gone!"

Bylyre grabs Gralyre's arm, and jerks him up from where he huddles, crying against my chest. His little feet skid on the flagstones, as the King pulls him roughly against his purple robes. Bylyre's face is red and angry. "I needed an alliance and had no choice but to wed a Dream Weaver Witch! But by all that I hold sacred in this land, Alyssa, I will not see your foul sorcery taint my son!"

The king spins Gralyre to face him, though he twists and reaches out for me. "Momma!" Gralyre screams.

The ugly welt on my forehead is making my thoughts misty. The sound of my son's distress propels me to try to rise, though I cannot seem to coordinate my legs beneath me.

"Stop your blubbering, boy! From this day forward, your mother is dead to you! If you use this evil power within you again I will have you whipped, and cast into the darkest dungeon in the castle!"

"Bylyre! No! Please!" I stretch out a quivering hand to stay

his edict. "Do not take him from me! Do not do this! He is only a
boy. He does not understand. If he is not trained to control his
powers he could come to harm!"

The King ignores me, and tries to force Gralyre from the
room. His little shoes tap and kick, as he bulks once more.

"Momma!" Gralyre screams. Stones materialize from the air,
and begin to pelt his father.

"Gralyre! No! You must not!" But he is in the grips of a
tantrum, and does not heed me. I am terrified for his safety and
struggle harder to rise, to go to him, to calm him.

"My Liege! Beware! The Dream Weaver Witch attacks you!"
yells Fennick. He is always nearby, the wizard who stares so
hard at my son. He steps into the nursery from the hallway,
where he has been lurking, and swings his staff. I have no
defence to offer. There is pain. There is nothing.

ᏚᏜᏣ

"No!" Gralyre flinched away in horror, as though his had
burned his fingers upon the surface of his Mother's Godwomb.
He bent at the waist, and howled into the golden light of the
Thewr 'ap Noir. He had experienced every moment leading up
to her death through her eyes.

"I am sorry! I am so sorry, Momma!" The child in him still
craved and mourned for her, and still blamed himself for her
death.

'No. Not my fault! It was Fennick!' He was no ally, but the

worst of villains!

Gralyre had almost died today because he had not remembered his mother's fate. Until now, he had held a vague recollection that she had passed in childbirth. But not this! Never this! How had he forgotten?

Gralyre clenched his eyes, as memories of his own were suddenly released from a dark well into which he had hidden them so long ago.

ᙣᙦ

...Fennick crushes Momma's skull with a blow from his staff. She slumps limply back to the rough stone floor.

I scream. I am inconsolable. I want them both to die. They deserve it for hurting my Momma! I create more stones to rain down upon them, and add a rushing thunderous wind, as I scream for her, "Momma!" She is crumpled, a discarded doll. I want her back! "Let go of me!" I roar, but the King's grip only tightens until I fear my little arm will be plucked from its socket.

"'Twas not her! 'Tis the boy!" yells the King. "Fennick do something!"

Fennick, his dark robes whipping around him in the storm of rocks and wind, slams his staff into my groin.

I have never experienced such pain. I cannot breath. The King releases me, and I drop to the flagstones, retching and crying. From where I lay, I can see Momma's blue eyes slowly glazing over. There is a dent in the left side of her skull from the impact of Fennick's staff. Her cheeks are wet from the tears she had shed.

"Sire! The boy's power must be quashed! He is too powerful! If his magic grows unchecked, the nobles will never accept him as their King. There will be rebellion!"

The King glares down at me. A sneer twists his lips. There is blood on his face from where one of the stones has struck him. I am glad. For the first time in my young life, I understand hate. "See to it, Fennick! Take the magic from him!"

Father leans down low to stare at me. I am sobbing so hard that I can barely make out his words.

"'Twas your fault all this came to pass, boy!"

He straightens and brushes down his royal purple doublet with a pompous snap. "To the dungeons with him. Whip him first to be sure he has some pain to keep him company in the darkness! Five by five, so that he remembers."

"As you wish, my King. What of her?"

The King turns his back, and struts from the room, sparing not a glance for Momma. "Send word to her family that she has died in childbirth."

෨ඏ

Gralyre's gaze rolled with revulsion. His forgetfulness was not of the same ilk as the black wall that had once hidden his past away from his reach. This was an ancient memory that he had suppressed as a child, out of pain and terror, in order to survive. This one glimpse into the abyss prompted a tsunami of emotions and memories to crash down upon him.

ৡৎ

The darkness is unrelenting. Sometimes I think that it is a monster that has eaten my eyes. Once a day, torchlight appears at the small grate set high in the heavy oak door. Food is shoved through a slot in the door near to the floor. I must scramble to reach the plate of thin gruel and stale crusts before the light fades away with the Gaoler's retreat. Before the rats return to challenge me for the small morsels.

I can no longer remember how long I have been in the darkness. I ceased to count the number of times the meals have come after ten, for that is as high as I can count. I am only six years old.

The gnawing, scrabbling sounds of rats scare me. I try to be brave, but in the darkness, the rodents sound like monsters. The scent of the dried blood on my back from the whipping keeps the rats coming for me, with scrabbling claws, slithering tails, and nipping teeth. I have learned to stay huddled upon the rough bench, with my bare toes tucked up under my long shirt to keep safe from their bites. I do not use the narrow cot, for I wet it in my sleep on my first night, and it has been damp ever since.

When I can stand it no longer, I close my eyes and concentrate, like Momma taught me, and I make the rats think that I am just a rock on the bench. It does not stop them from running all over me, but at least they do not stop to take a taste of my flesh.

A gut-twisting fear suddenly churns through me. What if Fennick knows I am using my evil magic to make the rats stay away? Crying bitter, silent tears, I release my hold on the rat minds, and endure their renewed attacks, as best I can.

Fennick. The court wizard scares me more than the rats do. If I use my evil sorcery, the wizard will lash me again. It is because I used my evil magic that Momma has died. They have all said so. It is my fault she is dead. "I am sorry, Momma."

I am bad. My magic is evil. I can never use it again. I must send all the magic away or they will whip me again, and lock me away forever in the black cold with the rats! I stare blindly into the unrelenting darkness, concentrating on pushing the quality I know as magic out of my mind and body, to purge myself of the evil.

"You are a scaredy-cat!" An unexpected voice states from out of the unrelenting darkness.

"Who is there?" I ask, terrified. I did not hear anyone come into the cell. I must have drifted to sleep. Time moves in strange ways in the cold dungeon.

"Scaredy-cat, scaredy-cat!" the voice taunts.

"I am not!"

"You are scared of the rats, and you are scared of Fennick!"

"He killed Momma!" I whisper, and terror quivers my voice.

"You are lying! You killed Momma. It is your fault. Fennick said so."

"Yes," I manfully try to hold back my tears so that my new friend will not know I am a crybaby, as well as a scaredy-cat.

"Fennick is a bad man! Momma always said so."

I cock my head to the side, confused by the other's sentiment. "Is my Momma, your Momma to?"

"Of course, dum-dum. You know who I am. I have always been with you."

I gasp with understanding, "You are my magic! You are bad! You are the one who killed my Momma! Get! Get away from me! Get! Get!"

"I could kill Fennick for you."

"No! I promised Momma I would never use magic to harm people. Magic is evil!"

"I am evil?"

"Yes, you are!"

"Momma's magic was not evil. She used to make us beautiful toys to play with."

"Leave me alone! You have to go away! If Fennick knows I have been talking to you he will hurt me again!"

"Alright, Scaredy-cat!"

Silence. The scrabbling, gnawing sounds of the rats growing bolder, coming nearer... "Wait! Come back!"

"Ha!"

"You did not leave! You were only pretending." I giggle in relief. It was a funny trick to play.

"Do you want to play a game?"

"Yes!"

"We will play 'Scare-the-rats'!"

"The rats?"

"Scared, scaredy-cat? Scared to scare the rats?"

"I am not! I can scare the rats! I will show you!"

Giggling and laughing, my friend in the darkness and I rush around the small cell, chasing after the scrabbling, unsubstantial sound of the rats in retreat.

A rat gives a horrific squeal, making me jump, and then freeze in place. There is a crunch of tiny bones, and the squeak of pain stops. "What are you doing?" I ask anxiously.

"Killing rats!"

"Momma said not to use magic to hurt…"

"They are just rats! Besides, 'tis fun to make them go pop!"

I back away fearfully. One by one, with high-pitched screeches of agony, the rats die. I have no liking for rats, but I have no stomach for killing them. Not like this.

"Maybe I will make Fennick go pop too!"

"No! Stop! If he finds out, he will hurt me again!"

The rats stop squealing, and the voice seems to vanish. I feel my way back to my bench, afraid of more than just the darkness now. What if the evil magic wants to make me go pop too?

Torchlight appears in the grate, only this time the door is thrust open. I am exposed in the light, blinking my watery eyes. I am alone in my cell. Ten dead rats, burst and bleeding lay around my feet.

"Ye are free, Prince Gralyre," says the guard roughly, yet not unkindly, and beckons me to walk towards him.

His head cranes to count, as he waits for me to come to him. "What happened here? Did ye kill all o' these rats?"

I shrug. "My friend did it. He is not here any more."

The guard propels me from the cell, his big hand gentle upon my shoulder. His other hand holds a torch to light our way. "Sometimes being in the dark for too long can prey on your mind, and make ye see things that are no' there."

I absorb this silently. "How long was I in there?" I have only vague memories of the dim passage we are now walking in. There is light at the end, warm red light, like a fire. I am so cold.

"Twenty-five days, lad, curse them." The guard spits with disgust onto the floor. "Five times five days 'twas the orders I was given. Five times five days ye were locked away." He pats my thin shoulders awkwardly. "They canno' break ye less ye allow yourself t' be broken, lad. Ye remember that."

I blink down at my filthy little fingers, past all of the rat bites. Twenty-five is ever so much more than ten.

"Ye hear me, lad?" the guard asks gruffly, giving me another little shake.

"Yes, sir," I say obligingly, but I do not really understand. My answer seems to please him.

The guard makes a noncommittal sound in the back of his throat. He delivers me to an awaiting nanny who takes me directly to a warm bath in the nursery. I have never seen her before. Momma always cared for me herself.

The new nanny does not speak to me, nor I to her. She scrubs me with lots of suds and a rough sponge. Then she dresses the wounds from my whipping, and my numerous rat bites.

I am given a sumptuous meal befitting my status as Heir to the Kingdom, which I wolf down with hunger, and promptly spew forth again when my stomach cannot support the weight of the food...

ℵℵ

Gralyre shed desolate tears, as he drifted limply outside his mother's gently bobbing Godwomb. She seemed so serene in her eternal rest. A slight smile lifted her lips. He wanted nothing so much as to reach within and feel her loving embrace comforting him. But even in the Thewr 'ap Noir, such was not possible. That window in time had been closed to him many years ago by a degenerate Sorcerer and his puppet King.

Feeling as though it was a betrayal of sorts, he turned from his Mother, and moved away from her Godwomb. He vowed to return soon to discover all else that remained hidden from him. Looking back on his upbringing through the eyes of an adult caused a deep and abiding bitterness. The beatings! The weeks of isolation in the blackness of the dungeon! Damn them both for doing such things to a helpless child!

Had it not been for the Weapons Master who had taught him the ways of the Sword Dance, Gralyre would have been a crushed spirit ripe for Fennick's possession. Which had likely been the point of it all.

Gralyre breathed deeply for a moment, to settle his roiling

hatred, before firmly slamming the door upon his disquieting past. For now, it had no place in his present.

He drifted amongst the large cluster of magenta orbs, brushing lightly against each to learn the names of his ancestors, whose souls slept within. Gralyre began to realize that he was descended from a powerful line of Dream Weaver Sorcerers. There were so many! He would be sure to learn all about this as well. Fennick and the King had stolen so much of his life!

At last, Gralyre found the orb that contained the sleeping soul of Gedrhar. He pressed his fingers to the soft surface of the Godwomb, and was relieved to learn that all was well with the army. Rewn's mask was holding. The Prince's absence had gone unnoticed.

Gedrhar was surrounded by thousands of souls bobbing gently in the amber glow of the Thewr 'ap Noir. Jacon resided within the nearest, and the rest held the army of Dream Weavers who travelled with the Rebels, comrades of like enterprise grouped together. Somewhere within this pack, Gralyre hoped to find the healer.

He cast the ether for Ninrhar, and followed a current that pulled him deeper into the cluster. At last, Gralyre spotted a lone magenta flash, and knew that he had finally found him.

Gralyre pressed both palms against the warm surface of Ninrhar's Godwomb, hoping that the Dream Weaver would know of a way to tend his burns. And he did. Gralyre absorbed the wisdom of manipulating Godsmagic to heal.

When he was certain he understood the procedure, Gralyre

rose up out of the Thewr 'ap Noir, drifting slowly towards the surface of his pool. As he went, he pulled upon the certain strands of energy that infused his flesh with the pulse of life, aligning his Godsmagic for healing and health: this power made skin grow, this invigorated the life force against infections, this rebuilt strands of muscles.

Far away, the pain in his flesh eased, as his wounds began to knit together. His blisters receded back under his skin, and his burns crusted over.

He reached the surface of his Godsmagic, and waded to the shore near to his Tree of Life. He was not yet prepared to return to the world outside to confront his loss, so he lingered, drawing strength from the source of his power, and gathering the courage to say goodbye to Little Wolf.

Gralyre glanced over at his Tree of Life to reassure himself that the virulent black cord was no longer syphoning his powers, that it was truly gone. It was then that he spied a weak glow at its roots.

What was that? Was a tainted seed from Fennick lying in wait to poison him further?

What began as a calm walk towards his Tree of Life, became angry strides, that became a full battle charge, as he raced around the shoreline of his Godsmagic. A challenge of rage ripped from Gralyre's throat, as he lost control, becoming inarticulate in his primitive need to destroy all traces of the enemy who had killed Little Wolf. A burst of Dream Weaver magic, filled his hands with a longsword, double-edged and sharpened to a fine point. Fennick would never find him defenceless again, he vowed, as he rounded the thick roots of his Tree.

Gralyre skidded to a rough halt, feeling as though his heart had been punched from his chest. The sword evaporated to mist in his grasp, as he released its magic back into the Deep Dreaming.

A weakly glowing wolf spirit was sprawled between two of the thick roots of the Tree of Life, unmoving.

"Little Wolf!" Gralyre gasped. He crouched to the ground and gathered his pup's soul into his arms, much as he had cradled the wolfdog's body in the world outside. Little Wolf did not awaken. His paws dangled limply.

Gralyre pushed his thoughts outwards and into the spirit of his pup. *'Little Wolf. I am here. I am here now.'*

Bite... Chew... Mouth... Burn... Hurt.

'I know, I know. I will save you, just as you saved me.' Gralyre did not know what to do. He cursed his ignorance of magic that left him so helpless. All he knew was that healing Little Wolf's soul could only come through the use of Sorcery.

Gralyre had survived Fennick's attacks through immersion in his pool of Godsmagic. It was all that he could think to do to aid Little Wolf.

Lifting the wolfdog in his arms, Gralyre carried him into his fount of magic, submerging them both. He ignored his memory of Gedrhar's warning, that without the powerful sword to aid him, as it had with Catrian, he would save Little Wolf only at the expense of his own ability to sustain his body. He did not care. He could deal with only one problem at a time. Using his connection to the wolfdog, he freely shared the light of his life force with his pup.

The shimmering brightness of Little Wolf's spirit grew more intense. Within Gralyre's arms, Little Wolf's legs began to kick urgently as he roused. It was working! Encouraged, Gralyre continued to carefully soothe his pup's hurt, and bolster his strength.

Little Wolf stilled, opened his eyes, and looked up at Gralyre.

Gralyre was humbled by the perfect purity of trust that shone there for him. Love. Family. They seemed weak words to describe the depth of their connection. The tears that fell from his eyes were now of joy, not grief.

Gralyre released Little Wolf from his arms, and together they paddled to the shores of the pool. Gralyre did not note any ill effects from aiding Little Wolf, and wondered why. It would be a question to pose to Gedrhar when next they met, though he suspected it had something to do with the fact that his magic had not been spent in replenishing a body, but in bolstering a soul.

Grateful beyond measure, Gralyre smiled gently down at Little Wolf. It was inevitable that he would outlive the wolfdog, for such was the fault between the span of years granted a human and a wolf. But please Gods, not yet! "'Tis time to return to your body. Time to open your eyes to the outside world, pup."

Little Wolf put his nose to the ground, and made a wide circle upon the shore. His loose, lupine stride made short work of the distance, before he returned to Gralyre's side. *'The trail is lost. Eaten by the cold snake. My home is gone.'*

Gralyre withstood his dismay, as he realized for the first time that the glowing lifeline that should have connected Little Wolf's spirit back to his wolf body had vanished, destroyed by Fennick. The flesh would not long survive without a soul.

Wait! Fennick had spanned the distance from his Wizard Stone in order to possess Gralyre. Could Gralyre create a similar bridge for Little Wolf's soul to return to his body?

He sent his consciousness forth into the outside world, seeking the wolfdog's husk, but only Jord and Aneida were glowing brightly to his magical senses. Gralyre narrowed his focus to sense only Godsmagic, and there, finally, he felt the shivery presence of life. It was so very faint, a raindrop where there should have been a waterfall, but now that he had found it, it remained a beacon in the darkness to move towards.

"Come," Gralyre beckoned Little Wolf's spirit. "I will take you home." Gralyre laid a hand upon Little Wolf's neck, gripping tightly to the fur, and pulled them both outward from his centre, and into the wolfdog's body.

A frightening, dark emptiness surrounded them, and Gralyre was reminded of what he had found in Catrian's mind when her soul had been trapped in her Wizard Stone. It was like walking through an abandoned house. Without his glowing connection to his Godsmagic that made him the owner of this empty husk, Little Wolf was as much a visitor now, as Gralyre was.

Gralyre understood a little more of what Fennick had

attempted to do to him. In order to possess his flesh, Fennick had needed to sever Gralyre's connection to his Godsmagic, and replace it with his own. The black umbilical cord would have completed the transformation unchallenged, if Little Wolf had not sacrificed all to help Gralyre destroy it.

They moved deeper, to where the wolfdog's remaining Godsmagic was still working to beat his heart, and fill his lungs. Even as Gralyre watched, Little Wolf's small silver pool shrank, the lake of power receding from the shore like the ebb of a tide. Little Wolf's Tree of Life was wizened and ailing. A single dark leaf dropped into the small pool of Godsmagic that remained. It was clear that there was not much time remaining before the ability to live would be gone forever, and Little Wolf would die.

"Little Wolf, get into your pool." This had to be where the severed could be made whole again!

Little Wolf trotted into the light, and stood with the Godsmagic lapping upon his belly, waiting. Nothing happened. He cocked his head to the side quizzically.

Gralyre was stymied. How was he to weld Little Wolf back into his body? When he had helped Catrian, her lifeline had been an integral part of her Godsmagic pool, like a thread descending from a skein of wool. Somewhere in Little Wolf's pool was the severed end of his soul's tether.

Fennick had been supplanting Gralyre by syphoning from his Godsmagic, an unnatural act from a foreign entity. Little Wolf needed to do the same. It had to work!

Gralyre hovered his palm above the draining pool, and

imagined a lifeline similar to his own, glowing with light and life. The surface of Little Wolf's Godsmagic pool roiled for a moment and then the line appeared, lifting up out of the settling waves. It was like holding a light beam; it held no weight.

How was he to reattach it to Little Wolf's spirit? Gralyre remembered how Fennick's virulent black cord had stabbed into his soul like a lance when he had been coerced to surrender the power of the Thewr 'ap Noir. He remembered the pain of it. Would the same operation save Little Wolf?

"I am sorry, Little Wolf. This is the only way that I know of. It will hurt," Gralyre warned. He passed his forearm across Little Wolf's neck to anchor him. "You must not move until it is over." Holding firmly to the tether of light, Gralyre plunged his hand into Little Wolf's spirit, directly above his heart.

Little Wolf howled with pain but Gralyre did not relent, focussing his sorcery upon stitching Little Wolf's soul to the lifeline. The wolfdog's Tree of Life burst into verdant bloom and began to rustle urgently, as from a high wind. There was a surge of life within the empty husk, as the flesh and soul were reunited through the conduit of Godsmagic.

After a few seconds, Gralyre slowly withdrew his hand from the wolfdog's soul. It was done. Little Wolf panted harshly as he recovered, but his connection to his body was intact.

഻ഊ

Aneida caught movement from the corner of her eye, and

turned away from the loosened soil she was digging in to look more fully. Gralyre was sitting still, his eyes shut, cradling Little Wolf, just as when she had last checked on them. His wounds had crusted over, and the redness of his burns was fading. He appeared well on his way to healing fully.

Suddenly, all four of Little Wolf's paws trembled, as though he were dreaming of chasing rabbits. It was the same movement that had drawn her gaze.

Aneida's eyes narrowed. Though it was not unusual to see a dead body twitch, something else had just occurred to her. "When did ye say ye found Little Wolf?" she quizzed Jord.

"It was before the fire. Before dawn." Jord grunted, as he dug in his warped spade for another shovel full of dirt.

Aneida's face flushed with ire, and she punched him in the arm.

"Owe! What was that for?"

"Ye did no' think it strange that he had no' yet stiffened?" she condemned, noting that there was no rigor mortis in Little Wolf's flesh.

Jord coughed in surprise, hopping back out of her reach. His spade slipped from his loosened hands. "Gods! He is alive!"

𝔰𝔬𝔔

Gralyre returned to the world of ash and blood, but for the first time since the Stalker had taken Catrian, his spirits lifted. He bent his ear to the wolfdog and heard stronger breathing.

"Little Wolf, open your eyes," he whispered softly.

Jord and Aneida watched on in awe, as Little Wolf awakened and his tail began an enthusiastic tattoo upon the ground. With exclamations of joy, they crowded around Gralyre, reaching out to touch the wolfdog, welcoming him back from the dead.

CHAPTER TWENTY

"We must be far away from this place by nightfall," Gralyre warned. "They will be searching for us!" Briefly, he recounted his epic battle with Doaphin and Fennick. He told Jord and Aneida of the Master's evil presence infecting the hall of the Demon Lords, which had unexpectedly saved his life. "As powerful as he is, even Doaphin fears this Master. We would be wise to heed this."

"We have a full moon o' travel ahead o' us t' reach the Towers, assuming we are still set upon rescuing Catrian?" Aneida asked.

Gralyre nodded, heartsick with the delay to reach her. "'Tis more important now than ever that she stands with us. I cannot fight Doaphin alone, and we need to reclaim the sword. 'Tis too powerful to abandon to the enemy!"

The crusted scabs covering his healing wounds itched, so he rubbed at them. They loosened and fell, flaking away to reveal new, unmarred skin.

"'Tis remarkable. There are almost no scars!" Aneida smiled.

Gralyre examined his hands. Where once had been melted, damaged skin, there was now only normal, healthy flesh. He was not a vain man, but he found himself gladdened that he would not bear the scars of his defeat for what remained of his life.

Wagons sounded upon the open road behind them,

approaching the ruined city. Gralyre sent his attention winging outwards, and smiled grimly, as he realized what it was. Wagons were still arriving from the countryside, carrying the female survivors of the purges. Doaphin, it would seem, did not wish to be wasteful of his resources.

"Tithe Wagons," he announced.

Jord grinned and his daggers came forth to dance. "Better t' ride than t' walk."

Aneida tossed Gralyre her short sword. "Take it! I will act the bait," she grinned her familiar, maniacal smile, and took position in the centre of the road, with her arms firmly planted upon her hips. The others hid in the ditches.

The wagons cleared the curve, and spotted her. She waited impatiently, as they drew rein and halted their team.

"What are ye doing out o' your cage?" One of the 'Riders demanded, as they dismounted and started towards her.

Little Wolf howled, and launched out of the woods, taking a 'Rider to the ground in a spray of blood. Jord popped up from the ditch he hid in, and his knives began to flick through the air in rapid session. Four more Demon Riders dropped.

The rest of the platoon hesitated, confused by the sudden deaths. The creatures were used to docile, fearful humans. They were slow to realize that they were under attack, and so they never noticed the swordsman approaching at a run from their rear.

Gralyre waded through their ranks, his sword a blur of destruction, leaving fifteen twitching corpses in his wake, as he hardly broke stride.

Aneida whistled appreciatively, as he tossed his borrowed sword back to her. "I have no' seen ye move that fast in a long time."

"Get the heads. We need no Deathren nipping at our heels."

The prisoners in the back of the caged wagon watched on with dull, defeated gazes as Gralyre smashed the lock and bade them exit. "Where are we supposed t' go?" one woman asked.

Gralyre considered for a long moment. "We need to find Hektar."

೫෮ஐ

"What are we supposed t' do with them?" Hektar demanded of Gralyre, indicating the group of a hundred women. They were sick and weak from their hard weeks of travel in the cages.

"Make for the village of Ghent, on the coast. Do you know it?"

"Aye," Hektar muttered grudgingly.

"From there, the resistance is evacuating people out over the sea to the Western Fortress."

"How do I know ye are telling the truth?"

"Stay and find out," Jord suggested with a sneer. When the Rebels had seen Gralyre, they had displayed surprise and guilt enough to inform Jord's spy instincts to the truth. He had not forgotten watching them flee the city the night before. He needed no one to tell him that they had left the Prince to die. "Ye will know for sure by nightfall. By then Doaphin will have thousands o' Stalkers and Deathren swarming this forest seeking ye. Ye can put the question t' them."

"Why should I?" Hektar continued to bray truculently.

Gralyre grabbed his shirt and slammed him into a tree. He leaned close, threateningly. "Because otherwise you are of no use to me. And I will kill you for trying to murder me last night."

Hektar scowled, but nodded his compliance. He was no fool.

ℰ⊗ℭ

Doaphin's Towers

Catrian lay upon the musty mattress, doing her best to rest. Her shivers of fear crested and ebbed upon a sea of terror. She prodded at her mind, seeking her Godsmagic. If only she could reach it, she would be able to fight her way out of the Towers. Or die trying. Without it, she was vulnerable, blind and powerless to halt the inevitable.

So far, she had been treated well. She had been delivered of a sumptuous meal of roast chicken and ale. They wanted her hale. She would not ignore such favours for the sake of martyrdom. It did not affect her decision to take her own life rather than submit to impregnation with the evil spawn of Demon Lords.

When would she do it?

Tears slipped down her cheeks as despair crashed over her.

Why not now? It would free Gralyre from any misguided
attempts to save her. It would free her, before the worst
happened. Why wait?

She sat up with a clank of chains, and opened her hand. The
nail that she had pried from the table leg had made deep
impressions in her palm after clutching it so tightly. The nail was
three inches long, and rusted from the dankness of the cell. Still,
it had a sharp point and would do the job.

Catrian pressed the tip to her wrist, and drew forth a small
bead of blood. With all her being, she wanted to live! She closed
her eyes, and imagined herself in Gralyre's arms. The memory
of their passionate embraces in her Wizard Stone gave her the
strength she needed to do what she must. She would not allow
the beauty of their love to be tarnished by the horrors to come!
One quick thrust to open the vein. She steeled herself…

Godsmagic struck her face, snapping back her head, and she
collapsed unconscious. A shadow soared from out of the corner,
and slapped the nail out of her hand.

"She is safe now," the shadow whispered into the darkness. It
undulated, over Catrian's prone body. It had no shape or form.
"You were correct. She tried to end her being."

"Watch her always," the Demon Lord commanded, from his
warm, luxurious chamber several floors below. "Let no harm
come to her."

"As you wish." The shadow retreated into the darkness made
by the angle of the walls of the cell. There, it waited and
watched from its perfect camouflage.

The End

Of

The Prince

Lies of Lesser Gods – Book Four

Coming Soon

The King

Lies of Lesser Gods – Book Five

DO A GOOD DEED FOR A GREAT READ!

Post a Review

Please take a moment to post a review or click a star rating for **The Lies of Lesser Gods** anywhere you purchase books or eBooks online, such as Amazon, Chapters/Indigo, Kobo, Kindle, or Apple Books.

Independent authors don't have corporate backing. I owe all of my success to the support of my incredible fans who promote **The Lies of Lesser Gods** to their friends and family through posts and online reviews.

Your opinion lets me compete on the same field with authors like Stephen King, George R.R. Martin (Game of Thrones), and J.K. Rowling (Harry Potter).

Each fan's <u>honest</u> opinion helps my books rank higher in online search engines and in best seller lists, which in turn helps more people to discover these great stories.

Thank-you for being a part of my dream of being a best selling author. I'll make you a deal! If you keep loving my stories, I'll keep writing them!

With Thanks
~ LGA McIntyre

About the Author

L.G.A. McIntyre grew up in the wilds of British Columbia, Canada. After a successful career as a Producer and Director, she has returned to her roots, and now teaches at the College of New Caledonia. A self-proclaimed writing addict, she has devoted her life to a pursuit of the creative arts.

Connect with the Author

Visit our website for insider news and giveaways
http://www.lgamcintyre.com
Like us on Facebook
http://www.facebook.com/lgamcintyre
Follow us on Twitter
@LGAMcIntyre
#theLOLG

Made in the USA
Middletown, DE
17 August 2020